"Tell me that ten minutes ago you weren't trying to pull me down to kiss you."

Madeline kept her smile in place. "Of course I tried to kiss you. I'm a whore. It's my nature."

Gabriel laid her down on the bed, but his arm remained behind her head. "Yet it wasn't the coquette who tried to kiss me, but the woman. A woman who even now strains toward me."

Heat invaded Madeline's cheeks. She relaxed her neck and shoulders, settling more firmly into the pillow.

"There is something between us that cannot be explained away. And neither you nor I wish for it. Unless I am wrong." He slid his hand through the opening of her robe, engulfing her breast in his hand. "And you do wish for it. In which case, all you have to do is ask."

His lips dropped to her neck.

Her breath hissed though clenched teeth. *Yes, please, yes!*

Romances by Anna Randol

SINS OF A VIRGIN
A MOST NAKED SOLUTION
A SECRET IN HER KISS

ANNA RANDOL

Sins of a Virgin

AVON

An Imprint of HarperCollinsPublishers

AVON BOOKS
An Imprint of HarperCollins*Publishers*
10 East 53rd Street
New York, New York 10022-5299

To my husband, who is always my hero,
and my mom, who is always my biggest supporter

Sins of a Virgin

Prologue

Three glasses of the finest French brandy lingered untouched on the desk. Sir James Glavenstroke tapped his own half-empty glass with nervous fingers. He never should have poured the drinks before they entered the room. That had guaranteed they wouldn't imbibe. Which was a damned shame. Alcohol would have made the upcoming ordeal easier.

At least for him.

The Trio, they called themselves—La Petit, Cipher, and Wraith. The finest agents he'd ever created. More soldiers owed their lives to them than to Wellington himself.

Pride burned in Glavenstroke's chest, but he coughed it away. After all, any one of them would gladly slit his throat for the hell he'd damned them into.

Not that they'd be any happier when he kicked them out of it.

Glavenstroke ran a hand through his thinning gray hair, then sipped his brandy. Madeline Valdan, La Petit, watched his fidgeting with far too keen a gaze. The past ten years had transformed Madeline from a breathtaking youth to the most achingly beautiful woman he'd ever seen. He tried to still his nervous motions, but he knew that, in and of itself, would be a sign.

"What are you stewing over, Glavenstroke?" Madeline asked. "You know you can't hide anything from us."

No. He'd been unable to do that since he plucked them from their fate on the gallows. In exchange for their lives, they'd agreed to hone their particular skills on behalf of His Majesty's government. They'd each originally possessed talents that had led him to select them over the other condemned souls in Newgate, but once they'd received formal training, they'd become an unstoppable force. A wickedly sharp dagger used to eviscerate Napoleon and his allies.

But now the war was over.

"Out with it." As always, the voice of the Cipher, Clayton Campbell, remained perfectly calm, yet drew a shiver up Glavenstroke's spine.

With a sigh, he removed the bank drafts from the drawer and laid them on the oak desk. "The Foreign Office thanks you for your hard years of service on His Majesty's behalf."

"But?" prompted Madeline.

"There is no *but*. You've served your country well and are free to resume normal lives. You each have, of course, received full pardons for your past transgressions."

Madeline and Clayton stared at him. It was a measure of their level of shock that they permitted that much of a reaction.

Ian Maddox, the Wraith and third member of the Trio, was the only one who remained unsurprised. But Glavenstroke knew that stemmed from his low expectations of humanity in general. Unlike the other two, Ian was a product of the mean streets in London's West End. No level of cruelty or greed surprised him. The government could have ordered their immediate execution and he wouldn't have batted an eye.

Madeline tucked a strand of chestnut hair behind her ear—the one nervous gesture he'd never been able to break her of. "Why?"

Ian's powerful frame relaxed in the chair, and rather than diminishing his strength, the pose made him resemble a tiger the moment before it pounced. "What dear Glaves here is too polite to say is that they don't need us anymore. Now that we're of no use to them, having us on the payroll is too much of a risk. Can't afford to let the sweetly docile populace discover they're employing the hangman's leftovers."

Ian was correct as always. In fact, with his ability to gain access to whatever location he desired, it was likely he'd known about this forced retirement before Glavenstroke did.

With an uncomfortable cough, Glavenstroke delivered the final insult—the bank drafts.

"This is the first pension payment?" Clayton's hand tensed on the slip of paper.

Ian snorted. "Sorry, they can't have us on the pension records, either."

Madeline stiffened. "I've whored myself on behalf of this country. A foot soldier would have made more than this."

Glavenstroke took a large swig of his brandy, welcoming the muted burn at the back of his throat. He'd called in every favor owed him to arrange for even this much. But he hadn't reached his current position by being soft, so he didn't apologize. After all, without his help, the three of them would've been dead a decade ago.

Clayton rested his hand on Madeline's arm. "With proper investment—"

"And what, another ten or twenty years of waiting? I know you're a genius with numbers, Clayton, but even you cannot miraculously transform this into anything other than the insult it is." She rose to her feet, and the other two followed.

"What do you plan to do?" Glavenstroke asked them, despising himself for the weakness the question betrayed.

Ian glanced back over his shoulder, a slight smile quirking the corner of his mouth. "Won't that thought keep you up at night?"

As the door closed silently behind them, Glavenstroke poured himself another glass of the amber liquid. They'd land on their feet. He'd taught them well.

Hopefully, they'd continue to use their skills to help society, because if any one of them turned—he knocked back the second shot of brandy in a single gulp—heaven help Mother England.

Chapter One

When lightning didn't strike Madeline Valdan as she strolled through the hallowed doors of White's, a wicked smile curved her lips. She'd seize her positive omens where she could.

While the footman by the door kept his gaze studiously averted, she slipped the heavy bag of gold sovereigns into his pocket and then rose up on tiptoe so her lips brushed the air inches from his ear. "Thank you, John." He still didn't deign to speak to her, but an adorable blush spread above the starched points of his shirt collar.

As she sauntered down the corridor, Madeline couldn't resist a quick gawk at this bastion of manliness. Marble pillars jutted out from deep, plush carpet to join with the ornate plaster of the ceiling and reflect the rippling patterns cast by the crystal chandeliers. The club reeked of power and entitlement.

And most importantly, money.

Madeline smoothed the flowing lines of her black domino. The silk used to make the cloak had been an extravagant expense, but as she'd learned, presentation was everything.

She strode past the coffee room and straight into

the card room. After all, she was offering a gamble—hopefully, a very expensive gamble.

The murmur of masculine voices rumbled through the expansive space, punctuated by an occasional bark of laughter. Faro cards slapped onto tables and dice clacked across tables.

She scanned the room as she'd been trained, noting the number of men and classifying them: those actively gambling, those pretending to gamble, and those watching; those holding a winning hand versus a losing hand. From her brief glance, she also knew which men were dangerous and which posed a threat only to their after-supper pudding.

As Madeline walked to the center of the room, the tables she passed quieted, then burst into jumbled exclamations.

She selected a table directly in the center of the room under an immense glittering chandelier. She couldn't have asked for a better stage.

She smiled at the nervous young man who had turned to gape at her as she approached. She held out her hand. "Be a dear, Algie?"

Algie's training as a gentleman didn't fail her, and he offered his hand without thinking. She grasped it, stepped on his thigh, and then onto the middle of the table.

Madeline now held the attention of the entire group of assembled men.

Two determined footmen arrived at the edge of the table. "Miss, this isn't that type of establishment. You must leave or we will remove you."

Madeline threw back the hood of her cloak.

"Madeline . . ."

"Who's mistress . . ."

" . . . seen with the Regent himself last . . ."

The voices testified that the last six months had served their purpose. They all knew who she was.

She'd spent every last dime of the paltry government stipend on being seen and heard around London. Dressed to scandalous perfection. Always on the arm of a different man and always on the cusp of something utterly outrageous. Soon the gossip sheets hadn't been able to write enough about her. Gentlemen lusted after her and ladies despised her.

She opened the front of her domino, revealing her emerald gown. The bodice skimmed her breasts and barely covered her nipples. In fact, when she'd tried it on, a misplaced sneeze had produced quite shocking results. The sleeves were practically nonexistent, and the lack of petticoats molded the skirt to every curve of her hip and leg.

She raised her voice to carry above the noise. "What do you think, gentlemen, shall I leave, or do you want to hear what inspired this dastardly stunt?"

The shouts clamoring for her answer overwhelmed the cries for her ousting, so the flustered servants stepped back a pace.

Madeline trailed a hand slowly down her hip. "I bring you something for sale." She nodded at offers shouted by several of the bolder gentlemen to share their beds for the night. "Not quite. I'm here to inform you of an auction."

"What's being sold?" asked the overdressed and overfed Colonel Willington.

She scanned the room, gauging the reactions. Excellent. Every single one of them strained for her answer. She waited three more heartbeats before answering. "My virginity."

Disbelief and outrage echoed through the room. Forgotten cards drifted onto tables as fortunes sat neglected in the center. She didn't even try to speak for several minutes. But when she did, everyone listened. "The bidding book will be at Naughton's for the next fortnight." Most of the men here knew of the gambling den firsthand, and those who didn't wouldn't be bidding regardless. "At the end of those two weeks, the man with the highest bid wins."

"What exactly does he win?" a dark-haired fellow asked.

She tapped her cheek. "Hmm . . . my virginity?"

The crowd laughed, but he pressed on. "But what exactly does that entail?"

"That's simple. One night with me and a chance to succeed where every other man in London has failed."

A voice that she couldn't quite match with a face spoke from the corner of the room. "If you're a virgin, why not marry?"

She'd rather be dragged over broken glass by a herd of gout-ridden turtles. Yet she allowed none of her thoughts to show on her face when she lifted her eyebrow. "Is that an offer?" As she waited for the chuckles to die down, she untied her cloak, dropping it so it pooled at her feet. Eyes once again riveted to the ample amount of bosom she'd arranged for display. "I think you gentlemen know—mistresses have more fun."

Murmurs swelled again through the crowd until Baron Weltyn, a perspiring gentleman with a salmon-colored jacket and slightly bulging eyes, snorted. "But why would we want to bed an innocent?"

"While I may be a virgin . . ." She reached up and unbuckled the specially designed clasps on the shoulders of the gown. With a slight shrug, the dress joined the cloak on the ground, revealing her tightly laced black corset, matching satin drawers, and sheer stockings. "I'm definitely no innocent."

Men jumped to their feet, some driven by outrage, some by lust. Friends pounded the elderly Duke of Avelsy on the back as he choked on his brandy.

She surveyed the uproar with satisfaction. The only bad reaction was no reaction at all. For this auction to succeed, the scandal needed to sweep London. The more this night grew in infamy, the better she would do. Madeline reached up and plucked the pins from her hair so the dark chestnut strands tumbled over her shoulders and cascaded down her back.

The room again quieted.

Desire pounded hot and almost palpable in the room.

"How do we know you're a virgin?"

Finally, someone had the nerve to ask the question she'd seen burning in everyone's eyes. She peered into the darkened corners of the room. Ah, the not-so-honorable George Glinton.

"You've been escorted around London by nearly every peer in this room. How do we know you're still a virgin?"

"Can any of you claim to have bedded me?" She reached leisurely to her feet and retrieved her dress and domino, treating the men in front of her to the view of her breasts threatening to overflow the cups of her corset, while the men behind her watched the fabric of her drawers tightening over her backside. Satisfied that she had their full attention, she draped her clothing over her arm and held out her hand so Algie could assist her to the ground. With swaying hips, she walked toward the door.

"Wait!" another voice shouted. "You didn't answer Glinton. How do we know you're a virgin?"

She peered back over her shoulder and smiled that seductive smile she'd been forced to perfect during countless hours of training by the Foreign Office. "It is a gamble, is it not? And that, gentlemen, is why you will have to bid and bid well."

Chapter Two

Gabriel Huntford kept his arms folded so he didn't beat some sense into the man. "Of course it's the same murderer."

Jeremiah Potts, magistrate of the Bow Street Office, mopped his perpetually damp brow with a square of linen. "Girls are strangled in London all the time."

"My sister's body was arranged exactly the same."

"In a nightgown in a bed. Half the blasted corpses we find have been murdered in their beds." Potts sat heavily behind his desk. "Why would the murderer have waited so long to kill again? It makes no sense. Your sister's case was put aside seven years ago."

Only in the official records. Not a day had passed when Gabriel hadn't searched for some clue he might have missed. Or for the mysterious gentleman his twin had mentioned before her death. Now he finally had suspects. Solid leads. Unfortunately, they resulted from another dead girl. "I'm the best Runner you've got."

Potts sighed, the lines creasing his forehead suddenly more pronounced. "Not for this case. If it's related to your sister's—and I'm not saying I agree with you on that—you're too close."

"You hired me because of my work on my sister's case."

"It was either that or arrest you for disturbing the public peace." Potts continued, "It took me over a year to smooth the feathers you ruffled. I'm not going to let you run roughshod through the richest, most powerful men in England based on the word of a half-blind, pensioned-off coachman who spends his days drunk in a tavern."

"A tavern directly across from the school where the dead woman taught. The man does nothing but sit and watch people come and go. He's a witness. He saw Miss Simm meet a gentleman and leave in his coach."

"A rented hackney."

"But the gentleman in the hackney had visited to the school before."

"In a coach with a coat of arms containing some sort of animal. I know. I read your report. I also read that your witness had no physical description of the man other than that he was tall, well-dressed, and blurry. You will not accuse innocent men on such unreliable evidence."

"In other words, you'd rather let a killer go free than risk questioning the aristocracy."

"Those gentlemen are the ones who assign us a budget every year. You may not like it, but if they cut our budget again, we'll lose two more Runners. Do you realize how many more criminals will remain on the streets if that happens? Besides, the Simm murder will be investigated. Just not by you."

Gabriel reminded himself that he respected Potts on most days. And he didn't envy him the groveling he performed to keep Parliament happy. But in this he was wrong. No one knew the details of this case or his sister's as he did. He was the one who had interviewed the witnesses from both murders. He was the one who'd recorded every detail from the scene of the crimes. He couldn't risk someone else not being as thorough. Or risk them not pressing hard enough because they were afraid to offend the high-and-mighty aristocracy. "I'll investigate on my own."

He'd finally been given what he'd searched for these past years. Suspects. After his sister's murder, the only thing he knew was that she'd been seen with a mysterious gentleman. But now with this new murder, he'd been able to cross-check his list of the noblemen who'd been in London at the time of his sister's murder with a list of men who had daughters at the school. And since the school, for the most part, housed bastard daughters of rich aristocrats, the list was quite small. When he'd further tightened the list to those with animals on their family crests, he'd been left with a list of seven names.

"Do you think your suspects will talk to you without the authority of Bow Street behind you? They won't even let you in the door. And if you go against my word on this, you'll no longer be . . ." Potts stared at something outside his office door, his mouth gaping.

Gabriel turned, curious as to what had rendered Potts speechless in the middle of one of his prized threats. The only time he could recall Potts at a loss for words was when that albino man and his camel—

Gabriel's breath escaped as if he'd been punched in the gut.

A woman stood in the doorway.

No. That would be like calling the Holy Grail a drinking cup.

If his every dark, midnight fantasy had somehow come to life, they would have created this woman. And since she'd been drawn from his dreams, he already knew the rich, dark curls artfully arranged on her head would be silky to his touch. He knew when she turned, a few lucky tendrils would have escaped to tease the slender column of her throat. He recognized the pert, straight nose, ached to run his finger over the delicate curve of her ear.

But it was her lips he couldn't look away from. Lips his imagination never could have conjured. Lush, sensuous, and dark, as if she'd just sipped a glass of fine red wine. He wanted to bring his mouth to hers, sample her flavor, and grow drunk on her sweetness.

A slight mocking curve of that mouth brought his attention to her eyes. After his intense study, it was a bit of a shock to find she wasn't looking at him at all, but rather over his shoulder at Potts.

She stepped into the room, the small, graceful movement drawing Gabriel's attention to her body. Her gown was no different from ones he saw every day in Hyde Park, yet it was infinitely more provocative. The bodice offered up the lush perfection of her breasts. The narrow skirt highlighted the tiny span of her waist and gentle flare of her hips.

"Mr. Potts, I can wait if you need more time," the woman said, her voice the perfect mixture of sugar and seduction.

Potts lumbered out from behind his desk and caught the woman's hand, bringing it to his lips as ruddy color darkened his cheeks. "No, Miss Valdan. I let time get away from me. We were finished."

The name doused Gabriel's lustful appreciation. Madeline Valdan. The courtesan's name had been on every male's lips for the past six months. Yesterday, with the start of her ridiculous auction, it had grown ten times worse. Hell, at the murder scene yesterday, the other constables had been unable to focus on anything save their lamentable lack of funds for bidding on her.

Potts led Miss Valdan to the worn leather chair across from his desk and motioned for her to sit, then turned to Gabriel. "Huntford, the matter is decided. You have other cases. Other people who deserve justice."

When Potts said his name, Miss Valdan finally directed her gaze to him. It swept over him like velvet, leaving his skin hot and itchy. But Gabriel resisted the urge to straighten like a green youth; instead, he met her eyes with a glare. He had a murder to solve—a murder he would solve quickly if Potts would just see reason. But he now had to waste precious time as Potts fawned over London's favorite courtesan, forgetting he was old enough to be her father.

"That will be all, Huntford."

Potts might tolerate Gabriel's arguments in private, but Gabriel knew better than to question the man in public. "Yes, sir."

Miss Valdan watched them with amused tolerance, somehow making the cracked leather chair look soft and comfortable, as if she'd climbed onto the lap of a lover.

He had better things to do than provide amusement. Gabriel strode from the room, glad to be out of the stilted air of Potts's office so he could pull oxygen more easily into his lungs.

Potts quickly shut the door behind him.

Chaos erupted as the criminals and constables alike regained their senses now that Miss Valdan was no longer in sight. The shouting started. The crying. The gruff orders.

Gabriel ignored them, locked his arms over his chest, and waited. What could she need? Help finding some bauble she'd misplaced? He had a murder to solve. Despite Potts's denial, there was no doubt that it was the same murderer. Both women had been strangled and their bodies arranged in a cheap rented room. They had both been dressed in a white nightgown with a mourning brooch pinned at their throats. Gabriel fingered the brooch in his pocket, the one that had been pinned to his sister. It held a lock of her hair sealed under glass. The one pinned to Miss Simm had held a piece of hers. The brooch was a taunt by the murderer to show he'd known his victims in advance—known them well enough to get a lock of hair. Every day Gabriel was tempted to crush the damned thing beneath his heel. But he couldn't. It was a clue, one of the only ones he had.

The door suddenly opened, and Miss Valdan appeared. "I shall expect him at eleven tomorrow."

Potts bowed deeply from his place near the door. "It's our pleasure, Madeline."

Gabriel held his ground outside the doorway so Potts wouldn't be able to avoid him. Miss Valdan would have to step around him to exit, but she could survive the slight inconvenience. Everyone else might bow to her whims, but Gabriel had more important priorities.

Yet rather than skirting around, Miss Valdan sauntered straight forward as if he weren't there. For a second, Gabriel feared she might careen into him, but despite the possible collision, he wouldn't scamper out of her way. She could damned well alter her course.

She didn't.

Her chosen path brushed so close to him that her dress caressed his leg and the hint of vanilla in her hair teased his nostrils.

A small smile lifted her lips. "I'll see you soon."

She had to have been talking to Potts. Yet dread settled in Gabriel's gut.

Potts cleared his throat. "You have a new assignment, Huntford."

Madeline handed the heavy bouquet of scarlet orchids to the wan-faced girl who waited at the kitchen entrance.

The girl's eyes widened as she tucked the blossoms into her basket. "Lawks, miss. I doubt any of the fellows on the street will be able to afford this."

Madeline tried not to notice the threadbare patches on the girl's shawl. After paying her butler and coachman for the two remaining weeks of the auction, and her trip to Bow Street, she was about equally poor. Besides, advice was worth far more than her few remaining farthings. "You have two options. Either break it down into smaller bouquets or sell it to one of the flower shops. These are from the Duke of Umberland's private hothouse. They're the only ones of their kind in England. Don't take less than a guinea for the bunch of them."

"Thank you, miss." Tears glistened in the girl's brown eyes.

Madeline stepped back. Why did they always complicate things by becoming emotional? "Just make sure you don't spend the money on trinkets. Use it to buy more flowers."

The girl nodded, holding the basket to her chest. "Think you'll have more flowers for us girls tomorrow, miss?"

"Undoubtedly." Did the men of London think she

wanted to drown in them? "Oh, and there's a forbidding man standing at my front door. Can you leave without him seeing you?"

The child's head bobbed. "I'm good at that."

Madeline shut the door, aware of her butler hovering behind her. "Orchids make me sneeze," she explained.

"And the roses, and the daffodils, and the peonies? I must say your sneezing was becoming bothersome."

"Terrible curse." Madeline crossed her arms and silently dared him to contradict her.

"Indeed, miss."

Madeline eyed her butler, her eyes rising to the top of his head. "The feather does look better on you."

Canterbury patted the ostrich feather on his hat. "Indeed, miss." The jaunty trimming she'd given him fluttered over his high-crowned beaver, a new addition in his seemingly endless supply of unusual creations. "Thank you."

She still wasn't sure how her butler knew Wraith. Neither of them would speak about it. All she knew was that Wraith had hired him for her because he was trustworthy. And Wraith didn't think anyone was trustworthy. "Well, as you said, it never suited my lavender bonnet."

Canterbury glanced toward the doorway. "Shall I answer the door now, miss?"

Madeline walked in the opposite direction. "Give him another minute, then put him in the study."

"Shall I tell him you will attend him shortly?"

"No. Our appointment isn't for another half an hour." She had no problem making the Runner wait until then. She was hiring him, not the other way around. If he was going to prove impossible to work with, she needed to know immediately.

"Very good, miss."

Madeline hurried up the stairs to the parlor. The room provided a clear view of the front door where Huntford waited.

As before, a tingle slid down her spine. It was a primal response, one she'd experienced only when her life was in danger. She shouldn't be in danger now, yet her senses sharpened. The clatter of each horse hoof. The glint of the sun on the puddle behind him. She became aware of the weight of the knife sheathed at her calf.

Even though Huntford's second knock had gone unanswered for several minutes, he still waited on her doorstep. He didn't fidget. He hadn't turned away in frustration. He simply waited. Still and silent like a wolf.

An arrogant wolf.

Below, the door opened. Huntford must have been surprised by her butler's hat—she often had to fight the urge to blink owlishly at him herself—but the Runner's posture didn't change. He simply removed his own hat and stepped inside.

Madeline moved to the door that joined the parlor to the study. Cracking the door open, she waited as the footsteps sounded on the stairs.

A moment later, Canterbury ushered Huntford inside. "Miss Valdan will see you when she is available."

Huntford nodded once. When the door closed silently behind Canterbury, Huntford remained in place while his eyes searched the room. She didn't doubt he saw everything from the ink stain on the desk to the threadbare patch on the rug, and he never once allowed his back to be to the door.

Perhaps he might be of some use after all.

She also liked the way he stood, weight centered, arms loose. There were scabs on his knuckles, too—at most, a week old. The calluses on his hands were far older.

His clothing gave her pause, however. Ian had said he'd earned a fair amount of money from his private investigations, but she wouldn't have picked him as a man to spend much of it on clothing. But there was no doubt that his clothing wasn't some ready-made attire. It had been tailored specifically for him, skimming his broad shoulders and trim waist. The cravat at his neck was tied simply, but with crisp, clean lines. His boots, while not new, were polished to a shine.

Who was he trying to prove himself to?

Not her. He'd been dressed just as precisely at the police office yesterday.

Huntford's gaze swung to the door she was hiding behind. He couldn't see her. She knew that. She'd hidden this way a hundred times before. She was out of sight. Her breathing was light and shallow through her nose. There were no shadows under the door. There was no way he could know she was there.

Yet when his attention lingered there, she had to fight the urge to back away, her heart fluttering in her chest like that of a cornered rabbit.

Madeline narrowed her gaze, annoyed at her body's betrayal.

Huntford suddenly disappeared from sight and Madeline had to shift to find him again. He stood at her desk, flipping through the blank sheets of paper on top. After a quick pause, he moved behind it and opened a drawer. When he discovered that the only thing inside was a list of her current bidders, he'd be disappointed.

Madeline smiled. She'd intended to make him wait

until eleven but this was too good an opportunity to pass up. Keeping her steps silent, she left the parlor and walked to the study door.

Gabriel's hand rested on the brass drawer handle. He'd meant to come here and refuse the assignment, a task Potts thought so important that he'd reassigned not only the Simm murder, but all Gabriel's other cases until Miss Valdan's job was complete. But now Gabriel stared at the page of names. It must be a list of the men bidding on her.

Lenton. Billingsgate. Darby. The names seared across his mind. They were three of his suspects.

Potts had said she wanted to hire a Runner to investigate the men bidding on her. What if he could use her investigation to hide his own? Potts was right, most of his suspects would do everything they could to avoid a murder investigation. But if they meant to win Miss Valdan, they'd be willing to—

The door suddenly swung open.

Miss Valdan paused in the doorway, eyebrow raised, her gaze on the paper in his hand. Gabriel straightened but he didn't bother to scramble away from the open drawer. It was too late for that. But why hadn't he heard her coming? And damnation, his cheeks were heating like he was an errant child.

She inclined her head. "Can I help you locate something?"

Gabriel shrugged. "I thought since you were occupied, I'd leave a note and come back when you were available."

She glanced pointedly at the blank paper and ink on the top of the desk. She didn't believe him, but then he hadn't really expected her to.

"Like at eleven, our appointment time?"

"I'm afraid I have a pressing matter to attend to then." Because he hadn't thought he'd stay here longer than it took to refuse her job.

Madeline checked the clock on the mantel, then gestured to the door with a flick of her hand. "Well, it's almost eleven now. If you cannot stay, feel free to send someone in your place."

Gabriel almost agreed. But those three names on the list beckoned, too tempting to ignore.

No, he needed to stay even if it meant giving her the capitulation she sought. "The other meeting can be postponed." Hopefully. His witness, the old coachman, Bourne, was always at the tavern. Gabriel could ask his additional questions later.

"Good. I assume Potts told you what I will require?"

"He did, but perhaps you should tell me so there will be no misunderstandings."

She walked toward him. Gabriel moved to the other side of the desk, reluctant to have her near him again. Rather than claim the chair as he'd expected, she stopped and glanced out the window.

The daylight poured across her face, and Gabriel studied her afresh. Surely the unforgiving rays of the sun would reveal some flaw. A freckle. A pockmark. A heavy dusting of rice powder. But if anything, the sun rendered her skin more radiant. More pristine.

His teeth ground together as lust rose unbidden. Everything from the lush cupid's bow of her lips to the way her fingers rubbed at a knot in her lower back whispered of sensuality. It surrounded her like fine perfume. It wasn't gaudy or overpowering, but rather a subtle fragrance that drew one closer to explore the complex notes.

Her eyes lifted from the window, sweeping him with similar methodical intensity. And being male, part of him was very curious what she concluded.

Hell. He didn't want Miss Valdan. He wanted to catch a murderer. "What is it you require?" he asked, his voice curt even to his own ears.

She shrugged, drawing his eyes to the luscious hint of bosom visible above the neckline of her cream-colored dress. "Contrary to what you obviously believe, Mr. Huntford, I'm not a fool. I need to be sure of two things—first and foremost, that the man who wins can pay. I need you to examine the bidders' financial records and discover if they have the blunt to honor their bids." She sat and straightened the papers on her desk. "I'm not going to hand over my virginity on the empty promise of being paid in the future. I want my money as soon as the deed is done."

Gabriel looked for any sign that she wasn't as cold about the pronouncement as she appeared. But she met his gaze without flinching. He further resolved to ignore his baser urges. A woman who could sell her virginity without any hesitance must have ice in her veins.

Or wasn't truly a virgin.

Yet that suspicion didn't matter if she gained him access to what he needed. If he had his suspects' financial records, there was a chance he'd be able to find some tie to both murders. The purchase of the mourning brooches, perhaps?

Yet in his experience, gentlemen weren't eager to part with anything, let alone their most private financial dealings. "What makes you think anyone will comply with your demand for proof?"

"Because I'll ask them."

Curse it. Perhaps it would be best to refuse the assignment after all. If that was her plan, she had about as much chance of succeeding as he did on his own. "And if they don't agree, Miss Valdan?"

The steady calm in her gaze fractured and she rose to her feet. She chewed nervously on her lip, leaving it moist and rosy. "Madeline. My name is Madeline." She peered up at him with wide eyes. "They will agree, won't they? I mean, it makes sense." She placed her hand on his chest, its weight light, uncertain. "I didn't want to do this, but what other option do I have? What lady would trust me in her house as a maid? And I'm not well-bred enough to be a governess."

Despite the seductive warmth of her touch, he wasn't about to feel sorry for her. He removed her hand. "You chose this."

She drew in a deep breath. "You're right. And I do have a plan."

"Your plan is to *ask* them?"

"It's a good plan. The men are gentlemen. They'll honor their bets." When her hands trembled, she tucked them behind her.

Heaven save him from naive fools. Without her veneer of bravado, she appeared barely out of the schoolroom. "Just because they're gentlemen doesn't mean they'll act like it." He wanted to brush his thumb across her lower lip to save it from the abuse of her teeth, but he feared if he touched her lips, he'd want to touch the slender column of her throat. And once his fingers had skimmed over her throat, he'd be unable to stop them from dipping lower.

And he wasn't one of her lovesick swains.

"You'll help me?" She reached for him again but then dropped her hand as if afraid of rejection.

The small sign of vulnerability ensnared him in a way her seductive glances never could. "I'll do what I can."

Her breath came fast and shallow, causing her breasts to strain against her bodice. "I know."

He swallowed roughly as she leaned toward him. He needed to tell her he wasn't interested. But when he spoke, his voice was raspy and deep. "Madeline—"

She pulled back with quick determination. "That is why they'll agree."

He stared at her through the muddled haze of lust. "What?"

She dusted off the front of her gown as if to rid it of any hint of their interaction. "Every man has a weakness. Pride, vanity . . ." She allowed a deliberate pause, a mocking grin curving her lips. "The desire to protect. Any weakness can be turned to my advantage."

Gabriel stalked to the far corner of the room until the urge to wrap his hands around her neck faded. She had played him. She hadn't even needed to snap her fingers to bring him to heel. "You intend to manipulate every man in England?"

"As amusing as that would be, it isn't necessary. Once the first few agree, I'll point out that anyone who refuses must have something embarrassing to hide."

He exhaled through clenched teeth. *Forget she made a fool of you.* He'd wanted her to have a plan, and apparently, hers was far better than he'd given her credit for. But fury, and a disturbing amount of frustrated desire, still drove him. "So you plan to dupe them into paying you a fortune?"

She frowned. "No. They'll get what they pay for. My virginity. I'm merely trying to ensure they don't cheat me."

"By preying on their weaknesses."

She crossed her arms. "It's not a crime to discover fantasies. You do the same thing."

He glared at her. "Nonsense."

"When you capture a suspect, you ferret out their weaknesses first, do you not? You watch for the lies and the fears, then you exploit them to gain a confession. The only difference is that my process ends with a pleasant interlude in bed and yours ends on the gallows."

His fists tightened until his hands ached. But Miss Valdan was right, curse her. Besides, he couldn't risk provoking her further. The more he thought about it, the more perfect this opportunity was. By working for Madeline, he could investigate the men of the *ton* without their knowledge. Hell, perhaps they'd even help. "What else do you need me to do?"

She hesitated, and for a moment, he was positive his bitterness had lost him the assignment.

The door opened and the butler entered. This time a blue ribbon and pheasant feathers trimmed the man's hat. He carried a tray containing tea and biscuits, which he set on a small table. Madeline didn't spare the butler's strange attire a second glance. Instead, she lowered herself onto the settee and motioned to the chair across from her.

Gabriel sat. He'd be harder to throw out if he was drinking tea.

She poured with a grace more befitting a lady of the manor than a woman of the streets. Even his mother would have approved. She offered him a plate of biscuits. "I will also require the sexual histories of the top bidders. That information, I assume, they will be less anxious to part with."

At least she'd decided not to throw him out.

"My desire to fulfill fantasies only goes so far. I won't share a bed with a madman, no matter how much he pays. Nor do I want to end up with the pox as a memento of the evening. While financial information can be supplied by a banker or solicitor, this portion of the assignment will require an investigator familiar with the darker environs and back alleys of London."

That he was. Since Susan's death, he'd spent little time anywhere else. The more violent and depraved the criminal he hunted, the better. He held out hope with each arrest that someone would have a clue that would lead him to his sister's killer. As the months and years had passed, he'd recognized the growing improbability of that hope. Yet he couldn't stop.

Besides, if Miss Valdan wanted a proper investigation, not only would he look into the whorehouses and bordellos, he'd have to interview her bidders' staffs as well—butlers, valets, maids. All people who would know of their masters' proclivities.

And their whereabouts the night of the Simm murder.

Gabriel nodded in acceptance.

"Also, for the next fortnight, I need you by my side when I'm seen in public."

"What?" That sneaky cur Potts had left out that detail. "I can't investigate if I'm escorting you."

"I'm not asking for much time. A couple hours in the morning when I drive in the park and in the evening when I appear at my chosen entertainments. The rest of the day belongs to you."

It sounded reasonable, but he had no desire to spend that much time in her company. "I didn't think you lacked for escorts."

"Do you know Lady Golpin?"

Gabriel shook his head at the change of topic. "Not that I remember."

"She owns a fantastic diamond necklace. It is enormous. She only wears it if she is accompanied by two armed footmen."

He took a bite of his biscuit and waited. Although he might dislike her methods, he'd begun to suspect that a calculating, logical mind worked inside that beautiful head.

"Everyone is so impressed by the security that no one has thought to question the actual worth of the piece."

"And they should?"

Madeline smiled, a mischievous grin that harkened back to girlhood pranks. "It's paste. She's actually only a stone's throw from losing everything to her creditors."

A matching grin threatened to form on his face until it occurred to him that her smile was likely a ploy calculated to draw that reaction from him. To gain his compliance.

"It is in my best interest to look like I have something worth protecting."

He stilled as another correlation to Lady Golpin occurred to him. "Lady Golpin uses this tactic to hide the truth. Are you doing the same thing?"

Would she admit it?

"Are you asking me if I'm a virgin?" She looked thoroughly entertained by the question. "Why do you care, Mr. Huntford?"

Gabriel placed the biscuit on his plate. He didn't care, yet he found himself leaning forward. "I think I should know the value of the commodity I'm protecting."

"Immense, of course." She blew gently on her cup of tea.

Tiny pinpricks covered his arms as his body reacted to the imagined sensation of that air moving over his skin. "It's my reputation you're hiring as well as my skills. Are you a virgin?"

She sipped her drink and swallowed, sending a ripple down her throat. "What else could I be?"

"Very clever or foolish. Are you truly untouched?"

The sparkle in her eyes dimmed, and she returned her cup to the tray. "I never claimed that. If you want further assurance, you'll have to bid on me yourself." She rose to her feet. "Now I also must be clear that I have several rules I will insist upon. First, all information you discover will be reported to me, no matter how insignificant it might seem."

Gabriel nodded. He'd give her any information that might affect her auction. He would not be telling her, however, about his own private inquiry. He'd do everything she'd hired him for. If he chose to do more, that was his business. He quelled a stab of guilt. He hadn't lured his suspects into bidding on her. With or without his involvement, they'd still be pursuing her. In fact, she was safer because of him.

"Next, your investigation into my bidders' private lives remains private. I won't risk scaring potential bidders away."

That suited his purposes perfectly. "Anything else?"

"One last thing. Your only payment will be monetary. Under no circumstances will I sleep with you or pleasure you in any way." Her gaze swept over him, lingering on his lower body. "No matter the size of the bulge in your trousers. Are we agreed?"

Resisting the urge to look down, Gabriel gave a curt nod. "I'm at your service."

Chapter Three

"Ready?" Madeline asked, taking her bonnet from Canterbury.

Huntford glared at her from where he'd propped his shoulder against the door frame. The morning light pouring in behind him rendered his face difficult to read. "I'm here, aren't I?"

She pinned on her hat. "Feel free to continue glowering. It will quite add to your authoritative air."

He didn't reply to her sally. She opened her mouth again, then paused. She didn't have to keep him enthralled. He could be dour and bitter all he wanted and she had no responsibility to coax him from his black mood. She savored the novelty of it.

Perhaps she shouldn't have tormented him yesterday, but it had seemed easier to show how she planned to ensure her bidders' cooperation rather than argue. And truth be told, his arrogance had nettled, and she'd wanted to take him down a peg.

Madeline walked toward him, doing her best to give no indication of the way energy sizzled around him, raising the hair on the back of her neck. While he was not precisely handsome, she'd dealt with enough men to know he'd undress well. But that didn't explain why his proximity increased the rate of her heart. She kept her gait steady as she passed, hoping to determine the cause of her agitation.

Most likely it was the way his eyes never left her, and the fact that it wasn't lust binding his gaze. She was unused to people seeing past her beauty. It unnerved her. Her secrets were her own.

Beyond the carriage, a footman ducked behind an oak tree.

Not knowing what about him had caught her attention, she lifted her skirts and hurried across the street. She knew better than to ignore her instincts. The crunch of gravel informed her that Huntford followed. She didn't look back, hoping that if she ignored him, he wouldn't speak until she could see the man behind the tree.

It was a vain hope. "Madeline—"

The man darted out, his pace just short of a run.

"Henry!" Madeline called out, hoping to startle him into turning around. But the man didn't slow. Short of breaking into a run herself—and she knew she'd never be able to explain that to Huntford's satisfaction—she wouldn't be able to catch him. She studied what she could: the awkward swing of the man's arms, the slight outward turn of his feet, his boots. The boots were by Hoby—there was no mistaking the quality. And they were new and perfectly fitted.

Shoes never lied. A wig or coat could be thrown on, but shoes were too bulky. And if he'd planned his disguise so poorly, he wasn't a professional.

But neither was he a footman.

Huntford watched her as if she'd gone mad.

"I could have sworn that was the footman I sent to deliver letters. But I must have been wrong." While pretending to adjust her skirt, Madeline studied the grass under the tree where the man had been standing. Well trampled. He'd been waiting there for some time.

If he'd been an assassin, she'd be dead.

Huntford's eyes bored through her again. "You often run after servants?"

Far too observant.

She raised an eyebrow. "He also left with the silver."

As she'd hoped, Huntford's attention lifted toward where the man had disappeared. "Do you want me to go after him?"

Madeline shook her head. If the man came back, she'd be ready for him. "It wasn't him. Henry was shorter." She crossed the street and climbed into her carriage.

"Lenton, Billingsgate, and Wethersly are your top three bidders," he said as he sat across from her.

She nodded. Apparently, she'd been granted a reprieve for this morning's oddity, but she didn't for a moment believe he'd forgotten. "I received a report on the bid book as well."

"What do you know of them?"

"You've had their names since this morning. What did *you* find out?"

His shoulder hitched upward. "Lenton is young and horse mad, inherited a large amount of money from his maternal grandmother. Billingsgate is a gambler and floats between wealth and poverty on a weekly basis. Wethersly, I haven't heard much about, but from what I could discover, he's an old man with an eye for pretty women. What do you know?"

She saw no reason to hide the fruits of her own carefully placed questions. "Billingsgate has won more than he's lost the past few weeks and prefers faro."

"Do you know him?"

"Only very slightly. We met in the park last week. He's charming, if a bit cold."

"Cold in what way?"

She could hardly explain that she'd noticed how his hands tensed whenever someone touched him. Or that he always positioned himself in the dominant position in any conversation. "Does it matter? My main concern is that he has money."

Huntford leaned back in his seat, somehow failing to appear any more relaxed. "So it doesn't matter if you like the man who wins?"

She'd never expected to. The government had been assigning her to seduce men since she was fourteen. Any romantic notions she might have once held were long dead. "What matters is that *they* think I like them."

"You see no issue with the deception?"

"Don't act so offended. Half the world pretends. Doesn't an heiress become more desirable the larger her dowry? Dukes have more admirers than their character and wit warrant. A modiste always swears the most expensive fabric looks the best. In my case, I'll make the winner think the fortune he paid for me was a bargain. We both win."

Huntford frowned. "You have a disturbing ability to make your justifications seem valid."

"Is that a compliment?" she asked.

"No."

But that pleased her even more. Flattery was meaningless; accusations seldom were.

The carriage slowed as they approached the tree-lined roads of Hyde Park.

"What do you know of Lenton?" Huntford asked.

"Quite a bit. He—" A familiar round face rode toward them. "See for yourself."

As she beckoned, she tilted her head and parted her lips. While ensuring her body was artfully arranged on the cushions, she peeled off her gloves, baring even more flesh. By the time Viscount Lenton reined in his spirited bay gelding, she was ready.

A grin split his cherubic face and he doffed his hat with a wide sweep of his arm. "My fair Miss Valdan, it's been far too long since you allowed me to escort you to Vauxhall. Your beauty is like the first daffodil in spring."

Drat, Canterbury won. She'd laid her money that the first compliment would compare her to the sun. Madeline extended her hand, and Lenton brought it to his lips for a lingering caress. Then he froze, his wet lips like two lethargic slugs. With an uncomfortable cough, he jerked upright. The sudden motion provoked the gelding to snort and yank against his bit.

Lenton kept a wary eye on Huntford as he calmed the skittish animal. "I say, you're that Runner, aren't you?"

Huntford inclined his head. "Gabriel Huntford."

"You're the one who caught the Chetfeld killer?"

"Indeed."

"What ever happened to him?"

"I sent him to the devil with a noose around his neck."

A chill trickled down her spine. But she had nothing to fear. He wasn't investigating her. She simply shouldn't wear such low-cut gowns in April.

Madeline allowed Lenton to process Huntford's less than cordial expression before redirecting his attention back to her. "Enough about him." She gave a dismissive wave in Huntford's direction.

The flicker of her hand spooked the horse.

With a grunt and pull on the reins, Lenton again settled the bay.

She widened her eyes. "Is that magnificent creature one of Cooing Dove's line?" It was, unless her sources failed her.

"Got him at Tattersall's last week. I outbid Barton for him." His eyes roved over her with renewed interest. "Not many women recognize prime horseflesh when they see it."

Such a high-strung animal wasn't fit for a country lane, let alone the streets of London, but she trailed her gaze deliberately over the viscount. "I make it a point to take note of all fine flesh—horse or"—she paused, drawing her hand along the edge of her bodice—"human."

Although Lenton's gaze locked on her fingers with feverish intensity, it was another set of eyes from across the carriage that intruded on her senses, snagging her breath in her throat and tightening her breasts.

Her hand froze for less than an instant. By the time she'd named the novel feeling, she knew how to turn it to her advantage.

Like anger or fear, lust was simply a physical reaction to external stimulus. And although its severity was unexpected, there was no reason to waste such a perfectly genuine reaction. She slowed the motion of her hand so Lenton would notice her taut nipples.

As she kept her gaze locked with him, she savored the idea of grasping the front of her bodice and lowering it as Huntford watched. His scowl would no doubt remain in place but his eyes would darken, turning the pale green into a more human color. His gaze would narrow, held captive by her actions.

Fanning her face with her hand, she highlighted the flush heating her cheeks. A slow blink drew attention to her dilated eyes.

And Lenton, the poor fellow, thought it was all for him.

She spoke while the throaty quality still clung to her voice. "Please tell me you've bid."

Lenton tugged on the front of his jacket. "I did. And I won't let another man top me."

"I hope you'll let *me* top you."

His hand clenched on the reins, and his horse pranced, its eyes rolling. "When I win you, I—"

"If you win." Huntford's bored tone cut through Lenton's fervency.

"You never did say why he's in your carriage."

To irk her, apparently. Some things required gentle coaxing, not a blunt blow alongside the head. "With the attention this auction is garnering, the authorities feared for my safety."

Huntford's lips thinned, but he didn't deny her claim. Good, he'd forced her hand to begin with.

"I would protect you," Lenton protested.

"I know. But I don't know if I could trust myself with you until the end of the auction. But Mr. Huntford . . . well, he poses no threat in that area."

Perhaps Huntford would think twice before intruding again.

Lenton favored the Runner with a pitying smile. "Keep her safe for me."

"She'll come to you in the same condition she's in now."

Whatever that might be. He didn't voice the words, but she could feel them dangling in the air.

Luckily, Lenton seemed oblivious to anything but her bosom. "I will do what it takes to win you."

Madeline smiled. "Good. Then you agree. I knew a wise man such as yourself would see the logic."

"Pardon? Agree to what?"

"To let Huntford verify your financial situation."

"What?"

"I know you have the honor to win the auction legitimately, but there are men who might try to outbid you, claiming funds they don't possess. You don't want that to happen, do you?" She leaned over the edge of the carriage, providing him with a brief glimpse down her bodice. "Now that I know you truly want me, I don't want anyone else to win."

Lenton nodded to Huntford. "My secretary will provide you with whatever you require."

Madeline clapped her hands. "I knew I could rely on you."

Lenton reached to capture her chin, but his beleaguered horse revolted. Its hooves clacked on the cobbles as it pranced sideways, then galloped from the park onto the street, narrowly missing a lumbering refuse cart.

Madeline leaned back against her seat. The pleasure of a perfectly executed plan had no equal. "I told you all I had to do was ask."

Huntford pinned her with his gaze; the earlier heat now blistered her flesh. "Forget this auction and become my mistress."

"What?" The word croaked from her throat in an embarrassing manner. After all, men made that offer every day. She had a dozen witty jests to decline a man while still stringing him along and twice as many cutting responses to put him in his place.

Huntford leaned forward.

She pressed back, regaining the few inches of separation.

"If you're so intent on having me, why not end this auction now?"

The smugness drained from Madeline's expression, leaving her face blank.

Hiding what? Shock? Revulsion? Anger? But it didn't matter; the opportunity to settle the score had been too tempting. "That's what your suitor would've said if he had half a brain. What would you have done if he'd called your bluff?"

She relaxed. "I would have appealed to his sense of honor and fair play. After all, the auction has already begun. It would hardly be gentlemanly of me to pull out now."

"You aren't a gentleman."

The animation rekindled on her face. Her head tipped to the right as she laughed, exposing the smooth, pale skin of her throat. The pose practically begged a man to set his lips against the delicate flesh. How long had she practiced to perfect it?

Rather than a sultry murmur, her laughter skipped light and bright along carefree notes. He might have believed it to be genuine, if not for the fact that several men, including a few escorting respectable ladies, swung around at the sound.

And Madeline's eyes darted briefly in their direction, noting every single one. "I might not be a gentleman, but those bidding are. The thrill of trouncing other men is half the pleasure of winning."

"And the other half?"

She cocked an eyebrow. "Oh, very good. If I were any other woman, I would be firmly under your heel where I deserve to be, I assure you."

If he had her under a part of his anatomy, it wouldn't be his heel.

As the carriage progressed through the park, she worked her charms on any male foolish enough to enter her territory.

She was good.

The small niggling of admiration alarmed him, yet the fascination remained. As each man approached, her response altered. A touch more ribald with one, more shy with another. One by one their eyes darkened, stripping Madeline naked. She encouraged the reaction with careful movements of her hands, directing the men's attention to her body with the skill of a dockside sharp running a game of shells.

Her finger tapped against her lower lip as she spoke, drawing attention to its generous curve. The poor sap she currently conversed with swallowed with a noisy grunt. Even though Gabriel recognized her action for the ploy it was, his thumb tingled as if he'd touched her.

He clenched his hand.

She was a manipulator. And a liar. As talented as she was at convincing each man that she was his perfect mate, there was no way someone hadn't bedded her.

But she'd managed to do what she'd promised. Each of the men agreed to allow Gabriel access to his records. Gabriel fingered the warm, smooth angles of the mourning brooch in his pocket. He now had access to Lenton.

But what were the odds that it was Lenton? And what were the odds the man had recorded anything of use?

Damnation. He refused to give up the first hope he'd had in years. Besides, he wasn't constrained to the records. To find out the other information Madeline required, he'd have to speak to the man's servants. They might know something.

Madeline's current follower scrambled off to place his first bid and another man jostled for a turn to speak with her.

Even though this man wasn't a suspect, Gabriel studied him as he had all the others. It was habit now. He'd spent far too many hours scrutinizing various members of the *ton*, trying to figure out which of them was the new suitor Susan had spoken of before her death. But this man was too young. He couldn't have been the man who wooed her with promises, then lured her away to strangle her.

"Huntford, do stop growling. I'm sure David isn't afraid to prove his bid." Madeline gave Gabriel a quick, searching glance, then returned to smiling at the nervous man.

"What?" David asked.

"It is quite the amazing thing. Gentlemen are serious about this auction. They have no tolerance for those who bid without the resources to pay."

The young man who'd moments before been comparing the color of Madeline's dress to freshly churned butter, paled. "There was a fire a few months back and whatnot. My solicitor might not be able to, um, put together proof of my finances in a timely manner."

Gabriel waited for Madeline to mock the lad's obvious avoidance.

"I'll understand if you must handle those matters first," Madeline said.

The young man grasped the excuse. "Yes, yes. Those matters might not allow me to bid."

Before the next man could speak, Madeline motioned to the coachman, who set the carriage in motion, scattering the large crowd of gentlemen sniffing about.

Gabriel studied her, suspicious of her kindness. "Why leave before wooing all of your potential deflowerers?" And before she'd been approached by his other suspects.

Madeline glanced around, then closed her eyes, dropping her head back against the seat. "Always leave your audience wanting more." One eye peeped open at him. "And always leave before you want to murder your audience."

He snorted. "You control them well. They'd probably throw themselves off a bridge to save you from having to lift one dainty finger."

Both eyes snapped open and she grinned. "If only there was a way to get them to pay me for that."

Of course she was charming. She'd hardly be able to pull this off if she wasn't. But he refused to be cozened. "Most people don't find death a joking matter."

Her smile remained on her face but it fled from her eyes. "Most people spend their lives miserable and poor."

The coach drew to a halt outside her home. Gabriel helped her descend, but she withdrew her hand as soon as her feet were on the pavement.

A small, white paper fluttered on her steps next to the door, and she paused to pick it up. She read it but then tucked it in her bodice. "What a horrendous poem." She tucked a stray wisp of chestnut hair behind her ear. "I need you tonight."

That inspired far too many images. "I must start the investigation."

"Your supervisors are concerned for my safety, remember?"

"Second only to England herself." He'd responded to her teasing tone without thinking. That annoyed him. He didn't waste time on banter. "What are your plans?"

"Something shocking."

"Nothing shocks me."

She slid her hand down his cheek. "We'll see about that."

Chapter Four

Madeline shivered in a draft of cold air as Clayton Campbell stepped inside, shaking rain from his dark hair. The brisk sunlight of the morning had given way before the habitual rain clouds of London.

"Have you decided to give this insanity up then?" he asked as he handed his coat to Canterbury.

She shook her head. The man had always had too many morals for a spy. "And live off the scraps the Foreign Office paid us?"

"My investments have already doubled."

"Twice a pittance is still a pittance. And how can you lecture me about insanity, Mr. I-Will-Seek-Revenge-with-My-Dying-Breath?"

"Justice. Not revenge. A fine distinction, but one that makes all the difference."

She snorted.

"Why did you send for us?"

"I'll explain as soon as—"

"I show up?" Ian Maddox sauntered in behind them.

She gave Ian a mock frown. He received some sort of perverse pleasure from mysteriously appearing out of nowhere even when the front door was perfectly accessible.

"You're late," Clayton pointed out.

"Someone's butler not only locked but barred the other doors and booby-trapped the windows."

Canterbury took Ian's coat and hat. "It's to keep out the ruffians, sir."

"No wonder I got in so easily then, old man."

Canterbury sniffed, holding Ian's battered hat away from his body with two fingers. "It appears I need to be more diligent."

"So other than pining for my handsome face, what are you up to, Madeline?" He ruffled her hair, ignoring the fact that it was elegantly coiffed. Or had been.

She blew a disarranged strand from her face. "Come." She led them to the study.

Clayton grimaced as he perched on a spindly, filigreed chair. "Tell me you didn't select this furniture."

"No, the house came furnished, which is one of the reasons I let it."

"I see no problem with it." Ian draped himself across the entire settee.

Rather than taking one of the uncomfortable hard-backed chairs, Madeline knocked his feet onto the floor and sat next to him. "I'm being watched."

"Who in London is not watching you?" Ian asked, but his head lifted from the arm of the settee.

Clayton stood, abandoning the creaky chair. "Did you recognize him?"

Madeline shook her head but listed the footman's identifying characteristics. When she mentioned the boots, Ian sat fully upright. "Have you seen your reluctant admirer since?"

"No, but I found this on the doorstep." She pulled out the note and handed it to Ian.

He scanned it once, then read the message aloud.

" 'I remember you from Paris. I know you for the liar you are. You will pay for your deception.' " Ian grinned. "Does he know how little money you have?"

Clayton took the paper and inspected it. "Really, criminals are becoming too lax with their research."

"And they could've been more specific. How many times did we run missions in Paris? Twenty-two? It would be a miracle if someone *didn't* see you in Paris."

Their familiar banter soothed the edginess that had nipped at her all day. She could handle whoever was fool enough to threaten her. And with Ian and Clayton lending assistance, the man might as well have signed his name to the note and asked to be eliminated. Even if they'd refused to help her with the auction, no one threatened a member of the Trio and lived.

Clayton flipped the paper over, examining the other side. "The paper quality isn't fabulous, but neither is it cheap. I doubt we are dealing with your typical guttersnipe. They'd have better uses for their money than purchasing nice new paper for threatening letters."

Ian leaned back on the settee. "As a former guttersnipe, I concur."

"Former?" Canterbury entered with a tray of cold ham, cheese, and bread.

"I haven't dropped a single *aitch* all day, old man. Seen the writing before, Clay?" Ian asked.

Madeline surveyed her butler once again. Ian trusted him enough to speak about Trio business in front of him? How did they know each other? Ian would only say Canterbury was an associate from a former life. But which former life? His life as a thief or his life as a spy?

"No, I don't recognize it."

Which meant the author wasn't someone whose documents they'd stolen in the past. If Clayton didn't recognize the writing, then they'd never encountered it before. Everything he'd ever read was etched into his mind, never to be forgotten.

"So who in Paris wants to kill you?" Ian asked.

Clayton snorted. "Shall I alphabetize the list?"

Ian tapped a lazy finger on the back of the settee. "You wouldn't have this problem if you'd let me eliminate the bastards after we retrieved the information we needed."

She knew Ian's comment was only half in jest. "Yes, because a slew of dead bodies in our wake would have been so subtle."

He shrugged. "Dead bodies wouldn't threaten you."

Ah, but they could haunt her, as she well knew. She wiped her hands on her skirt.

Clayton rose to his feet and began to pace. "Back to business. So if our friend knows you from France, we assume he's French?"

"Not necessarily." She'd been mulling over that question all afternoon. "If he was there while we were assisting Louis the Unavoidable back onto the French throne last year, he could be any nationality."

"Damnation," Clayton swore. "I'll compile a list of those I think most likely to be holding a grudge."

Ian sat up and began loading his pockets with food. "I'll start making inquiries with the savory fellows that I know. See if anyone's heard anything. Speaking of inquiries, how do you like Huntford?"

"I worry that he might be a bit too observant." Madeline wished the words unsaid as soon as she'd spoken them. Both men turned to her in disbelief.

"Too observant? When have you ever been worried about the local police?" Clayton asked.

"She's been pensioned off, remember. Perhaps her skills have gone into decline."

How could she explain the feeling to them when she couldn't even explain it to herself yet? Disgruntled at her show of weakness, Madeline stood and walked to the window. She was careful to keep to the side so she could look out without anyone below spotting her. Her watcher had not yet returned.

"Does Huntford know about the threat?"

"No. There's no way to explain that without explaining my work for the Foreign Office, and that I'm not willing to do. If anything arises, I'll handle it myself."

"Yourself? In that case, I think I'll head down to the tavern—"

She glared at Ian. "You two don't count."

He winked at her. "To begin asking questions, of course."

Clayton paused directly in front of her so she had to crane her neck to see his face. "As much as I don't like giving in to a murderous criminal, I still say you should stop the auction." Although his voice was cold, concern darkened his gaze.

She sighed. It would be much easier if he were really as unfeeling as he pretended to be. "We've been over this already."

"If anyone else connects you with La Petit, there are many powerful men who stand to be quite embarrassed by your virginity."

"The chances of that are slight. The only danger is if someone sees me and recognizes me as this man must have done. Even if the men from our past compared notes with each other, who would think to connect Madame Juliette with Marie the chambermaid or Sasha the royalist?"

Ian took a large gulp of tea. "Become Madeline,

the happily wed mother, and there will be even less chance of them making the connection."

"You know why that will never happen." Or at least as much about it as she'd told another living being. The rest of her story would make the devil himself cringe. Perhaps she'd test that theory when she met him. "I choose to sell myself for the night, not for the rest of my life."

"What if someone else makes the connection to La Petit?" Clayton asked.

She snatched the last sandwich from the tray before Ian pilfered it. "If they do, they can bid on me with the rest. I'm finishing this auction."

The barmaid rubbed her heavily perfumed bosom across Gabriel's back as she set the tankard of ale on his table, but he kept his focus on the inebriated man sitting across from him.

The man reached for the alcohol with an unsteady hand as she stalked away. "It's right generous of you, sir. Now where was I?"

Gabriel rested his elbow on the smooth pine table. Lenton's valet had agreed to meet him at the Irish Hag, a tavern frequented by the servants of the aristocracy. The place was moderately clean and the ale decent, although it seemed the latter characteristic was the main enticement for the valet. If Lenton's servant kept demanding ale for each bit of information, he'd soon be useless. "Where was the viscount last Tuesday, William?"

"Well, in the morning he had me prepare his blue superfine and dove gray waistcoat. He only wanted his cravat tied in a simple mathematical, so I have to assume he was going to visit his mother. She despises anything showy." William sniffed, his pinched nostrils flaring.

"Then later that afternoon?" Gabriel had to wait for his answer as the valet took several large gulps.

"He had me change him into his new green riding jacket with gold buttons and braiding. He didn't specify, so I selected his yellow waistcoat with the holly embroidery." William sat back with a sigh. "Fine piece of craftsmanship that. Although I must confess I've always thought that if the tailor had gone with a slightly larger leaf, the whole thing would—"

"Did he say where he was going that afternoon?"

The man's eyes widened and he blinked blearily a few times. "Tattersall's, perhaps?"

It would be easy enough to check with the grooms and see if that's where he'd gone. "Then that evening, where did he dress to go?" Gabriel asked, hoping to forestall another extended discourse on fashion.

But William apparently couldn't think in any other terms. A sappy grin slid over his face. "That was the evening I finally perfected my personal triumph—I call it the Timid Swan. The folds of the cravat feather down from the chin in graceful wings . . ." William lifted his cup for another sip, but then glared into his empty tankard and glanced up expectantly.

Gabriel motioned to the barmaid. Her face twisted in a sneer and she sat on the lap of the man she was serving, twining her arms around his neck and giggling when he pinched her backside.

William tapped his mug on the table for a few seconds, then pushed back his chair. "Well, I've only got a few more hours of my day off so I think I'll find myself a drink."

Gabriel pointed to the chair. "Sit down." He'd perfected the tone over years of dealing with reluctant criminals.

William sat, but his face turned sullen. "There's no call to talk to me like that. I'm helping you, remember?"

Gabriel wished once again for some of his sister's skill with people. As twins they'd shared many of the same talents, but it was Susan who gained people's trust and friendship with her big, honest smiles.

Gabriel, on the other hand, relied on blunter methods. "Where was Lenton on Tuesday night?"

William shrugged. "The theater."

"Was he escorting anyone?"

"No, I think he was meeting friends in the pit."

"Who?" Gabriel asked.

The valet swallowed nervously. "He didn't say."

"What time did he come home?"

William pushed his tankard with short jabs of his finger. "Sometime after three."

"And how was he dressed?"

The valet looked up from the mug's progress in confusion. "I just told you. My cravat—"

"I mean, was there any damage to his clothing or signs of a struggle?"

William shook his head. "Nothing like that." Then he paused. "Actually, now that I think on it, his cravat was mussed. I called him to the carpet over it, not that he even heard me."

"Why wouldn't he have heard you?"

"He was too foxed."

Gabriel stood. "If you remember anything else about that night, let me know."

He tossed a shilling on the table, which William snatched up, his face lightening. "Why are you asking so much about His Lordship?"

Because, curse it all, he'd give anything to see Susan's smile again. To have her tease him about his big ears even knowing hers were just the same. But instead he said, "It's my job to see London safe."

Gabriel paid for the drinks, then walked out into the damp evening. His breath fogged in cottony clouds as he hailed a hackney. It wasn't until he'd climbed inside the coach that the old fear returned. Gritting his teeth, he focused his gaze on the street outside, counting pickpockets and thieves that he passed. But that couldn't banish the gnawing centered low in his gut. The uncertainty, the fear that he'd missed something. The fear that if he were better, smarter, or more vigilant, he might have been able to catch the murderer.

His failure seven years ago had cost Molly Simm her life.

Gabriel rubbed the heels of his hands against his eyes. He refused to let it happen again. Unlike last time, he had solid leads. He had suspects. He'd find the killer and personally see him kicking on the end of a noose.

As the coach slowed in front of Madeline's house, Gabriel stared out the window at a light flickering in what must be her bedroom window. He told himself the anticipation he felt was because she was going to bring him closer to his killer.

In fact, she'd bring the killer to him.

Chapter Five

"*H*ave you ever been to a Cyprians' ball, Huntford?"

"No." Gabriel frowned, hoping to quell Madeline's chatter as the coach jolted toward her evening entertainment. He suspected she took some unholy glee in trying to provoke a response from him. And the less he looked at her in that accursedly tempting dress, the better.

"It might shock you."

"So you said. What precisely will astound me so?"

One delicate shoulder lifted, threatening the tenuous hold her sleeve had on the pale curve of her upper arm.

He held his breath, unsure whether it was with dread or anticipation.

"You don't strike me as a man given to carnal pleasure."

Hell, how was he supposed to respond to that? Argue that he loved a good swiv as much as the next man? That if he gave in to his baser instincts, he'd pull her on top of him right now and pleasure her with all sorts of carnality?

Gabriel exhaled. In some regards, she was right.

He'd seen the vile underbelly of London far too closely to make use of the loose women he often dealt with. He'd seen what had driven them into that life, and no matter how randy he was, the idea of making love to a woman who'd been forced into that sort of profession held no appeal.

Neither did he want to bring some bride into the ugliness that was his life. Susan was the one who wanted to marry and make a passel of little children. She'd even picked out names for her future little ones, knitted bonnets and booties, for pity's sake.

Not that he was a saint. He'd enjoyed the occasional relationship with a well-off widow, as long as it was purely for mutual physical satisfaction.

The carriage drew to a halt outside Chatham House.

Madeline placed a hand on his knee when he would have exited. "Just so we are clear, you're not here as my chaperone. I don't need your interference."

"What are my orders then?" he asked, ignoring the hand massaging his knee.

"You are to glower occasionally and follow me about."

"So I'm to be your lapdog?"

"Do you want to be in my lap?" She grinned at the dread he felt imprinted on his face. "No, unlike a dog, I will not have you on a leash. You're free to pursue any of the lovelies you meet. Actually, I recommend it." Her hand inched slowly up his thigh. "We don't want anyone to mistakenly think you might want me."

He clamped her devilishly distracting hand in his own and removed it from his person. "Hardly likely."

She tugged free and climbed from the carriage, assisted by a groom. "I don't intend to stay long."

"Good."

She tilted her head and glanced at him over her shoulder. "You might find you'll enjoy yourself if you allow it."

Not bloody likely. Being crammed into a too-small space with a bunch of gentlemen with no concerns other than whom they'd next bed was not his idea of fun. But it was another chance to investigate his suspects. He jumped from the coach and followed her through the stately columned entrance.

"Enter the ballroom a few steps behind me. I need to appear eminently attainable, yet tantalizingly out of reach."

"That makes no sense." Yet as her softly rounded hips swayed as she preceded him into the ballroom, strangely it did.

The boisterous notes of a Scottish reel pulsed around him as he entered. As at most London balls, couples cavorted around the dance floor, but here their motions were more exuberant and carefree. Fingers stayed intertwined longer than necessary and hands wandered with unconcerned abandon during promenades. Eyes rested with blatant hunger on breasts and backsides carefully displayed in dresses that had more in common with handkerchiefs than their namesakes. Emerald, violet, and sapphire advertised the bodies beneath with reckless ferocity.

When Madeline paused, he stood next to her. A seductive smile graced her lips, but her gaze was calculating as she surveyed the crowd.

"Find your prey?" Gabriel asked.

She didn't look at him, but the right side of her lips quirked higher. "No, the trick is to arrange myself so my prey hunts me."

Gabriel grabbed her arm and dragged her backward as a couple fumbled past, nearly careening into them. The woman's dress was little more than pink gauze draped over her generous form. Her dark nipples were clearly visible through the bodice.

In her ivory dress, Madeline looked positively virginal by comparison. But that, no doubt, had been her intention all along.

Despite being already occupied, the woman shot Gabriel an admiring look as she continued past.

"The improbably named Miss Victoria Vixen and Mr. George Tundell," Madeline supplied. "She's between protectors right now. If you want her, she appears to be interested."

The overblown woman held little appeal. It would be like making love to the Alps.

"Hmm, so you're not a breast man."

She was doing it to him again. He wasn't about to protest that he liked bosoms quite well, just not a hideous excess of them. "I prefer your breasts." That should put an end to her teasing.

She didn't even blink. "I'm sure we'll be able to find someone with similar measurements."

So much for the attempt. "I didn't come here to find a mistress."

"Most men would leap at the added benefit."

"Most men would be oblivious to your attempts to manipulate them."

"Madeline!" Viscount Jamison practically skipped to her side, his grin vanishing as he looked at Gabriel. "Huntford." He spat the name.

Seven years ago, Jamison had been a prime suspect in Gabriel's investigation into Susan's murder, but in the end he'd proven innocent. Yet Gabriel felt no guilt about the level of his scrutiny. If Jamison had bothered to answer the questions he'd been asked and treated his maids better, there would have been no need for Gabriel to delve more deeply into his past transgressions.

Jamison's lip curled. "I doubt you can afford a single night with one of these women let alone one as your mistress."

Gabriel knew he was wealthier than the constantly impoverished Jamison. But since Jamison was no longer a suspect, he wasn't worth an argument. Gabriel merely inclined his head. "I'm here as an employee of Miss Valdan."

Jamison's sneer shifted into a superior smirk as he tugged Madeline toward the dance floor. "Dance with me."

She laughed. "I like boldness in a man, although most would have asked me to dance before leading me away."

Jamison bowed his head in mock contrition. "I could hardly say what I wanted in front of your servant." His gaze darted over his shoulder to ensure Gabriel had heard.

Madeline's reply was lost in the sway and press of the crowd. When she appeared on the dance floor a few seconds later, she was on the arm of the Duke of Spencer. He liked to think she'd disliked Jamison's attitude, but it was more likely that the duke was wealthier.

Dozens of perfumes and colognes vied in the damp, warm air, coating Gabriel's throat. He edged his way toward an open window, always keeping Madeline in his line of sight.

Madeline smiled at something the duke said and leaned in to respond, her eyes gleaming as if she were about to impart the perfect secret. Gabriel only just stopped himself from leaning in to try to hear even though he was half a ballroom away. Another gentleman to his right lacked his control and inched forward. As she spun about the dance floor, she radiated wicked sensuality, as if she might suddenly decide to scandalize everyone at any moment. And none of the gentlemen present would risk looking away and missing it.

Gabriel took advantage of their distraction to survey those in attendance. From his investigations this afternoon he'd tightened his suspect list to five: Lenton, Billingsgate, Hurley, Wallace, and Stedman. The other two had been eliminated when he'd confirmed their whereabouts the evening of the murder. Of the remaining suspects, two were here tonight: Lenton and Billingsgate.

While keeping Madeline in sight, Gabriel worked his way through the crowd until he stood a few feet to the right of Billingsgate.

The man's long black hair was tied back in a queue, but a piece had come free. He kept shoving it out of his face with impatient swats of his hand. A curvy, blond woman lingered by his side even though it was apparent his attention was on Madeline. "There is something about her I cannot resist."

"You used to like a thing or two about me." The blonde inched closer, finally wrapping her hands around his waist and pressing herself fully against him.

Billingsgate lifted his hand and roughly fondled her breast through her bodice, but his gaze stalked Madeline on the dance floor. "You were never more than a passing tolerable swiv."

When the woman swatted his hand away with an annoyed huff, Billingsgate shoved her from his side and prowled closer to the edge of the dance floor.

Gabriel intercepted the woman as she regained her balance.

Her brown eyes swept over him with an appraising gleam. "Are you looking for some company?"

Gabriel shook his head. "Answers."

"Why don't you come with me and I'll see what I can do?"

"I want information on Billingsgate."

Her tongue darted nervously over her lips and she checked to ensure he was still hovering by the dance floor. "I didn't come to waste this evening talking."

"I will make it worth your while."

Her eyes skipped to Billingsgate's back again. "He won't know I talked to you?"

Gabriel led her toward an alcove. "No."

Her smile returned, this time bloodthirsty. "What do you want to know?"

"You were his mistress?"

She shrugged. "Not quite. He visited me a few times, but we never had anything formal."

"When?" Gabriel asked.

"About two years ago."

She would know nothing about his whereabouts for either murder then. But perhaps she could link him to Miss Simm. "Did he ever mention a daughter?"

The woman's eyes widened. "No, he's not precisely the sentimental type. He—"

Billingsgate had glanced behind him, and even though he wasn't looking at them, the woman bolted before Gabriel could stop her. Before he'd paid her.

That bespoke a lot of fear. And that fear definitely moved him to the top of Gabriel's suspect list.

Gabriel threaded his way back to the edge of the dance floor so Madeline could find him when she finished this set. Where she went, Billingsgate and Lenton would follow.

He tried to picture either of them as the suitor Susan had spoken of. Not that he knew much. He only knew the man was handsome and titled. Gabriel hadn't let Susan get any further in her description before cutting her off. He'd come back from Oxford so full of himself and yet stinging from dozens of slights doled out by his aristocratic classmates. He'd been sure her suitor couldn't have honorable intentions. He'd been so certain he knew what was best for her he hadn't even bothered to ask questions. Instead, he ordered her away from the man. Ordered her, as if Oxford had made him all-knowing.

He might have been right about the man, but he'd been a fool about his sister.

Madeline returned to his side as the next set formed. The dance had brought a flush to her cheeks, making him long to let her warmth chase away the chill that surrounded him.

A sparkle lit her eyes. "You can't play nice with the other children, can you? What did you say to Laura to chase her off?"

Ah, he hadn't inspired the look, the chance to taunt him further had. That was easy for him to believe. "Laura?"

"The blonde."

Gabriel saw no reason not to tell her at least part of the truth. "I was investigating Billingsgate. Where's suitor number one—or rather two?"

"I sent him to fetch me a glass of wine. Don't you ever pursue women for the sake of enjoyment?"

"Not when I'm working."

She leaned in so close that, if he lowered his gaze, he'd be able to stare down the enticing valley between her breasts. "Are you ever not working?"

"No."

Her lips widened into a grin. "I can just picture you ordering a woman to bed with you."

Gabriel knew he should be insulted, but all he could focus on was the slight crinkle on her nose. It turned her smile from perfect to something far more real.

She straightened, fixing her smile on an approaching man. "Lenton! I feared you wouldn't make it tonight."

The crease on her nose was gone, returning the smile to mere perfection. A hollow smile.

After his initial certainty, Gabriel frowned, studying her again. There was nothing to confirm his suspicion. Her eyes still sparkled. Her face was glowing and animated.

A spurt of disgust tightened his lips. No, he was a fool and she was far too good at her job. No doubt Lenton found some quirk in her that he thought was only for him.

Sickening.

As if to confirm his suspicion, Lenton caught Madeline around the waist. "Come away with me. You don't want these others."

With a graceful twist, Madeline disengaged his arms in a clever maneuver that left her hands clasped in his. "But I had so hoped to dance with you this evening."

The poor sod didn't even realize she'd escaped him. "When are you free?"

"In only four sets."

Lenton groaned. "I shall persevere until then."

The other slavering gentlemen descended, forcing Lenton back, but Gabriel refused to cede his place near Madeline. He didn't try to hide his expression of thinly reined tolerance, and either that or his reputation was fierce enough to win him a handbreadth of distance from the press of bodies.

Madeline, laughing at some inane folly, whipped open her fan and brandished it flirtatiously in front of her, accomplishing the same separation from the crowd. As the men laughed at one of her sallies, she drew toward Gabriel, lifting her fan to conceal her mouth. "Your scowl could eclipse the sun."

He directed the aforementioned expression at some striped popinjay who attempted to insert himself next to Madeline. "Good."

"I'm not paying you enough for this much diligence."

She'd provided him more than she'd ever know— the perfect opportunity to watch Lenton and Billingsgate interact with the others. "I do my job. You do yours."

"For the record, I wish I could scowl rather than wave this fan. It is much less tiring."

The corner of his mouth quirked, ruining his scowl. "You're welcome to try it."

"I should. So many men fantasize about dour-faced women." A comical grimace flashed across her face for the barest instant before Madeline redirected her energy back to the pack in front of her.

After several minutes, the other courtesans, realizing the shifting interest of their customers, wove their way through the men around Madeline, hoping that the dejected supplicants would turn to them for comfort.

But they'd underestimated Madeline's skill.

She held court like a pagan queen—jesting, flirting, drawing them all in while keeping them at bay. Except for a few fellows who wandered over to examine the commotion rather than Madeline, she kept their rapt attention.

Which, unfortunately, left the eager, ambitious women at loose ends.

As they grew more bored, his scowl reduced in proportional efficiency.

He batted away a hand that slid down his side.

"Can I borrow that fan?" he muttered, inching a step closer to Madeline.

She cast him a glance from the corner of her eye. "Perhaps a sword?"

A hand pinched his backside, startling him into taking a step. His back pressed into Madeline's. "Tell me that was your hand."

She laughed. "You should hope. But never fear, it's time to break up this mob. I need to leave them longing, not trampled." She accepted the hand of an older gentleman to the cries and groans of her other admirers, then let him lead her to the dance floor.

Without Madeline luring them closer, the group of men slowly dispersed, snared by Madeline's competition.

Gabriel rolled his shoulders a few times, relishing his newfound space.

Lenton appeared next to him, an untouched wineglass held dejectedly between two fingers. "It's almost my dance with her, isn't it?"

Who knew what the woman had planned? But he wasn't about to give up the chance to speak with Lenton if he was feeling sociable. "She'll return after the set. Is she the type of woman you normally fancy?"

"She's like the air in my lungs. I've loved her as long as I can remember."

"How long have you known her?"

Lenton blinked. "Oh, same as everyone, I suppose. Since she showed up in London six months ago."

Gabriel followed her laughing progress across the floor. "Where was she before that?"

Lenton sighed. "I never asked. Heaven, I suppose. Or Shropshire." He frowned at his wine. "I need something stronger. I'll return."

As Lenton wandered away, Gabriel reviewed all

the gossip he'd heard in the past months. Her name had been on every man's lips, noble and common, until he'd been sick of it. She featured so prominently in the scandal sheets it had been difficult to learn anything else. But before that, he couldn't think of any mention of her.

If she'd been in London for only the past six months, where the devil had she been before that?

Madeline disentangled herself from Wethersly. Really, the man was more octopus than octogenarian.

She searched out Huntford, now blessedly isolated from the swarming mass of humanity that filled the ballroom.

Not that his cocoon of space would last once she returned.

She kept her step light and carefree even though she wanted nothing more than to dive through the nearest open window. Why had she come tonight?

Her stomach gave a very undainty rumble. Ah yes, money.

A drunken gentleman stumbled into her path and she skirted around him, leaving him to the dubious comfort of the woman he'd selected to entertain him tonight.

Alcohol had flowed abundantly throughout the evening, and, as she well knew, wine and lust were a potent duo. She skipped around a hand grabbing for her backside. But there was a fine line between inspiring lust and fending it off. It would soon be time to leave.

Huntford's jade eyes locked on her as she approached. Under his gaze, the natural sway of her hips felt exaggerated and wanton. Her bodice tight-ened uncomfortably over her breasts. And again the awareness returned. Not of her seductiveness, she knew that tool too well to pay it any heed, but of the woman beneath it who wanted to be seduced.

That woman was a stranger. And a terrifying one at that.

But it was more than just physical attraction that slowed her steps as she returned to Gabriel. When she'd stood back to back with him earlier, she'd been surprised by the warmth that spread through her. It wasn't the heat of an additional body pressing against her or even the simmering lust. No, it was something far more singular in her experience—security. There weren't many people she'd trust at her back in a fight. As a matter of fact, there were only two.

Three now, apparently.

She wanted to pinch Huntford's scowling cheek. "Come, let's get you some food. I won't have them saying that I'm a cruel taskmaster."

"I believe Lenton hoped to find you."

"You're right. We'd better hurry before he suc-ceeds."

He tipped his head in acceptance, and she led the way to the dining room. She stopped just inside, a snort of laughter escaping before she could contain it. She'd promised Huntford scandalous, hadn't she?

On the table in the center of the room, a nude woman had arranged herself across several silver platters. Fruit had been placed over her body. As the men selected the fruit, more of her bare skin was re-vealed.

Perhaps they should stay away from the fruit table. In fact, the beef looked rather good. But Madeline couldn't resist peering back at Gabriel. "Hungry?"

Gabriel's scowl deepened. "Not anymore."

"Madeline!" A gentleman called out, pausing in the act of lifting a bunch of grapes from the woman's hips.

Madeline repressed a grimace as a new group of men formed around her, cutting her off from the food.

"Shall I get you a plate?" one of the men asked.

Only if it didn't come from the table with the woman.

A fast-moving object flashed in the corner of Madeline's vision. She reacted without thinking, her body jerking to the side. A large strawberry hit the man next to her square in the chest.

"Greedy witch! The men were supposed to be falling all over themselves for *me* tonight! Do you know how long I had to stay still while they arranged all that fruit?" The formerly food-bedecked woman had risen to her feet, her colorful costume in piles at her feet. She picked up a bowl of cream and hurled it in Madeline's direction. Gabriel stepped in front of her to block the projectile. Luckily for him, the woman's tantrum affected her aim, and the bowl sailed through the air and bounced off a man four feet to Madeline's left.

"My best waistcoat!" With a huff, he flicked the cream off his chest. The foamy treat splattered over the man next to him, who looked down at his sleeve with the bleary intensity of one who'd had too much to drink. Then with a laugh, he tossed a pastry from the nearby table back at the man.

Suddenly, pastries and globs of gravy were flying around the room as the rest of the gentlemen joined in.

Madeline caught Gabriel's arm. "It's nice to know the future of England is in such responsible hands." They dodged a spinning slice of beef as he led her out a side door. As they exited, a footman carrying a tray of almond biscuits entered. Without pausing,

Madeline snatched three of the sugary treats with him none the wiser.

"Were you ever a pickpocket?"

Only once or twice; that had been Clayton's area of expertise. "At least we know these biscuits haven't been worn. Let's find a less crowded place to eat. Through here, I think." Except that she didn't think, she knew. She'd scouted the location dressed as a scullery maid earlier this afternoon. She'd gotten lax about such things the past weeks, but she could no longer afford that. She hurried through a set of doors at the far side of the corridor and down a narrow, dimly lit passage.

He glanced up and down the narrow space. "Servants' corridor?"

"One of them. This one leads to the laundry and cellar." The space smelled of coal dust and lye, perhaps not the most appetizing aromas, but she'd eaten in far worse. Madeline handed Huntford a biscuit and lowered herself onto the top step.

After a moment, Huntford followed suit. "I didn't picture you as the type to sit in a stairway."

She paused with the pastry halfway to her mouth. "I'm surprised you pictured me at all."

He shrugged, ignoring her bait. "You don't seem the type to tolerate dingy wooden steps."

She feigned a delicate sniff. "Indeed, this exquisite derriere only condescends to grace the finest furniture." She bit into the treat. "Unless I'm hungry, then I'll sit anywhere."

Gabriel's lips twitched, then he lost the battle and grinned.

Her pulse skipped in her veins. His smile wasn't one that transformed a striking man into a heart-rendingly handsome one. No, the change was far more wickedly subtle.

It made him approachable. The pale green of his eyes softened and the tension that normally narrowed his lips disappeared.

She choked on the powdery sugar coating the biscuit.

He eyed her warily. "Are you well?"

She nodded and focused on eating. The confection was one of her favorites so she prolonged her enjoyment with small dainty bites, allowing herself full immersion in the rich, nutty flavor and the occasional pleased moan.

Huntford hadn't touched his.

Perhaps she could ask him if she might have his— but no, she'd already eaten two to his one.

With a sigh, she raised her fingers to her mouth and began to lick each finger clean.

His sharp curse echoed in the narrow space.

With a swift movement, he placed the biscuit on his knee and caught her hand, pulling it toward him. His palm was warm and callused under hers. "I can help with that."

His thumb rubbed small circles on the delicate skin on the inside of her wrist, spiraling throbbing sensations to the sensitive places between her legs.

What did the man think he was doing? And why was she letting him? "Huntford—"

"Gabriel is better, don't you think?"

She knew Gabriel's type. There was no place for a woman in his life except as an occasional bedmate. And that she couldn't be.

As much as she might be tempted to—

A handkerchief plopped into her hand.

"That should take care of the mess." Gabriel released her hand with a satisfied smirk.

The beast!

But as her sexual frustration ebbed, an answering

smile formed on her lips. She supposed she *had* deserved that. "Well done."

He picked up his biscuit. "I thought so."

That didn't mean she was going to let him get away with smugness, however. "Have you enjoyed the evening?"

"Which part? The mobs or the food fight?" He dusted the sugar off his knee. It was her turn to watch the muscles bunch along the hard line of his jaw as he chewed. "I think you coerced me here under false pretenses. Other than seeing you eat stolen biscuits on the servants' stair, I haven't seen anything that shocks me."

When would the man learn she couldn't resist a challenge?

Madeline reached out and flicked a crumb from his lip, letting her finger drag over his smooth, firm skin. "That's because you've hardly left the ballroom."

Chapter Six

Why in the blazes did he allow her to goad him so easily? Gabriel followed Madeline around a half-nude couple fornicating in an open doorway. The man's trousers hung down around his ankles revealing hairy, spindly legs. The woman under him emitted high-pitched sounds reminiscent of a screeching violin. Gabriel grimaced. They couldn't make it another two feet into the room and shut the door behind them?

Gabriel hurried Madeline around the corner to escape the couple's increasingly loud grunts. "That couple classified as more revolting than shocking."

Her nose wrinkled. "You do have a point—" She froze placing her hand on his chest. "Listen."

"I'd prefer not to." But her sharp look silenced the rest of his snide comment. He struggled and failed to hear anything besides the overexuberant couple. Madeline, however, took off in a silent lope down the hall.

What the devil? No mysterious footmen were in sight this time.

She stopped abruptly. He collided against her. Only his arm wrapping around her ribs saved her from tumbling face-first into the carpet. The heavy weight of her breast pressed against his arm. If he turned his hand he'd be cupping—

A woman's cry of pain aborted his lustful thought.

Madeline jerked her head in the direction of a door to their right. A man's laughter spilled from the room.

She shoved at the arm encircling her, and Gabriel released his hold.

She strode toward the occupied room, her voice loud and shrewish. "I swear if you don't find something to remove this gravy from the hem of my gown I'll scream. I give you two minutes to locate a maid with laundry powder. I'll wait here." She flung open the door.

A woman stumbled out, clutching her ripped bodice to her chest. A line of crimson dribbled from her mouth down her chin. Grotesque swelling around one of her eyes sealed it tightly shut.

"Get back here, whore!" a gravelly voice bellowed from inside the room.

With a terrified glance from her one good eye, the woman fled, revealing bloody stripes harrowed across her bony shoulder blades.

Rage built until each heartbeat thudded in Gabriel's ears with deafening percussion. "Stay here." He set Madeline to the side and strode into the room. Dealing with brutes like this was familiar territory.

A balding, heavy-jowled man stood inside. Dr. Horace Webster. "I thought we had discussed your problem before, Webster."

Gabriel had investigated him seven years ago, not because he thought his sister would have fallen for the corpulent mass, but because his reputation for violence had made it impossible for Gabriel to ignore him. Unfortunately, the doctor had been in Bath at the time of Susan's death. Four separate sources had confirmed it.

Webster stood in his shirtsleeves, no doubt to allow him a better range of movement to swing the riding crop in his hand. "Just enjoying a bit of sport, Huntford."

"I don't think the lady would agree."

"That woman is a whore who I intended to pay. Now you've robbed us both of our satisfaction."

"Then why isn't she here complaining?"

Webster cracked his knuckles. "Probably embarrassed she enjoyed it so much. Perhaps I should finish up with that pretty thing you brought."

Gabriel slammed Webster against the wall, his forearm pressed into the spongy column of his throat. Fury corded the muscles of his arm but he forced himself to stop an inch before he crushed the man's windpipe. "You're the only one who receives any enjoyment. But that's what gets you off, isn't it? The pain? Their terror?"

Webster's throat twitched under Gabriel's arm as he struggled to breathe. His words emerged in a hoarse rasp. "It ain't a crime for a man to show his woman a little discipline."

"She's not your woman unless you have marriage lines to show me. Your discipline's a felony."

"To have a felony, you need to have a crime." Webster wrenched Gabriel's arm from his neck and shoved him back. Gabriel crouched, preparing for the doctor to charge. Waiting for it. Anticipating it. The doctor outweighed him by a good five stone and was no stranger to violence, but he wasn't accustomed to a target that could fight back. And Gabriel intended to fight back hard.

The doctor's chapped fists balled at his sides, but then unfolded to rub his neck. A mocking smile stretched his face. "It wasn't a crime. Ask her. I bet she won't say a thing against me."

Webster was right. His victims were always too afraid to stand against him, and without the victim to prosecute the crime, Gabriel was powerless.

"Without her complaint you can't charge me with anything."

Gabriel's brows lowered, revulsion warring with his anger. "Except being a purulent cyst of a man."

Webster growled.

"Or having the breeding of horse manure." Gabriel tensed, hoping the man would take a swing at him. He couldn't arrest him, but at least he could flatten the man's ugly nose.

Unfortunately, Webster stormed to the door, spitting at Gabriel's feet as he passed. "Bastard."

"Indeed. Now leave."

Gabriel followed the doctor into the corridor. If the man even looked in Madeline's direction, Gabriel would shoot him in the back.

But Madeline was nowhere to be seen as Webster lumbered away.

Gabriel peered around with a frown. Had she returned to the ball? After a brief search, he found her sitting on a chair in the corridor a few passageways down. Her arms were tightly folded across her chest and her head was bowed.

"Madeline, I'm sorry if he frightened you. He's gone now."

Her head jerked up. "Frightened? No. If I had stayed I would have cut off his ballocks. And I didn't want to stain my dress."

Gabriel would have snorted in agreement but her eyes held no humor.

"Did you at least hit him a few times?"

The bloodthirsty wench. "No. He wouldn't take the bait. I did call him a purulent cyst."

"Purulent?" A glimmer of a smile tilted the corners of her mouth.

"It seemed apt."

"Perfectly. Well, we'd best return swiftly to the ballroom."

Gabriel couldn't suppress a grimace.

"As your reward for being a white knight, I'll say my good-byes and we can go home."

They worked their way past the amorous couples littering the house toward the ballroom.

"There you are!" Lenton hurried forward. "It is my dance now."

Madeline smiled. "I was just coming to look for you." With an apologetic grimace at Gabriel, she allowed Lenton to lead her onto the floor.

Curse it all, another dance meant at least fifteen more minutes. But as much as he might wish to escape, the additional dance meant more time to study Lenton. Gabriel watched the man twirl Madeline about. The man was a fop and not overly bright. Gabriel doubted his guilt, but until he had solid proof of his innocence, he'd remain a suspect.

Gabriel stepped around a pillar to keep them in sight. He might not have told her of his murder investigation, but he refused to endanger her.

Lenton and Madeline edged toward the terrace doors.

"Huntford?"

Gabriel turned toward the vaguely familiar voice.

A large, solidly built man strode toward him. "I thought it was you."

Gabriel tipped his head in greeting. "Danbury." Finding a friend in this mess, even one he hadn't seen in years, came as a surprise. Yet despite his satisfaction, Gabriel's attention returned to Madeline.

She said something to her escort and they drifted back toward the other dancers.

"I see you avoided the food fight," Danbury said.

Gabriel spared a glance for his friend. "You appear unscathed as well. And quite brown. How are your family's plantations?"

"Quite well. They are flourishing under my leadership. Where have you been keeping yourself? I haven't seen you since Oxford." A crease marked Danbury's broad forehead. "Wait, I think I heard mention that you'd become a Runner?"

"Indeed."

Danbury gave a low whistle. "I envy you that. Saving the fine men of this town from criminals and ne'er-do-wells. Far more noble than any of this lot."

If nobility meant wading through filth, violence, and death. But he said, "We try our best." After all, Danbury had always held grandiose opinions on justice. There was no reason to disillusion him. "How long are you in London?"

"I had planned to return but there were some repairs needed on my father's ship. Stalled me here. And then I became fascinated by this auction." Danbury gave him a conspiratorial look. "Why did you and the delectable Miss Valdan disappear together for half an hour?"

"Our relationship is professional."

Danbury peered intently at him. "Her profession or yours?"

Nothing would ensure Madeline turning him out quicker than rumors of that sort. "I'm assigned to protect her. I'm not wealthy enough for anything else."

"If she's not yours, Huntford, then do you mind if I bid?"

He did mind, actually.

Because he didn't want Madeline to cozen his friend, of course.

Gabriel forced his shoulders to lower. "You're welcome to do as you wish."

The final chord of music faded and Madeline's court converged around her. Gabriel ignored his spurt of satisfaction as Lenton was pushed to the perimeter.

Danbury followed his gaze and grimaced. "Perhaps I'll let my bid speak for me rather than brave that insanity." He frowned as he noticed a couple behind Madeline. "I wonder if Tenet knows that woman's last protector had the pox. I suppose I'll go warn him. See, Huntford? I can do my part to save the men of society, too." He grinned and strode off in the direction of the pair.

"Ready?" Madeline's voice spoke next to him. She stood at his side, eyebrow raised. She laughed at his scowl. "Let's go then."

A footman handed Gabriel his hat and greatcoat as they left, and they walked down the steps at the front of the building.

Fingers of fog twined through the streets, shying away from the torches burning outside Chatham House.

"I'll expect you at ten tomorrow," she said, shivering in the cold mist.

He resisted the urge to share the warmth of his jacket. She'd no doubt dislike the impression that would give. "Where's your coach? I informed the footman you were preparing to leave."

She rubbed her arms briskly. "I thought you planned to hire a hackney. Your obligation to me is finished for the evening."

"I should leave you on a dark street in the middle

of London?" Apparently, his mother's teachings had rooted deeper than he realized. A gentleman never deserted a lady. Not that he was a gentleman or she a lady, but he still couldn't leave her standing there in the cold.

The hollow clatter of hooves drummed on the cobblestones, and her coach drew to a shuddering halt in front of them.

The coachman doffed his hat. "St. Mary's was full, so I took her to them good Quaker women on Green Street."

St. Mary's was a charity hospital. What business did Madeline have—

The other courtesan.

"Did you—"

"As I said, it's none of your concern. Don't you have a hackney to hail?"

Not with such an intriguing puzzle before him. "I think I'll ride with you."

Chapter Seven

Madeline sat stiffly in her seat, keeping her face averted from the pale green eyes watching her from across the dark confines of the coach. Why had she let him bully his way into her coach? Now the entire way home she had to endure his smug expression as if he knew some great secret about her.

He didn't. He didn't know anything.

She'd seen his satisfied expression before. Her physical beauty always led men to search for proof that she was beautiful on the inside, too. When they thought they'd confirmed it, they relaxed, everything stable and rational in their world. She'd used that susceptibility to gain the trust of men all over Europe. Used it to lull state secrets from their mouths and classified documents from their pockets.

She wouldn't have pegged Gabriel as the gullible type.

"I helped the woman because I didn't want her to distract from my performance. Nothing makes British gentlemen more uncomfortable than a bloody woman in their midst. It plays havoc with their concentration. I want my name to be the one on everyone's lips tomorrow, not the poor wretch who had the bad luck to catch Webster's attention."

"Of course," Gabriel said, but a patronizing half smile creased his face. "Why are you holding this auction?"

He couldn't truly think—but he'd leaned toward her, elbows braced on his knees, his appearance condescending. Oh, this was too much.

She folded her hands tightly in her lap and allowed a hint of anguish to sculpt her features. "My grandmother is ill and the doctors cost so much. I can't let her starve. I won't."

Gabriel reached for her hand but she dodged him and pressed her fist to her mouth. She was just warming to her tale. "I have a younger brother, too. He has to go to school. I won't let him live life on the streets like I have. And the enclosures have robbed my father of the farm he's worked his entire life. His father and his father's father all worked that land, but now it's gone, with nothing to show for it but the calluses on his hands."

With each sentence, Gabriel's smile dwindled until his face shuttered to the cold mask to which she was accustomed. "And your mother?"

"Worked herself blind as a seamstress to provide for all of us. But now she's dead. The influenza last winter. I couldn't even afford a marker for her—"

"The true reason?" Gabriel reclined back against his seat, the shadows further obscuring his face. But his tone could have iced the Thames.

"Money." There was nothing more to it than that. No great and noble reason waited to exonerate her.

"You obviously had money. I looked into your financial situation. You don't owe the shops any money. You aren't in debt."

No, she preferred selling her body to selling her soul.

He continued, "The house is rented, but you own your coach, horses, and clothing. They cost a good deal. Why not just live off of that money?"

"So I can live the rest of my life in genteel poverty? Counting each piece of coal? Forever patching and mending and trying to hide the fraying edges of my gowns with castoff pieces of ribbon?" She refused to go to bed hungry every night. She refused to sleep on the floor because there were lice in the mattress. She'd left that life behind and she wouldn't return to it.

She couldn't see Gabriel's face, but the stiffness carved into the broad lines of his shoulders announced his disapproval. "It's better than selling yourself."

"Why? Where's the nobility in suffering in silence when I have other options? Men are told to better their lot, but because I'm a woman, I'm supposed to huddle in shame and accept the pitiful situation life has flung at me?" Her lungs pumped, and she drew a measured breath to bring herself back under control. Her rationale was logical and precise. There was no reason for her explanation to devolve into trite emotionalism.

"You could marry."

And give some man control of her money and body? Give him the right to rape her and beat her nightly until she complied with his wishes? She'd seen what that had done to her mother, how it had hollowed her out until nothing was left inside. "No."

He was silent and she knew he waited for her to expound, but like everything else in her life, it was none of his concern.

"Where were you before you appeared in London six months ago?" he finally asked.

Unfortunately for Gabriel, she'd been taught how to avoid interrogations by the masters. "Dallying with the czar in St. Petersburg." Ah, the truth was far better than any story she could have invented. "He's a terrible kisser, by the way." She slid onto Gabriel's bench, her fingers trailing across his lips. He remained motionless, but the muscles at his jaw tightened. "Before that, I was with Grand Marshal Prutoz. He didn't even want to bother with kissing." She pressed her lips against the knotted muscle at his jaw, then worked her way up to the hollow under his ear. "He just wanted me to unbutton his trousers and take him in my mouth." She slid her hand down the hard planes of Gabriel's torso, but he caught her hand before she reached his waistband.

His hand tightened on her wrist, not tight enough to be painful, but strong enough that she couldn't pull away.

Gabriel's gaze scalded her. "Then Bonaparte himself before that? What did he want to do?" He traced the neckline of her gown with his free hand. "Did you offer him these enticing mounds?"

Her skin was suddenly too tight, her breasts heaving against his hand. "I never met Napoleon. But his brother, King Joseph, had the annoying habit of referring to them as twin bastions of perfection."

He examined her as he might an insect.

Satisfaction unfurled in her chest but it didn't warm her. No, she wasn't kind. He wouldn't make that mistake again. Not even Ian and Clayton were fool enough to believe that.

"I intend to find out who you really are, Miss Valdan."

She twisted her wrist to the weak point in his

grasp and broke the hold. "Save your scrutiny for my bidders." Her secrets were none of his concern.

She remained seated next to him, unwilling to flee back to her side of the coach. Once they halted in front of her town home, Gabriel didn't rise to assist her, but allowed the coachman to help her.

She gave orders for the coachman to take Gabriel home.

But he climbed down. "I believe I'll find my own way."

She shrugged, marching toward her stairs and refusing to let herself watch him depart. "Good."

Chapter Eight

"Another drive in the park?" Gabriel asked as Madeline walked past him down the front stairs. A frothy, lavender carriage dress floated around her form, begging a man to sample her and see if she tasted of spun sugar.

He gave thanks he'd overcome his madness yesterday. For a moment, he'd forgotten her mastery of the game. Forgotten how talented she was at manipulating every situation to her advantage.

He still wanted her. She ensured that every red-blooded man did. But he had come sickeningly close to letting her beguile him, and that was completely unacceptable.

Even if he had the money to bid, he wouldn't waste it on a single night of frivolous pleasure.

Of ecstasy.

He ignored his body's painful disagreement.

Daintily lifting her dress to keep the hem from the damp pavement, Madeline grinned. "I can hardly make morning calls. Nothing would scare potential bidders away quicker than showing up at their homes."

"Their wives might not appreciate your appearance."

Not a trace of guilt crossed her face. "I do try to spare them that much."

"So you have no issue if the winning bidder is a married man?"

She bent over to adjust the buckle of her shoe, providing him with a perfect silhouette of her pert backside. "Why should I?"

He resisted the urge to swat that generously offered piece of anatomy. "The man has made promises. Promises he shouldn't betray." He settled for grabbing her around the waist and all but tossing her in the carriage.

She raised a delicately arched brow at his action, but settled gracefully onto the seat. "How delightfully prudish. I shall make you a deal. If you find that one of my bidders has never strayed from his wife, and that I'm the devilish harlot that's about to lead him into a life of sin, you inform me. I'll see that he takes himself out of the running."

Gabriel gritted his teeth. Every single one of the men changed mistresses almost as often as they did cravats. And she knew it. The carriage creaked as he climbed in across from her.

With her nod, the coachman cracked the whip and the carriage lurched into motion.

"It's their responsibility to keep their vows, not mine," Madeline added, smoothing her skirt as the breeze rippled it around her legs.

"But what about their wives? Do you care nothing for their feelings?"

Her lips tightened. "I'll be doing them a favor."

"A favor?"

"It is foolish to ignore what their husbands truly are."

How had he been taken in by the wit and charm he'd seen yesterday? Cynicism ran through her like steel. "Not all men are like that."

She laughed. "You're different, I suppose? Never mind. That hardly matters. The top three bids are now Lenton, Wethersly, and Danbury."

Gabriel frowned. "Danbury? He wasn't on the list when I checked this morning."

"He is as of half an hour ago." She shrugged. "I have my sources."

He had no issue with the near strangers vying for her, but the idea of his friend bidding made his teeth grind. Why was it different? As with the other men, Danbury had kept mistresses before. He wasn't even married. That made him better than most.

Gabriel focused on an oak tree far in the distance until his emotions were back under control. Whether she slept with his friend or the Regent himself it didn't matter; what mattered was finding the killer.

"What can you tell me of the Earl of Danbury? I've never spoken to him. He's a friend of yours, is he not?"

Gabriel returned his gaze to her. The sunlight filtered through the few curls that had escaped her bonnet, turning the chestnut strands to copper. One whispered over her cheek, the slight flaw in her appearance only highlighting the rest of her perfection. He wanted to reach out and tuck it behind her ear, return her to her previously pristine—and more easily ignored—condition. But he hadn't paid for that privilege and he damned well wasn't going to, so instead he drummed his fingers against his knee. "How did you know that?"

"I saw you speaking to him, and it was the only time last evening that you didn't look ready to commit murder."

She'd been half a ballroom away. How did she know whom he'd been speaking with? He'd never seen her attention waver from Lenton.

"How did he come by the scars?" she asked.

How had she even noticed them? The three thin lines crossing Danbury's cheek had faded since Gabriel had last seen him. "He was engaged to wed while we were at school. On one of his trips home, there was a carriage accident. He was injured and his betrothed was killed."

Madeline's face softened, her brows dipping. "He never married?"

"No."

Her concern vanished under a calculating gaze. "Will you have issues determining his suitability as a bidder?"

To be honest, he hadn't considered the idea, but his foul mood prevented him from admitting it. "I will do my—"

Madeline suddenly switched seats so she sat next to him, her hip flush against his thigh.

He cleared his throat. "—best."

She reached up and pulled her bonnet off. "My hair is driving me mad. If I don't fix it now, it will be down around my shoulders by the time we arrive at the park." She pulled a few pins loose and held them out to him. "Pin the loose strands up, please."

Gabriel stared at the bent pieces of metal and then at the rich mass of hair he wanted to dig his fingers into. "I'm not your maid."

She shrugged, sending a few more curls bouncing to her shoulders. "As you wish." She tilted her head slightly and spoke to the driver. "I need a bit more time, Jenkins. Would you turn right on Ash Street?"

The coachman grunted in agreement.

Madeline stiffened next to him. "Oh, blast. I

dropped one." She pointed to where one of the pins skittered across the floor of the coach toward the other seat. "Could you get that for me?"

Gabriel only just hid his exasperation. Potts thought this more important than apprehending criminals? But his mother's training proved difficult to ignore, so he leaned forward to retrieve it.

"Turn right again here, Jenkins."

That made no sense. If they turned right again, they'd be heading in the wrong direction. As Gabriel's fingers closed around the pin, he glanced back at her.

Madeline's attention wasn't on him or even on her hair. She was riveted by something behind them.

Gabriel followed her gaze to the hackney a few blocks back. It had been behind them earlier as they headed to the park, but he had barely taken note of it. It must have turned with them onto Ash. As he watched, it followed them as they turned right onto a narrow lane.

It made no sense for anyone to have purposely chosen that route. Blood began to strum in his veins. "Who's following us?" he asked.

Madeline's lips thinned, and she considered him with either surprise or annoyance, he couldn't tell which. "I'm not sure. Probably just a devoted admirer." She eyed the coach again. "But that doesn't mean I'm not curious. Pull over, Jenkins. Let this poor man pass."

Jenkins pulled the carriage as far over as he could. The wheels were a scant inch from the building wall. The hackney would have to pass them. The lane was too narrow for it to turn around and there were no streets it could escape down to avoid them.

Suddenly, it stopped completely. A man leaped out and disappeared down a gap between two shops.

As Madeline whispered epithets, Gabriel leaped to the ground. Men with good intentions didn't lurk, and innocent men didn't flee.

His boots struck the cobbles and the air streamed in and out of his lungs. Grim satisfaction filled him. For the first time in days, he was doing something. Not struggling through the mire that was his investigation, not playing nice with Madeline's suitors. He increased his speed as he followed down the alley where the suspect had disappeared.

He caught a glimpse of the well-dressed man just as the fellow turned out of sight. Gabriel pushed his body until his legs burned. He darted around the corner and nearly ran into the other man. A solid brick wall abruptly ended the alley and the man's escape.

Gabriel's hands shot out, grabbing the man by his shoulders and slamming him face-first against the wall. He recognized the color of his hair and the set of his shoulders. It was the man who'd been in front of Madeline's house the other day. "Who are you?"

"You have no right to hold me thus. I've done nothing wrong." The man struggled in an attempt to knock Gabriel away.

But Gabriel had restrained far larger and more experienced criminals. He kept the man's face against the bricks. "I will repeat this only once. Who are you?"

"Timothy Haines! Confound you. I've done nothing."

"Why are you following Miss Valdan?"

"She is my muse!"

Gabriel loosened his grip. That was certainly not one of the answers he expected.

"Didn't you hear, Gabriel? I'm this man's muse.

Let him go, by all means." Madeline stood at the entrance to the alley.

Why wasn't he surprised she didn't have the sense to wait in the carriage? But he let go of Haines.

The young man stepped away from the wall, a grin lighting his face as he brushed the front of his jacket. "I knew you'd understand. When I see you, it's as if a fire is lit in my soul. I knew you'd feel the same. No other woman has ever entranced me as you have."

Madeline lifted her eyebrow. "So you're the one who left the note on my doorstep?"

Gabriel frowned until he remembered the paper she'd picked up yesterday.

Haines scowled as he picked at a tear on the front of his jacket. "I didn't leave a note. My poem's not even completed yet."

Madeline shrugged. "Well then, while I'm flattered to be your inspiration, next time you want to see me, I suggest you place a bid."

"But I can't place a bid," Haines moaned. "My quarterly allowance is already spent and that accursed publisher hasn't gotten back to me on the book of poems I submitted." He tried to step toward Madeline but Gabriel blocked him with a hand to his chest.

Madeline might not take the lad's adoration seriously, but Gabriel had seen too many of these situations escalate to violence.

"I knew if I talked to you, you'd feel the same passion licking the confines of your soul. I'll cherish you as none of the others ever could. You are my first love." A mess of dark hair flopped over his forehead as Haines spoke.

Before Gabriel could warn Haines away, Madeline spoke. "Are you a good poet?"

Haines's chest expanded. "Quite good, my mother claims."

She lowered her voice. "I feared that. That is why you can't see me again."

"What?" Haines cried.

"What makes a good poet? Passion, anguish, unrequited love?"

"I suppose."

Madeline clasped her hands primly in front of her. Her eyes gleamed with regret. "If you won the first woman you loved, you'd never experience the searing crucible of heartbreak. For the good of your work, I'll give up what we might have had. Can you, Timothy? Can you sacrifice for the good of future generations?"

Haines's mouth had dropped open in codlike fashion. "But—"

"You must, Timothy."

"Don't come near Miss Valdan again," Gabriel ordered, not content with Madeline's coddling.

Haines grunted, his face drooping into sullen lines. "You cannot prefer this thief taker over me."

Madeline laughed. "No, I prefer the man with the winning bid."

Glaring venomously at Gabriel, Haines stalked away.

"How did you know you were being followed?" Gabriel asked as he led Madeline back to the carriage.

"I've learned to be cautious."

Gabriel studied Madeline. Every time he'd thought he found his footing with her, she knocked him back a step. She'd handled that skillfully and been surprisingly subtle with that young fool's pride. But she had to have a motive. He just needed to figure it out.

Madeline exhaled slowly, finally admitting to the nausea heaving in her stomach. Ignoring it was only making her dizzy. She forced herself to look across the carriage at Gabriel. There was no bullet hole in his forehead. Madeline forced her mind to process the information. No one had been waiting to catch Gabriel in an ambush. Haines hadn't even been the one to leave the threatening note.

Gabriel was fine.

In fact, he was looking at her with that assessing gaze again. The rest of her panic cleared. He was doing it again, trying to decipher her. At least this time he didn't have the half smile playing around his lips.

Well, he could believe what he wanted. Last night had been an aberration. Today she wouldn't let his smug benevolence goad her into explaining anything.

Yet it did.

It was as if she wore ill-fitting boots and could think of nothing else until they'd been removed. "Giving the boy a reason to stay away was more effective than threats," Madeline said. "I can't have my full attention on my bidders if I'm worried about him disrupting the auction."

"He might not be over his obsession."

"I know." She forced a laugh. "But I've grown used to that." Keeping her gaze from drifting to Gabriel's face, she searched for her suitors as they reached the gravel path of the park.

She had much more important things to concentrate on like— Blast. She couldn't concentrate at all with his gaze boring through her. "I think I'll walk."

The coachman drew the carriage to a halt and Gabriel helped her down.

Even though it didn't linger, his touch at her waist

was too warm, too personal. "Get behind me. I don't want you to scare off any suitors."

Gabriel tipped his head and fell back, the space allowing her to think. He was right. Haines was still a threat. She should have calmly discussed a plan to implement if he returned. Instead, she was running like a frightened doe.

Perhaps a bullet in her head would force some sense into her.

But before she could turn to Gabriel, Viscount Lenton hailed her from across the park. He cantered over on a glossy black stallion that appeared much more stable than his bay of yesterday. "May I walk with you, my lovely?"

The smile she gave him was genuine as she slipped back into the familiar role of coquette, relishing the brief respite it gave her from self-recrimination.

He dismounted and led his horse by the reins. Gabriel slowed further to allow room for the horse.

More of her tension eased. Gabriel's gaze might still bring the hairs at the nape of her neck to attention, but that was far preferable to the lightning that danced over her skin when he was near.

She tucked her hand around Lenton's arm. "I hear you've bid again."

He smiled down at her. "I told you I'll win this auction." He glanced over his shoulder. "You can tell the Runner that my records will be ready later this afternoon. I would have had them yesterday, but I don't keep seven years of reports in London. I had to send to my country estate."

"Seven years?"

"He insisted on it." Lenton frowned. "Isn't that what you asked for?"

Madeline stole a brief peek at Gabriel, but he was

too far behind to hear the conversation. "Of course. I'd forgotten. That's why I have someone else handle the business." She brushed her bosom against Lenton's arm. "I much prefer taking care of the pleasure."

Ian had claimed Gabriel was thorough, but this was something else. Either he was seeking to make things difficult for her bidders, which she wouldn't tolerate, or he had his own reason to want to see the records.

She tugged on Lenton's arm, slowing him. "Let me inform Huntford before I'm distracted by more"— she ran her tongue over her lips—"enjoyable things."

Lenton's Adam's apple bobbed several times.

She released his arm and strolled back to Gabriel, hating how her breath caught at the familiar expanse of his shoulders. How her fingers wanted to explore the line of his jaw and smooth the tired creases by his eyes. She subdued the sensations by focusing on her irritation. Why couldn't she have this reaction to one of her bidders? It was beyond aggravating. "Lenton's financial records are ready for your perusal this afternoon."

Gabriel acknowledged her with a slight inclination of his head.

"All seven years' worth."

His eyes narrowed, but he gave no other reaction.

"I'd forgotten I was so demanding. Remind me why I decided on seven years."

"Your friend is getting lonely."

Madeline glanced back to find Lenton shifting from foot to foot, fingers tapping on his leg. "I expect to hear my brilliant reasoning later."

He bowed, his expression bland, but his gaze was anything but obedient.

She let her stubbornness clash silently with his for a second before resuming her place by her suitor's side. "That man can't wait to be through with me." The words roused a strange discomfort. She frowned. That sentence shouldn't have bothered her. It was the truth, after all.

Lenton didn't disappoint. He pulled her close. "I, on the other hand, can't wait to win you."

His flirtation didn't soothe her vanity as much as she might have wished. Yet she brightened her smile and kept Lenton—and the other gentlemen who joined their group—enraptured until she'd finished their circuit around the park. She dispersed the fellows with promises of future dalliances and rounded on Gabriel.

He gave her a brief bow and began to walk away.

Oh no, he wasn't about to leave without an explanation. She caught his arm. "Walk me to my coach."

"It's two feet away from you." He halted, glaring at her hand. "I believe my duties are fulfilled this morning."

"Apparently, your sense of duty knows no bounds. Seven years?"

"It will be hard for your suitors to hide the truth of their situations from me. They might counterfeit a few months' worth of financial records to win you, but they won't be able to falsify seven years' worth, not in the amount of time I give them." His voice was noncommittal, as if he wasn't even interested enough to try to convince her of the truth of his words.

"That's the best lie you could come up with?" Anger burned across her cheeks, warming them. He'd even had extra time to come up with a better one. "Why seven years?"

"You'll know if they have the money, which is what I was hired to find out. As you're so fond of pointing out, the rest doesn't concern you."

But it did. He was hiding something. And as someone who had done that professionally, she knew not to trust secrets.

Or the person who kept them.

Chapter Nine

Madeline handed Ian a cold towel.

He pressed it to the back of his head and collapsed into a chair. "Really, old man, you knew it was me."

Canterbury's face remained expressionless. "I had no idea. I took you for a common thief."

"You accuse me of being common when you hit me over the head with a frying pan? That would have done a fishwife proud."

Canterbury sniffed, causing the scarlet plumes on his hat to jerk toward his face. "You should know. You are the one who has far too much experience with wives of all kinds. Now I must prepare the tea." He bowed to Madeline and backed from the room.

How did they know each other? They bickered like an old couple.

"So did you find out anything about the note?" she asked.

Ian groaned. "Give me a moment to collect what remains of my meager mental facilities." He stood and poured himself a brandy.

Madeline snatched it from his hand and poured

it back into the decanter. "You know that brandy is only for show."

"But it's excellent brandy. I bought it."

"With my money. You also know the one bottle is all I could afford. What will I do if I'm forced to entertain some gentlemen?"

Ian reached for the decanter. "Offer them tea?"

She slapped his hand away.

"But it's your butler who—" He held up his hands. "Fine. You win. I haven't been able to discover anything about your note. No one's heard anything unusual. I took Clayton's list of the fellows who hate you the most but could find no trace of them in London."

She sighed. "It seems quite wrong that people are threatening to kill me, but I no longer get paid for it. Do you miss it?"

"The hunger, the cold, the lice, the rats that gnawed holes in the soles of my feet as I slept? I awake yearning for it every day. Why, do you?"

No.

Yes.

When she was a spy, there had been no Gabriel to pester her thoughts and desires. And if someone had threatened her life, she would've either killed him or moved on to another mission. She hated feeling like an overstuffed Christmas goose awaiting butchering.

"Am I nice?" Madeline wished she could recall the words. She was having this conversation with the wrong member of the Trio. Clayton would have scolded her for being foolish and said something deep and profound that would have soothed her fears.

Ian, on the other hand, laughed. "Why would you want to be nice? You're well trained. That's far better."

But was that all there was to her? Training?

More importantly, did she care? She hadn't a week ago.

Ian lifted a glass of brandy to his lips.

She glared at him. Of course, he hadn't listened.

"It's only a sip, I swear."

Why did she bother trying to stop him? He was the Wraith, after all. What he wanted, he got. "The brandy will cost you."

He sipped the amber liquid. "Of course. Everything does."

"I need to find out all there is to know about Gabriel."

"Huntford? Why?"

"He's using the task I assigned him to pursue some personal agenda."

"Have you asked him what it might be?"

"Yes. But now I need the truth."

Ian patted her on the head. "I did train you well, didn't I? He's a bastard, you know."

"I've experienced it."

Ian laughed, handing her the rest of his brandy. "No, as in there is no Papa Huntford. I did some research before I gave him to you. His mother was a governess who found herself in the family way and changed her name to Mrs. Huntford before she gave birth to twins."

"He has a brother?" For some reason, the idea of two of him running around was as amusing as it was frightening.

"No. He had a sister. She was murdered seven years ago, strangled. They never caught the killer. That's why he became a Runner."

Poor Gabriel. No one took the death of a family member lightly, but to lose a twin sister . . . And Madeline had seen the body of a woman who'd been strangled. Even though she hadn't known the woman, the horrific image had stayed with her. What would it be like to go to sleep with the image of his sister like that imprinted on his thoughts—

Seven years.

"Gabriel asked for seven years of financial information from my suitors."

"So he seeks something to do with his sister's murder? I'll see if I can find out what he's looking for."

"And anything else about him you think of interest." The words slipped out before she could stop them, and she'd sooner face a Russian execution squad than explain her sudden yearning to know every last detail about Gabriel.

Ian massaged the back of his head. "Explain to me why I'm working while you spend the night at the theater?"

She wished she could simply delegate the investigation into Gabriel's motives to Ian, but the puzzle nagged at her. "I'll do my portion."

"Will you torture or seduce the information from him?"

"I haven't yet decided." At the moment, both ideas appealed equally.

Grimacing, Ian rose to his feet, complaining about butlers who were fast with frying pans yet slow with tea. He paused by the door. "Are you sure you want to know what I find?"

She ignored the way her stomach dipped. "Isn't it possible there's nothing dark lurking in his past?"

Ian met her gaze with unflinching intent. "Everyone has secrets."

Chapter Ten

$\mathcal{I}$n the middle of her dramatic, agonizing death, the actress on stage paused to glare at Madeline. Gabriel couldn't blame her. No one had paid the redhead the slightest heed since Madeline had glided into the pit at the end of the first act. The ladies above peered over the sides of their gilded boxes with varying degrees of disgust, outrage, and envy. Their gentlemen escorts kept their heads averted, but after a few moments, although their opera glasses remained trained on the stage, the eyes behind them drifted to the far more entertaining performance below.

The gentlemen surrounding Madeline didn't try to hide their ogling. Or their groping. Gabriel knocked away a hand reaching for her.

The actress on the stage finished dying to a smattering of halfhearted applause. She miraculously revived and flounced offstage before the curtain had fully closed.

With the pause on stage, more men gathered around Madeline. A drunken Corinthian, eager to press closer, stumbled into Gabriel, driving him backward into Madeline. He reached to steady her but two of her admirers were already hoisting her back to her feet.

Madeline laughed with abandon, as if she could imagine nothing more delightful than being tossed about by overanxious theatergoers. But rather than keeping the crowd at arm's length as she'd done the night before, she pressed back against Gabriel, the softness of her derriere flush against his thigh. "It's time to make a strategic retreat to the corridor."

He threaded her through the mob of men surrounding them. "I thought you were succeeding well with your impression of a lively barmaid."

"Barmaid? I'll have you know that was lonely opera dancer to perfection."

Gabriel couldn't help grinning at her look of exaggerated affront.

"But I swear, if I get pinched once more, I won't be able to sit for a week."

People were already strolling about, taking advantage of the intermission. "I doubt you'll be safer in the corridor."

"I can keep my back to the wall. And if I'm in the corridor, the gentlemen will be able to create an excuse to leave their boxes and wander past me."

He should have guessed even her escapes were carefully orchestrated. "You're frightening."

She laughed, this time a breathy chuckle meant only for Gabriel's ears. "Why do I love your compliments the best?"

The refreshment vendor must have adored her because, true to her prediction, nearly every gentleman present found himself possessed of great thirst and in need of lemonade from the vendor directly to her left.

Gabriel settled against a wall a few feet away, allowing her free rein with her wooing.

Danbury arrived at his side a few minutes later. "I

don't know if I envy or pity you having to keep an eye on her."

"You're the one who bid on her. I'll need the past seven years of your financials, by the way."

"You know I'm good for the money."

Gabriel did know. The man was incredibly wealthy, but Madeline was right—he couldn't excuse his friends. "Same rules for everyone."

Danbury focused on where Madeline stood sipping a drink, her lips moist and red from the spiced ratafia. "I suppose I will do what I must. Although I doubt she's actually a virgin."

"She claims she is."

"Come now. There's a ship at the docks waiting to take me to the other side of the globe. The only thing that holds me here is this auction. Surely you know the truth."

Gabriel preferred not to think about Danbury taking Madeline to bed. "If you question whether she's a virgin, why did you bid?"

One of Madeline's bidders careened into Danbury. Grabbing the man's port before it spilled, he steadied the man. "These men will bring shame on our entire gender if I don't save them from themselves." Danbury handed the glass back to the drunken man. "Do you suppose she cares if I woo her before I bed her?"

Slowly, Gabriel uncurled his fists. She wasn't a lady whose reputation he needed to protect, after all. "No. Your bid is all that counts."

Danbury exhaled dramatically. "Good. Then I'd better return to my box. I'm escorting the youngest daughter of the Earl of Riverton tonight. If she suspects where I've been, I'll never hear the end of it. The woman can't keep her mouth closed to save her life." Danbury bowed and hurried off.

The ringing of the porter's bell signaled the close

of intermission. As the gentlemen returned to their seats, Gabriel worked his way upstream to Madeline's side. "Are we returning for act two?"

She reached for him through the press of people. "Not a chance. Let's—" She lurched, and her hand caught his in a viselike grip. Her head whipped around and she peered at the men jostling around them, her fingers digging into his hand. "—go."

Despite the radiant smile on her face, the color had drained from her cheeks.

"Are you all right?"

Her free hand pressed against her stomach and her next step wobbled. "Who would've thought the punch wasn't watered down?" She laughed, but then released his hand and folded both of her hands at her waist.

She darted and wove her way through the darkly clad gentlemen to the front entrance, her scarlet dress making her easy to follow. Several men called to her but she pretended not to hear.

Something was definitely wrong.

Frowning, Gabriel increased his pace. He caught her arm as she ran down the stairs in front of the theater. "Madeline—"

"Get my coach."

"What is wrong?"

Her hands were shaking where they clenched against her stomach. "Curse you, just do it. Please."

He spoke briefly to one of the lads nearby and tossed him a coin. The young man ran around the corner to where her coach was waiting.

The faltering lamps cast dark shadows over her face. "Madeline?"

She refused to look up.

Gabriel tucked his finger under her chin and tilted it up into the wavering light. "Are you ill?"

Shaking her head, she swallowed twice and lifted her gloved hands slightly from her body.

Odd. Why would the red dye from the dress—

Bloody hell.

He grabbed her wrists and pulled them fully away from her stomach. A dark, wet spot marred her dress where her hands had been. "You're bleeding." His pulse pounded loudly in his ears. What had happened? How had he missed it?

She wrenched her hands free and pressed them against the wound. "Shh. Not here. The cut's not a deep one."

She must be in shock. He pulled out his handkerchief. "We must tend to—"

The carriage appeared at the end of the street and she hurried toward it.

Did he need to wrestle her to the ground? He trapped her again, clasping her shoulders with his hands. First, he needed to see to the bleeding. "You're injured. Wait for the carriage to come to us."

She glared at him. "I can't risk anyone from the theater seeing me like this. It won't help the auction if I'm seen bloody and hurt." She winced. "It's not precisely the image I've been trying to portray."

Did the woman even have a heart beating in her chest? "We tend it now."

The carriage stopped. She pulled away from him and opened the door, but when she tried to climb in, a muffled moan escaped.

If he put her in the coach, at least she'd have to hold still. With one hand tucked under her arm and the other at her backside, he lifted her in. Madeline fell back onto the seat with a gasp.

Swearing, Gabriel followed her, shutting the door behind him. He leaned over her. A thin slit, about the width of his palm, cut through the bloody circle in the middle of her dress. "You were stabbed?" Rage blurred the edges of his vision.

Madeline's breath emerged in short, quiet pants. "So it appears."

He removed his cravat. "Who?"

"I don't know. There were too many people around me."

"Why the hell didn't you scream or cry out?"

She pressed her bloody glove against the cut. "I—"

"The dress is ruined no matter what, is it not?"

Her brows lowered, but she nodded.

He grasped the thin silk and ripped it, splitting the bodice open. A crimson stain glared against the white linen of her stays. The wound still bled, but it didn't gush. She was right. It most likely wasn't fatal. At least not if cleaned and properly dressed. But it must hurt like the devil.

Madeline studied her bloody undergarment, only a faint dotting of perspiration betraying her discomfort. "I never thought I'd say this, but thank heavens for my stays. The knife thrust hit the whalebone in the center and glanced off. If the criminal was more adept at stabbing women, I'd be dead. It was quite inexcusable."

"On their part or yours?"

"Both, I suppose. But it was foolish of me to allow it."

She sounded as if she were annoyed she'd left her reticule behind, not as if she'd nearly been killed.

During his watch. Hell, right under his nose.

Gabriel contemplated removing her stays, but now that the bleeding had slowed, he didn't want to risk aggravating the wound while in the limited confines of the coach. He pressed his cravat against the gash with steady pressure. "Who did this?"

"I don't know."

"Do you have any enemies?"

Her lips quirked in a wan smile. "Only half the population of London."

"But most of them don't hate you enough to kill you."

"Fine. A quarter of the population of London."

He couldn't bring himself to smile. "How are you taking this so calmly?"

"Would it help if I panicked?" She gave a half hearted cry. "Eek?"

He shook his head. His cravat was becoming sticky with blood, so he added a bit more pressure to the wound. "If there's anyone threatening you, tell me. I'll protect you."

"I don't think I'm paying you enough for that."

He frowned. "I don't care if you pay me. Who is it? I will deal with them."

A brief uncertainty flashed through her eyes, then was gone. "I don't know who stabbed me."

The coach slowed. Gabriel placed her hands back on the cloth while he removed his coat. But when he tried to tuck it around her, she flinched away. "It will be ruined, and I can't afford to pay to have it replaced."

He draped it over her with a growl. "Not everything comes with a price. I don't give a damn about your money. You're injured and half naked. Take the blasted jacket." He leaped from the coach, then pulled her into his arms and strode to her door.

"I can walk," she protested, her voice muffled against his chest.

He was finished arguing. Her slender frame weighed hardly anything. She couldn't afford to lose more blood. "No."

Canterbury opened the door as they approached, a blue and yellow striped nightcap topping his head. His eyes widened with concern. "What happened?"

Gabriel walked past. "She's been injured. I need hot water and bandages."

Without wasting time on more questions, Canterbury hurried off to the kitchen.

"Where's your bedroom?" he asked as he carried her up the stairs.

"You sure seem eager to get me in—"

Gabriel interrupted her witty comment. "Where?"

She sighed in defeat. "Third door on the right. I don't need your help, but I don't suppose you'll listen to me, will you?"

"Do you have much experience dealing with knife wounds?"

She was silent.

"I thought not. I've treated them before. Let me help you, then you'll be free to throw me out."

Her shoulder twitched in what he supposed was a shrug of agreement. Despite her quips, she was in too much pain for much else. Her face hadn't regained color and her lips were compressed in a thin line.

He entered her room. Next to an ornate mahogany bed, a single candle had been left burning on the nightstand, no doubt in preparation for her return. The small flame did nothing for the dark greens in the room except make them appear more forbidding. The color proclaimed it the bedchamber of the former master of the house rather than its mistress. "Why not use the lady's rooms?"

"The bigger bed has its advantages."

He didn't need images of why Madeline might require a larger bed. He laid her gently on the mattress. "I need to remove your stays so I can examine the wound." He pulled his knife from the sheath in his boot.

When she nodded, he grasped the top edge of her

undergarment and carefully sliced the fabric to where it ended at her waist. He peeled back the wet, bloody cloth, revealing her crimson-stained shift.

The door opened behind him. Canterbury rushed in with a basin of steaming water and a stack of neatly folded bandages. He stiffened when he saw the blood, his hands trembling as he lit all the candles in the room. "What do you need me to do?"

To not pass out and add to Gabriel's list of patients. "Put the supplies next to me. Then get me towels." Canterbury complied and then fled the room.

Gabriel's fingers hovered only for an instant before untying the ribbon at the neck of her shift and then slicing the garment from her upper body.

He made only brief note of the lush perfection of her pink-tipped breasts before focusing on the bloody mess below.

The cut still bled, but as Madeline had claimed, it wasn't mortal. However, she would need the wound sewn shut. "I'll call a doctor."

"No. You said you've dealt with wounds before. Can't you help me?"

"I can." As a Runner, he'd dealt with enough of his and his associates' wounds to be able to handle them without a second thought.

But then she shuddered, a tiny quaking that she tried to disguise as an attempt to shift on the bed. His gut clenched. The thought of piercing her time and time again with a needle and thread sickened him. He couldn't. Not to her. Not to Madeline.

"I'll call a doctor, regardless."

She grabbed his arm, her bloody gloves wet on his sleeve. "They'll just botch things. Please. You help me."

Hell. He owed her that much. He'd failed abysmally at protecting her. Gabriel swallowed, forcing the nausea to a tolerable churning. He peeled the bloody gloves from her hands, then wiped them clean.

Canterbury reentered with towels.

"I'll need needle and thread. And brandy, if you have it." He looked at Madeline, giving her a chance to rethink her mad request, but she simply nodded in agreement.

Canterbury returned with the other supplies, then quickly skittered from the room. Gabriel removed his waistcoat, then rolled back his sleeves to just below the elbow.

"See? So much more pleasant than a doctor would've been."

He glanced up to find her intent gaze on him and a half smile playing on her lips, but her seductive expression couldn't mask the fear in her eyes. He tucked towels under her, then spent far too many seconds ensuring the towels were straight.

He exhaled through tightly clenched teeth. *Get it done already.* He dipped a cloth in the steaming water, then wrung out the excess. "I'm sorry for this."

She closed her eyes. "So am I."

He wiped off the excess blood as well as he could, then picked up the crystal decanter from the bedside table and poured brandy into the cut.

Her quickly stifled cry of pain echoed in his chest until he had to struggle for his next breath. He concentrated to ensure that none of his fury at her attacker translated into the cleansing strokes of the cloth, but another whimper escaped her lips.

He rinsed the cloth in the porcelain basin, darkening the water to that red-orange color particular to drying blood.

Gabriel wiped away the remaining blood with quick efficiency. A gunshot wound to his thigh had taught him it was better not to have the process drawn out. He poured her a glass of brandy. "Drink this. It will dull the pain."

She shook her head. "I can't keep the stuff down."

"Madeline—"

"I can handle it."

Yet as he attempted to thread the needle, Gabriel's hands shook so badly he had to stop until he regained control. Perhaps he should have drunk the brandy himself.

When Gabriel poised to begin, she jerked under his fingers. "I lied. Please, I need something to distract me. Talk to me, Gabriel."

Madeline sincerely hoped she looked better than Gabriel did right now. Perhaps she should've let him call the doctor.

But then she would have given up the perfect opportunity for interrogation. Guilt was far too valuable a tool to waste.

"What do you want to talk about?" he asked.

"Where are you from?" Start simple. That was the first rule of interrogation. Ease them into it. It was amazing what men would let slip before they realized the questioning had gone too far.

"London."

She flinched as the needle sank into her flesh, and his jaw tightened still further until she could see muscles bunch.

"Cheapside," he continued as he pulled the thread. "My mother teaches deportment to the daughters of rich merchants."

She focused on the way his lips formed the words as he spoke, distracting herself from the friction of the thread slithering through her flesh.

"She taught you your manners?"

The worried furrows knitting his brow eased a fraction. "She taught, I just didn't learn."

"Does she enjoy"—she closed her eyes at the next stab—"her work?"

"I suppose. She doesn't have many other choices. She's too wellborn for trade but not wellborn enough to have connections to help her."

Madeline could imagine how difficult it would be. It must eat away at her, knowing she'd been seduced, then cast aside. To have to raise the children of the man who had betrayed her.

Madeline never intended to have children. No child would want her for a mother. "And your father?" she asked.

"He was fortunately out of the picture by the time I was born."

Two quick stitches robbed her of the ability to speak. The embarrassing squeak wasn't feigned. "He passed away?"

He hurried on, his voice gruff. "No, he was never . . . married to my mother. He seduced her, then refused to do the right thing after he'd . . . done what he did."

His words were awkwardly chosen for so well-spoken a man. He hadn't told this story often, if ever, before. She'd found that once a person told a story, he called on the same words again and again without having to search for them. In fact, the more emotional the memory, the more he relied on his memorized phrases to get through it. Like the lieutenant in Corunna who'd had a leg blown off by a cannon. He kept referring to a resounding blast, first to her when he thought her a tavern wench. Then later as he begged for mercy before he was hanged for selling secrets to the French.

Her hands gripped the sheets until the taut wrinkles imprinted on her palms. "Who was your father?"

He dabbed a warm trickle of blood off her stomach. "The brother of her employer."

She wanted more of the story so she moaned.

"He was already promised to another woman." Gabriel's eyes swept her face. "I don't think I've ever related this story before."

An unwelcome sensation gnawed at her chest. He wouldn't have shared the story with her if she hadn't manipulated it out of him. The pain in her stomach was preferable to her guilt, so she focused on that. Besides, it wasn't as if she'd asked to be stabbed. And the agony of his ministrations was far too real. "Don't worry, your secret is safe. Did you . . ." *Have any brothers or sisters* had been what she was going to ask, but the words stuck in her throat. Curse it all. Madeline wasn't without a conscience, but she normally did a far better job of quieting it. For some reason she couldn't ask him about his sister. At least not like this. Shame flickered in the corner of her thoughts.

Why? the cold, logical voice in her head asked. She'd done far worse as a spy. She had pried men's most private truths from them. Gabriel was no different. He was hiding information from her. That was unacceptable at best and life-threatening at worst.

The ill-timed pause in her scheming left her with no distraction. The next poke of the needle sent the hot tears she'd been willing into nonexistence dribbling down her cheeks. She pressed her eyes tightly closed, hoping Gabriel was too involved with his task to take note of her humiliation.

A soft, smooth cloth skimmed over her cheek, drying it. "We're almost done."

She turned her face away from his hand. She didn't

need her tears dried. Ian and Clayton had never tried. They'd given her food when they were starving, saving back none for themselves. Once Clayton had waited for her at a rendezvous point to warn her they'd been compromised even though that had allowed the French to capture and torture him for two days before she'd been able to free him.

But they hadn't dried her tears.

Not that she'd cried much after the first year. She would've gone mad.

"I've told you one of my secrets, you tell me one of yours," Gabriel said, clearing the tears from her other cheek.

She would have done anything to avoid the feelings stirred by his simple touch. Trapped by her own machinations, she spoke. "What do you want to know?"

"Where are you from?"

"London."

"Then where were you six months ago?"

The pointed question cleared the weakness from her mind. Apparently, she shouldn't have felt guilty over her interrogation. "I only agreed to give you one secret." And she was a fool for giving him that.

"Yours hardly equals the one you were given."

"But it does. You told me something that no one else knows and I have done the same—" She sucked in a sharp breath at the jab of the needle.

"Done." Gabriel knotted the thread and pulled back from her with a weary sigh. He rubbed his hands over his face, then picked up the glass of brandy. "Just once more. It will help keep infection from the wound."

She nodded. As the cool amber liquid ignited her skin, she writhed in pain, her fingers locking around his forearm as if she could stop what he'd already done.

With his free hand, he brushed strands of hair from her face. "It's almost over. Almost," he whispered.

She clung to the deep murmur of his voice to maintain her sanity.

Gradually, the burning began to fade, ebbing back to the bearable agony of the wound itself. As it did, she became aware of the weight of his arm where she clutched it to her naked breasts. The hard masculine strength of it. How the dark hair sprinkled over the back tickled her with each breath.

She loosed her hold on his arm, wincing at the red crescents imprinted by her nails. "Sorry."

He glanced down. "After what you endured, you expect me to complain about those?"

She managed a smile, but then his gaze focused on the breasts on either side of his arm. The smile faltered on her lips. Eager for his attention, her nipples contracted into hard nubs.

His eyes darkened until the pale green was nearly obliterated by the black of his pupils.

The muscles in his arm contracted, and even that small shift stole the air from the room. For a moment, she thought he'd lower his hand and caress her. Thought. Hoped. Prayed.

Instead, he jerked toward the supplies beside him, retrieving another cloth.

The air became breathable again, and Madeline exhaled. She must've lost more blood than she thought.

She'd wanted him to touch her.

Oh, she'd desired men before, but she'd never allowed it to go further than that. She'd enjoyed the novelty of the sensation but then she'd noted her body's reaction for future use and moved on.

It was past time she moved on. She would get the information she sought about Gabriel, and then if satisfied, allow him to continue working on the auction. If not, she'd be rid of him.

Using her pain as an excuse, she closed her eyes, blocking Gabriel and his accursed jade eyes from her sight. Guilt was no longer the most effective tool. She'd wasted that.

He hadn't taken advantage of her when he had the chance. But not only hadn't he taken advantage, he'd turned away. He was trying to resist her. A man didn't need to resist something he didn't want.

He'd handed her a weapon just as potent as the one she'd thrown away.

Desire.

She'd relished not having to entice Gabriel. She no longer had that luxury.

She would do what she did best—seduce the truth from him.

Chapter Eleven

Keeping his hand light, Gabriel dabbed the wound dry again.

Madeline lifted her head a few inches and peered at his work, the row of thin, black lines, fifteen in all, that held the edges of the knife wound together. "If you ever desire to cease being a Runner, you have a chance at making a tolerable tailor."

He unclenched his aching jaw. "For a moment I feared you were going to say surgeon. If this ever happens again, I'm sending for a doctor."

"Don't worry. It's my intent to avoid all knife attacks in the future."

The question remained why this attack had occurred in the first place, but he'd finish dressing her wound before addressing that. Gabriel pressed a square of cloth against her stomach. "I need to bandage the wound. Can you hold this?"

She kept the pad of fabric in place as he removed the wet towels, cut off her bloody bodice, then draped a long strip of cloth over her stomach. When he slid his hand under her back, his palm skimmed over the satiny skin at the base of her spine. As he worked, he kept his eyes on the bandage, refusing to note that it only highlighted the round, firm contours of her breasts.

His hand dipped under her again, and she gave a small moan. Pain, no doubt. But the luxurious delicacy of her skin tried to lull his exhausted brain into thinking otherwise.

He needed something to keep him sane. "Who was behind the attack?"

"I don't know."

He circled the bandage several more times until she was securely wrapped. "Who was near when you were stabbed?"

Her voice was weak and breathy. "Everyone. I didn't even know I'd been stabbed at first. It just felt like someone had struck me. When I realized what had happened, I tried to identify my attacker, but there were too many people."

"No one in particular struck you as odd? Someone badly dressed? Walking too fast?"

Her brows pleated together. "I keep running through the situation in my mind, but cannot think of anyone."

The furrow remained on her face. Without thinking, Gabriel reached out and smoothed it with his thumb. "You have an excuse. I, on the other hand, deserve to be flogged."

Her breath misted over his wrist, alerting him his hand had meandered to her cheek. "Hmm . . . If that is what you enjoy." Her eyes sparkled with a hint of mischief, but then grew serious. Turning her head, she touched her lips to the inside of his wrist. "Thank you for helping me." Her lips brushed against him as she spoke, then settled more firmly for a lingering caress. Her tongue flicked out and traced the vein on his wrist. "I should think of a way to reward you."

Although her mouth touched only a tiny portion

of his skin, the resulting heat was more than enough to burn him alive.

Her eyes rested on the bulge his breeches were unable to hide, then with a slight smile, she laved a slow circle on his wrist.

As if either of them doubted where he was imagining those lips.

With a throaty breath, she turned her head slightly, catching the tip of his thumb in her mouth. She suckled it gently, letting the flat of her tongue rasp over the end. His groin throbbed with each pulse of her tongue.

Then she moaned, the low, gasping sound of a woman enjoying herself.

Liar.

He'd heard that moan before when she'd allowed one of her suitors a lingering kiss of her hand. Despite the temptation to allow her erotically skilled lips to continue on to every other part of his anatomy, he pulled away. "Why do you do that?"

She raised an eyebrow. "Reward men that please me?"

"Play the seductress." He pulled the sheet over her torso.

Only a heartbeat's pause betrayed her surprise. She traced his lips with her finger, the movement dislodging the cover he'd placed over her and revealing the pale edges of her breasts. "I like to play, and I imagine you'd like some of my games."

His body agreed, but his mind took note of the exhaustion that lurked in her eyes and the wan cast of her complexion. Not to mention the pile of bloody towels and clothing next to them. He caught her wrist and lowered her arm back to her side.

"Don't you want me?" Confusion warred with shock in her eyes.

Hell, yes.

"I want you to sleep. You need to rest if you're to recover." He lifted the sheet up again, this time adding a coverlet from the foot of the bed for good measure.

She studied him through slightly narrowed eyes as if she didn't know what to make of him. As he suspected, her eyes started to drift closed.

But then she blinked them open. "What did you mean, play the seductress?" Sleepiness slurred her words.

He frowned. "It's as if you decide to become the courtesan, like an actress playing a role."

Her head rocked side to side. "No. I'm afraid it's who I am."

"I'm not sure I believe that."

"Then you're doubly a fool." She grabbed the top of her blanket and pulled it all the way to her chin.

"You hide behind the façade of seduction."

"What if that's because I'm hiding something worse?"

His role as a Runner couldn't let a question like that go unaddressed. "Are you?"

She closed her eyes. "Nothing you need to concern yourself with."

"I told you I mean to discover who you really are."

"You say that as if there's something to find." Only the smallest slivers of her eyes were visible, so it was impossible to read the dark emotion that lurked in them. "I'm tired. I'll see you tomorrow morning for our drive in the park."

Perhaps he should have taken her to Bedlam rather than home. "No. You need to allow your wound time to heal."

Her eyes snapped back open. "Impossible. I don't have time to waste lying abed."

"I'll use the time to further investigate your bidders. You'll hardly impress your suitors if you faint at their feet."

She sighed. "I'll rest one day, and I expect to hear your report tomorrow evening."

"Two."

"One, but I will only go on my morning outing on the second. I heal quickly."

"You've been stabbed before?"

She shrugged. "Once or twice."

The devil! "When?"

She settled into her pillow. "You don't think I'm serious, do you? You must be as exhausted as I."

He didn't know what to believe about her anymore. But her refusal to rest concerned him. "Why does your life mean so little to you?"

"Why does it mean so much to you?"

Gabriel didn't have an answer, so he smoothed a strand of dark hair from her forehead. "I don't get paid if you're dead."

She chuckled weakly at that. "Trying to appeal to me in a language I understand? I'm touched."

He folded his hands behind his back to keep them from wandering again. "Go to sleep, Madeline."

She huffed at his order, but after a few moments she lost the fight with her weariness, and her breathing settled into slow, even whispers.

The candlelight cast a warm, golden glow over her face, revealing a vulnerability she tried so hard to obliterate while she was awake. Who was she really?

With a grimace, Gabriel stood, pulling his jacket on over his bloody shirt. The coat was undoubtedly stained as well, but at least the black fabric disguised it. If he lived to be a hundred, he would never be able to divest himself of the agony on her face as he'd closed the wound.

But he had many such memories.

Madeline gave a quiet whimper in her sleep.

Gabriel hesitated, then continued to the door. He'd done his duty by her. Yet his hand refused to grasp the tarnished brass handle.

She wriggled in her sleep.

Damnation, she might reopen the wound. The thought carried him back to her side. Trailing his fingers down her cheek, he soothed her back to stillness. Perhaps he should stay tonight in case she needed him.

The satin softness of her skin entranced him, and he traced the delicate features of her face. The arched wings of her brows. The high, delicate cheekbones. The lush, rosy mouth.

Enough.

Gabriel wrenched his hand away. He didn't want to be entranced, especially by her. He wanted to solve the puzzle that she presented. The puzzle was what captivated him. Why his every other thought lingered on her. There were too many things about her that didn't add up.

He glanced again at her sleeping form tucked neatly under the blankets, then around the dark room. If he wanted information, she'd provided him with the perfect opportunity.

Chapter Twelve

What type of woman had no personal effects at all? Gabriel closed the dressing room door as silently as he'd opened it. The room contained her clothing and shoes but nothing more. No love letters poked out from among her stockings. No small keepsakes or mementos rested in her jewelry box. Her toilette table held only a wooden comb and a box of pins. No ornate silver brushes or expensive perfume.

Perhaps she kept those things locked away elsewhere.

He paused, listening to ensure no one was about, before he stole into the adjoining bedroom.

The light from his candle illuminated pale blue wallpaper, but holland covers shrouded everything else in the room. If she had a secret hideaway, this wasn't it.

Gabriel moved back into Madeline's room. He would have searched further into the house, but he suspected her butler lurked nearby in case he needed to be of assistance.

Gabriel set the candle on the side table. He knew no more than when he'd started, although that shouldn't come as a surprise—

The thin, cool blade of a knife rested at his throat. Sharp. Short.

His muscles tensed in unison. The bastard had come to finish the job on Madeline.

With an explosive movement his arm shot up, tucking under the wrist holding the knife to his throat and wrenching it away while simultaneously throwing his head back into the face of his attacker.

Gabriel spun away while holding the man's wrist, maintaining control of the knife. A quick blow to the man's armpit sent the knife clattering by Madeline's bed.

But his assailant had already compensated. A powerful fist connected with Gabriel's kidney. He sucked in a breath as he darted back, kicking the assailant's knife into the corner of the room. By his next breath, Gabriel had pulled his own dagger from his boot and balanced the familiar weight.

His eyes adjusted to the dim glow cast by the fireplace.

The other man waited where Gabriel had left him, a new knife brandished in his hand. His placement between Gabriel and the fireplace ensured Gabriel couldn't discern his face, just a hard, lean outline.

"Well done. You held up far better than I anticipated." The man's voice was deep and cultured, but Gabriel didn't recognize it.

"Drop your knife."

The man shrugged. "I just honed this one. I'd rather not chip the blade. But I will put it away." True to his word, he sheathed the knife at his waist in a smooth motion.

The man's lack of weapon didn't lull Gabriel into following suit. He'd seen how comfortably the man controlled his blade. "Who are you?"

"A friend of Madeline's. Canterbury sent for me."

"Forgive me if I don't believe you."

"I would be disgusted if you did."

Gabriel sidled to his left, and as he hoped, the other man turned as well. The reddish light from the coals slid across his face, illuminating a dark, rugged countenance. A crescent scar marked his right cheekbone.

"So who are you?"

"Most call me Wraith."

In Gabriel's experience, two types of people used a name like that: lunatics and criminals. He would put this man in the latter category. "And the others?"

The man's lips curled in a cold smile. "Ian Maddox."

"Who are you to her, Maddox? A former lover?"

A touch of real humor entered his smile. "I wish she were awake enough to hear you say that. How is she?" His humor faded as concern swept his face.

Gabriel didn't lower his arm, but his muscles relaxed slightly. "She'll live."

Maddox exhaled slowly. "I should've known not to believe her damned nervous butler." His eyes narrowed. "Now, where the devil were you when she was stabbed?"

The man's anger did more to allay Gabriel's fear than anything he could've said. But he wasn't about to risk Madeline. "Three feet away from her." He studied Maddox, awaiting his reaction.

But the other man's expression didn't change. "Did you catch him?"

"No. She didn't tell me she'd been stabbed until we were out of the theater."

Maddox's grunt was half amusement, half acceptance. "Did she see who attacked her?"

"No."

Maddox ran his hand through his hair. "Damned sloppy."

The sentiment echoed Madeline's a little too closely. "How did you say you know her?"

"I didn't."

Gabriel was too exhausted to tolerate any more ambiguous partial answers this night. "Then go."

"I'm supposed to leave her with a man who skulks about her house as soon as she's asleep?"

The door to the room opened, spilling a stream of light into the darkness. Another man swept in as Canterbury hovered in the doorway.

The new gentleman was taller than Gabriel and Maddox and leaner. However, like Maddox, the man moved with the grace of a trained fighter.

"How is she?" the newcomer asked.

"Wound's not mortal," Maddox answered with an annoyed glance at the butler. "Unlike the dire predictions I was fed."

Canterbury sagged against the door frame. "Thank heavens."

Maddox nodded toward Gabriel. "Gabriel Huntford, may I present Clayton Campbell?"

Gabriel was tempted to say no, but he inclined his head. "Campbell."

Campbell's eyes narrowed as they moved from Madeline's prone form to the knife still in Gabriel's hand.

"He's not the one who stabbed her," Maddox said.

"We're sure?" The gleam in Campbell's eyes promised that a swift death hung on his answer.

Gabriel was glad he still held his knife.

"We only have his word for it, do we not?" Campbell said.

Gabriel met Campbell's glare with one of his own. "Just as I only have your word that one or all of you aren't the assailants come to finish the job."

Canterbury straightened. "I assure you *I'm* not."

All three of the men glanced at Canterbury.

"Well, I'm not. And I would thank you all to save your violence for later. It isn't proper to fight in a lady's bedchamber."

Maddox raised his brow. "The parlor or the drawing room is preferable then?"

Canterbury pointed his finger at Maddox, his bushy, white brows drawing together. "In the gutter. I think you are quite familiar with it."

Campbell walked over to the bed and drew back the quilt covering Madeline. His glare turned black as her breasts were revealed. "Enjoyed yourself, did you?"

Gabriel readied his knife as Campbell lunged toward him.

Maddox stepped between them. "See to her life, then worry about her virtue."

Gabriel grabbed Campbell's arm before he could disturb the bandage. "Are you a doctor?"

Clayton shook him off with a cold look. "No, but then neither are you."

Gabriel pressed his knife to Campbell's side. "Move away from her."

"Would you gentlemen move your pissing contest out of my room?" Madeline cracked open one eye, let it drift closed, then opened both with a sigh. "You're all still here."

"Are you all right, little one?" asked Campbell. For the first time since he'd entered, ice didn't drip from his words. He traced his index finger along Madeline's nose.

Gabriel sheathed his knife with slow precision, the idea of running Campbell through far too appealing for his peace of mind. Besides, Madeline obviously knew the other men to the extent she didn't question why they were in her room. Or mind them seeing her half naked.

"Yes. Someone tried to stab me, but they failed miserably. Gabriel took care of me."

Campbell lifted the edge of the bandage and made a quick but thorough inspection of the wound. "You have experience with doctoring, Huntford?" He tucked the sheet under her chin, and Gabriel's brain resumed its normal functioning.

"Some. None of it by choice." Gabriel watched Madeline as her gaze drifted between the others. Not once did her coy, flirtatious manner appear. She was at ease with them. Yet he couldn't trust her decision. She was paying him to keep her safe.

Or at least paying him to appear to keep her safe, but there was no way in hell he'd allow her to be harmed again. "How do you know each other?"

"Would you believe cribbage partners?" Maddox asked, his face a mask of sincerity.

"No."

"Cousins?"

Gabriel leveled him with a glare. "Are you going to tell me the truth?"

"Not likely. Unless Madeline does."

"I could have you thrown in prison until you rot."

Campbell shifted so he was shoulder to shoulder with Maddox. "It would be comical to see you try."

"Would you—" Madeline pushed up on her elbows, then fell back, the hint of color she'd regained during her rest leaching away. Her shuddering breath propelled Gabriel to her side.

Unfortunately, it had the same effect on the other two.

Gabriel blocked them. "I'll see to her."

Campbell's lip curled. "I don't think so. Your work here is finished."

"*Canterbury!*" Madeline's shout interrupted their dispute.

"Miss?" The butler hurried in from the corridor.

"The gentlemen are leaving now."

Campbell frowned. "Madeline—"

"I'm tired and in pain and you are all making it worse."

Canterbury motioned to the door. "I believe Miss Valdan made her wishes quite clear."

But Gabriel remained by the bed. She might have made her wishes clear, but that didn't mean they were in her best interest.

"Send for us if you need us." Maddox tipped his head toward the corridor, then he and Campbell strode out without looking back.

"Mr. Huntford?" Canterbury cleared his throat with deliberate force.

Gabriel remained where he was. "I need to ensure she didn't reinjure herself when she moved."

Madeline's lips thinned, but she sighed. "Fine. But you leave as soon as you finish."

Gabriel nodded. "Agreed."

Canterbury bowed and backed from the room.

Gabriel hesitated before lifting the sheet covering Madeline, willing himself to be a gentleman. *Check the dressing, nothing else.* It was no different than when he'd tended Bartles after the man took a knife to the shoulder.

And Gabriel was the Prince Regent.

She was perfection from the gentle, pale slope of

her shoulders to the slender span of her waist.

Which was covered in a bandage. Blood had already seeped through.

Gabriel's teeth clenched together. "I told you to rest." He unwound the fabric covering her stomach.

She nodded, her eyes already drifting closed again.

He placed a fresh square of fabric over her stitches. "How do you know Maddox and Campbell?"

"They're old friends."

Gabriel finished securing the bandage again. "You know each other from London, then?"

"Initially."

A lock of her dark hair had fallen across her shoulder and Gabriel smoothed it away as he covered her. Her elegant coiffure was crushed beneath her on the pillow. It couldn't be comfortable. And for some reason he couldn't explain, that bothered him. "Did you become friends because of your mutual talent for giving ambiguous answers?" He began removing the pins holding the curls in place, unraveling the satin coils across her pillow, sifting them through his fingers until the strands lay straight.

She sighed again, but this time it dangerously resembled pleasure. "No, that was beaten into us later."

Gabriel's hand paused on her hair. "Beaten?"

"A figure of speech, nothing more. Please don't stop."

He resumed stroking her hair.

"It's soothing. My mother used to do this when I couldn't fall asleep. She—" Her brows jerked together, then drifted apart again. Her breathing deepened.

Each slow inhale exactly matched its exhale in duration. The tension drained from her face. Unlike her fitful slumber from earlier, she slept like an angel.

He almost believed her. "Your mother?"

Not a single twitch betrayed that she'd heard him.

Gabriel smoothed her hair one final time. "Coward."

Chapter Thirteen

Mid-morning light brought respectability back to the uneven cobbles of Cheshire Street. The townsfolk unfortunate enough to live near Lady Aphrodite's Love Grotto began to venture timidly out of their houses like rabbits in spring. They peered left, then right, then left again, noses practically twitching as they checked for signs of drunken revelry before descending down their stairs.

Gabriel's rap with the well-polished brass knocker on the door to Lady Aphrodite's sent a middle-aged woman and her maid scuttling back into their home across the street, barely swishing their skirts out of the way as the door slammed shut.

A young, barrel-chested footman appeared. Gabriel handed him his calling card as he stepped inside, removing his hat. "Is Lady Aphrodite available?"

The man's brow wrinkled and his head tipped to the side as he read the card. "I don't think she sees anyone this time of morning. She don't wake up too early."

Gabriel would bet this simple-minded man was assigned elsewhere when customers began to arrive in the evening. "I'm a Bow Street Runner. This is business." It was past time he delved into the sexual histories of Madeline's bidders. Lady Aphrodite's wouldn't cater to the more depraved proclivities, but it was popular, so it would be a good place to start.

The footman's head bounced with uneven bobs as he nodded. "Let me go ask Her Ladyship."

Gabriel was left standing in the foyer while the man trundled off to check. The decorations at Lady Aphrodite's were surprisingly tasteful. The colors were soft, muted blues rather than the crimson and gold preferred by so many of its competitors. The chairs were worn but of good quality and smelled of beeswax. No doubt, it looked quite elegant by candlelight. It was easy to see why Lady Aphrodite's had exploded in popularity during the six months since it opened. Bawdiness in the decor was limited. A few neatly wrought paintings depicting fornicating nymphs scandalized the walls. And in the center of the entryway stood a large marble statue of a nude woman with her head thrown back in obvious ecstasy.

Gabriel froze.

It couldn't be.

While feeling like a schoolboy stealing peeks at the naughty bits of the Greek statues in the British Museum, he circled the translucent stone.

Madeline.

He stopped directly in front of it, no longer caring if he was caught staring.

The sculptor was either inept or had never seen Madeline naked. Madeline's breasts were fuller. Her waist narrower.

Gabriel moved his gaze upward.

And the Madeline he knew would never meet passion with such languid acceptance. She would climax with eyes wide open, her fingers digging wildly into her lover's back.

Unless the winning bidder preferred her more docile.

Gabriel exhaled harshly and turned away from the sculpture. No wonder she'd done so well with the auction. Who wouldn't pay a fortune to be the man to bring that look of rapture to her face?

Had she arranged for the statue? Planned for it to be in the center of the *ton*'s most popular new brothel? Planned for the men to see, and then, consciously or not, want her? Gabriel no longer underestimated her skill at strategy.

"Sir?" The young footman scrambled back into the room. "You're lucky. Lady Aphrodite says she'll see you." He drew a deep breath, seeming to recall the solemnity of his position. "I mean, if you will follow me, sir."

Gabriel nodded at the man, wondering how he'd come to be hired. He'd not yet met Lady Aphrodite through any investigations, which was remarkable in this line of work. Had she hired the footman to save on funds? Or to be kind? The answer would go a long way to revealing her character.

But as much as he tried to focus on those questions and the way he would address his investigation, another question kept intruding—how did she know Madeline?

The footman ushered him into a study. A blond woman reclined on a settee, a pale yellow dressing gown draped over her full, rounded figure. Her gown gaped in the front, revealing a generous amount of bosom. She slowly uncrossed her legs, flashing slender ankles and calves. She shrugged, allowing the gown to slip from her shoulders and display the lack of clothing beneath the robe. After Madeline's subtle finesse, the woman's offer couldn't have been more blatant if she'd thrown him to the carpet and ripped off his clothing.

Yet Gabriel didn't feel a thing in response. Not a bloody thing. Not a single flicker of lust. All he could think about was that he preferred dark hair. Not just dark, but deep russet brown with a few streaks of auburn only revealed by the sun. And shoulders so delicate they appeared fragile until one held them and felt the carefully disguised strength.

Damn Madeline.

"Mr. Huntford, please have a seat." A hand heavy with a rainbow of jeweled rings motioned to a wide footstool near her feet.

"I'll stand, thank you."

Lady Aphrodite straightened. Light streaming in through the open curtains diffused through the rice powder dusting her cheeks and skipped across the fine creases hiding near her eyes. "This is business, then."

"Indeed."

"That will be all, Michael."

"Yes, Franny—I mean, Lady Aphrodite." The man's face crumpled at his mistake, then brightened. "Your sleeves are slipping. Let me help." He tugged the fabric up over her shoulders. "That's what brothers are for, after all."

She cast a quick glance at Gabriel, but still smiled gently at the other man. "Thank you, Michael."

The footman hurried from the room.

"What is it you require?"

"Information on a few of your clients."

The humor faded from her face. "That, I cannot give you."

Gabriel pulled several golden coins from his pocket. "I'll pay."

She made no move to take the money. "Do you think my clients will come if they think I give out their secrets? Is it official business that brings you here?"

"No. The inquiry is on behalf of a private client."

"Who?"

Gabriel debated what to tell her; after all, Madeline couldn't be all that well liked in the circles of the demimonde. Yet he saw no reason to lie. "Madeline Valdan."

Lady Aphrodite swept him with a penetrating gaze. "You work for Madeline?"

Gabriel nodded.

A smile blossomed on Lady Aphrodite's face. "Then bugger my clients, you may have whatever information you wish."

He couldn't help a niggling of suspicion. "Indeed? How do you know Madeline?"

What would he do if Lady Aphrodite said Madeline had worked for her?

Gabriel still didn't know what to make of Madeline's claims to virginity. Part of him had almost begun to believe her, but a single flick of her tongue over her lower lip or a swivel of those perfectly curved hips made him doubt her all over again, and he wasn't a man given to uncertainty.

"I met her at a brothel."

Gabriel's chest constricted.

"I'm no longer young, and society has no place for aging courtesans. I'd just sold my last piece of jewelry from my former protector but it hadn't brought in what I'd hoped. As you saw, I have Michael to take care of, so I was at my wit's end, I suppose. I was going to sell myself to a brothel. But when I arrived, I couldn't bring myself to enter. Madeline walked past as I sat on the curb. Oh, how I hated her grace and beauty. But then she turned and sat next to me. I bemoaned everything. Rather than pity me, she suggested I take every last penny from the necklace and open my own brothel. And she told me how much to charge." Lady Aphrodite laughed and shook her head. "I thought she was mad, but she told me people equate money with class. The more expensive it is, the more people will want it. I've always had a touch of the gambler in me, so I did what she suggested, thinking if I failed, I could still sell myself. I only had enough for two weeks' rent on this place." She waved her heavily adorned hand. "That was six months ago."

Gabriel exhaled slowly, a bit disgusted with the amount of relief coursing through him. After all, Madeline had counseled a woman on how to open a successful brothel. "I noticed the statue."

She smiled. "It is an ode to a courtesan far more skilled than I."

Gabriel pulled a copy of the list from Naughton's from his pocket and handed it to her. "These are the bidders so far. What do you know about them?"

"If you are looking for more colorful information, I don't know how much help I'll be. I keep things simple here."

"Then the ones you don't know will be just as useful as the ones you do."

She pulled a pair of silver spectacles from the table next to her and perched them on her nose. She scanned the list slowly. "I have only seen Danbury once since he is not normally in London, but no complaints about him. Although he's fastidious. He brings new nightclothes for the girl he selects. Lenton comes here as well. Has a fondness for variety. Never wants the same girl again, much to her dismay."

"Then your girls have no complaints about Lenton? He's never shown any hint of violence?"

"No, I've slept with him myself. He is a demanding lover, but his demands are nothing unusual." She looked at the paper again. "Wethersly, I haven't seen. He keeps several mistresses from what I hear, and he's older than the crowd I attract." Her finger trailed along the list as she read, tapping when she came across a man she recognized.

Gabriel resisted the urge to call the recitation to a halt. He'd known the gentlemen of the *ton* to be rutting beasts under all their fine trappings, but as Lady Aphrodite revealed their secret perversions, his rage built. These were men Madeline was eager to attract?

Lady Aphrodite's hand suddenly clenched on the paper. "Is Billingsgate still in the bidding?"

"He hasn't bid for a few days, but I believe so."

Lady Aphrodite's lips puckered as though she might spit on the carpet, but thought better of it. "He's an animal. He likes his girls tied and bleeding."

Gabriel had heard the man was fond of violence. And his other lover from the ball had been scared of him as well. "He comes here?"

"No, that bastard knows I'd shoot him."

"You know him personally then?"

Lady Aphrodite smiled coldly. "You could say that." She pulled aside the neckline of her robe, revealing pale, puckered scars on the side of her breast.

"You were his mistress?"

"Only for one day. I wasn't fool enough to stay with him longer than that."

"Why did you accept him at first?" Gabriel asked.

"He's handsome and charming. He hides his dark side well."

"Charming?" Susan had said her suitor was charming.

"I think it adds to his sense of power to make the women infatuated with him."

The hope that Gabriel usually managed to keep chained deep in his chest threatened to break free. "Didn't his other mistresses complain about the violence?"

"He pays well, too."

"Do you think he could get violent enough to kill?"

Lady Aphrodite twisted the ring on her index finger, hesitating. "Possibly. He needs to feel in power. If someone took that from him, he might overreact."

"Was he ever violent in any other way?"

She shook her head. "Just with the knife."

Gabriel's teeth ground together. Even if the man wasn't responsible for the murders, he'd see him dead in the street before he'd allow him near Madeline. "I could have him arrested."

"Arrest a peer of the realm for roughing up a whore five years ago?"

Gabriel held her disbelieving gaze. "Even if the charges didn't hold, it might take him down a peg."

"You'd do it, too, wouldn't you?" But then she sighed. "As tempting as that is, I won't risk losing this place. But not many men would be willing to risk angering a peer." She ran her index finger along her collarbone, then between her breasts. "Are you sure there's nothing I can do for you this morning? It would be my treat. As much as I love Madeline, with her current ruse, she can't be keeping you satisfied."

"Ruse?"

"About her virginity . . ." She paused, her brows jerking together. "I shouldn't have said anything."

Gabriel ignored the betrayal slamming through him. It didn't matter. He had access to his suspects. Whether she was virgin or whore didn't matter.

Yet his tongue was suddenly clumsy in his mouth. "How do you know?"

"I—" Lady Aphrodite straightened a large ruby on her finger. "When she sat next to me on the curb. Her eyes. It's why I never mistook her for a lady. In this profession you do things you wouldn't wish on the devil himself." She absently rubbed at the scars through her bodice. "And Madeline has the eyes of a woman who's been through far worse than I."

Chapter Fourteen

After the laborious journey from her room, Madeline rested her head against the cool glass of the study window. The wound in her side throbbed in time with each breath, but there seemed some victory to be claimed in not heeding it. She trailed a finger absently in the condensation collected near the sash. The windows in this place needed to be repaired. But that was an expense for another tenant.

It was funny. She'd stayed in this house longer than anywhere else in the past ten years, but it didn't feel like a home.

But then again, how could it? This was just another mission. Just another carefully arranged illusion.

When she was done with this, she'd buy herself a nice little cottage with a thatched roof and garden. Crochet doilies. Or did one knit doilies? Regardless, how much more homelike could she get than that?

She flicked a droplet of water off her finger. Or would that existence be another illusion? Her way of playing the role of a normal, boring country widow.

After fifty years, surely she'd begin to forget it was pretense. Glavenstroke had always warned that if a spy stayed too long in an identity, she might begin to lose herself.

Please Lord, let it be so.

Although at this rate, she might not live long enough to forget anything at all. She shivered and tugged her nightgown tighter around her, wincing at the increased pressure on the stitches. This was utter nonsense. Her assassin could sneeze and do away with her.

Well, curse him anyway.

Or her. Madeline was hardly one to discriminate.

She gingerly lowered herself into a chair by the window. Perhaps she should tell Gabriel about the threat. But he already knew someone wanted her dead. It wasn't particularly important why.

Besides, if she told him, he'd undoubtedly do something noble and altogether foolish, like insist on staying with her. Her stomach fluttered at the thought of meeting him in the kitchen over a plate of coddled eggs, his shirt unbuttoned and his feet bare, a touch of stubble darkening his chin . . . Madeline rubbed her knuckles against her eyes. She didn't even like coddled eggs, for pity's sake.

The truth of the matter was that she couldn't trust herself with him, which was ten times more dangerous than any doubts she had.

Thank heavens she was no longer a spy.

Madeline took refuge against the damp glass of the window, her breath adding to the droplets obscuring the view.

A dark cloaked figure turned the corner below, moving with athletic grace, his pace neither fast nor slow. Even the capes of his greatcoat couldn't hide his strong, purposeful stride.

Gabriel.

Although his head remained straight, she could

feel the way his attention spread around him, noting everything she'd seen from her window.

Most people were oblivious to the world around them. Anything that didn't stumble directly into their path passed by unobserved and unnoticed.

But Gabriel had the finely tuned senses of a hunter, and even from this distance, she could feel the energy crackling around him. On some level, his talent for observation terrified her—she'd spent too long as a spy for it not to.

Yet at the same time, it had become increasingly hard not to ask him if he noticed the same things as she did. If he'd noticed the owl nestled at the top of the oak as they drove around Hyde Park or the footman who clanked as he walked because he was making off with his employer's silver.

Madeline smoothed her nightgown as Gabriel mounted her steps. She should have left it in the recesses of her closet where it belonged, but she'd been tired and miserable. Now there was no way her legs would hold long enough for her to return to her room to change.

Well, he'd wanted to find out more about her.

Her smile faded. The dangerous part was that she desperately wanted to know what he discovered.

Gabriel paused at the entrance to the study. Madeline rested in a high-backed chair near the window. She was swathed in a high-necked, white flannel night rail. The thing had to have more material than three of her normal dresses combined.

All she lacked was a little cap and she'd be the perfect little wife awaiting her husband.

He exhaled, surprised at the hot rush of desire

sweeping through him. How the hell had she known that image would be erotic? That he'd feel like she'd been waiting up for his arrival. That he'd feel he could go to her side, and she'd smile, then offer her hand so he could lead her to their bedroom. That he'd hardly be able to wait to rip the clothing from her and reveal the exquisite body beneath. A body that was his alone.

The surge of possessiveness brought him back to his senses.

Possessive? Of a courtesan about to wager away the virginity she didn't even possess?

His hands clenched at his sides. What the hell was wrong with him that the picture she presented was even appealing? If he were fool enough to marry, he'd tramp in at three in the morning, knuckles bloodied from apprehending a criminal, the filth of the streets caked on his boots, and his wife would run revolted from the room. Or worse, cry copious tears because he'd missed her dinner party.

So there was no reason for Madeline's picture of domesticity to affect him so. Not one damned reason.

There was also no reason for her to be out of bed. He latched on to the thought, his first sane one since entering the room. "What are you doing up?"

Her brows drew together. "I feel quite well. Thank you for asking."

He strode to her side. As he'd feared, the skin around her mouth was pale from pain, and purple smudges lingered in the delicate skin under her eyes. "You do not. Can you even walk? Or did you push yourself too far?"

Her chin lifted a fraction. "I can walk."

Gabriel offered his hand. "Prove it."

She stared at his hand as if inspecting bread for

weevils. "I'm the one with reason to be in a foul mood today. What's your excuse?"

That Lady Aphrodite's assertion about Madeline had tumbled about in his mind until he felt he'd go mad. Lady Aphrodite had no proof about Madeline's background other than her assumptions, but something in it had rung true. He'd seen glimpses of haunted disillusionment in Madeline's eyes when she thought no one watched.

Yet as angry as he was that she'd lied about her virginity, it didn't begin to compare to the rage that consumed him at the thought of her suffering at the hands of other men.

But he wasn't about to share that with her. Hell, he wished he could clear it from his own mind. "Besides not sleeping last night and prowling the bordellos of London this morning?"

"Bordellos? I would have thought that would put you in a better mood."

"Not if it meant discovering Lord Plimpington has an unnatural fascination with feet."

She grimaced. "What else?"

Gabriel listed what he'd found out at Lady Aphrodite's as well as a couple other seedier brothels toward the docks.

Madeline nodded as he spoke, not once betraying a flicker of surprise or horror at any of the habits of her suitors. She tapped absently at her lower lip with her index finger. "Manton and Kramer are out of the running then."

Only those two?

"How are you going to ensure that?"

"Using the same skills that encouraged them to bid in the first place."

"And the rest? You're fine if Lord Plimpington

wants to suck on your toes? Or Sir John wants you to take a cane to his pudgy arse?" The fury that had been building inside him coated his words.

Color mounted on her cheeks. "For the fortunes they are willing to pay, I find myself most tolerant."

He wanted nothing more than to grab her shoulders and shake her until her teeth rattled. Until she recoiled from what he'd told her like any other woman of his acquaintance would.

"What of Billingsgate?" she asked.

Gabriel hesitated. He was scheduled to meet with Billingsgate's solicitor soon. He couldn't risk having her cut ties with the man before he'd had a chance to view them. "I hope to have information on him by tomorrow."

He exhaled and strode toward the door, using the movement to rein in his guilt. His duty was to his sister and the dead girl. He forced himself to picture the bodies, perfectly laid out on their beds, swathed in white with the damned brooch pinned at their throats.

Susan had been a blameless innocent when some bastard sullied her neck with those ugly, mottled bruises. She deserved justice. Her murderer deserved death.

He stared at the grid of fibers in a threadbare patch of carpet. He'd tell Madeline before the auction ended. Even if he hadn't solved the case, he wouldn't let her choose Billingsgate. So why did it feel like he was sacrificing one woman for the other? "Now that you know all the information I gathered, you need to return to bed. Shall I call for your maid?"

"What maid?"

He frowned. "You don't have a lady's maid?" He hadn't thought about the lack of one last night, but now the absence was glaring.

"I'm hardly a lady."

"Who changed your bandages this morning?"

"I managed."

Gabriel swore. There was no way she could have secured the bandages correctly by herself. "Who helps you with your hair before you go out?"

"Is it so outside your realm of understanding that I can survive on my own?"

"Survive, yes. Get in and out of those contraptions you women dress in, no."

A reluctant smile tilted her lips. "An observant point. I have a coachman and a butler. We have a maid-of-all-work, who comes in occasionally to help. When I want to do something elaborate with my hair or dress, however, Lady Aphrodite sends over one of her girls."

"She thinks highly of you."

Madeline snorted. "Lady Aphrodite simply admires that she found someone more mercenary than she."

"Did you know about the statue in her entry hall?" Gabriel regretted the question as soon as the syllables tripped off his tongue. For it was impossible not to stare at Madeline and imagine her posing for it.

Then he no longer needed to imagine.

She tipped her head back, letting her eyelids drift half closed, her lips parting.

Bloody hell.

Straightening, she dusted an imaginary speck of lint from her sleeve, but her ducked head couldn't hide her grin. "What statue?"

A laugh escaped in a rusty bark. How did she do it? A moment ago he'd been furious at her. "Was it your idea?"

"What kind of vain creature do you take me for?" She peeked at him through her lashes. "I did, however, suggest she move it closer to the front door."

The curve of her lips widened, then twitched as a laugh escaped.

"Ow." Her gaiety ceased and she pressed a hand to her side.

Gabriel lifted her into his arms before she could protest. "I'm taking you to bed."

"It was the statue pose, wasn't it? And to think, I complained the expression on the statue didn't look convincing."

"You have a sally in response to everything, don't you?"

"Of course." She relaxed against him, her cheek resting against his chest. "I suppose after all my talk of independence I should protest this treatment, but I really was dreading having to drag myself back to my room."

Gabriel breathed slowly through his mouth as he carried her, trying to avoid the subtle scent of vanilla clinging to her hair. If he shifted her more tightly against him, it was only because he wanted to keep her steady as he climbed the stairs, not because he wanted to feel those silken strands against his chin.

The late afternoon sun rendered the dark green walls and walnut paneling of her room only slightly less oppressive. He laid her on the edge of the bed. Without the life-or-death threat of the night before, it was impossible to ignore his body's immediate response to the simple gesture. "Let me check your stitches." His voice sounded gravelly to his own ears.

"You'll do anything to see me naked, won't you?" She grimaced. "I do that without thinking, you know. Turn everything into innuendo. The words form more out of habit than anything. Thank heavens I avoided meeting the pope. The shock might have killed him."

Behind the self-mocking tone, a forlorn note

lurked. The sudden desire to banish it overwhelmed him. "So you don't want me to see you naked?"

She jerked slightly against the pillow and her eyes widened. "That is neither here nor there. The point is, I would've made the comment to anyone."

"But would you have then confessed it?"

Sighing, Madeline closed her eyes. "I don't need my head to ache, too. Just strip me naked."

The thought of slipping the clothing from her body was slightly less unsettling than the thought of her undressing for him, so Gabriel unfastened her bodice, keeping his fingers light so they touched only cool, round buttons and soft fabric. Even so, the heat from her skin radiated over his fingers, luring them closer. He swore silently as his fingers fumbled.

Madeline opened her eyes and caught his hand. "No wonder you cut my clothing off last night. I would've bled to death by the time you finished. Let me."

Gabriel nodded, pinning his gaze to the windows. Four panes of glass per window. Three windows.

Her fingers unfastened the button between her breasts. The material slowly parted in her wake—

That would make twelve panes of glass. Now a pane of glass that size would most likely cost fifteen shillings apiece, which would—

"All done." Amusement tinted her words, but since he'd managed to survive the disrobing without ravishing her, he was content to allow her humor at his expense.

After all, urgency and exhaustion had consumed him last night. There was no way reality could live up to what his memory swore he beheld last night. No woman could have been so flawless—

"Hell." Gabriel's oath wasn't silent this time. She was more than perfect. Desire grabbed him by the throat, making him fight to draw in a breath.

She's tired and in pain. Repeating the mantra over and over in his mind was the only thing that kept Gabriel from making a fool of himself and cupping one of Madeline's rosy-tipped breasts in his hand to test its weight.

He quickly moved the bandage. The wound appeared to be healing. No redness or swelling encroached on the cut. He wrapped her with brisk efficiency.

"I don't mind if you see me naked."

"What?" Gabriel paused in the middle of tying the bandage in place.

"I didn't answer when you asked earlier. Besides, you saw the cavalry last night."

"Cavalry?" He'd apparently lost the ability not only to create sentences, but to understand them.

She winked, then glanced pointedly down at her breasts. "You know, upfront and flashy but of no real use."

For the second time that afternoon, a chuckle escaped him. But under her intent gaze, his laugh faded.

Her breath hitched through softly parted lips. He stared at those dewy lips until self-preservation drove his eyes downward. As her rib cage rose and fell, her breasts quivered, her nipples straining toward him.

He jerked his gaze upward to her face. Her eyes still watched him. She could hardly have missed him gawking at her breasts.

If any other sound had filtered into the room, he would've missed the slight increase in the cadence of her breath. He would have missed the dry gulp as a swallow rippled down her throat.

But there was no other sound.

His hand drifted upward until his knuckles grazed the underside of her breast. Her breath escaped in a tiny *hic* of pleasure, and he gloried in that one awkward sound far more than in a dozen of her perfect moans.

When he would have continued his caress higher, the bandage he held in his hand pulled tight, stopping him.

Damnation. What had happened to his control?

He finished tying the bandage with a quick yank, then drew her nightgown closed.

"Gabriel—"

A knock sounding on the door interrupted Madeline.

"Miss?" Canterbury poked in his ostrich-feather-adorned head. "Glad to see you resting." He held out a slip of paper. "The updated list from Naughton's."

Gabriel retrieved it from him. He scanned the list, then froze. The blood drained from his head, then rushed back with a deafening roar.

"Who is currently the top bidder?" Madeline asked.

"The Marquess of Northgate." Gabriel crumpled the paper and threw it into the grate, watching in satisfaction as flames dragged it into oblivion. "My father."

Chapter Fifteen

Madeline turned her face into the shadows dusting her pillow to disguise her shock. "Your father is a marquess?" It did explain a lot. For instance, Gabriel's Oxford education.

Gabriel looked as though he wanted to pull the list from the fire and stomp on the ashes for good measure. "The man is a lecherous reprobate."

"Then he should fit in well with the rest of my bidders."

Gabriel's frown deepened, but he didn't respond to her jest. He ran his hand through his short-cropped hair. "I have other things I must see to this evening."

Madeline barely stopped herself from grabbing his sleeve to prevent him from leaving. "You can't make a statement like that, then not expound."

"Indeed, I can."

Not if she tied him to the chair and held a hot poker to his feet. The idea held merit at the moment. "Do you want me to take him out of consideration?"

Gabriel shrugged. "Do what you will. I've had nothing to do with the man in thirty years. He means nothing to me."

A man doesn't burn the name of someone about whom he's ambivalent.

"So you don't care if I make wild and passionate love to him in this very bed?"

A muscle twitched in his jaw. "No."

Stubborn man. "If he strips my gown from me and kisses his way down my body?"

"No." But the tendons had corded on his neck.

"If I lie back on this bed and wrap my legs around his waist as he—"

"Damnation, Madeline! What do you want from me?" He stalked to the bed and braced his hands on the edge, inches from her shoulder. So many dark emotions churned across his face she couldn't begin to decipher them all. In Moscow, she'd once seen a man taunt a bear, poking and prodding until suddenly the animal snapped, lunging and snarling.

But in Moscow the bear had been chained.

Gabriel's knuckles gleamed white where they clenched her bedding. "Some heartfelt tale of a little boy longing for a father? Is that what you are looking for?" He caught her chin between his forefinger and thumb. "Because you won't find it. That man is worse than the dung on the streets, but if you want him, by all means have him. I have no doubt he has plenty of money." He jerked his hand away from her face with a growl.

"Gabriel—" She froze. She had no idea what she wanted to say to that. She simply knew she didn't want him to stride out the door. Not yet. "What happened between him and your mother?"

He gave a harsh bark of laughter. "Do you really need me to explain where babies come from?"

"You said he took advantage of her."

"Why do you want to know?"

"I don't know." And that was the truth. It wasn't

the question she should be asking. It didn't affect her or the auction like the information he was hiding about his sister. "It would help fill the time, keep me in bed," she finished lamely.

"You want me to share my family secrets because you're bored? If you want a reason to stay in bed, I can give you a much better one." His finger dragged along her jaw in a rough caress, then softened as he traced her lips. He leaned in until she could see every nuance of jade in his pale eyes. "Do you feel like getting out of bed now?"

She hardly remembered she had legs.

His hand lowered to the neckline of her night-gown, hovering just above the tiny ruffle below her throat. Each inhale brought the sensitive skin of her chest against his fingers. She found herself holding her breath to maintain the contact.

"How about now?" he asked, parting the edges of her gown, his mouth lowering to the space between her breasts, briefly caressing it. "Why would I want to tell you some tawdry tale when I can be doing this?"

Her skin burned as if he'd branded her. "Because if you do, I'll repay you in kind. I'll tell you something about me."

His lips left her skin, and she cursed her stupid tongue.

Gabriel fastened her top button, his gaze intent. "What will you tell me?"

"About my own parents." Why was she bargaining? It was an ineffective tool that left far too much in Gabriel's control. And a bargain meant she had to give something up.

"The truth?"

But it did seem to be working. "Yes."

He stared at her for a moment, his eyes searching her face in an unnerving manner. Then he spoke. "My mother was a governess, the only child of a vicar. She worked for Lord Simon. One summer, his older brother, the Marquess of Northgate, came to stay with them. Even though he was engaged to marry another woman, he seduced my mother. When he knew she was pregnant, he refused to do the right thing and marry her."

She reached for him but he stepped away. "How did your mother take it?"

He gave a short shake of his head, and color darkened his cheekbones. "She makes excuses for him. He had her so enthralled with his lies, I think she still believes him and his promises of love." Behind his anger lurked embarrassment that his mother had allowed herself to be so gullible. Gabriel was not one to excuse foolishness.

"Have you ever met him?"

"No. He attempted to come to my sister's funeral. But I refused him. As if he hadn't made her a bastard and robbed her of the life she should have had as a lady."

"And you the life as heir to a marquess?"

Gabriel snorted. "He and his title can go rot for all I care. But Susan deserved better. And my mother."

Madeline tentatively grasped the opening he provided. "What happened to your sister?"

"She was murdered seven years ago."

"What—"

"Enough. Your turn."

Madeline inhaled slowly, smoothing over the panic that rippled through her at the thought of revealing a piece of herself. *Stop it.* There was nothing dangerous in the information, nothing that could be used against her. Her father and mother were both dead. She was no longer a spy with an identity to hide.

But there had to be some way he could turn the information against her. There always was.

She concentrated to force the words past her years of training. "My mother was Elizabeth Valdan, the daughter of a rector. She was married to Thomas St. John, a traveling actor." She exhaled. That was more than enough of that.

Gabriel was silent. "And?"

"That's it. I only have the two. I believe that's the way of things."

"We had a bargain."

"We did, and if you choose not to be more explicit in your bargaining, that is no fault of mine." Hurt sharpened her tone. But of course, he didn't know what that small morsel of information had cost her.

With a growl, Gabriel braced his hands on either side of her head, his face inches from hers. "You know that's not what I intended."

The position should have made her feel trapped. After her mother had died, Madeline promised herself she'd never be confined again. The first day in gaol, she'd beaten and clawed against the door and bars until blood dripped down her arms, mingling with the dead man's blood already staining her clothes.

She should do the same thing now. She should pound her fists against Gabriel and free herself. It would be easy. A blow to the chin since she didn't want to hurt him too badly.

But when her hands connected with his body, they weren't fists.

She slid her palms up his chest, her fingers sliding easily over the fabric of his coat, the muscle underneath as smooth and hard as polished stone. Keeping one hand on his pounding heart, she wrapped the other around the back of his neck. She slipped her fingers through the hair at his nape, relishing the smooth, even texture. "What is it you intended then?"

He lowered his mouth until his lips were an inch from hers. "To find out the truth about you."

"So you keep saying. Why? Why do you want to know about me? I'll be out of your life in little more than a week. I mean nothing more to you than you mean to me." She tugged on his neck, trying to close the distance between them, wanting nothing more than for the tingling in her lips to cease.

But he resisted, his mouth remaining impossibly far from hers. "I wish to hell I knew. You torment me, Madeline." His words weren't the thwarted cry of a desperate lover. They were accusatory, almost angry.

She knew that if she lifted her lips to his, he would be lost. She could see the hunger glowing in his eyes. The desire. Lust was her weapon of choice and she wielded it well. He was strung as tight as a fresh-made bow. If she pressed, he would snap, giving her what she wanted. What she needed.

Yet she shifted under him, an unaccustomed uncertainty stealing over her. "You don't sound pleased by that."

"I'm not. I don't want to want you. I have more important things to do than wonder how your lips would taste. How your breasts would feel in my palm. How you would react when I slipped my hand under your skirts."

Her body throbbed as if he'd done the things he said.

He continued. "I don't approve of this auction. You give advice to whores about opening brothels. You manipulate those around you without batting an eye." He exhaled, his breath shuddering through him. "So why, in heaven's name, can't I dislike you?"

She despised the burning in the back of her throat as much as she despised her inability to push him away. "I never asked you to like me. I make no apologies for who I am." Why would she? Apologies wouldn't bring her absolution.

"I know."

Drawing on the wellspring of her pride, she placed both hands on his chest and shoved. "Good. Then you'd also best remember that I don't want you to like me. You don't have the wealth to make it worthwhile."

For a moment her attempt to move him proved ineffectual, but then he drew away, his jaw tense, his lips tight. "Madeline—"

Glass shattered as something crashed through the window.

Madeline's gasp was smothered as Gabriel's weight landed on top of her. He swore, then rolled off, tearing off his jacket as he moved.

Ignoring the pain searing her side, Madeline sat up. Flames licked the carpet under the window, sending tendrils of black smoke crowding against the ceiling.

Madeline leaped up. Two yanks removed the counterpane from the bed. The smoke scratched in her lungs, and she blinked through watering eyes so she could see.

Gabriel was already beating at the fire with his coat. His coat landed with rapid cracks against the floor. She joined him, throwing the heavy blanket over the remaining flames threatening the curtains.

An orange glow flickered in the room.

Where had they missed? She could find no more flames.

Sunset. She closed her eyes. The orange glow came from the setting sun outside her window. Her exhale ended in a choking cough. Pain exploded through her side as her hip connected with the floor. She opened her eyes in surprise. Had she really just fallen? How utterly inexcusable.

Strong arms lifted her into the air. "What the devil were you thinking?"

"That my house was on fire." The flames had only intensified her unsettled emotions. Proximity to the hard, mesmerizing line of Gabriel's jaw didn't help, either.

"Did you hurt yourself?"

She frowned. "I don't think so."

"Did the glass cut your feet? Can you stand?"

"I can stand." She wouldn't let his grudging concern soothe her.

"Good." He moved away from the glass and set her on her feet, then crouched behind her. His fingers brushed over her backside.

"What—"

"You sat in the glass."

She stepped away. "I'll just take the blasted thing off. I don't want you cutting yourself."

Gabriel turned away before she shed the garment. His boots crunched on the glass as he returned to the charred portion of the room.

Her night rail fluttered to the floor and she limped into her dressing room. She sighed as she donned a red satin dressing gown. It clung to her breasts and hips, barely closing in the front. Not that she had much choice, her others were worse.

Leaning against the dressing table, she gathered her strength and a witty retort if Gabriel dared to think she'd dressed this way for him.

"I told your butler to ready another room for you." Gabriel appeared in the doorway. Inky streaks of soot marked his cheeks, settling darker in the creases by his eyes. He scowled as he saw her, but held out the neck of a broken bottle. "It appears to have been a brandy bottle filled with lamp oil. The attacker stuffed a rag in the top and lit it on fire."

She shrugged. "Not the most efficient way to kill someone." A shiver raced down her spine. Yet it wasn't the least efficient, either. If she had been asleep or more severely injured, the fire might have raged out of control before she could contain it.

"This makes the second attempt on your life in less than twenty-four hours. This cannot be allowed to continue." He strode forward, stopping a mere inch from her. He reached out and wiped his thumb over her cheek. Then he drew back, his finger tinged with soot. "You cannot remain here with only your eccentric butler. I'll see to it you're protected."

Madeline held herself still, refusing to give in to the need to clean the smudges from his face. There were a dozen reasons why she couldn't allow him to stay with her. Thirteen, if she counted the heat pooling between her legs fed by the desire in his eyes. It would be like setting the wolf to guard the sheep.

Make that fourteen reasons. She wasn't a sheep— what a disgusting metaphor. She was capable of taking care of herself. She'd fended off assassins in the past. Real assassins, not fools who threw bottles through windows.

Besides, he couldn't investigate her bidders if he was protecting her constantly, and that was the real reason she'd hired him.

So, no matter how tempted she was to allow him to—

"I'll assign another Runner to watch the house," he said.

"I cannot allow— Pardon?"

"There are several men I trust. I'll assign one of them here. He'll pose as your footman."

Madeline attempted to step back, but the movement only pressed the rounded edge of the table harder against her thighs. How had she misread his intentions so entirely? "I—" Now she was stammering. She covered the humiliation with another cough. "I cannot afford a footman, let alone another Runner."

"You don't need to. You have been stabbed and your house set on fire. This is an official Bow Street investigation now." Cool aloofness ruled his gaze as he lifted her into his arms again.

The thin material of her dressing gown provided an insufficient barrier to the warmth of his chest. She held her body stiffly as he carried her to the bed in the next room, but every inhalation brought the scent of sandalwood, bay, smoke, and him deeper into her lungs until it flowed in her veins.

Gabriel adjusted his grip, bringing her flush against him. "I don't want to drop you."

"Or you don't want to want to drop me?" Of all the dunderheaded things to say. Yet Madeline kept a smile on her face.

Gabriel stopped walking, his hands tightened on her, but his voice was weary. "Tell me you don't desire me. Tell me that ten minutes ago you weren't trying to pull me down to kiss you."

Madeline kept her smile in place. "Of course I tried to kiss you, I'm a whore. It's my nature."

Gabriel laid her down on the bed, but his arm remained behind her head. "Yet it wasn't the coquette who tried to kiss me, but the woman. A woman who even now strains toward me."

Heat invaded Madeline's cheeks. She relaxed her

neck and shoulders, settling more firmly into the pillow.

"There is something between us that cannot be explained away. And neither you nor I wish for it. Unless I am wrong." He slid his hand through the opening of her robe, engulfing her breast in his hand. His thumb teased her nipple to a hard peak. "And you do wish for it. In which case, all you have to do is ask." His lips dropped to her neck.

Her breath hissed through clenched teeth. *Yes, please, yes!* But her logic refused to cede dominance to the new, reckless desire of her body. "You make it sound extraordinary. Lust lies between us, nothing more."

Easing the satin of her robe out of the path of his mouth, Gabriel's lips skimmed the line of her collarbone to her shoulder. "And what do you want to come of this lust?"

How could she answer when breathing seemed a horrible distraction from the silken touch of his lips? For all her fine words, she'd never felt lust like this. A molten crucible of desire that burned away all else, until nothing remained but the surety that she would give up everything for another kiss.

The realization terrified her.

And terror was familiar territory. She'd dealt with it every day for the past ten years. "Nothing will come of it"—she drew her sleeve back up her shoulder—"unless you're so weak you cannot control yourself. I assure you I have no such problem."

Gabriel straightened, the lines of his face hard and unreadable. "Good. I'll hold you to that."

Gabriel studied the maid. She shifted nervously, clutching her skirts in her fists. When a carriage clattered by, she pressed herself more closely against the wall.

"You are sure Haines didn't leave at all this evening?"

Her head bobbed and her pale face disappeared into the shadows. "His mother is entertaining. He was at dinner, then they retired to the parlor for one of Her Ladyship's fortifying reads."

"There was no chance for him to have slipped out?"

"No. His mother has him paired with Miss Eustace and she's been clinging to him all evening."

Gabriel sighed and handed the maid a guinea. She tucked it in her skirt and ducked back into the Haineses' house.

It wasn't Timothy Haines, the would-be poet, who'd thrown the bottle tonight, and Madeline's overzealous admirer hadn't been at the theater yesterday. Gabriel kept to the far left of the sidewalk to avoid the water splashed by the coach wheels. Haines wasn't the person trying to kill Madeline.

Gabriel flipped up the collar of his greatcoat to keep the cold drizzle from his neck. She had put herself in the public eye. It was inevitable that she would attract some negative attention along with the notoriety. But this was more than an impulsive attack.

He should be the one protecting her. Not Kent. Kent was a good man, sharp, and totally devoted to his wife and baby. Only the knowledge that Gabriel was to meet with his murder witness kept him moving in the right direction. Away from Madeline's house.

Assigning Kent to watch her had been the right thing to do. They had made their boundaries clear tonight, and the less time they spent together the better.

When an empty hackney approached, Gabriel motioned to the driver and climbed in. It was only a short walk to the tavern but with his concentration wavering, he didn't want a knife in his ribs because he wasn't paying attention. She did this to him. Madeline tangled his thoughts. He didn't like not being in control of himself. He'd been honest when he told her that earlier. He needed focus right now and the very thought of her disarrayed his mind. He didn't trust himself and he sure as hell didn't trust her.

The coach drew to a halt in front of the tavern and Gabriel climbed out. He'd already questioned the drunken coachman, Bourne, once, but he hoped the man might have remembered some more details. He stared for a moment at the school across the street. This was why he needed focus. Another woman was dead. He wouldn't allow any more.

"Huntford?"

Gabriel turned at the familiar voice. Danbury strode toward him, a smooth black cane in his hand.

"I had no idea this was such a popular bit of London. I just passed Billingsgate a few moments ago. What brings *you* to this part of town, Huntford?"

If Billingsgate was lingering around the scene of the crime, that made him all the more suspicious. "Bow Street business. And you?"

Danbury pocked his cane down the street toward the docks. "My father was expecting a ship he'd invested heavily in to arrive."

"Any luck?"

Danbury grimaced. "Do you think I'd be wandering home like a dog with its tail tucked between its legs if it had? It's over a month overdue and no one has heard anything about it."

"Can he take the loss?" Gabriel asked.

Danbury snorted. "The loss of the ship is nothing more than a pebble on the mountain of his fortune, but money is money. And he won't be happy to lose it."

Gabriel had met Danbury's father once when he and Danbury were down from Oxford. The man had refused to acknowledge Gabriel even though he'd been standing next to his son. Gabriel was too lowly to even warrant a tip of the hat. Even though Gabriel had laughed it off, it had pierced his youthful arrogance.

A few days later Susan had tried to tell him that a fine gentleman fancied her. Remembering the sting of humiliation, Gabriel had refused to listen to her and mocked her naïveté.

Danbury eyed the tavern. "Do they have decent ale here? I'm not in a hurry to make my report to my father."

"The ale might burn a hole in your gut but it will get you drunk enough. I'll join you for a glass after I finish talking to someone." Gabriel rarely drank but he found the idea quite appealing tonight.

Laughter and bawdy songs spilled through the door as they entered. A comfortable fire glowed in the hearth, and with a few tallow candles sputtering on tabletops, the place almost managed to look inviting.

"Who are you here to see?" Danbury removed his hat. Droplets of water dripped to the rough wooden floor.

"A witness in one of my cases."

"What's the case?"

Gabriel had never believed in discussing his work. The cases weren't entertaining stories; they were the pain of real people. "I'd prefer not to talk about it."

Danbury shrugged. "I'll get us a table."

Gabriel nodded, then turned to where Bourne normally lounged.

The chair was empty.

Gabriel pulled his watch from his pocket. He was precisely on time. As the barmaid, Loretta, shuffled by, Gabriel stopped her.

She blew a lock of rusty red hair from her flushed face. "I already told you I didn't see anything that night. I don't have time for any more of your questions. I've got customers."

"Have you seen Bourne tonight?" he asked.

She shifted her tray of glasses to her other hip and glanced over her shoulder. "He's over—" Her brow furrowed. "Well, he was. He's still got half a pint of ale over there. I can't think he went far. Maybe into the alley to take a piss?"

A group of millworkers called for her and she hurried away.

Gabriel sat at Bourne's customary table by the window and waited. After several minutes, the coachman still hadn't returned. Gabriel went out to the alley, but other than the odor of human waste and a few rats, the alley was empty.

Gabriel swore. Bourne must have staggered home only a few minutes before he arrived. He shouldn't have tried to meet him at night. The man would likely be more sober in the morning.

Frowning, Gabriel reentered the tavern. Danbury had secured a table next to the fireplace. Danbury waved him over and Gabriel settled into a chair. It was stained and worn, but at the moment, perfectly comfortable.

"No luck, eh?" Danbury asked.

Gabriel shook his head. "Not tonight."

Danbury grimaced. "I'll drink to that." He waved the barmaid over. As Loretta approached, he smiled lazily at her, then flipped her a guinea.

She flushed and straightened, the sway of her hips

exaggerated. The anticipation that lit her eyes made years of hard living melt from her face. "What can I do for you, my lord?"

"Bring a pint for my fine Runner friend here."

She curtsied low, her eyes never leaving Danbury, her fingers playing with her bodice. "As you wish, my lord."

Danbury patted her on her backside. Loretta giggled and tapped him playfully on the lips before sauntering away.

Gabriel raised a brow. "I would have thought you'd outgrown barmaids by now."

Danbury chuckled and leaned back in his chair. "Do you know what I like about barmaids? They're honest. There's no hiding behind the pretense of morality. They are what they are." He lifted his mug in an imaginary toast. "And I'm quite grateful for it."

Gabriel shook his head as Loretta hurried back with a tankard. She clanked it down on the table and pressed plump breasts against Danbury's arm. "Anything else?"

Danbury met Gabriel's gaze. "See? Honest." He shook his head. "Not right now, love."

She sighed, glaring at Gabriel as if it was his fault Danbury had refused her. "Let me know if you change your mind."

Gabriel sipped the liquid, then grimaced. "This is worse than I remembered."

Danbury nodded but took a swig from his half-empty tankard. "It gets more tolerable after the first pint."

Gabriel pushed the mug away. "I don't think I'll test that."

"So did the man you were going to meet have to do with Miss Valdan?" Danbury asked.

"No."

"Miss Valdan. Now there is a woman who could use a lesson from the barmaids in honesty."

Gabriel's muscles tightened across his shoulders at the other man's words. "You don't have to bid."

Danbury didn't seem to notice Gabriel's quelling tone. "Of course I do. Do you know how she is going to fake her virginity?"

When Gabriel remained silent, Danbury looked at him incredulously. "You don't actually believe her, do you?" He slapped his knee. "Perhaps you aren't the crack Runner I thought. I knew most of my peers are too blind to see her for what she is, but I thought the truth would be obvious to you." He leaned in, propping his elbows on the table. "Well, let me tell you. I'm sure she's not. Other men might be paying for her virginity. I'm paying to see how she intends to get around not being one."

The tension in Gabriel's jaw made it difficult to speak. "As I said, there's nothing forcing you to bid."

Danbury gave a bark of laughter. "She's gotten to you, hasn't she? So much that you can't even talk about her. But how well do you really know her?"

Gabriel stood, the idea of prowling the dark streets of London in the icy rain suddenly preferable to sitting at this tavern with Danbury. "She's an assignment. As to her virginity or lack thereof, I simply don't care. I apologize, but I have other business I must attend to this evening." He flipped a shilling on the table, the thought of Danbury paying for his drink no longer palatable.

Danbury shrugged and motioned the barmaid over with a smile. "I have business this evening as well."

Chapter Sixteen

$\mathcal{A}$s they exited the milliner's, Madeline handed Gabriel a large package. "You don't mind, do you?" Her lips curved into a beguiling smile, her eyes sparkling.

And Gabriel had never hated an expression more.

His hand tightened on the cord encircling the box. Since he'd collected her this morning, she'd teased and flirted and laughed. But it was as if she were a pretty china doll with nothing behind the glossy eyes and sable curls.

And she hadn't changed. That was the worst part. As he watched her banter with the other men, she was exactly the same as she'd been every other day. They fawned and lusted and she responded in kind, still as gorgeous and teeth-achingly seductive as always.

The difference was, now she treated him the same as her other male acquaintances.

The occasional wry glance when one of her suitors said something particularly outlandish was gone. Absent, too, were any hints she was something more than she appeared: a desirable, young courtesan eager to hold court over her swains.

He should be happy. She was upholding her bargain.

Yet his jaw ached from grinding his teeth together. He was mad. Who but a madman would want her to be cold? To ignore him? To be angry at his words last night? To be anything but this glossy caricature?

It was as if he'd been tossed from the wings of the stage into the audience with all the other fools.

But that didn't make him one of her suitors, eager to jump at any small task to win her favor. "Perhaps instead of buying a hat, you should have hired a footman."

She laughed. "Why, when you'll be providing me one free of charge?"

"I've assigned you a guard. Two very separate things."

"Really? Do you think he'll hesitate to assist me if I ask?" She ran her tongue over her lip.

"Kent has a wife and child."

"Well then, he shouldn't be tempted by me."

"Don't torment him because you're angry with me."

"I'm not angry with you. I would have to care about you to be angry. Besides, I don't dally with my servants, remember?" Her tone was cheerful and patient. She could have used that tone to ask after the health of his mother. "If the package is too heavy for you to carry to the carriage, I can have the milliner send it around later," she added.

He shifted the large box to his other hand so he'd be free to draw his knife, then paused. The box actually felt remarkably light, even for a bonnet. "What did you buy?"

"The box."

"What?" He jostled the box from side to side. "There is nothing in here."

She grinned. "I know."

That made no sense.

"I didn't actually buy a hat. I only need to appear like I have."

But she'd looked incredibly beguiling in the black riding bonnet, and he'd seen the way her fingers trailed over the brim. "Why didn't you buy the hat?"

She shrugged. "Perhaps once I have my fortune. But until then, I only buy what I can pay for, which at this point is an empty box."

"Why shop then?" Why not sit in the comfort of a coach, rather than forcing herself to saunter about London on foot? Not once, even when they were alone, had she given him a glimpse of the agony she must feel from her wound as she strolled around Bond Street.

Madeline winked at a gentleman passing by on his horse. "Appearances. I'm bright, beautiful, and expensive. Do you think I'd be nearly as appealing if I appeared poor, downtrodden, and desperate?"

She could be dressed in burlap and still be appealing.

He should let this conversation go. As much as he wanted the real Madeline again, it was easier for them both if she stayed hidden away. He'd done remarkably well resisting beautiful faces over the years. But she had gotten to him somehow. Perhaps through the damnable way her eyebrow twitched before delivering a quip, the way she wore huge flannel nightgowns when she thought no one would see, or her ability to delve to the core of every situation.

Yet Danbury was right last night. He still knew almost nothing about her. "Are you desperate?"

She shrugged, smiling at two pinch-faced matrons. They sniffed, wielding their fans like shields as they skittered away. "Desperation is a relative term, is it not?"

Let it go.

But he couldn't. Gabriel wanted to blame it on his years as a Runner. Or the mystery she presented. But although the contradiction she embodied intrigued him, the woman responsible for creating the contradiction intrigued him more.

Gabriel placed the box prominently on the seat of her carriage. "I'm sure the store would've extended you credit until after the auction."

Her lips thinned, the first time that rosy flesh had expressed anything but polite cordiality. "And if something happened and the auction was never completed? Do you know what debt does to a person? The duns that knock on your door and take the linens from your bed? How the threat of prison flays you until you're willing to sell your wife to put an end to it?" Her charm deserted her, replaced by a desolate intensity.

One of the things Gabriel watched for in an interrogation were the outliers—facts, stories, and tidbits that weren't asked for but the subject gave. "Selling a wife? That seems a bit extreme."

Madeline inhaled deeply, her mask dropping back in place. "You're right, of course." But her jaw was too tight and her lips stretched too far.

Interesting. He continued to probe. "Lose too much in a game of piquet?"

But her brief moment of candor had passed. She laughed, tilting her head to her precisely practiced seductive angle. "I never lose."

He stepped to the side, forcing her to alter her pose. "You're skilled at cards as well?"

She placed her hand on his arm and stood on tiptoe, her breath whispering over his neck as she spoke. "My skills are moderate at best." Her breasts brushed against his arm. "But my partners find it difficult to concentrate."

Lust resumed its familiar cadence in his groin. But she hadn't befuddled him as completely as she might have hoped. He trapped her hand when she would have trailed it down his arm. "I find that difficult to believe." He traced a slow circle on the delicate skin on the inside of her wrist, unable to resist making her suffer as he did. "Oh, I believe men find it difficult to concentrate around you, but I don't doubt you know the card each man holds before he plays it."

Her brow lifted with idle amusement he might have believed if not for her pulse fluttering under his finger. "You're accusing me of cheating?"

"You might indeed cheat on occasion, but I'm referring to your talent for observation."

She freed herself from his grasp and strolled away to peer at a fanciful display of fans in a shop window. To anyone else she would've seemed enthralled with the merchandise, but Gabriel could see her eyes studying him in the reflection.

"People watch me, not the other way around."

He walked behind her and met her gaze in the glass. "You watch with a trained eye." He knew the truth of his words as soon as he spoke them.

She whirled away, allowing two agitated strides before her pace slowed and her hips resumed their customary sway. "Well, I'm trained in many arts." Her voice rose slightly as she spoke, snagging the attention of a gentleman riding past.

The portly man reined in his horse and, with several strained grunts, dismounted. "What arts, Madeline?"

Her arm barely encircled the gentleman's pudgy arm as she attached herself to his side. "What arts are you interested in, Percival? I've many interesting abilities. You served in India, a few years back, did you not? I've gleaned a few interesting talents from that area of the world." The slender curve of her back presented an effective wall, cutting Gabriel from the conversation.

"No, I could never make a choice now. I need to leave room for one of you to surprise me." Madeline laughed, clinging to the ornamental cement railing behind her. She desperately hoped the pose looked languid and carefree, unlike truth—that if she let go, she'd collapse.

Her suitors continued to press in around her, jostling and vying for a better position on the bridge. Their brightly colored waistcoats swam around the edges of her vision in gaudy blurs. A cool breeze blew off the Thames below, its sour, fishy smell fueling her desire to be done with her morning outing.

"Come now, Madeline, if there were no money involved, which of us would you pick?"

With lingering consideration, she scanned the dozen eager faces around her, proud as she kept her gaze from straying to where Gabriel stood a few feet behind the crowd. "I think that man knows who he is."

As if pulled by marionette strings, all the gentlemen straightened, their chests expanding in unison as each of them came to the conclusion she'd intended.

A flicker of movement to the left caught her attention. She shifted, trying to see past the male bodies pressed around her without appearing as if she were giving anything less than her complete interest.

What had captured her attention?

There. A disjointed flicker of color in the gap between two men's shoulders. To their left, in the space created as Tupe lifted his hand to smooth his balding pate, she glimpsed another flash of dark.

A group, then.

Her smile at Lenton drew him forward and allowed her a brief glimpse of the men approaching. It was a pack of dockside toughs dressed in assorted castoffs, moving with the ease and arrogance only youth provided. Seven of them.

While they were a good distance from docks, Ranleigh Bridge connected the more fashionable shops of London to the brothels and gaming hells on the other side of the river. All types frequented it.

Yet the youths had captured her attention, and she'd learned to not take that lightly.

"Well, gentlemen, since you're obviously my favorites, there is a little thing I'd like to tell you." She leaned forward as she spoke, hushing her tones, drawing in the circle of men until they provided a solid layer of protection. Or at least as much protection as Englishmen who thought boxing at Jackson's preparation for a real fight could offer.

Although Madeline could no longer see him, the knowledge that Gabriel stood a few feet away soothed her far more than the wall of flesh surrounding her.

"I've been thinking about the night I'll spend with the winner." She closed her eyes and released a pleased sigh. "Do you know what I am looking forward to most? How I will—"

"Move your bloomin' arses. This ain't no drawing room," a coarse voice said.

"How dare—"

"What is the meaning—"

Madeline's suitors erupted into chaos as the youths pushed their way through the center of the circle, jostling and shoving gentlemen from their path, puncturing her wall as if it were paper.

"Spare a few coins, guv'nor?" A few of the lads held out their hands and dragged their faces into pitiful expressions, then guffawed when her bidders blustered and attempted to shield their pockets.

"Move along, lads." Gabriel's voice sliced through the ruckus, his authority lifting the heads of the youth.

"Bloody 'ell! It's Huntford."

"Didn't tell us he'd be here."

"Do it, already—"

The young man nearest to Madeline turned to her and smiled, two perfect dimples on his swarthy cheeks. "Sorry, love."

With a quick movement, he grabbed her by the waist and tossed her over the railing.

Gabriel's dive into the river was clean, but it still hurt like the devil. Madeline had hit the water in an awkward, half-twisted angle. If she'd lost consciousness, there was a chance he might never find her.

Fear strengthened his kicks as his head broke the surface. Putrid water dashed into his eyes and mouth. Gagging against the salty filth, he scanned the river, searching for Madeline.

A few feet away he saw her, bobbing on the current, her hair running in thick rivulets over her face.

"Madeline!" he shouted. Or at least he thought he did. It was impossible to hear his own words over the churning water and the relief buzzing in his head.

Yet she turned toward him, her eyes wild as she slipped below the foamy gray water.

Three rapid strokes brought him to where she'd disappeared. He sucked in a deep breath, preparing to follow her under, but then her head reappeared.

He caught her with one arm, relieved when she

had the sense to immediately cease struggling. But even then, he had to fight to keep them both afloat and moving toward shore, his legs numbing from the exertion and icy water.

"My dress and petticoats. They keep tangling around my legs and weighing me down. If you can remove them, I can keep myself afloat." Despite her shaking, her voice was steady.

If they wanted to reach shore, they'd have to try. Gabriel wasted a glance at the gentlemen lined up along the edge of the bridge, but none of them seemed poised to leap in and assist.

Gabriel nodded, and she pulled away, her legs kicking.

He grabbed the fabric between her shoulder blades and yanked, but the cold had sapped the power from his fingers, and they skidded painfully across the wet silk rather than ripping it. A second attempt was no more effective.

Gabriel spun her toward him. "Can you stay up a few more moments?"

Her face was chalky, but her head jerked into a nod.

When Gabriel stopped kicking, the water eagerly accepted his still form. In the inky darkness of the water, he fumbled with his boot, drawing his knife. The water grew thick as he again clawed his way toward the air. Madeline's hands gripped his shoulders and yanked, freeing him from the water.

He swam behind her, and with a quick slice, removed her dress and other heavy layers. The fabric coiled around his legs before slithering away.

"Without the dress, I think I can make it to shore on my own." The skin around Madeline's lips had darkened to a purplish blue.

Gabriel eyed the hundred or so feet to the shore.

He had to get her out of the water. If she could swim on her own, they'd reach it quicker than if he pulled her. "I'll stay beside you the entire way."

He watched her first few strokes. Her movements were jerky from the cold but competent. He followed, focused on the pale arc of her arms as they dug through the Thames. Twenty feet from shore, her arms no longer cleared the water and her attempt at a breath ended in choking convulsions. Gabriel grabbed her before she sank, and after a few more strokes, risked trying to stand. His feet squelched in silt on the river bottom as he struggled upright with Madeline in his arms, the water sluicing down his chest.

He stumbled the few remaining steps to the shore and collapsed to his knees. The edges of the rocks bit into his knees as he shivered. The men on the bridge shouted inquiries but Gabriel ignored them as he laid Madeline as gently as he could on the stones. Her eyes were closed and her breath shallow.

Unlike him, she wasn't shivering.

Hell.

He needed to get her warm.

She wore only a shift, rendered transparent by the water. Standing, he struggled out of his wet coat. It wouldn't do much, but it would be better than nothing.

"Gabriel?" Her eyes squinted as if the cloudy morning was too bright for them.

He brushed a finger over her cheek. "I'm here. I'll take care of you."

"Don't cover me with your jacket. If the bidders had to see me nearly drown, at least they can take away a pleasant mental image."

White-hot rage chased the chill from Gabriel's blood. "To hell with your bloody auction." He scooped her up, wrapping his jacket tightly around her as he climbed up the embankment.

Lenton waited at the top beside a glossy black coach. "I've had my carriage brought around. I'll take her—"

Gabriel strode past him. "I'll see to her." He set Madeline in the coach and followed her onto the expensive leather seats. He gave the coachman an address.

Lenton shifted from foot to foot as Madeline remained slumped, unmoving, against the seat. But then he nodded, giving his servant permission to follow Gabriel's orders. "I would've assisted but it appeared you had things well in hand—"

"Did anyone detain the men responsible?"

Lenton's face reddened. "No. We tried but they put up a fight—"

Gabriel shut the door, interrupting the viscount's excuses. He'd have to track the attackers down himself. He pulled Madeline onto his lap, sharing what little warmth his body still radiated. Her head lolled unresistingly onto his shoulder, the color of her face alarmingly close to the white of his sleeve. Her chest fluttered with small, brittle breaths.

"Stay with me, Madeline." He chafed her arms, willing energy and warmth into her slender form.

This made the third time in as many days that someone had tried to kill her. He glanced down to where a red stain leaked through the bandage and onto her shift. New worry increased the tempo of his hands. The killer might succeed if Gabriel didn't get her warm and her wound clean.

And yet if she lived, she'd insist on continuing the auction. He didn't doubt that.

But why? The question had hounded him since he met her, but now it reached a deafening crescendo in his mind. Despite her claims, he wasn't ready to believe money was the only factor. She was too smart not to realize that the money from the auction would do her no good if she were dead. There had to be something he was missing. "Come on, Madeline. Stay with me."

"We're heading south. Why aren't we going home?" Madeline's voice was slurred and weak, but she was awake.

"How do you know?" She hadn't even opened her eyes to note the surroundings.

"The sun's on the left side of my face."

He stroked that cheek with the back of his hand, her damp skin far too cool. "I'm taking you somewhere closer."

Her eyes still didn't open. "Are you trying to be ambiguous?"

"I'm trying to keep you talking."

"I'm hardly about to die from a little swim."

Gabriel gloried in the stubborn tone of her words. "That's what I want to avoid."

The carriage clattered to a halt in front of the comfortable brick town house.

Madeline forced one eye open. "That *was* fast. Where are we?"

Gabriel kicked open the door of the coach. "My mother's house."

Chapter Seventeen

$\mathcal{M}$adeline screamed as she was plunged into boiling water. "*Nyet! Ya ne znyoo!*" She wouldn't tell them anything. She couldn't let go of her story of being a simple peasant woman. She had to give Ian and Clayton time to get the information out of the country. Even if her skin blistered off her body. They hadn't forced her to talk with the rocks they piled on her chest or by eviscerating that poor woman inch by inch as she begged Madeline to confess to spare her.

Hands clamped on her arms and Madeline struggled against them, desperate to escape or, failing that, to burn some of her torturers along with her.

"Madeline." Arms wrapped around her upper body. "I know it hurts, but the water's only warm. It's not burning you."

Gabriel.

This wasn't St. Petersburg.

She stilled. What had she given away?

"Master Gabriel?" A stately voice roughened with age rumbled over Madeline. She tried to pry open her eyes to see the man who addressed Gabriel like a little boy, but the lead in her eyelids refused to budge.

"Everything is all right, Jones. Her hands and feet are thawing, and that's a painful process. Is my room prepared?"

"Indeed, sir. It is as warm as we can make it, and clothing is laid out. I placed the lady's things in there as well. Are you sure you do not require a maid?"

"I'll ring if we have need of anything. Warn my mother we're here when she arrives home." Gabriel's deep, velvet voice seemed to vibrate in Madeline's head.

Then the room was silent but for the gentle lapping of the water.

Madeline knew she'd spoken as she awoke, screamed most likely, if the soreness in her throat was any indication, but she had no idea what she'd said or in what language she said it. Gabriel remained quiet. Perhaps she hadn't said anything. Perhaps she'd only screamed mindless nonsense.

The burning in her fingers eased until only delicious heat remained. With careful deliberation, she curled her toes. When they responded to her direction, she drew in a shuddering breath. By some miracle, she'd survived. No, not a miracle—Gabriel. When she was fighting the river, she'd known he'd come if she could stay alive long enough for him to reach her.

"The water should warm you quickly."

Her eyes finally obeyed and opened. Submerged under the water on either side of her was another pair of legs encased in dove gray breeches. Just to ensure she wasn't going mad, she pressed back into what should have been the edge of the tub and instead rubbed against the wall of Gabriel's chest.

She should pull away. Although Gabriel hadn't spoken of it, it was possible she'd said something incriminating. Even if she hadn't, she'd sworn not to get close to him. Her desire for him made it too tempting. But she closed her eyes again, grateful weakness gave her an excuse to remain. She rubbed her cheek against the hard ridges of his upper arm.

It was the novelty of the position that enticed her, she reassured herself. Clayton and Ian had protected her, but in the end, they'd treated her as one of the team. If they had held her, it would've made it that much harder for them to risk her life.

In fact, no one had held her since that day her father had taken her to the park. Mama was crying when they returned, but the man Madeline's father had left behind with Mama seemed very happy.

Her father had taken her to the park on other days. Until one day, he didn't bother to take her away when he brought a man over to keep Mama company. Not long after that, her father had stopped coming home altogether.

A shiver shook her body.

No wonder she'd never let Clayton or Ian hold her. It made her disgustingly maudlin.

"You could have removed our clothing." Her voice wasn't as strong as she might have liked, but it broke the silence and dispelled the cloying security of his arms.

Or at least it should have.

He exhaled slowly, his chin resting on her hair for a moment. "We both needed to get warm as soon as possible. And it's not as if our clothing is salvageable."

She studied the gleaming copper tub that held the two of them. A large iron pipe trundled down the wall, ending in a spigot and knobs that jutted over the edge of the tub. "Where are we again?"

"My mother's. Can you stay upright if I lean you forward?"

She nodded more out of principle than surety.

Tucking his hands under her arms, he sat her upright. As he stood behind her, water sloshed in uneven waves. She gripped the rim of the metal tub as the ripples threatened to topple her. She'd survived the Thames. She refused to drown in the bath.

From the edge of her vision, Madeline watched as he climbed over the edge, peeled off his waistcoat and shirt, and dropped them into a wet pile on the tile floor.

She'd been right. He did undress well.

But his wasn't the body of a gentleman—a body trained by riding and sport. Gabriel's was the body of a warrior. Lean and hard. Muscle, sinew, and power held ready to be unleashed in an instant.

Peering from the corner of her eye wasn't nearly enough. She turned and reveled in the sight of him. Newly warmed blood burned into her cheeks and through her veins.

She wanted nothing more than to skim her finger along the smooth indentation that ran down the center of Gabriel's chest, bisected the ridges along his abdomen then disappeared into the waistband of his trousers. But she'd wasted her small store of energy by moving her head, so she had to content herself with following the planes of muscle with her eyes alone.

Gabriel tied a towel around his waist, then reached underneath to remove his trousers. He met her gaze with a raised eyebrow. "We're doing nothing about this lust between us, remember?"

She didn't look away, couldn't look away. "I haven't done a thing."

"It's in your eyes." His trousers hit the floor.

"If I remember my agreement, it was to *do* nothing, not to *think* nothing."

His brow lowered to his customary glare.

She sighed. "I'm half drowned and exhausted. If you have fears for your virtue, they can be set to rest."

"Good." But his glare was belied by the desire lingering on his face.

He pulled her to her feet. "Lift your arms."

She tried to comply but she couldn't lift them more than a few inches from her body. She was just tired. As soon as she'd rested, she'd be able to move them. She knew that. She did. Yet a sickening sense of vulnerability coursed through her. And a spy who showed weakness ended up stripped of secrets and dead.

She raised her chin. "And have you accuse me of seducing you with my nakedness?"

"You're bleeding through your bandage."

She should just tell him the truth. Did her training own her so completely that she couldn't tell the man who'd saved her life such an inconsequential detail? She had to disguise it with her sly comments? Yet her lips remained firmly together.

"Madeline—"

"I can't move them!" She spoke before she could think of more reasons she should not.

Gabriel swore quietly, but his expression softened. He untied the drawstring securing the neck of her shift and eased it off her shoulders, leaving her completely nude, save the bandage at her waist. He unwound the sopping cloth, then immediately wrapped a soft, white towel around her.

"Come." He picked her up once again.

The smooth flesh under her cheek smelled of clean, damp male—a scent far more erotic than any expensive cologne. She drew in slow deep breaths, fighting the darkness blurring the edges of her vision.

When she blinked her eyes open, she found a blanket tucked around her. Curtains were drawn over the windows, so she tried to analyze the intensity of light seeping in through the cracks in the fabric.

"You've only been asleep two hours. It's one in the afternoon." Gabriel sprawled in a large leather chair he must've dragged to her bedside. She should have been startled to find him so close, yet it soothed her, settling her more deeply in the lavender-scented sheets. He was dressed plainly in buff breeches and a white shirt unbuttoned at the collar. Leaning forward, he brushed his fingers across her forehead. "How are you feeling?"

"Alive." She couldn't say much more than that. She ached all over. With a fortifying breath, she shifted on the bed, experimentally flexing her arms and legs. It took effort, but she could slide them across the sheets. Her wound throbbed like the devil as well. She lifted the edge of the blanket to examine it.

He jerked his hand away from her. "Leave the blanket on."

Her hands slid over a new bandage at her waist, then down her hip. She was naked.

His pale eyes focused on where her hand rested under the blanket as if he could see her hand trembling against her leg. He'd seen her completely bare. The thought twisted along her spine and tingled between her legs.

"My wound?" she asked, her voice husky.

"Three of the stitches tore, but the others held. It should continue to heal if you rest."

"Impossible."

"Madeline—"

"Two days. I'll rest until the masquerade. But I

don't have the luxury of more. Rumors will already be circulating from this afternoon. If I'm not at Lady Wheeler's ball, people will assume I'm dead."

His jaw tightened as she'd known it would. "Is this auction worth your life?"

"Do you want me to end the auction?" Her breath caught as she waited for his answer. What would he say? She didn't know what she wanted to discover more—the truth about how he was using her auction for his investigation or that he'd be willing to set it aside for her safety.

"What you do is your choice."

Nothing. His answer gave her nothing. She forced herself to take the blow without flinching. Of course he wouldn't start sharing the details he'd been keeping hidden all this time. He didn't care enough to stop her, either. "Then you'd be fine if I ended it now?"

Gabriel glanced away. "It would be the wise thing to do."

"That's not what I asked. Do *you* want me to end it?" His opinion shouldn't matter because it wouldn't affect her actions, but her fingers tangled in the sheets as she waited.

Gabriel stood with an angry exhale. "Why must you always do this? Burrow under my skin?"

Her chest ached. "You stand back and cast out dire warnings when it seems you want this auction to go on as much as I do. I think you only protest because you know I won't listen."

Gabriel spun toward the fireplace, his hands clenched at his sides. "I don't want you dead."

"True. If I'm dead you will be unable to find whatever else it is that you're seeking. But, until you are honest with me, do not play the hypocrite and condemn me or my auction."

"Fine." Gabriel stalked back to her side. "But if

you are interested in honesty"—he pulled out her sheath and knife and laid them on the bed—"tell me why a courtesan wears a knife strapped to her leg and screams in Russian."

Madeline's leg flinched under the blanket, but her expression remained disinterested. "There have been two attempts on my life. Three, counting today. I'd be a fool not to protect myself."

And if there was one thing Madeline wasn't, it was a fool. But neither was he. Gabriel pulled the knife from its sheath. The blade was four inches long and freshly honed. "This isn't one of the pretty baubles they sell to women for protection." The leather on the handle was worn in places, as if the knife had been handled often. He knew if he put the knife in her hand it would match perfectly. "And this sheath is custom work. Designed to fit your leg alone. Where did you get this?"

She'd been stabbed and thrown into a river. Her house had been set on fire. She should be sobbing her story and begging for his help. Instead, an amused smile danced on her lips. "The knife is from Wraith and the sheath from Cipher."

"Cipher?"

"Clayton Campbell. Even without the recent attacks, the best of men are trying to ravish me, and the worst . . . well, that's the reason I have a knife."

"And the Russian?"

She propped herself up on her elbows. "I said I was a woman of many talents."

"Shall we list those talents?"

"No. It would quite go to my head."

"You're observant. You have a keen grasp of strategy. You excel at turning any situation to your advantage— *Fais gaffe!*"

Despite his switch to French, Madeline dropped flat at his warning and would have rolled off the bed if he hadn't trapped her there. "You also apparently speak French. And your reactions are quick," Gabriel said.

Her eyes narrowed at his ruse. "Yes, that explains why I've been stabbed and thrown into a river."

"Both of which you survived and accepted without a flinch."

"As I said, I'm exceptional."

Gabriel leaned in closer to her. He needed the pieces to fall into place. He felt as if he were walking with a pebble in his shoe and each of his steps landed slightly painful and off-balance until he could think of nothing else. "Where were you six months ago?"

"I had just arrived in the south of France."

He waited for her to laugh at the absurdity of her statement, but she just paused expectantly. Disgust roiled in his gut. Why did he think she'd be truthful?

Fine. He was used to interrogating liars. He'd let her entangle herself in lies, then use them to squeeze the truth from her. "Why were you in France?"

"Trying to win an audience with Napoleon."

"Did you succeed?"

"No, Wellington needed advice, so we were called away."

"Wellington wasn't in France six months ago." Let her lie her way out of that.

"I know. He was in Flanders," Madeline said.

"So you just wandered across France until you got there?"

"No, we—" Her lips pursed.

"Can't you think of another lie fast enough? Come

now. It doesn't need to be logical. Your entire story hasn't been. Did you walk? Skip? Take a hackney?"

"No." A mocking smile curved her lips. "Actually, I marched with the French army."

His patience evaporated. "Madeline—"

There was a polite cough behind him. "Who is this woman you rescued, Gabriel? And do tell me you have good reason to be yelling at her."

Gabriel nearly groaned. "Good afternoon, Mother."

Chapter Eighteen

*G*abriel's mother strode over to the curtains and pulled them open. "If you're both awake, I see no reason for us to linger in gloom. Besides, Gabriel hasn't brought anyone to visit me since Oxford."

Madeline blinked as streams of light poured into the room, illuminating the other woman. She wasn't what Madeline had been expecting. Instead of a thin, bitter husk of a governess, Mrs. Huntford was well-rounded with the type of plumpness that came to women who'd been voluptuous when younger. Her face was pleasing, although with more the look of a hearty farmer's wife than a lady of the *ton*.

It was her eyes that stood out, pale like her son's, but clear crystalline blue. They sparkled with life and good humor.

It was, in fact, the very expression that Madeline often tried to emulate. But Madeline's was always that—imitation.

How did his mother do it? She couldn't have had an easy life, yet she radiated energy—nothing as simple as cheer, but rather the assurance that people were good and things would work out.

It should have stirred pity or perhaps amusement in Madeline. After all, she knew firsthand that both those things were lies. Instead, an envious longing lodged in Madeline's chest.

The corner of Gabriel's mouth lifted. "I work with thieves and murderers, Mother."

His mother smiled, a sunny rearrangement of her face that crinkled her nose and reduced her eyes to crescents. "Bow Street's hiring practices must have grown lax of late."

As Gabriel tipped his head in concession to the jest, his mother walked to Madeline's side. "So which are you, thief or murderer?"

Both.

The older woman's face smoothed into concerned lines. "Are you all right? What happened? Jones said you arrived wet and reeking."

Gabriel folded his arms. "Someone threw Madeline into the Thames."

His mother's eyebrow twitched at his use of Madeline's first name.

Madeline spoke quickly before any inaccurate assumptions could form. "I hired your son to protect me and handle a small investigation."

Mrs. Huntford glanced back at Gabriel, pride obvious in her gaze. "Why do you need protection?"

Gabriel stepped forward to his mother's side. "I've been remiss. Madeline, this is my mother, Beatrice Huntford. Mother, this is Madeline Valdan."

Mrs. Huntford stilled a moment, a tiny crease marking her brow.

Madeline wanted nothing more than to slap the look of grim satisfaction from Gabriel's face. After all, it wasn't as if she'd thrown herself into his mother's path.

Oh, she took guilty pleasure in irking the snobbish

women of the *ton* with her presence. But for people like Gabriel's mother, who wouldn't be offended but just made to feel awkward, she tried to spare them contact.

Madeline inched the blanket up. Not only was she a harlot, but she was a naked harlot.

She hated the uncertainty assailing her. But if Gabriel thought she'd curl up in proper shame, he'd soon discover otherwise. "Your son neglected to mention my profession. I'm a courtesan."

Mrs. Huntford's eyes widened and Madeline knew she'd remembered why she recognized the name.

Madeline smiled. "I apologize for not rising to greet you, but your son has taken all my clothes."

Gabriel's self-satisfied smirk dissolved into a sputtered cough. "You were going to freeze to death otherwise."

"It does sound noble when you put it like that."

"That's how it happened." Gabriel spoke through clenched teeth.

"I never claimed otherwise."

His mother's gaze traveled back and forth between them, finally settling on Madeline. "Well, Miss Valdan—"

"Madeline. After all, your son already uses it."

"Then you must call me Beatrice." Her lips twitched. "It is a pleasure to meet you."

For some reason, the woman's acceptance cut through her bravado, unsettling her far more than she would have expected. Madeline didn't want scandal to harm the woman. "If you would lend me some clothes, I'll be on my way."

Gabriel advanced on her. "No, you won't. You need to rest and recover."

His mother held up a hand, blocking him from reaching Madeline's bedside. "I'm sure what my son meant to say is that I'd be honored to have you remain until you're feeling stronger."

Madeline shook her head. Perhaps the woman still didn't understand who she was. "I'm not precisely the ideal houseguest. There's an auction—"

Beatrice patted her shoulder. "I know who you are, dear."

The maternal pressure of that hand only spurred Madeline's determination. "The parents of your students—"

"All love me. If they ever find out, they'll trust me in this."

The woman must be batty if she believed that. Madeline tried a different route. "People have been trying to kill me. It wouldn't be safe—"

"Then you're safer here than at home," his mother said.

"But you are both in more danger." Madeline kept her resolve, ignoring her pleasure as something warmer replaced Gabriel's aggravation.

"Give in, Madeline. You're outnumbered," he said.

Madeline looked from determined pale green eyes to blue, then sighed. "Tonight only." The thought of having people fuss over her was too enticing to resist in her current state. And she liked the idea of spending the night with Gabriel even if he was in another room. For reasons she hoped never to examine, contentment poured into her.

Madeline closed her eyes, trying to will herself to sleep before the plan floating at the edges of her mind coalesced into something she couldn't ignore.

She wouldn't think about it.

She'd sleep.

Was one night free of her own constant machinations too much to ask?

Apparently.

As much as she tried to ignore it, this was the perfect opportunity to finally have her questions about Gabriel answered.

"I must admit, she isn't what I expected." Gabriel's mother tapped absently on her cheek.

"What did you expect?" The thought of his mother pondering courtesans at all disturbed Gabriel.

"There's a fragility about her."

Gabriel stepped away from the serving table in the breakfast room, balancing his plate. "That was from the near drowning. Normally, she's the least fragile woman I've ever met."

His mother sipped absently at her tea. "No. She's been hurt badly before."

Her words too closely mirrored those of Lady Aphrodite. "By what?"

"By whom, most likely. I'd like to find out."

So would he. Perhaps his mother would succeed where he'd failed. People willingly shared information with her that he would've had to drag from them with a team of horses. And his previous attempts to glean information from Madeline had been frustratingly fruitless. After all, he could only slam his head against a brick wall so many times.

"What would you like to find out?" Madeline asked as she glided in, her face innocent and curious.

She'd overheard everything then.

A cornflower blue gown swallowed Madeline's small frame, dragging on the floor behind her. If not for her breasts straining against the bodice, she would have appeared to be a little girl dressed up in her mother's clothes.

Not mother's—Susan's.

Gabriel sat heavily in his chair, his plate clattering slightly against the oak table.

"About you, of course. I apologize about the dress, but one of mine would have been even worse." His mother smiled, patting her ample hips.

An answering smile formed on Madeline's lips. "The dress is lovely. I can hardly blame you for my stature."

Had Susan been that tall? Gabriel hated that he had to think about it. To his desperate relief, he recalled that she'd only been a few inches shorter than him. He'd been fifteen before he'd finally surpassed Susan in height. She'd been furious until she realized her art teacher was only an inch taller. Then she'd stopped complaining.

Where had his mother found it? He'd thought she'd donated all of Susan's dresses years ago.

He'd been glad when she'd done it. The idea of Susan's things hanging in her closet when she'd never return to them had bothered him. It seemed like a false hope, as if they were waiting for something that would never happen.

The heaping portions of food he'd served himself no longer appealed, and he pushed the plate away.

Thankfully, his mother had hurried to Madeline's side to convince her to provision herself with enough food to feed an army, so she didn't notice.

Gabriel pulled his plate back toward him. If he planned to use his mother to pry loose Madeline's secrets, he couldn't allow anything to distract either of them. Both of them would notice if he didn't touch his food. For good measure, he also unfolded the paper so he'd have a valid excuse for not participating in the conversation.

As Madeline sat, Gabriel nodded absently in her

direction, then returned to the paper laid out beside his plate.

His mother and Madeline chatted for several minutes about inconsequential topics: the weather, favorite places to purchase gloves, the poor treatment of the soldiers recently returned from the war. The topics should have been inane, and would have been if his mother and Madeline had been normal people. As it was, twice Gabriel almost snorted tea from his nose at some especially witty observation from one of the women. Both times, he barely covered his choked laughter with coughs.

"Are you feeling quite well, Gabriel?" his mother asked.

Gabriel swore silently as Madeline peered at him over a bit of ham, her blue-gray eyes far too assessing. "Is the tea not to your liking?"

That she'd noted his coughs did not bode well for his small deception. Gabriel redirected his attention back to the news. "Quite the contrary, it's soothing on my throat."

"Unwell from our dip in the Thames yesterday?" Madeline asked.

"I'm sure it is nothing. Simply a passing cough."

"Anything of interest in the news?"

Although he'd been staring at the newspaper for the past fifteen minutes, he hadn't actually read any of it. He scanned it, hurriedly searching for something of interest. "You're mentioned."

Madeline leaned toward him. "Really? What does it say?"

Gabriel had to fight not to peer down her bodice. His mother was sitting two feet away, for pity's sake. Her eyes met his with a sparkle and he had the disturbing feeling that she was enjoying his internal struggle.

"That Miss V was attacked by some young miscreants and aided by the heroic Viscount L."

"Yes, if he hadn't offered his coach, I surely would have drowned. It's good to see the praise go to those deserving it."

The side of Gabriel's lip edged upward. He didn't care that he wasn't mentioned in the story. But he did like that Madeline seemed to take issue with the discrepancy.

"So has Gabriel always been this astonishingly heroic?" Madeline asked.

Gabriel hoped his mother would recognize his quelling look. He didn't want the conversation to turn to him. He needed it to revolve around Madeline. But his mother either didn't see or ignored him.

Madeline, however, noted it with a smirk.

"Shall I guess? Did he bring home pigeons with broken wings? No, that wouldn't be quite right. Did he soundly beat any and all neighborhood bullies?"

His mother chuckled. "Actually, he was rather bookish as a child." Gabriel again tried to catch his mother's attention. What happened to her intention to discover the truth about Madeline's wounded past?

But his mother continued. "But he did always protect his sister. Once, when they were seven, Susan claimed her kitten had eaten the biscuits missing from the tea tray. Gabriel interrupted, explaining all the reasons why it was impossible for the cat to have been the culprit. But then she started to cry so Gabriel claimed responsibility and took the punishment."

Susan had looked so betrayed when he undercut her argument, he'd had no choice. But it had been a ridiculous story. As if her kitten could have opened the nursery door and gone to the kitchen to eat the treats.

"Did you ever have a pet, Madeline?" his mother asked.

Gabriel exhaled. The conversation was back where it belonged.

A small, wistful smile drifted over Madeline's face. "No. We couldn't have fed one."

Damnation, now in addition to the lust, he had to battle pictures of a forlorn, hungry young Madeline longing for a kitten.

Madeline glanced at him and her introspective gaze vanished. Her lips were transformed by the same smile she gave her suitors. "Perhaps that was fortunate. There were times when we would have eaten the poor thing."

His mother placed her arm around Madeline's shoulders. "Is that why you thought up the auction? I must admit I find the idea of your auction quite ingenious."

Madeline's expression froze. Gabriel thought it was discomfort. After all, his mother's propensity for ambushing her friends with affection took time to accustom oneself to.

But then he noticed the slight flaring of her nostrils. She wasn't embarrassed—she was terrified, tense as a deer about to take flight. "I found myself with few resources other than beauty."

"But you've been quite intelligent about the whole thing. I quite admire that about you."

To keep from staring dumbstruck at his mother, Gabriel stirred his tea. Had she just complimented Madeline on turning to a life of prostitution?

Madeline rose to her feet, freeing herself from his mother's hug. She hurried to the side table and poured herself a cup of coffee. "Thank you, although I don't suppose it's something I should accept compliments on." Despite her haste to the coffeepot, she added her sugar and cream with leisurely care.

The woman had been stabbed, drowned, and nearly set on fire without a single flinch, yet his mother's touch sent her fleeing.

Perhaps he'd learned something of use about her this morning, after all. Unfortunately, without more context, he wasn't entirely sure what.

Madeline returned to her seat, subtly scooting the chair a few inches from his mother as she sat.

"Who are your top bidders?" his mother asked.

Madeline wanted to kick Gabriel in the shins and knock the panicked message from his face. Did he think her an absolute monster? She wasn't about to tell his mother that her former lover was one of the top bidders. "I haven't heard today. But Viscount Lenton is high on the list, as is Gabriel's friend, the Earl of Danbury."

Gabriel's mother leaned in, her blue eyes glinting. "I haven't seen him since they were at Oxford. Is Lenton as handsome and charming as Danbury?"

Madeline didn't know what to think or how to act for the first time in years. Why was his mother friendly toward her? Distracted, Madeline had to think to remember either man's face. "I haven't spoken to Danbury so I can't compare his charm, but Lenton is definitely dashing."

"A suitable bed partner then?"

Gabriel made an odd, sputtering sound to her left.

His mother shook her head. "You're welcome to cover your ears, dear."

"Either of them would be adequate." Madeline

wasn't quite sure what to say. She hadn't had a mother in ten years and she didn't need one. Even if she was tempted—which she wasn't—she had no idea what she should confide to another woman.

"Only adequate?"

If his mother hoped for romance to blossom from the auction, she'd be sadly disappointed. "As decadent as this auction might seem, it's business, nothing more."

"Your mother's no longer alive, is she?"

"No."

"Then let me tell you something I'm sure she would have."

Madeline would have paid a good amount of money to watch Gabriel's face as his mother explained what happened between men and women in bed, but she couldn't shake the fear she might blush as well. "I'm well aware of what to expect."

"Physically, yes, I suspect you are. But have you considered the emotional aspect?"

Madeline shifted, uncomfortable. "There isn't one. That's the whole point."

"But there will be. He'll be your first. That isn't something you'll be able to take lightly. He'll stay with you." Her brows knitted together. "I will confide something to you. The situation between myself and Gabriel's father—"

"Gabriel told me."

Her brows lifted almost to her hairline. "Indeed? Well, that will make things simpler. Even though it only happened once. He's with me every time I climb into bed. In my thoughts whenever I see a man and a woman together in the streets. But since we loved each other desperately, I don't mind him."

Gabriel's hands tightened on the edge of the table. As Madeline reached for her tea, she glanced more fully at him. His face was expressionless, but red darkened his cheekbones.

"I cannot imagine what it would be like to have a stranger in my thoughts for the rest of my life," Beatrice said.

Far too many men already crowded in Madeline's head for her to worry about one more. "I appreciate your concern." And she did truly. But she should be out driving in the park or flirting with potential bidders. Instead, she was sitting in a breakfast parlor. All because for the first time in ten years, she felt like a person. Not a spy.

Gabriel's mother patted her on the cheek. "In other words, keep your nose out of my business, old woman."

Madeline shook her head. "I didn't—"

She waved her hand in dismissal. "I know you didn't. Just keep it in mind. What would your mother have told you?"

Madeline could still feel the warmth of the older woman's hand on her face. Her confusion only increased. "To be practical at all costs."

More than that, she'd taught Madeline that emotions couldn't fill an empty belly.

The air roughened until Madeline couldn't draw in a smooth breath. Beatrice must have noticed, and she reached out to enfold Madeline in another hug.

Madeline spoke quickly. Anything to save her from being smothered by whatever emotion threatened to crush her. "My mother knew she was dying. After our rent, we barely had money for food. There was never any extra to save. So she made arrangements with the resurrection men." Madeline sucked in a breath at the memory of the filthy, hard-eyed man who'd agreed to buy her mother's body so he could sell it to the medical school. Mr. Hurke had fit his profession, his person as dark and moldering as the graves he robbed. "She arranged to sell her corpse to provide for me. She made me promise to tell them the same hour she died. They preferred the bodies fresh." Madeline shuddered. Despite her promise, it had taken her two hours to gather the strength to inform Mr. Hurke that he could collect the body. She almost didn't go, but her new position as an assistant seamstress wouldn't pay until she'd learned the trade. She'd been left with little choice.

All her mother had asked in return was that Madeline be good. Despair uncoiled in Madeline's stomach, writhing and twisting.

She had managed for two weeks.

Madeline lurched to her feet, her chair scraping behind her. Gabriel and his mother stared at her with identical stunned expressions.

She stumbled on the hem of the dress as she hurried toward the door. "I apologize. I'm not as recovered as I'd hoped." She knew the lie would fool no one, but she didn't care.

Madeline fled before she revealed anything else.

She heard Gabriel on the stairs behind her, but refused to acknowledge him. She didn't want his pity. She hurried into her room, but his boot stopped the door before she could push it closed.

"I'm finished talking, Gabriel."

He forced the door open and stepped inside. "My mother's worried about you. She's always been the nurturing type, but ever since Susan was murdered, she's been unable to resist anyone she sees as a stray chick. She never meant to upset you."

"It isn't her fault I'm a ninny."

He reached toward her cheek but she flinched. "Are you all right?"

"I'm fine. Now leave." She spun away, loath to have him read anything on her face.

His hands grasped her shoulders. "How old were you?"

"Fourteen."

His thumbs rubbed slow circles on the base of her neck and she wanted to slap him away as much as she wanted to lean back into him and accept the comfort he offered. Confound it, how had she let herself become such a mess?

Gabriel rotated her until she faced him. Madeline schooled her expression into the look of amused boredom she knew would infuriate Gabriel.

Anything would be better than the pity on his face.

"Did you like that story? I was perfect, wasn't I? It would make you forgive anything about me, wouldn't it?"

Gabriel's hands tightened on her shoulders, but he didn't roar or thrust her away as she'd hoped. "The story was true."

Madeline laughed even though it burned like glass cutting her throat. "I *did* do a convincing job."

"Because it was the truth." His fingers traced her arched brow and the mocking curve of her lips. "This is the lie."

Her smile trembled under the delicious friction of his finger, but she held it constant. "Why do you think that?"

"A thousand little things. Little flaws that the woman you're pretending to be would never allow, but the real woman cannot hide."

"I think my suitors would call you out for saying I have any flaws." But she couldn't keep her heart from thudding in her chest. When had she allowed him close enough to notice?

"That's because they want a pretty face in bed."

And that was precisely what she intended to give them. The rest of her wasn't for sale. "And you, Gabriel? What do you want?"

"To be put in an asylum, apparently." He lowered his mouth.

Although Madeline would never have admitted it aloud, she'd thought a time or two—or seven or eight—about what Gabriel's kiss would be like. She'd finally decided he'd be as dark and deliberate with his mouth as he was with his temperament. She thought he'd take charge and drive the kiss in the direction he desired.

Instead, his lips barely brushed hers. If she had flinched, the contact would have been broken. But she couldn't. Heaven help her, she couldn't.

His hands slid from her face and dragged down her spine, pulling her flush against him. Then he waited, his lips hovering over hers.

She'd never had a man hesitate to claim her. As inept or inexperienced as they might be, no matter what they had planned for the bedroom, they wasted no time plundering her lips. Did Gabriel seek permission? Madeline's heart tripped a beat. Or some sort of taunting revenge? That made more sense. That she could understand. Did he think to make her beg for a proper kiss?

But she couldn't. She couldn't beg any more than she could walk out of a house without her knife.

With a growl, Madeline closed the gap. If it was permission he wanted, it had just been granted. If it was revenge, he'd soon find it to be hers rather than his.

Her mouth pressed against him. For a moment she feared her desperation would be terrifyingly obvious, but then Gabriel matched her intensity and her fears evaporated, burned away as heat burst through her, hot and demanding. She'd kissed dozens upon dozens of men but never had it consumed her, robbing her of the ability to think, reason, breathe.

Soon the pressure of his lips wasn't enough. She wanted to taste him, to fill her senses with the flavor of his mouth and the rasp of his skin.

She flicked her tongue across his lower lip, reveling in the masculine taste of him. Even if she kissed a hundred more men, she'd never be able to mistake him for anyone else.

His hand tangled in the hair at the base of her neck, and his tongue swept hers with a lazy caress then continued on to explore the delicate recesses of her mouth until she could no longer remember which of her carefully perfected motions would bring him to his knees. All she could think about was—more, faster, harder.

Madeline clung to him, her fingers molding to the hard muscles of his shoulders as pleasure hammered through her, stealing the strength from her knees.

Her hips began to shift, driven by the tension building between her legs. The motion pressed the evidence of Gabriel's arousal against her stomach. The knowledge of her effect on him only inflamed her more. She knew she had the power to arouse men, but that meant nothing compared to the knowledge that she could arouse Gabriel. She rubbed against him, relishing the guttural moan that rumbled in his chest.

She wanted no one else. No one but him. No one—Madeline ripped her lips from his, the words echoing in her ears.

There *would* be someone else.

Madeline stepped back. Gabriel didn't try to stop

her. She smoothed a crease from her skirt, lingering over the movement until her breathing surrendered to her control. "That's one way to avoid answering a question."

Gabriel scrubbed his hand over his face. "Damn it, Madeline. Don't turn what just happened into a jest. It wasn't for me and it wasn't for you."

She opened her mouth to scoff, but he gripped her shoulders, his fingers insistent on her flesh. "Your lie won't work." His knuckle skimmed up her neck to the point just below her ear where her pulse still fluttered. "Your body tells the truth."

"Perhaps it's like that every time I kiss."

"Is it?" Gabriel demanded. "Shall we try again and see if the outcome is the same?"

Madeline wrenched herself from his grasp. "No."

"Then tell me that kiss was different."

"No!"

He caught her around the waist, drawing her toward him, his lips lowering. "Tell me."

She couldn't live through another kiss, not if she wished to retain her sanity. She twisted free. "Very well! A kiss has never affected me that way before. I'm at a loss to explain it. Does that satisfy you?"

Gabriel's lips curved into a wolfish smile and his eyes focused again on her mouth. "In part."

But she stepped away again, reminding herself that physical desire meant nothing. "I promised you nothing would come of this, remember? Please send for my coach."

After all, he might claim to see her flaws, but he hadn't seen the worst of them. Otherwise he never would have kissed her.

Chapter Nineteen

As they descended the stairs to the waiting coach, Madeline's expression was bland, her manner pleasant. She'd thanked his mother prettily for her hospitality and made light of her scene in the breakfast parlor. She didn't flinch when his mother hugged her tightly and wished her luck. She neither avoided nor sought out Gabriel's gaze.

If it wasn't for the residual heat pumping through Gabriel's veins, he might have believed that he'd imagined the kiss.

But he hadn't. There was no way in hell he could have imagined a kiss like that. It defied everything in his experience.

He lifted her into the vehicle, his hand tingling as it reunited with the supple curve of her lower back. Yet he didn't allow his hand to linger.

Madeline sat in the middle of the forward-facing seat, leaving no space for him on either side of her.

"Eager to escape?" he asked as the coachman urged the horses into a trot.

Patches of sunlight drifted over Madeline's face as she gazed out the window. "Your mother is a dear." The corner of her mouth nudged upward. "The poor thing. The first woman you bring home is a courtesan."

He wanted to explore that adorable smile with his lips—no, he did not. He wasn't thinking of kisses. Completely out of his thoughts. "She seemed to like you in spite of that. Do you plan to accept her invitation for tea next week?"

"I might. I liked her."

"I thought she made you uncomfortable."

Madeline's expression settled into more serious lines. "Her effusiveness surprised me, nothing more."

"Nothing more?"

Her pointed look gave him her response.

Gabriel frowned. "You answered my mother's questions. Why do I have to battle for the smallest bit of information?"

"Because your mother is much more charming." But then Madeline bit at her lower lip, a pensive expression entering her eyes. "Honestly, habit again, more than anything."

"So if I ask a question, will you answer?"

She shook her head. "Probably not. The answers *you* seek are dangerous."

"I don't know what is in your past, but I won't hurt you." The more he thought about it, the more he agreed with his mother. Something had forced her to hide away all the vulnerable parts of herself like they were something to be ashamed of.

Madeline studied him with a look that he'd seen several times before. It felt as if she was weighing the wisdom of sharing some part of herself with him. And this time, as with every time before, she found him wanting. "I know you wouldn't *intentionally* hurt me."

Gabriel straightened, disliking the emphasis.

But she spoke before he could. "We both know no

one can promise more than that." Madeline surveyed him again. "Besides, I'm more worried about your safety."

Ridiculous. "What do you know that could be of danger to me?"

Madeline folded her hands neatly in her lap. "If I told you, you'd already be in jeopardy."

"I'm well acquainted with risk. I doubt your information is more dangerous than the criminals I deal with."

Madeline shook her head, briskly this time, without a hint of indecision. "Then you don't need my information endangering you further."

The coach clattered to a halt in front of her town home. Before Gabriel assisted her down, he scanned the street. No attempt had been made on her life today, and considering the pattern of the past few days, that put him on edge.

A stout, iron-haired woman clad in stiff black bombazine waited on the steps, but she appeared to be alone. Most likely a religious woman intent on warning Madeline about the state of her soul. Still, he intended to warn her away before Madeline came near. "Wait in the—"

Madeline was already descending the steps of the coach, but she froze at the bottom.

The woman on the stairs shrieked when she noticed them. "I thought you were burning in hell!" She barreled down the stairs toward Madeline.

Gabriel stepped in front of Madeline, blocking the other woman's advance. The woman obviously was insane. Was she the one behind the attacks on Madeline?

But Madeline stepped around him into the path of the other woman. Her face was cold and haughty, but not afraid. "You did try your best."

The older woman stopped an inch from Madeline, her bulbous, red-tipped nose quivering with her rage. "How many guards did you rut before one allowed you to escape?" The woman's chest heaved and she rounded on Gabriel. "You're that Runner, aren't you? Arrest this harlot."

A faint buzzing filled Gabriel's ears. "On what charge?"

"She's a murderer by the name of Madeline St. John. Ten years ago she killed my husband, Arnold Ripley. She was convicted and sentenced to hang, yet here she stands." The woman's finger waved wildly in Madeline's face.

A murderer.

Gabriel needed to see Madeline's eyes. He needed to know her reaction to the charge. But her attention never wavered from her accuser.

Madeline stood motionless before the irate woman, her composure making her appear like a stone in the midst of a churning river. She was remarkably calm.

Or cold-blooded.

Gabriel's hands curled as he fought the impulse to grab Madeline by her shoulders and force her to look at him.

Despite Gabriel's suspicions about Madeline's friend Maddox, he'd never seriously considered that she had a criminal past. Was this what she'd been hiding? Had she spent the past ten years running from a conviction? Hell, had she been transported and only just returned to England?

But large sections of that theory didn't make sense. Why would she have hired him if she was a criminal?

Unless she thought he wouldn't find out. She had said her past would be dangerous for him to know.

And she still hadn't looked at him. Not once. Not

to gauge his reaction or to share her own. Unease tightened Gabriel's gut.

"Spread dirty lies about my dear Arnold, too. Took away my livelihood and that of my children. We're destitute without Arnold to care for us. My poor babes are starving."

Gabriel doubted that. The woman's dress was new and of quality material. Either she was a horrendously terrible mother or she exaggerated her poverty.

Gabriel expected Madeline to protest. Or to put the woman in her place with one of her carefully worded set downs. Instead, she held up her hand. "Enough. What will your silence cost me?"

"I can't be bought. I'm not of your ilk."

"Five guineas."

The woman's nostrils flared as if scenting blood. "Ten guineas, not a penny less."

"Done. My solicitor will deliver it to you at the end of next week. But if I hear these rumors from anyone else, there will be no money. And if you come back, you know what I'm capable of."

Gabriel grasped Madeline's arm, unsure if he'd been driven by her threat or by his desire to protect her from a blackmailer. "It will be easy enough to discredit the woman's claims."

Madeline brushed his hand off her arm and finally met his gaze. Her eyes were empty. "Not when they're true."

Chapter Twenty

Madeline's knees obeyed long enough for her to step through the doorway. "Shut the door, Canterbury. And don't open it for anyone." She sank to the floor, her trembling limbs halting her progress farther into the house.

Arnold Ripley. The name chased shivers along her spine. Like any childhood nightmare, she should have long outgrown the hold he had on her. Yet in some deep part of her mind, he still ruled her fears. Only two men had the power to wake her in the night, face drenched in sweat—Antov Markeff, the czar's preferred torturer, and Arnold Ripley, a no-consequence landlord.

She forced herself to picture him, tiny bloodshot eyes in a bovine face, jowls hanging like sandbags around his chin. He'd been nothing more than a cruel bully, selecting victims he could dominate and control. To the woman she was now, he wouldn't have warranted a flicker of concern. She could have managed him with a glare and perhaps a twisted arm if necessary.

But at fourteen, she hadn't been a woman yet.

"Is everything all right, miss?" her butler asked.

She pressed her hands against her face. If she'd had one less thing tormenting her today, she could have handled this. Perhaps if Beatrice hadn't reminded Madeline how she longed for her own mother. Or if she hadn't betrayed far too much about her past. Or if Gabriel hadn't kissed her.

Heavy boots thundered up the stairs. She shouldn't have left Gabriel with such a cryptic comment. There was no way he wouldn't follow her to find out more. It might be physically impossible for the man.

However, that didn't mean she had to see him.

"Lock the—"

Gabriel slammed open the door, his pale eyes narrowed. "What the devil did you mean?"

Canterbury blocked him, his lemon yellow tricorne tilting askew. "Miss Valdan is not at home to visitors."

"I don't give a damn what—"

Canterbury straightened his jacket, but when he raised his hand, an old dueling pistol glinted in his knobby, liver-spotted hands. "Someone is trying to kill the mistress of this house. If she says she's not at home to visitors, then no one gains entrance."

Gabriel's fury melted into shock. He held up his hands in a placating manner. "I'm the one trying to protect your mistress." Canterbury didn't flinch, and a wary respect glinted in Gabriel's eyes. With small steps, he tried to edge around her butler. "I mean her no harm."

But neither was he there to offer comfort. He was there for answers.

What if Gabriel had been the one to arrest her ten years ago? Would he have believed her sobbed, incoherent explanation over Mrs. Ripley's strident condemnations? Especially when the question was not if she had killed Ripley, but why?

She was suddenly grateful Glavenstroke had arranged official pardons for all of them, paperwork and all. She had no doubt if there was any question as to her guilt, Gabriel would arrest her himself.

He spared no pity for murderers.

But she no longer qualified as one. She'd been pardoned. In the eyes of the law, she was an innocent.

What she would be in Gabriel's eyes, however, remained to be seen. She shouldn't care, but she did. Oh, how she did.

"Thank you, Canterbury. Mr. Huntford can enter. He's not worth wasting gunpowder on." Madeline wasn't sure she'd be able to stand until she'd done it. "We'll be in the study."

Canterbury lowered his pistol. "If you are sure, miss."

Gabriel grabbed her arm in a viselike grip and his other hand rested on her waist.

This wasn't an escort—this was imprisonment.

Anger gave her momentary respite from the sickly, childish terror that had welled up when she saw Mrs. Ripley. Madeline jerked away from Gabriel, but smiled at Canterbury. "There won't be any need for tea. He won't be staying."

Canterbury bowed, keeping a glare fixed on Gabriel. As untraditional as Canterbury might appear, he took his position quite seriously. "Ring if you need anything."

She nodded, striding ahead of Gabriel to the study before he could apprehend her again. Summoning what strength she could, she sat behind the desk, leaving Gabriel to choose one of the faded chairs beyond.

"Did you kill Arnold Ripley?" he asked, his voice tight, unforgiving.

"Yes."

Gabriel surged to his feet. "You were convicted?"

The disgust in his eyes clawed a hole in her chest, making it difficult to breathe. "Yes."

"And sentenced to hang?"

"Yes."

Ask me, she silently begged. *Ask me what happened*. He knew more about her than anyone save Clayton or Ian. She needed him to be different from the magistrates, the ones who'd proclaimed her guilty even before she'd been tried. True, she'd refused to tell Gabriel much about herself, but he should know she wouldn't kill a man in cold blood. He might dislike her at times, but he couldn't think her evil. Surely he'd trust her more than Mrs. Ripley.

"Were you transported?"

"No."

"Then how did you escape from prison?"

It felt like he'd taken a razor to her heart and carved dozens of deep cuts. "Are you asking how many guards I spread my legs for?"

Gabriel's hand tightened on the edge of the desk. He didn't flinch at her question. "You've told me time and time again that you're a whore."

She *had* told him, and it was the truth. Yet hearing the word from his lips robbed her of whatever pretense she'd used to separate herself from the term. She felt filthy, like the muck on his boots. But she'd left whimpering and pleading behind her ten years ago. "I was convicted of Ripley's murder, but then I was pardoned." She stood. "Now get the hell out of my house and do not come back."

She was a murderer.

Gabriel strode down the corridor, wishing for

something fragile he could shatter against the wall.

How could he expect to solve his sister's death if he couldn't identify the murderer standing next to him? Hell, he'd even kissed her.

He made his living knowing truth from lies and yet he'd fallen for lies from a master liar.

Halfway to the entry hall, Mrs. Ripley's salacious accusations began to clear from his ears. His steps slowed.

She'd been pardoned.

The realization began to seep into his awareness. There was more to the story than she'd said. In fact, she hadn't told him the story at all.

Hell. He hadn't even asked.

His heart twisted. Ten years ago. How old would Madeline have been? Thirteen, fourteen? What had happened?

When had he become such a vindictive bastard that he'd convict someone without learning the facts first? And why had he been so quick to leave Mrs. Ripley unquestioned? He suspected she was more interested in the money Madeline offered than violence, but he'd been so blinded that he hadn't questioned her further.

He turned back toward the study. After Madeline had confessed, he'd been unable to hear anything but her guilt. Feel nothing but betrayal and humiliation that he'd begun to trust her. But it should never have been about him.

Ahead of him, Madeline slipped out of the study, her lithe grace marred by hesitation, as if each step was made by sheer willpower. She raised her hand to her face, and since her back was to him, he couldn't tell if she brushed away a strand of hair or a tear.

"Madeline."

She whirled toward him. "I told you to leave." The

chalky color of her skin transformed the delicate features of her face to porcelain. But the expression of loathing in her eyes was anything but fragile.

"What happened with Arnold Ripley?"

"Your question comes a bit late."

Gabriel reached for her, but she knocked his hand away and resumed walking.

"Is this why you wouldn't tell me about your past? Is this what you were protecting me from?" Gabriel asked.

A cold, brittle laugh drifted behind her. "Hardly."

Gabriel called after her. "Then why won't you tell me? Habit, again?"

She stopped abruptly as if his words had snagged her. "No. Whatever weakness might have tempted me to reveal anything about my past is gone. If you want to verify the pardon, check the official records."

Gabriel's hands fisted at his side, the cool tone in her voice flaying him. He couldn't let her walk away. "All I could think about was my sister's murderer."

"Ah, I'm in fine company then."

"Damn it. You didn't refute Mrs. Ripley's claims."

A tiny sigh escaped her lips and her shoulders sagged. "Did it ever occur to you it was because the woman makes me ill? Besides, my explanation failed to sway her ten years ago. I don't think anything has changed since then."

Gabriel crossed the few feet separating them, moving around her so he could see her face. "What happened with Arnold Ripley?"

When she lifted her head, the lost look in her eyes knocked him back a step. Gabriel only had an instant to steel himself before she spoke.

"After my mother died, I was on my own. I had no family, but I still had the small room my mother and I rented from Mr. Ripley. I had a job as an assistant seamstress. I came home one day and Mr. Ripley asked for the rent. I didn't have it with me, so I said I would retrieve it from my room. Mr. Ripley followed me."

As a Runner, Gabriel had heard hundreds of stories like this. Yet he longed to block his ears from this one.

"He attacked me. Threw me to the floor. Told me he deserved a little extra for letting me stay there." Her hands clutched the bodice of her dress as if pulling together torn edges. "I tried to fight him. But he was too big. Then I saw my basket of sewing on the ground. I grabbed the scissors and stabbed him. He tried to catch my arms so I stabbed him again. Mrs. Ripley must have followed her husband up to my room to make sure he got all the money. She started shrieking and called the constable." Madeline shuddered, her eyes unfocused. Gabriel wanted to pull her into his arms and hold her until the memory faded, but she'd no longer welcome his touch; he'd lost that privilege with his ham-handed accusations earlier.

So instead of soothing her, he stood a foot away, each word branding another layer of guilt deep into his skin.

"She said that I'd seduced him, then murdered him. Swore up and down that her Arnold had been a good, churchgoing man, whereas my mother had been a prostitute. I was a pretty girl living on my own. No one saw reason to doubt."

Rage at his own profession burned through Gabriel. Too many of his associates would have taken Mrs. Ripley's account of the events, grateful to have the forty pounds they'd earn for a murder conviction handed to them with no investigation needed.

"The magistrate didn't even need to be sober to sentence me to hang."

The residual terror on her face abruptly smoothed as she presented him with the sultry expression he'd grown to loathe. "Fortunately, someone higher up in the government took a liking to me and intervened. Enough tawdry history. I'll expect you at eight to-morrow night for the masquerade."

Everything she'd told him until the pardon had been the truth, but she was still hiding something. Yet Gabriel nodded once, recognizing the dismissal as well as the reprieve. "Rest until then."

Her chin lifted. "I'll do as I see fit."

Gabriel knew he'd thrown away the right to argue further. He bowed and walked away.

Chapter Twenty-one

Rather than renting a hackney, Gabriel walked to the Home Office, hoping the perpetual London rain would clear his thoughts. It failed.

He nodded as he passed a constable huddled miserably in his watchbox. All pardons came through the Home Office. If Madeline spoke the truth, there'd be record of it there.

After a few words with a clerk and a brief wait, Gabriel leafed through a pile of records. Most were conditional pardons, where criminals were given the option of being transported to Australia rather than face execution. Full pardons were rare. In fact, there were fewer than half a dozen in several years of records that Gabriel examined.

And none was for a Madeline St. John.

On the slight chance she'd received a conditional pardon and spent the last ten years in a penal colony, Gabriel read through every single pardon.

Then he read through them again.

Nothing. No Madelines. No St. Johns or even a single bloody Valdan.

He'd left her free in her house. Would she even be

there when he went back or would she have fled? Could he arrest her if he needed to? It was a miracle a woman with her beauty had survived prison the first time.

The clerk jumped as Gabriel tossed the heavy files back onto his desk.

"I need to see another year before and after this." His disgust must have colored his voice because the young man nervously straightened his cravat.

"Right away, sir. What are you looking for, if you don't mind my asking?"

"A pardon for a murderer named St. John."

The clerk's fingers ceased mangling the folds of his neck cloth. "I—just a moment, sir." When he returned, he was leafing through a new sheaf of paper. He glanced up. "A Madeline St. John?"

Gabriel rocked forward on his toes, nodding.

"Well, I have one here for the murder of Arnold Ripley."

Gabriel didn't notice the tightness in his chest until it eased, allowing a great, deep breath to expand his lungs.

The clerk, however, held out the paper with a frown. "But why were you looking at the records from ten years ago? The pardon was only handed down last September."

What the devil—

The door to the office flew open and one of the young constables from the Bow Street Office scrambled inside. His shoulders drooped in relief when he spotted Gabriel. "There's been another murder. Coulter says to come at once."

Gabriel examined the purple blotches on Bourne's throat. "Has the body been moved?"

Coulter shook his head. "Not by me, but I can't say if he was robbed before or after he was killed."

In this neighborhood, either was likely. Probably by the very people huddled around the entrance to the alley, watching.

The man's pasty white flesh had been stripped of everything that could bring a penny or two, including clothing and hat, and left in a crumbling alleyway. Gabriel took off his greatcoat and tossed it over the body. Damnation. He should have sought Bourne out immediately when he didn't make their appointment, but little other than thoughts of Madeline had filled his head for the past few days.

And that distraction had cost him.

Gabriel looked at the bruises again. It was impossible to know for sure if they were inflicted by the same hands that had strangled Molly Simm. But Gabriel didn't believe in coincidence. His only witness to the Simm case had also been strangled.

Coulter tugged the brim of his battered hat lower against the rain. He was the constable who'd been assigned the Simm case. He was also one of the few constables who valued justice more than the few pounds earned for condemning a man to hang. "No one saw anything?" Gabriel asked.

Coulter grimaced. "Never do. Do you think the killer found out he was our witness?"

"Probably. Bourne wasn't the reserved type. He dined off the story of his last sighting of her for days."

"A few other constables will be here soon to help me move the body." The warning in Coulter's words was clear. The other constables might report Gabriel's presence back to Potts. He had to be gone before they arrived.

Yet Gabriel pulled out his notebook from his pocket, hunching over it to protect the paper from the rain as he recorded every single observation. He couldn't risk overlooking anything. The same icy self-doubt that terrorized his nights wouldn't let him. What if he'd failed to catch the killer not because the murderer was clever, but because he himself had been inept?

But when he heard the cart clattering down the street to collect the body, Gabriel put away his notebook, pushed through the gawking crowd blocking the alley, and strode across the street to the building where Bourne had rented a room.

The landlord wasn't there to give Gabriel a key, but the lock opened easily under Gabriel's experienced hands. The normal hiding spaces—the mattress, the table, the assorted tins in the kitchen—held nothing of interest. Shouts sounded below as the other constables arrived and began dispersing the crowd.

He didn't have much time.

As Gabriel finished his examination of the crate that must have served as a chair, a scrap of paper on the floor caught his eye. He held it up to the dim light offered by the window, not daring to breathe. It was the crude outline of a family crest. A few misspelled Latin words had been scribbled at the bottom.

Billingsgate.

Gabriel had memorized damned near every family crest after hearing Bourne's original description of the coach he'd seen. He carefully tucked the paper into his waistcoat pocket. Perhaps Bourne still had something to say after all.

Danbury had said he saw Billingsgate lurking around the school the other night. What if he had found out about Bourne then?

Gabriel hurried down the creaking steps to the front door, but before he reached the bottom, a man stepped into his path. Another constable. Gabriel tried to step around him, but the constable blocked him. "Potts wishes to talk to you."

"Good. I have something to say to him."

"**Y**ou will do nothing!" Potts bellowed, slamming his hand onto the desk.

Gabriel tapped his finger against the drawing he'd displayed in Potts's office. "The paper clearly—"

"Is nothing more than a few lines drawn by a half-blind drunk. According to Coulter's investigation, Billingsgate was at his club the night of the murder."

"But can anyone say he was there the entire time?"

Potts's eyes narrowed to slits. "He doesn't have to. The other magistrates will take him at his word." His shoulders sagged. "Listen. Even if you have something—and I in no way say that you do—you do not have enough to convince anyone of his guilt. A scrap of paper is not proof."

Gabriel's jaw tightened.

"And if Billingsgate turns up dead in the next few days, I will not hesitate to see you arrested for it."

Damnation, but Potts was right. If he was going to convince the court that a peer was guilty of murder, he needed to have indisputable evidence. And he had a way to get it assuming he hadn't ruined things too completely with Madeline. "I understand."

Potts tugged at his cravat. "Good. I think—" He straightened and stopped fussing with his collar. "My lord."

Awareness prickled down the back of Gabriel's neck, and he turned slowly around. An older man stood behind him.

The Marquess of Northgate.

His mother had always said he looked like his

father. Gabriel had hated that when he was younger. He'd wanted no connection to the man who'd sired him. But now he saw there really was no other way to describe himself. He was simply a younger copy of the man standing in front of him. Gabriel resisted the urge to bare his teeth. "My lord."

The marquess inclined his head. "Huntford. I have come to make an appointment for you to view my financial records."

"You could have sent a note."

Northgate's brow lifted. "I feared that would be as unsuccessful as my previous attempts to contact you."

Gabriel had burned, unopened, every note he'd ever received from him. The only time Gabriel had corresponded with him was after Susan's death when the man presumed to send a letter to Gabriel's mother asking to be allowed to attend the funeral. "On the contrary, now you have a legitimate reason to be contacting me."

Northgate's eyes narrowed. "I'm intent on winning this auction. I won't let your animosity interfere."

"No, you've never been one to let anything interfere with your pleasure, have you?"

Northgate's expression froze for a moment, but then he shrugged. "I intend to get what I want."

"And damn anyone who gets in your way?"

"My lord, please excuse Mr. Huntford—" Potts had finally regained his wits enough to speak, but his eyes continued to dart between Gabriel and his father. He dabbed at his forehead with his handkerchief.

Northgate barely spared the other man a glance. "Does tomorrow at three fit into your schedule?"

Potts shuffled to Northgate's side. "Of course. Mr. Huntford will be able to meet with you whenever you think convenient."

As much as Gabriel wanted to throw the appointment in both men's faces, it would be best to have the deed accomplished. Then he wouldn't have to lay eyes on Northgate again. "I'll be there."

Chapter Twenty-two

Gritting her teeth against the pain in her stomach, Madeline laced her sandals, crisscrossing the golden leather straps to mid-calf. The white linen toga slipped over her head; the nearly transparent material dangled from one shoulder and ended in soft ripples at her thighs. Her hair tumbled loose over her shoulders, framing the pale oval of her face.

She turned from the mirror. She looked more like a virgin sacrifice than a virgin goddess. She defiantly reached for the rouge pot. She was a whore, wasn't she?

Through her open door, she heard Gabriel arrive below. His steps echoed as Canterbury led him to the study.

Madeline adjusted the neckline of her toga to allow more bosom to escape and squared her shoulders. She was dressed as the Goddess of the Hunt, after all; melancholy was hardly fitting.

As she strapped her dagger, outfitted in a purely ornamental sheath, to her waist, a faint frown pulled at her lips. Telling him the truth about the murder had been the sensible thing to do. She hadn't told him anything that would endanger either of them, and he would have kept digging until he'd discovered the truth, regardless. Yet he'd seen her defenseless, and that made her uneasy. And then there had been pity in his eyes—pity!—as if she had any use for it at all.

She caught her hair up in a simple arrangement and ruthlessly secured it with pins. She cared as little for his pity as she did for his opinion. Allowing herself to care what he thought had been foolish, a mistake she refused to make again.

Lust was the only thing that lay between them, nothing more.

For a brief time at his mother's this morning, she'd wondered how she'd manage to keep the distance between them. Thankfully, the little interlude with Mrs. Ripley had provided her with all the motivation she needed.

Gabriel's mission was to punish murderers. Perfectly understandable given his history, but even with her pardon, that eliminated any sort of rosy future between them.

And despite any camaraderie they might occasionally share, he thought her a whore.

Madeline picked up the gilded bow and mask that completed the costume, ignoring the residual ache in her chest. After all, whore was a role she was comfortable with.

She glided down the hall to the study. Gabriel stood by the fireplace, one shoulder propped against the mantel. A black jacket, waistcoat, and breeches hugged the hard lines of his body, emphasizing strength of shoulders and trimness of waist. His cravat was snowy white and, as always, folded in a simple yet precise knot at his throat. Only a small ruby stickpin added a drop of color to his attire. Although he wasn't in costume, he would have made an excellent Hades. As she entered, he straightened, his arms locking over his chest and his eyes following the short expanse of her toga from thigh to breast.

Her nipples hardened as if it were his fingers rather than his gaze lingering on them. "I assume this means the gentlemen at Lady Wheeler's will approve of my costume?"

Gabriel cocked an eyebrow in acknowledgment. "Diana?"

Madeline slowly traced her finger down the grip of her bow, and Gabriel's eyes obediently followed the motion. "Of course. Who is more fitting than the Virgin Goddess of the Hunt? History is not exactly full of interesting virgins."

"Good Queen Bess might disagree."

That almost surprised a smile from Madeline. Almost. She was a whore, not a friend. "Do you know how hard it is to display this much skin dressed in Elizabethan attire?" She lifted a foot onto the chair next to her, the dress slithering farther up her thigh.

Gabriel jerked into motion, striding past her. "Your carriage is waiting."

Madeline slid her finger across his shoulders. "Lovely. I hear Lady Wheeler has engaged a troop of acrobats to perform clad only in flesh-colored silk. I shall ask my bidders their favorite poses so I can replicate them for the winner. You'd be quite impressed by the things my body can do."

The tension in Gabriel's body increased with each sentence. He was aroused but he was angry about it. Good. Things would progress more smoothly if he remembered she was a harlot.

He assisted her into the coach and settled across from her. "How is your wound?"

"Healing." She didn't want his compassion. It harkened a little too closely to his pity. Hooking a finger in the bodice of her toga, she slowly eased it down toward the peaks of her breasts. "Would you like to verify that?"

Gabriel's hands clenched his knees. "Enough, Madeline."

She eased her bodice farther until the dark rings around her nipples started to show. "Are you sure you don't want a bit more?"

"You know that's not what I meant. Save your performance for the bidders."

Madeline shrugged but left her bodice where it was.

They rode in silence to the ball. Although he didn't speak again, his gaze never faltered from her face. With each jolt of the coach wheels, tension wound tighter along her spine. Yet she refused to ask him the reason behind his stare. Whether it was lust or something else, she no longer cared.

Lady Wheeler's town house glittered, an excessive amount of candles and torches lighting the street for the entire block before they arrived. Two identical gladiators garbed in chest plates and leather skirts flanked the entrance, trying desperately not to appear half frozen in the April night.

After they'd descended from the coach, Gabriel gripped her arm, detaining her. With a quick movement, he tugged up the neckline of her toga.

Madeline knocked his hands away, partly because of his presumption, but mostly because his fingers set her skin afire. Ignoring the breath frozen in her lungs, she sauntered past the shivering gladiators into the spectacle that was Lady Wheeler's masquerade.

Lady Wheeler's origins as a Venetian opera singer were clear in the display. Crimson silk covered the walls. Miniature Roman temples had been constructed around the room, providing privacy for those who desired it. Atop marble pedestals, the seemingly nude acrobats posed in a variety of positions, and at the sound of a gong, they flowed into a new stance. Outside the terrace doors was a large bonfire surrounded by low-lying couches, many of which were already in use. On one, a masked dairymaid straddled a cavalier and placed grapes in his mouth.

While the courtesans' ball had been for business, this event had been arranged for pleasure. Invitations were notoriously unchecked, so women of Madeline's ilk could mingle freely with ladies of the *ton* intent on illicit fun.

Madeline handed her bow to a passing footman, then scanned the crowd, looking for her suitors. Most were easy to find, for although they were masked, they did nothing to hide their mannerisms. The only gentlemen she couldn't identify were the ones cloaked in full dominoes, the voluminous folds of the robes hiding their movements.

The Earl of Danbury strolled up to them as they entered, his mask dangling from his fingers. He was dressed as a magistrate—black robes, white wig, and all. His costume made his intent gaze judgmental, almost predatory. Madeline smiled at him despite her shiver. It wasn't his fault his choice in costume was so ill-timed.

"Huntford!" He looked expectantly at Gabriel. "Hurry and introduce me before the pack of eager pups descend."

Gabriel's expression was polite but Madeline could see no indication he was pleased to see his friend. "Miss Valdan, may I introduce the Earl of Danbury."

Gabriel watched as she curtsied low so the earl could have a better view down her toga.

Madeline rose quickly, angry at the awkwardness

she felt. "You certainly may. It is a pleasure to finally meet my mystery suitor." She trailed her gaze over his black robes, appraising the body beneath. "I must say you're worth the wait." And it was true. He was tall and broad and his manner was charming. The scars on his cheek only lent him the air of a rakish pirate.

Surely it would be pleasant to be bedded by him.

At least that's what she tried to convince herself of as they bantered. "Huntford tells me you're soon sailing to your family's plantation."

"Indeed. You're the only thing keeping me here," Danbury said.

She peered up beneath her lashes. "I hope I'm worth it."

He brought her hand to his lips for a lingering caress. "I have no doubt you'll be everything I expect."

"And what do you expect?"

"A creature that bewitches everyone around her."

Gabriel was silent through the exchange, but Madeline knew from prickles along her neck that he was glaring. Madeline intensified her smile. If he didn't like Danbury bidding on her, he'd had plenty of opportunities to tell her so. "I am a goddess, not a witch."

Danbury released her hand with a grin. "The effect is still the same. That's why I have to save the rest of the men of London from you."

"You think they need saving?"

"Definitely."

Despite Madeline's desperate attempts, she couldn't crush a small jab of guilt from flirting with Gabriel's friend in front of him. And she couldn't help fearing that she'd feel just as guilty if Gabriel wasn't there.

That had to mean there was some hope for her, didn't it? If she could still feel guilt, perhaps she must have something akin to a soul left.

Soon several other men joined their group, for although she was masked, Gabriel's glowering presence made her easy to identify.

When Danbury dropped back to speak with Gabriel, she could finally immerse herself in her performance. She already knew which of her suitors were behind their masks, but it made for amusing conversation to feign that she didn't.

When another man in a black domino joined the group, Madeline recognized Billingsgate.

"Come away with me," Billingsgate said. But the flirtation in his words was overshadowed by something darker. Possession glittered in his eyes.

She laughed, but she knew better than to ignore her instincts. Later she would piece together what it was that made her wary, but for now she focused on removing him. She had enough bidders without him. "Goddesses do not consort in your realm."

When he opened his mouth to reply, she shifted her attention back to the other gentlemen.

Every time Billingsgate attempted to enter the conversation, she redirected the conversation, never giving him more than a cursory glance.

Gabriel murmured in her ear. "You are driving away your suitor."

"Precisely." Why did he care?

"Perhaps you shouldn't be so hasty."

"I would like a word, Madeline." Billingsgate's growing annoyance showed in the tightness of his jaw.

"That was already more than one word wasn't it?" she said.

The men around them laughed at her sally, and

Billingsgate's face darkened. With a scowl, he stalked from the group.

She risked a brief glance at Gabriel. But for the first time, he wasn't watching her, he was trailing after Billingsgate.

So she turned to Viscount Lenton and offered him her hand. "My noble knight. I believe this is your dance?"

The chain mail Lenton wore rattled as he pulled her close for the waltz. "I'm glad to see you suffered no ill effects from the river yesterday."

Thanks to Gabriel. When her eyes would have searched for him, she fixed a blinding smile on Lenton. "Thank you for the use of your coach afterward."

"How do you know who I am?"

Because he held his arms stiffly at his sides when he walked and had a tendency to scratch his nose when nervous. She leaned in close, her lips grazing his ear as she spoke. "As if I could mistake you for any other."

She flinched back as soon as she made contact, the caress feeling just as wrong as her interaction with Danbury. Annoyed at herself, she trailed her finger down Lenton's tabard. She'd never needed anything more than determination to seduce a man.

Lenton, thankfully, didn't notice her discomfort. He preened. "Well, my goddess, what is your preferred method of worship?"

From the corner of her eye, she could see Gabriel tracking her around the perimeter of the floor. Madeline licked her lips. "I'm the Goddess of the Hunt. Perhaps I like to be pursued." She clenched her teeth at her line of thought. *But not by Gabriel.*

"Ah, then I shall follow you to the ends of the earth."

An intricate spin brought her within inches of where Gabriel stood. If she'd reached out, her fingers would have grazed his chest. Even without touching him, a tingle started in the tips of her hands.

"I—" For the first time since she'd started the auction, she found herself struggling for a seductive retort. "I would be most pleased," she finished lamely. She compensated by pressing her body flush against Lenton, despite the links of armor jabbing her in uncomfortable places.

He led them to the edge of the dance floor. "Then grant me permission to take you to a temple and worship you properly."

Madeline caught herself glancing over her shoulder and estimating how many seconds until Gabriel arrived. *Enough.* She wasn't here to woo Gabriel. "Permission granted." She followed him through the crowd, until they reached one of the small temples.

Lenton grinned. "Let me ensure it's unoccupied by lesser deities, goddess." He climbed the two stairs to the silk-covered doorway.

An arm clamped around Madeline's waist, the loose black sleeves of a domino covering a strong, male arm.

Her light rebuke died in her throat as the arm crushed her waist.

"You think no one knows what you really are." A deep voice rumbled, so deep and gravelly she knew the man was disguising his voice. He also spoke in French, but he was not French. That she was sure of. "But I have plans for you." He thrust her forward with sudden violence. She gasped as a piece of her hair snagged on something and ripped from her head.

Madeline stumbled, barely lifting her arms in time to keep her face from smashing into the side of the temple.

"Good heavens, Madeline, whatever—"

Madeline didn't hear the rest of Lenton's concern. She spun around, trying to identify the man who'd threatened her.

But black dominoes dotted the tightly pressed crowd.

Curse it all. Why did so many men of the *ton* have to be unimaginative and wear the same blasted robes? Three men in dominoes were closer to her than the others, but they all appeared to be involved with other guests.

Lenton fluttered ineffectually in front of her, blocking her view. "Are you all right?"

Madeline laughed. "Someone stumbled against me and I lost my balance." But then she spotted Gabriel rushing onto the terrace. She winced dramatically. "Oh, I have a splinter in my finger." When Lenton tried to examine it, she tucked it protectively against her. "Please, would you fetch a maid to help me remove it?" Madeline smiled for good measure. "How lucky that you're always nearby when I need rescuing."

With a clink of chain mail, Lenton straightened and set off on his heroic errand.

Madeline followed Gabriel onto the terrace.

Gabriel pursued the billowing black cloak into the labyrinth of gardens surrounding Lady Wheeler's home. The man had accosted Madeline. He intended to find out who he was and why.

But he must have seen Gabriel trailing him because as soon as he'd escaped to the terrace, he'd taken off at a run

Away from the bonfire, the paths darkened. He lost sight of the man as the fellow rounded a corner ahead of him. Gabriel quickened his chase, but then swore as he reached the intersection. Three paths branched off in different directions. Gabriel froze, still and silent as he listened for a noise to indicate the direction his target had taken.

Nothing.

A tiny snap sounded behind him.

Gabriel pivoted around, right fist already flying toward his assailant. He registered a white toga and feminine form in the same instant he realized he wouldn't have time to stop his punch.

Madeline thrust her arm upward, deflecting his attack, and ducked under his arm.

Gabriel wrenched himself back. "Bloody hell!" He'd almost flattened her. Or perhaps more precisely, should have. His eyes narrowed. Her response had been instinctive and efficient. In fact, better than that—it was experienced.

She removed her mask and dropped it in the bushes next to them.

"Which way?" she asked. She didn't sound in the least winded despite the air bellowing in his lungs. "Did you—"

He held a finger to his lips and she instantly fell silent, the utter stillness of a cat on the hunt. Gabriel slowly turned his head, listening to the different angles.

Leaves rustled down the center path.

Gabriel jerked his head and sprinted in that direction. Madeline kept pace beside him in her oddly noiseless lope.

Five cloaked men scrambled onto the path. "What's she doing here already?" one shouted. The barrel of a pistol shone in the hand of the man directly in front of them.

Gabriel lifted his arm to shove Madeline from the

path, but she dove to one side, tucking into a neat roll that brought her cleanly to her feet behind the cover of a tree.

The gun jerked sloppily in her direction.

Desperate to draw the fire away from Madeline, Gabriel lunged in the other direction, taking the meager cover offered by a row of rosebushes.

Suddenly, a man shrieked and the gun fired. As the bullet hammered into the trunk of an oak tree, the gunman collapsed to the ground, a knife protruding from his forearm.

The gunshot launched the other men into action. One man fled into the garden. Two scrambled toward Madeline.

The last attacker advanced on Gabriel. With a quick elbow to a hooded head, Gabriel felled him before he lunged across the narrow expanse of gravel to aid Madeline.

One assailant was attempting to lift her around the waist, but she went limp and the man stumbled under the sudden increased weight. As he struggled to regain his balance, she flung her head back, slamming it into his face.

The last man charged her but Gabriel kicked out, knocking him to the rocky path with a satisfying crunch. The fallen man rocked side to side on the ground, moaning almost as loudly as the man who'd been stabbed. "Confound it, Haines. You said this was going to be a lark. I should have known your planning was as poor as your meter."

Gabriel met Madeline's eyes in the darkness. In unison, they ripped off the gunman's hood.

The ashen face of Timothy Haines, poet and imbecile, gawked up at them. Gabriel grabbed him by the front of his robe and hauled him to his feet. "Kidnapping is a hanging offense."

Haines would have collapsed if Gabriel hadn't still had hold of him. "I—I wasn't trying to kidnap her. She belongs with me."

With an exhale of disgust, Gabriel let the man drop back to the ground.

"Madeline and I are meant to be together."

The man was a raving bedlamite. Gabriel's thoughts must have shown on his face because Haines switched to addressing Madeline directly.

"I know you're trapped by this auction and this brute at your side. I only wanted to save you. Come away with me."

"I need my knife back," Madeline said.

"I thought the Runner had thrown—"

Madeline studied him for a moment, then reached down and pulled the knife from his arm with a swift yank.

Haines screamed, gripping the wound.

She wiped the blood on Haines's robe and replaced the blade in a golden sheath at her waist. "He's not the man from the ballroom."

Gabriel stepped on the corner of Haines's robe when he would have crawled away like the rest of his helpers. "You're sure?"

She poked at Haines with her toe. "The other man's hand was clean."

Beneath the blood on Haines's hands were dark splotches of ink.

"Damn."

Madeline nodded in agreement.

"I'm bleeding to death. One of you fetch me a surgeon!" Haines' voice was strained and definitely peevish.

Gabriel allowed him to stand. "No need. One of the prison doctors can stitch it up."

"Prison, I can't— Madeline, tell him there's no need for that."

Madeline laid her hand on Gabriel's arm. "He's right. He's leaving the country, after all."

Haines's triumph turned to surliness. "What? I most certainly am not. Why would—"

Madeline's demeanor was cold and merciless. Haines retreated toward Gabriel as she advanced. "Because if you do not, tomorrow morning on my ride around the park, I'll have one of your poems with me. By the time I finish one circuit of the park, your poem will be a farce. By the second, your name will be synonymous with worthless poetic tripe."

Haines' breath came fast and shallow. "You wouldn't. You—"

"The Regent is most fond of a good chuckle."

"Fine. I've always wanted to go to Vienna. The English don't have the necessary temperament for true art." He pulled away from Gabriel. "And its whores get above themselves."

Gabriel sent him sprawling with a punch to the jaw. Did the fool not realize that Madeline had just saved him from the gallows?

Madeline eyed Haines with distaste. "Shall we go?" she asked taking Gabriel's arm.

He nodded, but paused next to Haines first. "You leave tomorrow. Or I'll know about it."

They left Haines, whimpering and cursing behind them.

The weight of Madeline's hand tucked around Gabriel's arm felt right and, at the same time, novel. She'd always been concerned with ensuring no one thought there was anything between them.

She must be more shaken than she appeared.

Gabriel placed his hand over hers, enjoying her

light touch and ensuring she didn't escape before she'd answered his questions.

He led her to a hidden alcove containing a marble fountain that he'd passed during his pursuit. It was secluded, dark, and a distance from the lighted paths. No one would disturb them. "I thought you might wish to clean up before returning to the masquerade." He pulled a twig and then a leaf from her disheveled curls.

She glanced down at her toga, dusty and rumpled from her dive into the shrubbery. "Lovely." She sighed and reached up to run her fingers through her hair.

Gabriel exhaled through clenched teeth as her hair whispered over her neck and shoulders in a curtain of gleaming chestnut silk. His blood surged hot and fast and demanded he act on the seductive vision she presented.

But she spoke before he was fool enough to do so. "The man in the ballroom threatened me."

The simple statement refocused him. "Did you recognize him?"

"No, he disguised his voice." She threaded her fingers through her hair again, loosening other bits of greenery. "Last time he left a note."

"What last time?"

"Shortly after the auction began, I received a note threatening me."

"Why didn't you tell me?"

"Your protection was supposed to be for appearances only, if you recall." Madeline dipped her fingers in the water, then scrubbed at a smear of dirt on her arm.

"You have been stabbed, threatened, and thrown in a river. I think we're past that."

"I agree. That's why I'm telling you now. I never

intended for you to be in danger. I thought I could handle it on my own."

Gabriel stepped closer and ran his finger through the glistening droplets on her arm. Even if she could defend herself like a trained fighter, he couldn't leave her to fight alone. He intended to keep her safe and that required answers. "Who are you, Madeline?"

His question was intense, but for the first time, lacked the harsh demand he normally used. Rather than a Runner interrogating a suspect, he was a man asking a woman.

Perhaps he did have a right to know. Rather than the imbecilic Haines, it could have been the man from her past coming to kill her. If Gabriel didn't know what to expect, the amount of expertise and threat, it could cost him his life.

Madeline stared at the finger tracing circles on her arm. A slight swelling marred the first two knuckles where his fist had connected with Haines's jaw. It was altogether a nice, masculine hand, but there was no reason it should hold such sway over her.

Oh, but it did.

Heat spread from his finger up her arm and down into her breasts. She'd felt this warmth many times before, but never had it terrified her as it did now. Her anger and hurt from earlier had been left discarded in the pile of injured dandies behind them, leaving her with little to shield herself.

"Who taught you to do what you just did?" he asked. "Forgive my arrogance, but I fight well. Yet I suspect your skill trumps my own."

"It does."

A slight smile curved his lips. "And I worried about my arrogance."

Not arrogance, honesty. She'd been trained by the best and had spent ten years honing her craft. "What betrayed me?"

"Dozens of things."

Madeline felt her spine stiffen. Surely not dozens. She refused to believe she'd been that careless. "Such as?"

Gabriel smiled slightly as if amused by her challenge. "First of all, these betrayed you." His thumb slid over her eyelid and then circled back to the ridge of her cheekbone. "You see too clearly. You notice things about people they think hidden. You note things that would have passed by anyone else."

"That has nothing to do with my fighting."

"But it has everything to do with the puzzle you present, of which your fighting skills play a large part. Now, don't interrupt." His thumb dragged over her mouth with exquisite lethargy, and she clenched her teeth to keep from licking it. "This betrayed you as well. You're witty. But it's not just charm, no more than the sails of a ship are just pieces of cloth. Every comment has a purpose." His hand trailed down her neck to the edge of the toga. After lingering there a moment, he cupped her breast through the fabric, gently kneading. "Next, only a fool would fail to take note of this." Madeline's nipple tightened and gooseflesh spread over her arms.

Gabriel continued to caress, and with each squeeze, she pressed herself more firmly into his hand. "Your body is your weapon of choice. You know a man longs to draw these taunting little nipples into his mouth." His hand traced down her side to her hip, skimming his hand over the swell of it, then explored the sensitive curve of her bottom. "You know this coy asset flaunts itself with every step. But not only do you know it, you rely on it, driving men mad with lust and making a fortune seem a mere pittance for the chance to claim you. You know the precise angle to hold your head. The most seductive curve for your lips."

"Any whore knows that."

Gabriel set her back, the hooded seduction in his eyes gone. "Do not call yourself that."

"But it's fine if you say it?" Apparently, she hadn't left all the earlier hurt behind her.

A muscle flicked at the corner of Gabriel's jaw. "I was wrong. It will never happen again."

Madeline shrugged, wishing her question unsaid. "I can hardly be angry. It is the truth."

Gabriel shook his head, as if his determination would be enough to make it so. "No. It's what you want everyone to think is the truth. But I don't believe it, and I should never have said it, not even in anger. No matter your past actions, you're not a whore."

If only Gabriel's version of things was correct. However, she'd earned the title fairly.

"Forgive me, Madeline."

Madeline would have defied any woman to resist the regret that hollowed his green eyes. And even though he had nothing to apologize for, she couldn't resist it, either.

Refusing to linger in the suffocating warmth created by his words, she nodded. "You've yet to convince me you noticed anything unusual about my skills."

She should have been wary at the slight lowering of his lids, the banked desire that returned to his gaze, but wanton that she was, she gloried in it.

"Seduction is only your body's most obvious tactic." He raised the hem of her toga and heated the flesh of her thighs with his palms. "But not its only skill. You walk with the stealth of a cat." His hands surged upward, pulling her skirt with them. The breeze twined around her naked thighs. "You know how to throw a knife. You roll better than the acrobats in the ballroom. You know how to fell a man with a few simple moves. You don't think in a fight, you react like a trained soldier."

Madeline had to grip his shoulders to prevent her knees from buckling, as much from surprise at everything he'd noticed as from the pleasure of his touch.

Gabriel's hands locked around her lower back and pulled her flush against him. "Then there is one last thing—your pardon only came six months ago. Nothing about you adds up. So there's no point denying the truth."

She shifted against the bulge in his trousers, desperate to buy herself a reprieve from responding, even if only for an instant. "Just as there's no denying that you want me."

Gabriel's voice was hoarse. "I've never been fool enough to attempt that lie. Now tell me the identity of the woman I'm about to ravish."

"I will."

Gabriel's shock at her agreement matched her own. But it felt right. He'd be an asset in capturing whoever was threatening her.

"Tomorrow," she added.

Gabriel's hands dug into her shoulders. "Madeline—"

"It's not an excuse. I need permission to share my secret. It's not mine alone." She couldn't expose Ian and Clayton without their consent.

"I have your word?"

"You'd trust it?"

His gaze held steady.

"Then you have it, inasmuch as I can give it. If I can, tomorrow morning, I'll tell you everything."

Gabriel's growl sounded remarkably triumphant before his mouth crashed down on hers. His lips were fierce and demanding, but in her excited state, nothing less was acceptable. His tongue battled with hers, stroking, thrusting, and twisting until they broke apart to breathe.

The oxygen restored a small part of her brain. "Nothing we do can affect the auction."

"I didn't for a moment dare to believe otherwise."

Madeline smiled in anticipation, any disappointment at his quick agreement tucked away. If there was one thing she knew, it was how to pleasure a man. She tugged off his cravat and nibbled the flesh of his neck. He tried to drag her back to his mouth but she resisted. She dragged her fingernails over the expanse of his chest, the fine linen of his shirt rasping under her fingernails. His groan of pleasure told her he was no different from the rest of the males of the species.

Her hand slid down his abdomen, then over the waistband of his trousers. With a light finger, she traced the contours of his arousal, pausing at the tip to run her finger in a slow circle. He bucked against her.

She lowered her voice to a throaty purr. "You seem to like that."

Gabriel caught her hand and pulled it away. "I'm not looking for the seductress."

She tensed at his words. She'd warned him she'd earned the title of whore. Had he expected her to be timid and innocent?

But he kept talking. "I want no acting between us. You only do what you want to do, not what you think you should. I don't want the courtesan. I want Madeline."

Cold invaded every inch of Madeline's body, save

where Gabriel's hand rested on her wrist. She shivered. "I don't know if she even exists." She whispered the confession.

Gabriel outlined the edge of her jaw. "She does. I've seen her once or twice. Shall we find her?"

He led her to the edge of the fountain, removed his jacket, and laid it over the damp marble for her to sit on. He stepped back. "Now close your eyes."

She complied with a nervous breath.

His lips brushed hers with a feather-light caress. "Did you like that?"

"Of course, I—"

But his finger on her lips silenced her. "Don't give me the answer you think will please me. Give me the truth."

His lips barely caressed hers again.

This time she stayed silent and let the sensations from the kiss linger as she examined her reaction. "I want more."

"More?" he asked.

"More pressure. More speed."

His lips slanted across hers, the wicked, wondrous pleasure bursting into focus.

Her arms anchored her to the edge of the fountain, but then she realized she should probably put them to use. She started to twine them around his neck but he stopped her again.

Her eyes flew open.

"Do you want to put your arms around me? Or do you think you should?" he asked.

Madeline slowly lowered them back to her sides, but lifted her lips. This time solely for the pure, blissful reason that she wanted Gabriel to claim them again.

As he kissed her, he slid the single sleeve of her toga down her arm, lowering it until her breasts were exposed to the night air and moonlight. And his gaze.

Gabriel studied her, as if he were memorizing the sight of her body. She liked him staring, liked the taut control writ over his face. She flicked the few strands of hair that had fallen in front of her shoulder out of the way so he had an unobstructed view.

"You aren't shy at all, are you?"

A smile tugged the corners of her lips. Apparently, not all her wantonness had been an act. Should she be pleased or dismayed? She settled for bemused. "It would seem neither version of me is."

Gabriel knelt before her. "Good. It would be a crime to hide perfection like this." He leaned forward and kissed the valley between her breasts. With a slight turn of his head, his mouth moved on to the sensitive skin on the side of her breast.

Madeline's head fell back as his fingers encircled the aching flesh. Pleasure, wild, uncontrollable, and raw flowed through her. Other men had touched her breasts, even men she'd found attractive. And she'd enjoyed their touch, but never before had she been driven mad by it, as if a single flick of his fingers had claimed her. As if she'd cease to exist if his lips halted their ministrations.

No one had ever made love to her before.

Even in her fevered state, the thought jarred her.

Men had used her for their own satisfaction. If they bothered to fondle her, it had been to increase their own enjoyment. Any pleasure she'd garnered, she'd snatched in passing.

But Gabriel's touches were for her. To make the lights swim dizzily behind her eyelids. To make her lungs burn as if she'd just run the length of Hadrian's Wall.

Gabriel's lips continued their progress across her breast. He laved a slow circle over her nipple, then drew the aching nub into his mouth, alternating sucking and tracing circles around the dusky ring.

Madeline couldn't think rationally. Gabriel was making love to her outside on the edge of a fountain. It was freezing cold. He wasn't offering her money or information. He offered nothing more than this moment of bliss.

Yet every consideration fled as Gabriel licked his way down to her navel.

He rose to his feet and pulled her upright. With a few tugs, her toga created a white puddle on the gravel path.

Gabriel's lips returned to her mouth as his hands slipped to the edge of the soft curls between her legs.

"Wait."

Gabriel froze, but his breath came in harsh pants.

"This is about what I want?"

Gabriel's fingers danced over her face in a butterfly's caress. "Yes."

Madeline leaned forward and nipped his lower lip. "Then I want you naked as well."

Chapter Twenty-three

Gabriel wasn't sure if he could stand Madeline's hands on him. She'd barely touched him, yet he already verged on explosion. But he'd granted the temptress her desires, so he didn't interfere as she made quick work of his buttons.

Once they'd discarded his waistcoat and shirt, Gabriel pressed his hands along her back, nearly groaning at the sensation of her breasts against his bare chest.

A mischievous grin lit her face. "Trying to steal my body heat?" Her eyes were mysterious in the near darkness, but they were clear and honest with no hint of pretense.

The look was far more erotic than anything he'd ever experienced. "You think I am seeking your heat?" His hand slipped between her legs and she gasped, jerking in his arms, her head thrown back. "I think this is where I should look." He nuzzled the velvet skin beneath her ear. "Hmm . . ." He teased her with a slow finger. "Definitely hot." He dipped his finger a fraction inside her. "And wet—" He meant to say more, but he was distracted by her delicate, spicy scent. She smelled warm and feminine and entirely delicious.

Her breath emerged in shuddered whispers. She arched against his hand, begging for more.

He increased the tempo of his hand, and her cries increased to incoherent syllables. Her nails raked his shoulders as she bucked wildly against him.

Her hand found its way to the waistband of his trousers. Then lower.

With a growl, he placed her on the edge of the fountain again. She blinked up at him. "But I wanted to touch you."

It took every ounce of restraint not to take her up on the offer in her eyes. "But I'm not finished with you yet." He dropped to his knees in front of her and kissed the inside of her knee.

Her gulp was audible as his mouth worked up the creamy skin of her inner thighs. They were sleek and perfectly formed. As he reached the middle of her thigh, he moved his hands to her knees to widen them. She resisted for an instant, then let her legs fall open, granting him access to her soft feminine core. He pulled back.

Her eyes were wide with arousal but also a hint of wariness.

"I think you'll like this."

She responded with a flush that started at the swells of her breasts, then darkened her face. But she didn't flinch or look away. Not his Madeline.

"I rather think I will."

Then he lowered his lips and tasted her. After only a few brushes of his tongue, she clutched his hair. "Gabriel!"

Her fingers twisted in his hair as she welcomed the increased pressure of his mouth. Suddenly, she stiffened, his name a gasping cry on her lips. She threw her head back, her fingers digging into his shoulders.

Gabriel treasured each imperfect, broken moan that escaped her as she climaxed.

He swept her onto his lap and she smiled at him, the grin open and relaxed with just a touch of awe.

She was so utterly perfect.

His Madeline.

She stayed nestled there for a brief moment, then pulled away. Her hand slid down his chest to caress the proof of his arousal pressing against her thigh. "My turn."

Madeline knew Gabriel was tempted to stop her, but she'd have none of that. For the first time in her life, she wanted to use her skills not for an assigned task, but for the pure enjoyment of it.

Her body throbbed with residual pleasure as she tried to slide off Gabriel's lap, but his arm tightened around her waist, stopping her.

"You don't have to," he whispered against her neck. His hands covered her breasts as he spoke. The heat languidly moving through her veins instantly reignited.

"I know. I want to do this." She shifted against him.

"Are you sure you don't want this instead?" His hand trailed down to the aching place between her legs, effectively distracting her from her goal. She whispered his name again and again as he drove her to the edge of that blissful cliff and then sent her soaring over the precipice.

In her former profession, she'd been trained to always use endearments in bed. It removed the risk of shouting out the wrong man's name at inopportune moments.

But Gabriel's name tumbled from her lips. It felt as instinctive as breathing.

Rather than pondering that disturbing fact, she scrambled off him before he could tempt her again. "Now as I was saying before I was rudely distracted—"

"Rudely?"

She gave the question mock consideration. "Pleasantly."

"Pleasant?"

She laughed and darted out of the way of his grasp. If he caught her, she'd never have the chance to pleasure him, and she was strangely eager to do so. "Exquisitely interrupted."

Gabriel sat back, the hard muscles of his chest rippling from the simple movement. "Better."

"I want to pleasure you, Gabriel."

His exhale was harsh, and tendons bulged along his forearms where he gripped the edge of the fountain. "Madeline, I don't expect this of you. I don't think of you as—"

She stopped his words with a kiss. "Are you truly going to refuse me?"

He searched her face for an instant. "I'm not noble enough for that."

She tugged him to his feet, then unfastened his trousers, easing them down. With a smile of pure feminine satisfaction, she took his hard length in her hand, tracing the velvety contours. Gabriel tensed, his body stiff with control. If not for the heat pulsing under her fingers, he might have been a statue.

A very erotic statue.

She lowered herself on the side of the fountain and brought him to her mouth, her lips brushing him as she spoke. "So aren't you glad I'm not a lady?"

But he seemed to have lost the ability or perhaps just the inclination to speak. Except for the occasional groan, Gabriel was silent as she pleasured him. But she quickly learned to read his body's responses. The clench of his fists. The tightening of his buttocks. The ripple of the muscles in his abdomen. The twitch in his shoulders. All providing clues as to his most sensitive areas and his preferred sensations and tempo.

Madeline took note of each discovery, adding it to her arsenal, drawing on his favorites over and over again. Her experience had also alerted her when he was nearing his climax so she could draw him back, only to return him to the brink.

Madeline hadn't lied when she said this was for her. She loved him in her mouth and on her tongue. She loved that she had the power to give him this pleasure.

She also loved the way he looked at her as if he'd never seen anything so incredible. She'd never been vain about her looks. But Gabriel made her want to stroll through the ballroom with nothing on but a grin.

Although she feared she'd never have her fill of him, she took pity on him, drawing him deep and hard into her mouth. That finally broke his silence. As his hips jerked with tight thrusts, her name issued from his lips in a guttural growl she savored down to her toes.

After he stilled, Madeline slowly drew away from him. Gabriel's finger traced down her cheek in a lingering caress, then he drew up his pants and gathered her clothing and his own.

With their lust sated, the cold finally began to penetrate and Madeline shivered. She shook out the toga, then hurried and pulled on the meager protection.

Odd, but for as many men as she'd seduced in the past ten years, she'd never had to deal with an afterward. The sedative she gave them always took effect no more than a few minutes in. She left them sleeping while she escaped with the information she'd been sent to collect.

But it wasn't in her nature to be shy, not even in a situation like this. So she smiled at him.

The smile slowly faded. Neither was it in her nature to be foolishly sentimental. While Gabriel might feel warmly toward her, he had no intentions toward her.

Neither was he a man to want her back after she'd sold her virginity. And while that small piece of skin might still be intact, she had ceased being a virgin long ago.

She was a whore.

Hadn't she just proved it?

No, their lovemaking hadn't been soulless, yet not even in the darkest corner of her mind would she examine what it had been.

"Well, we no longer have that simmering between us." But she knew it for a lie even as the words left her mouth. All she had to do was look at him and the heat threatened again. "Or at least, we're adult enough to enjoy ourselves while not letting it interfere with our goals."

Gabriel's jaw tightened. "You can make love like that, then walk into the ballroom and resume your auction?"

Madeline smoothed her skirt with a flick of her hand. "I believe I've always been clear on that."

She strode back to the ballroom before he could speak again.

Chapter Twenty-four

"So you want to tell your Runner." Ian's question was more of a statement. He opened the lids of the few dishes arranged on the table a second time. "Is Canterbury spiting me, or is this really the way you've been eating?"

Madeline scooped half the eggs he'd helped himself to onto her plate. "If you're going to complain, Ian, you don't have to eat."

Ian pulled his plate closer to him with a scowl and shoveled a pile of eggs into his mouth.

Clayton watched them with resignation while buttering his toast with the same precision with which he addressed everything in his life. "Ian said Huntford was sneaking about in your room a few nights ago."

Madeline nodded. The fact, although new, was unsurprising. "Do you think I would have let myself rest if there'd been anything for him to find?"

Ian spoke with his mouth full. "Why the sudden urge to bare your soul?"

"If you think it will improve his opinion of you, you're mistaken. In the eyes of the English, a female spy is worse than a camp follower," Clayton said.

"I don't want his good opinion." After all, what would that do but make things more awkward?

Instead, she explained the two additional attempts on her life as well as the threat from the night before, repeating the exact words from the masked man three times at Clayton's request.

Clayton's knife had stilled. "Why haven't I heard of these other attacks?" His dark gaze could have been hiding anything from guilt to rage. She suspected it was a touch of both. It was often difficult to read Clayton, even for Madeline.

She sipped at her tea as she considered the question. She hadn't told them because Gabriel knew and that had seemed enough. Odd. She had long relied on Clayton to pick meaning out of chaos and Ian to lay plans to address it.

"I knew about the attacks," Ian admitted. He shrugged in a manner he thought mysterious, but had instead become rather irritating after the first month they'd known each other. All the shrug really meant was that he was determined to be stubborn.

"I told him." Canterbury strolled into the room carrying an additional plate of toast.

Ian sighed in resignation. "I'll lose my reputation for being omniscient if you reveal I learn information in such a mundane manner."

Canterbury set the tray on the table as far away from Ian as possible. "The only one who mistakenly believes that reputation is you."

Ian leaned across the table to claim a piece of toast even though two remained untouched on his plate. "Huntford *has* kept you alive through three murder attempts. That says something in his favor."

"But that the three events were able to occur does not," said Clayton.

"Yet she trusts him so much she didn't tell us she'd

been thrown into a river and nearly burned to death. I think the implications are obvious." Ian's brows waggled, but his eyes were serious.

Madeline kept her chin up and refused to look away. "That Gabriel's competent, nothing more. If he continues to guard me, his life will be in danger. I want him to approach the situation with open eyes."

Clayton nodded once. "Tell him then."

Ian pointed at her with a piece of toast. "Might as well. It's not as if the government thought to swear us to secrecy or any such thing. You could shout it from the rooftops if you desired."

Madeline sucked in a breath, feeling as if the floor had disappeared under her feet. She'd stayed awake half the night perfecting arguments to win them over. Now, their easy acceptance left her unbalanced. "But if he betrays us, none of us would be safe."

"If you thought there was any possibility of that, we wouldn't be having this conversation." Although Clayton was calm, he didn't look up from the tea he was stirring. She sensed that she'd hurt him by not coming to him first with her problems.

"Besides, if Huntford shows signs of gossiping, I'll kill him." Ian bit into his toast with far too much relish.

Perhaps if she'd been forced to argue her case, she would have convinced herself that telling Gabriel was the right thing, but as it was, she still hesitated. "But the knowledge might put him in danger—"

Clayton tapped his spoon dry on the rim of his cup, his gaze hooded. "As you pointed out, he's already in danger."

She twisted her napkin until it balled in her fist.

As Clayton watched her, a fraction of the tension eased from his expression. He retrieved the abused cloth from her hand. "We've told people who we are before."

Without the napkin, Madeline began creasing her skirt. "Yes, other spies, couriers. But even then they didn't know our real identities." The last syllable sounded distinctly like a whine.

Enough. When had she become so weak-willed and vacillating? Why did she care if Gabriel knew about her? If he thought her more detestable? She had to focus on her priorities, which were capturing the man trying to kill her and completing this auction.

Ian glanced pointedly at the mangled napkin on the table. "You've fallen for him, haven't you?"

The reminder of her goals bolstered her enough to laugh. "Not in any permanent fashion."

Gabriel rubbed the weariness from his eyes as Canterbury showed him into the study. The idea of sleeping had been laughable after he'd returned home from the ball last night, so he'd resorted to his favorite sleep tonic—prowling the streets of London for criminals and information until he was too exhausted to stand.

The first part of the night had been a waste. It had been far too late to question any more of Billingsgate's servants, and the few of the man's terrified former lovers he'd found could shed no light on the killings. But while that particular investigation had provided no new leads, the night had improved in a seedy, little tavern by the dock. If the information he'd discovered was accurate, it was worth far more than a night's sleep.

Madeline sat behind the desk, the first clear sunlight in days greedily clinging to her.

She looked clean, fresh, and altogether delectable.

He, on the other hand, had barely time enough to change out of his filthy clothes from last night and scramble over here in time for their meeting.

Their eyes met as he approached, and for a brief moment, awareness of last night simmered in her expression. He knew it must be in his as well because it was impossible not to remember his lips on her body, the imprint of her nails on his shoulders as he drove her to ecstasy.

Or to remember the way she flaunted herself at the ball afterward. But it had been too late. He'd seen her stripped of everything, clothing and defenses. He meant to have her. Just as he meant to finally learn the truth.

Whether or not her two dubious friends agreed.

Gabriel nodded briefly at Campbell and Maddox, who stood flanking the desk. Campbell observed him with barely disguised dislike and Maddox with fascinated amusement.

Had she decided not to tell him? Was that why she'd brought in the reinforcements?

Madeline drew in a deep breath and met his gaze, the heat now extinguished. "While I was in prison awaiting my execution, a man came to me. He offered me a choice. I could hang or I could work for him. For the past ten years, I have been in the service of His Majesty's government as a spy."

A spy.

Given her talents, Gabriel had expected something of the sort, but hearing her straightforward confession was a bit staggering. The revelation tumbled about his brain for a few moments before he began to grasp the ramifications.

With her beauty, there was no question about how they would have used her. She would have been a valuable resource. His gut clenched.

Hell. How old had she said she was? Fourteen? "Why did they choose you?"

She glanced down at her scanty bodice and the abundance of curves spilling over the top, then gave him a pointed look.

"But there must have been other girls—women—he could have selected."

"The guards hadn't touched me."

"What?" Gabriel asked even as a sick feeling warned him he wouldn't like the answer. He knew of abuses, especially to young, unprotected women in Newgate.

But he still sent women to prison, many in fact. It was his job as a Runner. What was his alternative? To leave criminals on the streets because they were women?

"I managed to convince the guards they didn't want me."

"How?"

"By doing the same thing I do now. I watched them. I knew who would fear me if I claimed to have the pox. Who had daughters at home I could compare myself to. Who would back away at the sight of vomit."

Her face was blank as she recited her list. This time, he didn't begrudge her the shield she pulled around herself. She shouldn't have to experience it again.

She shouldn't have had to experience it at all.

In the absence of guards for pummeling, he was tempted to throw Maddox and Campbell out the window. They were, after all, the only reason he couldn't pull Madeline in his arms.

Because of their presence, however, she was able to continue. "I knew which women would shield me and which would trade me to the guards. It turned out I had a talent for noticing little things about people and using them to my advantage. So I perfected that skill, and in return, I escaped hanging."

"Then why this auction?"

A thin smile pulled her lips. "Haven't you heard? The war is over. We were given our pardons and let go."

"*Our* pardons?" He should have known.

Maddox bowed. "Criminals, the lot of us. Well, not anymore, I suppose."

"You worked together then?"

"We were a team." Pride crept into Madeline's voice, the first emotion since she'd started her explanation. "Does that answer your questions about me?"

It hadn't even begun to, but he intended to find out the rest after he'd expelled their audience. "The attempts on your life?"

Madeline repeated what the note had said about Paris and about the threat.

"Do you know who would have a reason to hold a grudge in Paris?" Gabriel asked.

She tucked a loose strand of hair behind her ear. "The list is extensive, but everything we have pursued so far is a dead end."

"I have a lead."

Maddox and Campbell glanced at each other, then broke formation and approached, the animosity in Campbell's eyes tempered by interest. "What did you find?"

Gabriel hoped Madeline would follow them, but she remained seated at the desk, content with the distance between them.

"The fellow who tossed Madeline into the river. I've discovered his identity."

Madeline's lips parted with a swift inhalation. "Who is he?"

The tiny gleam of admiration in her eye made him

long to puff out his chest. "A man by the name of Nicholas Toole, who suddenly has a large amount of money to spend."

Campbell's brows lowered. "Where do we find him?"

"*You* don't find him anywhere. I will arrest him at a high-stakes game of cards he frequents."

"You'll spook him. You look too much like a Runner," Campbell said.

"And you could do better?"

Maddox clapped him on the back. "We'll deliver him to you in a nice package. Not too many pieces missing."

There was no way he'd trust Campbell and Maddox on their own, but they had a point. The organizers of the game hired spotters to raise the alarm if the law ever came too close. And Gabriel knew his face had become well-known to the criminals of London. "Meet me at the corner of Ash and East Thicket at midnight. I'll tell you where the game is to be held then."

Maddox shook his head at Madeline. "Not a very trusting sort, is he?"

Not of these two. He wouldn't risk Madeline's friends deciding to act without him.

Campbell's head jerked once. "We'll be there."

"Good. Now I need to discuss the auction with Madeline."

Campbell and Maddox glanced at Madeline and she shrugged. "I can handle Gabriel." As the door clicked shut behind them, Madeline leaned back in her chair. "So are you content? The puzzle of my existence has been solved."

The picture was indeed clearer, but he was nowhere near content. Gabriel closed the distance between them. "So all those stories you taunted me with, marching across France, the czar, those were the truth?"

His proximity did nothing to discomfit her. If

anything, it seemed to amuse her. "I've never lied to you." Her lips nudged upward at his dubious expression. "Just told the truth in an unbelievable way."

"Why?"

"Because the truth is far stranger than any lie I could have created."

Her tongue swept her lips in a gesture that might have been nervous if it wasn't so damned seductive. He followed the path of her tongue with his thumb. "So what happened last night?"

"Which part? The ball, the attempted kidnapping, or the pleasuring each other by the fountain?"

Had he expected her to be timid about it? "Definitely the fountain."

"What part confused you? Or do you just want me to recount it in erotic detail?"

His body was happy to agree, but he was determined to avoid thinking with certain throbbing pieces of his anatomy. "What did it mean?"

She sighed. "That neither of us can resist playing with fire."

"Should we resist?"

"Unless you intend to marry me."

Gabriel choked. "I—"

"Have no intention of that, correct?" Madeline asked, scooting her chair back, her voice wary. "You said you didn't." She looked as though he'd lied about having the plague.

"I have no intention of marrying anyone."

"Good. Then unless you have a fortune I don't know about, we can't risk another event like last night."

Gabriel's hand's tightened at his sides. "Does it have to be about money?"

She was fast coming to the conclusion that a romantic lurked somewhere deep inside Gabriel's heart. She didn't have the luxury of being one. "What else should it be about?"

He picked up a quill from the desk and trailed the feather along the edge of her bodice. "Pleasure."

She gasped, her eyes closing, not strong enough to draw away, not when she could so clearly remember the sensations of last night. He freed her breasts from the low neckline of her bodice and circled the already taut peaks with light flicks of the feather.

"What good is pleasure?" she managed to ask in a credibly audible voice.

He lifted her from the chair to the edge of the desk and raised the hem of her dress, baring her legs. The feather traced a torturous path up the inside of her thigh. "Do you really need to ask that?" His fingers replaced the quill.

Despite her resolve, her body was just as susceptible to him as it had been last night. But while he could distract, she wouldn't let him deter. "Do you think we could leave it at this? That neither of us would be tempted to take this further?" She wasn't that much of a saint. Even this very moment, she wanted to lie back on the desk and feel the smooth wood on her back as he drove into her.

"Would it matter if we did?"

"I'd be lacking my only valuable commodity."

Gabriel's fingers paused. "Then you were telling the truth when you said you were a virgin?"

Madeline scrambled away from his hand. "I told you everything I said was the truth." What good did it do to share her secrets if he still thought her a liar?

Gabriel caught her before she could escape him. "Then what was your role as a spy?"

"To seduce information from the men I was ordered to pursue."

If Gabriel had said anything at all or even just raised an eyebrow, she would've had the strength to let Gabriel form his own conclusions. But he was silent. And so she had to prove she was telling the truth even though she could think of no logical reason for the necessity. "In case you didn't know, there are more ways to pleasure a man than by spreading my legs. Like using my mouth," she said, her shoulders aching from the effort it took to appear nonchalant.

But Gabriel refused her bait. "There must have been men who weren't satisfied with that."

She hated not knowing if he believed her or not. "Ian procured a certain drug that when mixed with alcohol, had a strong sedative effect."

"You put them to sleep?"

She nodded. "Except for a few who refused to drink, then a blow to the head achieved the same effect. I arranged the room so they'd think we spent a tempestuous night together before they'd passed out."

The skin next to Gabriel's eyes crinkled. "You didn't happen to give me anything last night, did you?"

He believed her. Her heart could have floated from her chest. "Last night? Why? Did you think something happened last night—"

Gabriel caught her chin with a growl and kissed her. "I couldn't have imagined that."

Her blood was coursing too quickly through her veins to taunt him further. But when he would have claimed her lips again, she turned her head aside. She had to make him see the futility of this before she was lost. "How would I support myself while we spend our nights making passionate love?" And mornings and afternoons.

"I would provide for you."

"How is that different than whoring? Simply not calling it by its true name doesn't make it nobler."

"So every woman who sleeps with a man is a trollop?"

Madeline paused, Gabriel's point surprisingly valid. Was it possible to make love to a man simply for the joy of it? But she found the flaw in his question. "She is if she's using her body to support herself."

"But what if she isn't? What if she's with the man because they desire each other? Care for each other?"

The walls around her heart trembled. If she let Gabriel continue, they'd crumble. And the last thing she needed was for him to convince her that a night with him was worth a lifetime of poverty. She placed her hand on Gabriel's chest and pushed away. "If I meet that woman, I'll ask her."

Chapter Twenty-five

Gabriel knew which house belonged to the man who sired him much in the same way he knew which shopkeepers sold tainted meat. There was a foul stench that couldn't be disguised. The butler showed him into the study where Northgate stood next to a large pile of ledgers on his desk.

Gabriel stiffened. "There's no need for you to be here in person, Northgate."

"I'm quite concerned with the outcome."

Gabriel had to fight through his contempt in order to shrug. Every moment his time was wasted here was a moment when he wasn't finding the evidence he needed on Billingsgate. "Do as you will, it's no concern of mine."

Gabriel sat at the desk, leaving Northgate to find a chair elsewhere, and flipped open the first ledger. While Northgate wasn't his murderer, Gabriel did hold a slight, petty hope the man's solicitor was robbing him blind.

His fingers trailed down the neat rows of figures adding the numbers and checking for inconsistencies. Incomes from rents on three different estates were distributed to butchers, coal vendors, servant wages, and everything else required to run an empire as large as Northgate's.

Beatrice Huntford.

His finger stilled on his mother's name. Next to it was listed a particularly large outlay of funds. What the devil? Three entries down, the money was logged back in. As Gabriel continued through the pages, a pattern built—Northgate withdrew a large sum of money from his accounts in his mother's name, then a few days later, returned the funds. Gabriel's head throbbed as he flipped through the ledgers. Every month was the same. Every blasted month. The money went out, then was returned.

Gabriel finally looked up at Northgate through narrowed eyes.

The other man relaxed in a leather armchair, his fingers loosely steepled together. "How is your mother, by the way?"

Gabriel closed the ledger and slowly looked up at the marquess. Criminals often asked after their victims, receiving sick pleasure from the answer. It didn't surprise Gabriel that Northgate was the same. "You lost the right to ask that question long ago. Perhaps you should ask about the woman you plan to deflower instead."

A muscle ticked in Northgate's jaw. "I have no interest in Miss Valdan."

Gabriel couldn't savor the brief moment of relief. "Then why am I here?"

"I bid to force you to speak to me."

That's what this was about? Didn't he understand the implications of Gabriel's refusal to respond to his missives? Unfortunately for Northgate, Gabriel was immune to whatever manipulation he had in mind. "If you aren't bidding on Miss Valdan, I have no reason to be here." He stood.

"Don't you want to know why I send money to your mother? Or shall I shout it from the rooftops until you hear me?"

Gabriel stilled. He didn't take well to threats, but he couldn't have the marquess tear apart the reputation his mother had finally rebuilt. "Then speak. But keep in mind, you have nothing to say that I want to hear."

"I love your mother."

Enough. The man was still a liar as well as a cozening bastard. Gabriel had experience dealing with his type. He narrowed his eyes and glared at Northgate. "You ruined an innocent under your brother's protection, then left her to face the consequences alone. Where is the love in that?"

Northgate flinched but didn't lower his gaze. "Damn it. It wasn't something dirty and base. She knew my situation. We both knew. We didn't mean for it to happen. But I have not once in thirty years regretted our actions."

"You don't regret leaving her to raise two children in poverty?"

"I didn't know she was pregnant. She didn't tell me until after I had already wed."

"How fortunate for you."

Northgate raked his fingers through his hair. "After I found out, I tried to take care of her. Of all of you. You can have every last penny I have if you want it."

The man was a silver-tongued snake. What did he hope to gain by this? Even if what he said was true, his guilt came far too late. "You think you can buy forgiveness for what you did to my mother?"

"I wasn't trying to buy forgiveness. I was trying to do the right thing. But your mother would never accept any help, not even when you were destitute."

"Why would she take your money? So she could be your kept woman?"

"It wasn't like that."

"You took her innocence with no intention of ever making it right. You left her with nothing." The words stuck in Gabriel's throat, and he braced his hands on the edge of the desk.

"Are you all right, Huntford?"

Gabriel stared at the man whose face he shared. He was angry at Northgate for wooing his mother. For taking her virginity. For robbing her of the ability to provide for herself.

It sounded far too close to Gabriel's plans for Madeline.

"Huntford?"

It wasn't the same. Madeline knew what she was doing. She was hardly an inexperienced young woman. And while he didn't want to marry, neither did she. Besides, he cared for her—so intently, in fact, that he feared to examine it.

Gabriel strode from the room, ignoring Northgate's perplexed frown.

He wasn't his father. The very idea was ridiculous.

Yet Gabriel turned away from the mirror in the entry hall as he strode past, refusing to look at his reflection.

Chapter Twenty-six

Gabriel pulled his hat low over his face and turned up the collar of his greatcoat, drawing farther into the shadows and away from the splotches of melancholy light cast by the streetlamp. His attempts to gain evidence against Billingsgate had continued to prove fruitless. One of the footmen at his club claimed he'd seen Billingsgate leave early the night of the Simm murder, while another swore he'd been at the faro table all night. Gabriel had tried to meet with Billingsgate's solicitor to view his financial records but the man said he hadn't received authorization to do it.

In the distance, a church bell tolled midnight. Gabriel studied the road through the narrow space between his brim and the edge of his collar. He intended to see that apprehending Madeline's attacker proved more successful.

A rat with a blunt stub of a tail picked its way over a forgotten pile of rags cluttering the mouth of the alley across the way. A spindly man scuttled down the street, his hands clutched protectively over his pockets, no doubt on his way to empty them in the card game. As expected, he headed toward the two spotters who guarded the entrance to the night's entertainment.

A drunken man and a lightskirt stumbled down the street, the man singing loudly of a bonny farm girl named Bess. The woman clung to him and swung a bottle of cheap gin from side to side almost in time with the music.

She lifted the bottle in Gabriel's direction. "Hey, guv'nor. Care to join us? I think I'm enough for the two of you. Besides, old Togger here sometimes can't raise his sails if he's three sheets to the wind. If you know what I mean?" She took a messy gulp of the gin, some of the liquor spilling past two missing front teeth, down her chin to her bosom and the ample roundness of her stomach. "But he don't mind paying for a show, either, and that might get you a fine deal."

Gabriel drew farther back into the shadows, hoping the enterprising woman would take the hint. Where the devil were Maddox and Campbell? He'd give them two more minutes, then go after Nicholas Toole himself.

The woman tugged her customer across the street toward Gabriel. "Here now, luv. Don't be shy. You a bit low on funds? Well, I'm feeling a mite generous this evening. Just name your price."

Gabriel lifted the brim of his hat so she could see his glare. "Move along. I'm not interested."

She paused an instant, then let go of the other man and stumbled against Gabriel. "Coo-ee! Aren't you a balmy one? With a face like that, I expect you usually get it for free." She reached out, dragging a filthy, broken nail across his chest. "You drives a hard bargain, but I accept."

Gabriel pried her finger off him, his head swimming from the gin fumes emanating from her skin.

The prostitute tapped the edge of the bottle against

her lip. "I hear that you know how to give a woman unspeakable pleasure, too." Her voice lowered to a whisper and lost its accent.

Gabriel grabbed her shoulder, anger tightening his grip as he recognized the voice. "What in the blazes are you doing here, Madeline?" Gabriel dropped his hand to her stomach, his fingers examining the layers of wrapping that comprised her newfound girth.

The drunken man straightened, nearly tipping over backward. "Wait one minute, Bess. You can't leave me behind. I employed you fair and square. If he's going to tup you, I get to watch." He staggered toward them.

Gabriel's eyes narrowed. From the man's build, it had to be Campbell. Yet he pulled off his role to perfection: a sloppy, hopeful grin twisting on his face, his feet shuffling with the awkward deliberation of a determined drunk. He draped his arm over Madeline's shoulder for support when he arrived. Only the glittering intensity of his dark eyes confirmed his true identity.

Across the alley, the pile of rags suddenly stirred and coalesced into the shape of a man.

Gabriel swore under his breath as Maddox joined their little group. How long had they been a team? Ten years? Gabriel turned down the collar of his jacket, hoping the cold air would clear his head. He looked at them with new respect. No, that didn't quite describe it. That implied his preconceived notions had been near the truth. They could have walked right past him and he never would have known it. Hell, Maddox had been lying only a dozen feet from him the entire time he'd been standing there.

But there was one more person to this team than he'd anticipated.

"What are you doing here, Madeline?"

She smiled her drunken grin. This time he could see that her front teeth weren't missing, just blackened. "Why wouldn't I be here, luv? I think this concerns me rather personally, if you get my meaning."

Gabriel frowned at Campbell. "You shouldn't have brought her."

Campbell shrugged. "It concerns her. She had a right to come."

"This man tried to kill her."

"Only because he was paid," Madeline replied. And the three spies nodded at one another as if that excuse made perfect sense.

"It isn't as if she's a hen-witted innocent that needs to be left at home." Maddox patted him on the shoulder. "We're going to leave her here to keep watch over you."

Madeline tucked her arm through Gabriel's. "We didn't want ye to be lonely. Or," she added in a whisper, "to look like a Runner waiting to pounce."

Gabriel was tempted to send them all home. But he wasn't that much of a fool. He recognized the advantage they provided. Besides, if Madeline was with him, he could ensure she wasn't harmed. "The card game is in a room above the bakery." He tilted his head toward the building two blocks down the street.

Maddox nodded vacantly, then sauntered in the wrong direction. Campbell smoothed the lines on his cravat, balanced a pair of spectacles on the end of his nose, then hurried toward the bakery.

Madeline draped herself over Gabriel's chest. "Now, luv, what pleases you this evening?"

Even padded and reeking of gin, the feel of Madeline pressed against him stirred heat through Gabriel's veins.

Her newly hirsute brows waggled at him. "Unless you're one of them mollies, but then mayhap I can change your mind."

Gabriel swatted her on her padded backside, feeling cheerful for the first time as she yelped in outrage. He lowered his lips to her neck, avoiding the bulbous mole that now graced it. "Remember, I didn't want you here in the first place."

She nipped his ear.

It was his turn to yelp.

"Clayton is a parson's son desperate to recoup his losses before he has to confess to his father. Maddox will circle around behind to cover any other exits." Her eyes sparkled with glee.

"You like this, don't you?"

She squirmed against him, groaning loudly. "I didn't peg you for such a wild one. You want to tup me here in the street? Where anyone can see?" Her giggle ended in a hiccup he would have sworn was real, but her voice lowered. "Like spy work?" She frowned for a moment. "It was hell on earth. But I always knew who I was and never had to be anything more."

Gabriel grunted when she backed him into a wall. "There's no one about. You can cease your performance."

Her hand tightened on his jacket. "Wrong. You never know who's about. Who is watching from a window or rooftop. It could be anyone from a housekeeper to an assassin, and you never know what they will recall."

"I bow to your greater wisdom." Before she could speak, he switched their positions, lifting her off the ground and pressing her against the brick wall. "Why did you let your performance slip for me? Why did you ever let me know you were more than a courtesan selling her virginity?"

She wrapped her legs around his waist. "Am I something more?"

He gently rocked against her, relishing her gasp of pleasure. But then he stilled. He wasn't his father. He wasn't going to woo her with sweet words when there'd be nothing more between them. But a glimmer of uncertainty had entered her eyes at his pause and he wasn't beast enough to leave it there. "You are much more. I've seen it."

"What did you see?" she whispered. "A woman so wanton she'd take her pleasure where she could get it?" She threaded her arms under his greatcoat, as if suddenly cold.

"Would you have done what we did with anyone else?" He stopped her immediate answer with a finger across his lips. "If you weren't being paid a fortune."

The corner of her mouth quirked at his caveat, but then disappeared. "If he had information I needed."

"But if it was up to you alone?"

She seemed to truly consider his question. "No."

A primitive possession sealed his lips to Madeline's before he could think better of it. "I saw a beautifully passionate woman. One any man in his right mind would want to claim as his own." Gabriel choked on the rest of his words. What was he saying? He was coming damnably close to professing something he didn't feel.

Liar.

Well then, he was coming far too close to establishing bonds between them that would be difficult to sever.

But why was he so afraid of those bonds? He didn't want to be like his father. The simplest way around that would be to pursue Madeline with honorable intentions.

Yet that wasn't what either of them wanted, was it?

Madeline's fingers clenched in his hair. "Oh, ye swells know how to pleasure a woman right." She tossed her head from side to side and began to moan. "Harder, harder! Ye know how I like it when someone's watching."

Taking her hint about an observer, Gabriel wrapped his arms around her back, saving her delicate skin from the bricks, and increased the pressure of his hips against her.

"To our right, four o'clock," she whispered.

Gabriel turned his head slightly. Nicholas Toole. The man sauntered with the same cocksure stride as he had on the bridge. A new hat and jacket only added to his swagger. Bought with Madeline's blood money, no doubt.

Gabriel looked forward to grinding that hat and the face under it into the dirt.

Toole spared them only a leering snigger as he walked past. But then rather than continuing on to the card game, he turned a corner.

Madeline shoved Gabriel away. "Well, luv, that'll be five shillings." She reached into his pocket, pulled out all the money he had, then darted away with a cackle in the direction Toole had taken.

"Thief! You said three shillings." He hurried down the street after her.

Ahead of them, Toole ducked through the tattered purple velvet that covered the door of a brothel.

Gabriel swore at Toole's choice of establishment. "I'm afraid Mrs. Humphreys will not be eager to lend me assistance."

"You make friends everywhere, don't you?"

"I arrested her a while back for kidnapping young girls from the countryside and selling them to brothels around London."

Madeline grimaced. "Is there another exit out of the building?"

Frowning, Gabriel nodded. "Into an alley behind."

"Wait for Toole there. I'll send him to you."

Madeline shed padding as she walked. Toole was a prideful young pup. No one would believe he'd tumble good old Bess. She scrubbed the ink off her teeth with the back of her hand. And altered her walk into a brazen sway of hips. Now she was Betsy, a Covent Garden prostitute, going places in the world, thank ye very much.

"*Nicholas!*" Madeline shrieked as she flung aside the curtain obscuring the doorway. She pushed past the prizefighter who posed as a footman. "Did he just come in here? Sporting a new hat and coat, is he?"

A plump, white-haired woman hurried forward. No wonder she'd been successful in luring children into her clutches. The carefully painted glow in her cheeks overshadowed the cruel light in her rheumy blue eyes. "What's going on, my dear?" Her gaze stripped Madeline naked and assigned a price to every attribute.

Madeline flounced as Betsy would have done. "It's that Nicholas Toole. Gave me the pox. And he never paid me for my services neither, don't pay any of his women apparently. But I ain't one to take it."

Although Madeline liked to think the threat of the French pox swayed Mrs. Humphreys, she knew it was the risk of not being paid. Mrs. Humphreys nodded to the footman and he disappeared into the back rooms, moments later dragging out a hatless Nicholas Toole with his open trousers held in his fists.

Madeline clouted him on the head. "That's for

giving me the pox." She punched him in the stomach. "And that's for skinting me on my payment."

Toole struggled against his captor's beefy fists. "What in the blooming hell is the matter with you? I don't even know who you are."

Madeline smiled with false sweetness. "From the bridge three days ago."

Toole's gaze searched her face, then he paled. "Bloody witch."

With a wild kick backward, Toole broke free of the footman. Madeline had positioned herself between him and the front door, so he took off in the other direction, yanking up his trousers as he went.

Madeline ran behind him, cursing like a fishwife. A gentleman in the process of unlacing a prostitute's bodice stepped out of the way without looking up. As they raced past, the bored woman surveyed them with only slightly more bleary-eyed interest than she paid to her customer.

Toole skidded around a corner, flung open a door, then stumbled through it. Flesh hit flesh, and Toole grunted.

He'd found Gabriel, then.

Madeline followed him out into the alley, careful to latch the door behind her.

Gabriel had Toole slammed into the wall, his arm twisted behind his back. "Who hired you?"

"I don't know—" His words ended in a squeal as Gabriel tightened his grip.

"I have you for attempted murder, and that's a hanging offense. As you may have heard, I'm not a merciful man. But if you give me the name of the man who hired you, I might suggest transportation instead."

Toole struggled for another moment, then sagged against the wall. "I knew I should've run when I saw a beak like you there, Huntford. But the money was just too good. I don't know his name." He groaned as Gabriel applied pressure. "I swear it! But I can tell you about him."

"Then speak."

"He's a foreign gent. Not very old, but not too young, either."

"You haven't yet earned your way out of a noose."

The pace of Toole's words increased. "I met him in a tavern by the docks. The Bull and the Bear. I think he was staying there. But I don't know if he still is, I didn't exactly want to see him again after we found out you hadn't drowned. I just took the money he'd paid to secure our services and went my own way."

"More details." Gabriel's voice was cold.

"He was portly. Graying hair. Tried to dress poor but his clothes were too clean."

"Was he French?" Madeline asked.

Toole shook his head. "No. One of those bloody sausage eaters. Prussian or some such."

Gabriel looked in question at Madeline. She searched through her mental list of suspects, but shook her head. She'd dealt with plenty of Prussians but none in Paris. Who was she forgetting?

Gabriel easily handled Toole as he dragged him out to the main street and down several blocks to the night watchman's box. Gabriel gave a few curt orders to the constable there, and Toole was taken away.

Gabriel turned back to Madeline. "I'll go after him tonight."

"Yes, we will." As if she'd shuffle home and allow him to go alone.

"Madeline—"

"As Ian and Clayton quickly learned, you either take me or I go on my own."

Gabriel glared at her but nodded.

"We should take them as well. They might recognize someone I'd miss. I'll sneak into the card game pretending to be—"

Gabriel caught her chin, the gentle contact sending tremors through her body.

"Sometimes things can be simple," he said.

As he strode in the direction of the card game, he removed his hat. A man standing watch on the corner dashed into the building, and seconds later men streamed out, some running, some burrowing deeply in their coats and trying to saunter as if they had nothing to hide.

After the press of people disappeared down the street, two gentlemen strolled toward them.

"Either you're a fool, or you have news," Clayton said.

Ian surveyed the now quiet street. "My vote's on the former."

Madeline stomped on Ian's foot, then explained about Toole and the information he'd parted with.

Gabriel's lips twitched as Ian shook his sore foot. Well, Gabriel had done his share of protecting her; at least she could return the favor.

When a cold breeze snaked between the buildings and raised gooseflesh on her arms, Gabriel opened his greatcoat and wrapped it around her, sharing his warmth.

She should have protested, but the patched shawl she'd brought along did nothing to warm her. And it was pleasant. In fact, it was so pleasant that she didn't step on Ian's foot again when he viewed her new cocoon with a smug, knowing smile.

"The Bull and Bear is a common meeting place for all types of criminals," Gabriel said, continuing on as if it wasn't at all unusual to have a woman sharing his coat.

Ian nodded. "Ah, I thought I knew it. Just a few blocks east of here. We'll meet there in ten." Ian and Clayton moved off in different directions.

Gabriel removed his coat and draped it around her shoulders. She thought perhaps his fingers lingered on the nape of her neck on purpose. When he smoothed the back of the coat and his hand cupped her bottom, she knew he had.

His hand tightened for a moment. "Just staying in character."

She grimaced at the reminder and relinquished the delicious warmth of the coat. "No man, no matter how noble, would lend his coat to a lightskirt." She interrupted his protest. "The coat is worth more than you'd pay me. I'd most likely abscond with it, leaving you cold and unsatisfied." She cupped Gabriel's cheek, her finger tracing the stubborn set of his jaw. "I do appreciate the thought, though."

Madeline hugged close to Gabriel as they walked. A smile kept invading her face, so she turned it into a saucy grin she wouldn't have to hide. She *had* missed this. Not the missions exactly, but the sense of being on a team. Of knowing exactly what she needed to do and how to do it.

She also had missed the challenge of it. Once she put herself to pasture in the country, would she be able to survive without going mad? What would she do when she had nothing more strenuous to plot than where to plant the turnips?

But for now, all she had to worry about was keeping alive and unseen in the dark alleys . . . and not giving in to the temptation to let her hand brush Gabriel's as they stalked the shadowy, wandering lanes.

The Bull and Bear squatted dull and disreputable between sagging dockside warehouses. The animals on the sign were so crudely drawn it was impossi-

ble to tell which was the bear and which the bull.
The scent of onion, gin, and stale urine clung to the
weathered wood. A few fat tallow candles coated the
windows with greasy smoke, making the patrons
inside little more than dark smudges. Two familiar
figures loitered on a nearby corner.

"Maddox, Campbell, you cover the front and back
exits. Stop anyone who looks familiar," Gabriel ordered.

"You're sending yourself in?" asked Clayton, his
opinion of that idea perfectly clear.

"The innkeeper owes me a few favors."

"I'm going with him." Madeline pulled her neckline lower so Betsy's attributes would be on fine
display. Gabriel's eyes narrowed, but he didn't contradict her.

Upon entering, Madeline decided God owed the
innkeeper a few favors instead. None of the man's
parts matched. His tiny pear-shaped head perched on
a mountainous body held up with two stumpy legs
and flanked by arms that hung at different lengths at
his side. It was as if God had dredged him from the
leftover bucket.

The innkeeper's hooked nose twitched as they approached through the motley collection of sailors
and dockworkers. "Damn it, Huntford. I'm having
a good night. No one's broken a thing." The man's
voice was a surprise; rich, deep, and melodious. It
was a baritone that could have graced opera houses
in Venice.

Gabriel planted his hands on the counter. "Why
do you think that's going to change?"

"It always does when you're around." The innkeeper's eyes narrowed as he looked at Madeline, his
tongue sliding over his lower lip. "She with you or
looking for work? I find myself in need of a new bar-

maid, and she looks like she'd be willing to service my customers."

Gabriel grabbed the big man by the front of his shirt and dragged him over the bar until they were face-to-face.

The patrons fell silent, setting down their tankards of ale. Hands flexed experimentally, not from any desire to help the innkeeper but in anticipation of a brawl. Madeline moved closer to Gabriel, covering his back.

The innkeeper gulped. "No offense meant, Huntford. Obviously, she's with you."

That rumor would sweep the underbelly of London. The powerful Huntford dallying with a common whore.

Ian would laugh himself silly. She'd have to step on his foot again.

But since Gabriel had been fool enough to stand up for her honor, she returned the favor. "Me? Take up with a charley? Lawks, what a hoot!"

Gabriel released the innkeeper, who immediately returned to wiping mugs with a dirty towel at his waist.

"No, he's helping me find the man who stole my da's watch. Odd bloke thinks he's a bloody noble knight." She slid a hand down her hip. "How much would ye pay if I worked for ye?"

"Three shillings a week."

"Bah. I didn't think ye could afford me."

"I meant ten shillings—"

Gabriel interrupted their haggling. "Do you have a foreign gentleman staying here? Prussian, perhaps. Older. Gray hair."

The innkeeper smoothed the front of his shirt. "Sounds like Schinder. He's in the attic room. Think he might even be up there now."

Madeline winked at the innkeeper as she followed Gabriel toward the stair. "Twelve. It would take twelve shillings a week to win me."

The innkeeper grumbled in disgust behind her.

"Twelve shillings?" Gabriel asked. "Perhaps I should have a word with your bidders."

"It's all about seeming expensive."

"You are worth more than what you can convince other people to pay."

Before she could respond to that provoking comment, he motioned for silence. As they reached the top of the stairs, he counted with his fingers.

One. Two. Three.

Gabriel kicked open the door. "Schinder!"

The man inside had been in bed, but at Gabriel's bellow, he leaped to his feet, or at least attempted to. His feet tangled in the sheets and he sprawled forward onto the rough plank floor. He scrambled up, embarrassment and rage mottling his face. "What's the meaning of this?"

It took Madeline a moment to place him without his uniform. "General Einhern."

He gaped for a moment like a cod, then lunged at her. "You worthless whore!"

Gabriel caught the man by the back of his nightshirt as he charged past. With a quick tug, he sent Einhern careening back in the other direction.

"Einhern, you're under arrest for attempted murder."

"You are arresting me? What about that slut? She seduced me, then robbed me. I was humiliated and disgraced."

Einhern had been pompous as a Prussian general years ago; apparently, time and a change in position had done nothing to temper that. "You were selling supplies meant for the allied troops to the French. Do you know how many men died because they lacked ammunition and food?" She really should have kept her mouth shut, but the last time she'd seen him, she'd had to simper and do things with him that still revolted her. It was refreshing to finally be able to say what she wanted.

"They stripped me of my rank. Me! As if I hadn't given them thirty years."

"Now you will hang." Gabriel's voice sliced through the man's blustering.

"I will hang? For attempting to rid the world of a whore? The bitch drugged me. Did she try the same tricks on you? Did she rub her pretty tits all over you? Milk your prick in her hot little hand?"

Nausea churned in Madeline's stomach. Einhern was nothing but a vindictive bastard, yet everything he said was true. She'd done what she needed to discover the location of the documents proving his treason.

She forced herself to look at Gabriel. Muscles bunched at the corners of his jaw, his lip curled slightly.

She swallowed twice, but the burn in her throat didn't abate. Good. Now he would no longer pester her with awkward nonsense about her goodness and inner worth.

In some ways perhaps it was easier. She'd told Gabriel of her past as a spy, but she suspected he'd chosen not to dwell on the reality of it. Now he couldn't ignore the truth of what she was. Not when it was standing before them, crimson with rage, spittle flying from its mouth.

"How did you find out I was in London?" Madeline asked.

Einhern shrugged. "You want information? Why don't you spread your legs and earn the—"

Gabriel's fist connected with Einhern's face.

The general collapsed on the floor.

Gabriel shoved the unmoving man with his boot. "I'll have him taken to Newgate."

"No, I need to find out how he connected me with my past. If we take him to my house, Ian can get the information."

"Torture?"

Madeline shook her head. "He has other methods."

Gabriel lifted the body none too gently over his shoulder. "Pity. I was looking forward to seeing him cut into ribbons."

They headed down the stairs and located Ian and Clayton.

Luckily, in this part of London, the hackney driver didn't ask questions as they climbed into the coach carrying an unconscious man.

Chapter Twenty-seven

Madeline's eyes were fixed on the room where Maddox had closeted himself with Einhern. Gabriel moved into her line of sight, but she turned away again. Much to his frustration, she hadn't allowed him a chance to speak with her since the inn. Instead, she seemed to occupy herself by keeping her chin lifted high enough to prove she didn't care for any opinion Gabriel might have formed.

She wouldn't be able to avoid him forever.

True to his prediction, a few moments later, her gaze flickered to him. When she met his regard, her focus jerked to Campbell. "I think I'll go change out of this monstrosity." She gestured down at her garish dress.

Gabriel stepped to her side and captured her arm before she could flee. "Let me escort you."

"To her room?" The disapproval was clear in Campbell's voice.

If anything, Madeline's chin lifted even higher, but there was a hint of resignation in her tone. "It's fine, Clayton. It's not as if I have much virtue in need of protection."

Madeline led him to the room she had moved into

after the fire. It was decorated in fussy splashes of peach and white, and it suited her no more than the oppressive master suite. She needed a room with a clear view of the street so she could relax. A comfortable chair or two by the fireplace—he was picturing her in his own room. Hell, now it would be even harder to sleep there.

Madeline tugged on the neckline of her dress. "What is it you want?" Without the added padding, the bodice was large enough that she simply slipped it off her shoulders. Her eyes held a challenge as she disrobed, daring him to be shocked—or worse, he suspected, not be shocked at all.

Instead, he settled for honesty. His eyes skimmed the creamy perfection of her skin with appreciation before returning to her face. "Einhern is a bastard."

Her walk was provocative as she moved to the washbasin and rinsed the paint and rouge from her face. "But a truthful one."

Gabriel recognized a gauntlet when he saw one, but he was more than willing to pick this one up. "I don't judge you based on what he said."

She laughed as she wandered into her dressing room. "Whyever wouldn't you? Ignoring the facts is simply delusional." She emerged carrying a sage green gown.

"I don't ignore facts. I simply assign them their correct value."

"Shall I tell you how many more men there are like Einhern? How many other men I lured away? That I let kiss me and fondle me?"

"I think I'd prefer not to know." Anger pounded between his temples at the thought of her being forced to endure what she did, but he held it in tight check. "But if you need to tell me, I'll listen. It won't change my opinion of you."

She regarded him with a mixture of fear and pity, then whirled away and pulled her dress over her head, the hem rippling around her feet.

"How many soldiers did you save by eliminating Einhern?" he asked, stepping behind her to fasten her buttons.

She remained silent, but she trembled under his fingers.

"If you're going to take credit for all the wicked things you did as a spy, you must also take credit for the good."

"Life isn't a scale, Gabriel." The fight had gone from her voice. "Good deeds don't cancel out the bad."

He turned her slowly toward him. "You did what needed to be done."

"I also accepted the repercussions."

"I think you hide behind them."

She flinched away. "Enough. You may not like who I am, but claiming I'm something I'm not won't change anything."

"Neither will letting the past define you and hiding from new risks."

That sparked her temper. "I wouldn't call this auction fearing risk."

"I would. You're afraid to discover if you're anything more than a wanton. You refuse to give yourself the chance to find out."

She planted her hands on her hips, a flush sweeping into her cheeks. "I have known myself for twenty-four years. How long have you known me? Slightly more than a week?"

"And it's enough to know you're better than this."

"Better than what? Better than making a fortune? Better than arranging my life so I can live comfortably? What would you have me do instead? Marry? A man who will desert me for the next pretty face and lush body?"

"Not all men are like that." If he married Madeline—and he could no longer reject the idea out of hand—there was no way he'd be tempted to look at another woman. Hell, he wasn't even married to her and he already feared no other woman would ever interest him. How could he settle for someone else when he'd already tasted perfection?

"Congratulations to your future wife then."

"Why won't you consider marriage?" Suddenly, nothing was more important to him than her next words.

"Have you ever eaten something that makes you ill, and afterward you can't stand the sight of it?" Air escaped her in a rushed breath. "My father was a poor actor and an even worse gambler. When we had nothing left to sell to pay his debts, he sold my mother. He forced her to whore herself to pay off his debts. He said the men would kill him otherwise. When he left us, she had no other choice but to keep earning money that way. Tell me why I'd want to place myself in that situation?"

Madeline's shoulders were straight and her face calm, but her eyes stared with remembered horror. Gabriel knew she wouldn't welcome his touch, but at the same time he knew she needed comfort. He wrapped his arms around her.

Although she stood as if steel ran the course of her spine, tremors shuddered through her. "I often wonder why she agreed that first time. Did she still have feelings for my father or was she trying to protect me?"

Gabriel's hands smoothed small circles over her back.

He expected her to remain rigid until she'd regained enough control to push him away, so when she melted against his chest as if she no longer had the strength to stand, a moment passed before Gabriel gathered his wits enough to tighten his hold.

"She gave up everything so I wouldn't have to be like her." She snorted, but the sound emerged more like a choked cry. "After all she did, I couldn't even manage that one simple thing."

"Do you think she wanted you to die on the gallows?"

"I—"

"Your life may not have been the one she would have chosen for you, but I think she, of all people, would have understood."

"Why do you keep trying to convince me?" When she tilted her face toward him, anguish shimmered in her eyes. "Neither of us want anything more to come of this."

So she kept reminding him. Yet each additional second he spent in her company made his reasons seem more insensible. He felt like he was going mad, but it was a glorious madness.

"Just let it go," she whispered.

"I cannot."

"Why?"

"Because I see what you refuse to see."

"And what is that?"

"You—"

The door opened and Campbell strode in. His gaze turned glacial when he spotted Madeline in Gabriel's arms. "Einhern is ready to talk. Come, Madeline."

Gabriel dropped his arms and she fled to Campbell's side. Gabriel watched her leave, an odd dissatisfaction burning in his chest.

He wasn't even sure what he would have said if

he'd been allowed to finish. Something half-witted and trite. Anything that would have eased the emptiness and pain in her eyes.

And he would have meant every damned word, heaven help him.

He followed them to the study.

Einhern sagged in one of the chairs as if he'd been deflated. His face was chalky, and when he raised a hand to his hair, it shook. But as Maddox had promised, except for the purple bruise on Einhern's chin that Gabriel had put there himself, neither the room nor Einhern showed any signs of violence.

"How did you discover Miss Valdan's location?" Campbell asked.

Einhern wiped a glistening smear of sweat from his upper lip. "I received an anonymous letter. It claimed to be from someone who was as bitter toward her as I am—was," he amended with a frightened glance at Maddox. "They said this Madeline Valdan and the woman I had known as the Countess d'Moriet were one and the same. They sent me money, told me her location, and said the rest was up to me."

"Why did they contact you?" asked Gabriel. The whole thing was far too convenient.

Einhern's hands twisted in his nightshirt. "I may have voiced my opinion of her a time or two when I was drunk." His voice was whiny, begging for pity, but his eyes traced Madeline's body with sickening lust.

Gabriel stepped between them, shielding Madeline. She'd had to endure the monster once before, she shouldn't have to go through that again. "Yet you accepted the proposition. You tried to kill her three times."

"But I didn't succeed, so no harm done really."

Gabriel's fists tightened as he thought of Madeline's nearly lifeless, blue-lipped body as he carried her from the river. Her whimpers as he stitched closed her wound. Her desperate motions to put out the fire. "Attempted murderers hang just as surely as the ones who manage not to bungle things."

"It's not my fault things went wrong. My plans—"

"You wouldn't know a plan if it crawled into your bedroll." Madeline stepped to Gabriel's side, her eyes blazing.

He should have known she would never cower. Even from a monster such as this. If it wouldn't have ruined her performance, Gabriel would have kissed her.

"That's ridiculous, you—"

Maddox coughed.

"—you woman," Einhern finished, his nostrils flaring.

"Even a *woman* like me knows not to write a letter warning the person I'm about to attack."

Einhern's brows lowered. "A letter? Did someone warn you? It was that imbecile Toole, wasn't it? Or the man I hired at the theater?"

"The note, you fool," supplied Maddox.

"I don't know about any note—"

"The one you left on my doorstep."

"I've never been to your house before."

Maddox cleared his throat.

Einhern flinched, his breath wheezing in rapid puffs. "No need for that. I've been answering your questions."

"Yes, but I expected truthful answers."

"They are, I swear!"

"Then what do you know about Paris?" Madeline asked.

The man's eyes widened, his surprise unfeigned. "Enough trickery! I won't let you entrap me again. I know nothing of Paris. I dealt with you in Berlin."

"Curse it all." Madeline's dark words were barely audible. Her fingers clamped on Gabriel's arm.

Gabriel covered her fingers with his own. "Are you all right?"

"He's telling the truth. He's too short to be the man who threatened me at the ball. And if he didn't know about Paris, that means—"

Gabriel didn't need her to finish the sentence.

Einhern wasn't the only one who wanted her dead.

Chapter Twenty-eight

*M*adeline hadn't meant to go to Gabriel's mother's house. She'd meant to send a polite and regretful excuse, explaining that obligations kept her away. Yet here she was, ensconced in the cozy parlor while Beatrice bustled about in her comfortable way, pouring tea and heaping a pile of biscuits onto Madeline's plate and preparing a plate for the Runner outside who'd escorted her. Gabriel's mother moved with the simplicity of a woman secure in her own home and her own skin.

Madeline, for all her training, couldn't withhold a longing sigh.

"That came from the depth of your soul."

Madeline's lips curved wearily. "I'm just tired."

Beatrice studied her. "From more than the auction, I should think."

Ah, it was so tempting to share everything, to unburden herself to another woman. But it had been far too long since she'd had any female friends, and she found herself uncertain how to go about it. Yet even if she knew, Madeline could hardly share the root of her problem—Gabriel.

While she floundered for a response, Beatrice

moved on to soothing chatter about the weather and the antics of her pupils, giving no indication she noted Madeline's halfhearted responses. Madeline only had to chuckle at amusing stories, and let herself be distracted from the turmoil in her mind.

The butler glided in a few moments later with a calling card on a silver tray.

Beatrice glanced down at the card, her story cutting off abruptly. She lifted the card off the tray and ran her finger along the edge. "He's early today." She nodded at the butler. "I'm not at home, as usual." She set the calling card on the table and hurried to the window, careful to stay to the side so she couldn't be seen from below.

Madeline glanced down at the card on the table. Her breath caught.

The Marquess of Northgate.

Even though she knew it was unbearably rude, she rose and stood next to Gabriel's mother.

"There. That tall man in blue."

Madeline couldn't see Northgate's face as he walked away, but there was power and grace in his movement, much like his son, but also a hesitance in his step as if he didn't wish to leave. "Has he come here before? If he's bothering you—"

"No!" Beatrice grimaced ruefully and started again in a more subdued tone. "He isn't bothering me. In fact, if I were a better person, I'd tell my butler to send him away for good rather than taking his calling card every day."

"Every day?"

Beatrice walked back over to the settee and picked up a large lacquered box from the table next to it. Inside, in neat little rows, were hundreds of calling cards. "He has called on me every day since the proper mourning period for his wife ended."

"When was that?"

"Almost one year ago."

"He's come every day for a year and you haven't allowed him entrance?"

Beatrice nodded, picking the card back up, her lingering caress of the card speaking volumes. "As I said, I should tell him not to call. It would be easier for both of us, but I cannot bring myself to do so. Each afternoon I tell myself I will send him away once and for all, but every day I fail. Silly, is it not?"

No. Far too familiar. "Do you know what he wants?"

Beatrice placed the card neatly in the box and replaced the lid. "To claim me or see if that is a possibility."

"Is it?"

"I—no. If I married him, everyone would know that he's Gabriel's father. The resemblance is too great. I forced Gabriel to be a bastard all his life. I won't force him to publicly bear the title."

"You hardly forced him to be a bastard."

Beatrice patted the couch next to her. "Come here and sit. I forget that you've only heard Gabriel's version of the story."

Madeline complied, a guilty fascination refusing any other option.

"I was a governess for the Marquess of Northgate's brother. One summer Matthew came to visit. Although he was tall and handsome, I was too sensible to fall for him. After all, he was a marquess, and I only the governess. But it was summer and the weather fine so there was a constant supply of picnics and games. The children were of course invited with me as their governess. And although Matthew and I tried to ignore each other, we could not. No more than we could stop breathing. The marquess was already engaged, an arranged match to the daughter of a rich merchant. His family needed the money. His father had long since gambled the family deep into debt. We loved each other. Truly. Passionately." She closed her eyes. "It was glorious. A time out of time." She paused. "Perhaps I shouldn't burden you with the details of all this."

Madeline couldn't bear for her to stop. "Please, I want to know."

Beatrice smiled. "It does feel good to talk about him. Mrs. Huntford is an honorable widow, not a fallen governess. I can hardly share the details with my friends."

Madeline blinked, concentrating on swallowing the tea in her mouth. She'd forgotten Beatrice wasn't truly Mrs. Huntford. That it was a role she'd chosen to protect herself and her family. She'd been playing that role for far longer than Madeline. Yet she was so sure of herself. Had she become used to pretending to be Mrs. Huntford or had she maintained her own personality despite the pretense?

Beatrice continued. "The end of summer came and we agreed he had to keep his word and marry the other woman. Two weeks later, I discovered I was pregnant. By then it was less than a month until Matthew's wedding. I didn't tell him. Not until after, when it was too late for him to come after me."

"So instead he comes after you now."

Beatrice nodded.

"Why won't you see him?"

"I could have married several times in the past years. To good men, wealthy men. I could have given so much more to Gabriel and Susan. But I couldn't, not while I still loved Matthew. I deprived them of so much because of my stubbornness. Gabriel hates his father and I cannot convince him otherwise. I love my son. I cannot betray him like that."

Did Gabriel have any idea of his mother's sacrifice

for him? She suspected not. She saw the regard in which Gabriel held his mother. He wouldn't want her to be miserable.

Then again, she'd seen the way he reacted to the mere mention of his father. He wouldn't believe the man's intentions toward Beatrice were honorable. In fact, if they *were* honorable. Why had the man bid in the auction?

"So it's right to protect the people we . . . care for?" Madeline refused to ascribe any loftier name to the emotion she felt for Gabriel. She needed someone to tell her she was right to continue to push him away.

"Mostly, yes. But sometimes—" Beatrice's fingers coasted over the lid of the box. "Sometimes I wish I had been braver. That I'd thrown caution to the wind and married Matthew. We might have frozen to death in the crumbling ruin of a castle he owned, but we would have been together. Sometimes I wonder if by protecting everyone, I made things easier but not better."

That wasn't the answer she'd been hoping for. "Yet you still protect Gabriel."

"I do, but I hope I won't have to for much longer."

Madeline paused before taking a bite of lemon cake. "Why?"

"You, my dear."

Madeline wished she'd taken a bite, so she'd have had an excuse for the choked sound issuing from her throat. "Pardon?"

"When he's around you, he has a fire I haven't seen since Susan's death. When Susan was murdered, it was as if Gabriel gave up living as well."

"I would hardly say Gabriel was pining away."

"No, but for a long time, he ceased living for anything but justice. It was as if he felt guilty moving on with his life, since Susan could not."

Madeline didn't have the heart to tell her that Gabriel was interested in her for access to her bidders, not romance. And she still didn't know what precisely he hoped to find.

"What happened to Susan?" Madeline knew it was a rather bald question, but perhaps if she knew, it would help her make sense of Gabriel's actions.

Beatrice closed her eyes, pain slicing her expression. "Never mind. I shouldn't have—"

She opened her eyes. "No. If you want to understand Gabriel, you will have to understand this. Susan found a position as a governess with one of the families of the girls I teach. She had every other Sunday off. One Sunday while Gabriel was on holiday, she came to visit. She was bubbling with excitement. She said she'd met a man who was interested in her, and not just any man, but a titled gentleman." Beatrice rubbed her arms as if chilled. "I think Gabriel saw too many similarities between mother and daughter for his liking."

"Gabriel loves you."

Beatrice smiled slightly. "Indeed he does. He loved us both, but he had no tolerance for another female in his life professing love for a man so far above her station. I do not doubt that he thought to protect her as someone should have protected me. Another fault to be laid at my door." She picked up her tea and began to stir. "He told her the man was only toying with her affections. He ordered her to stay away from him. Susan wasn't one to take direction well, especially from her twin, so she stormed off. One week later she was strangled."

Gabriel paused at the foot of the stairs to catch his breath. Madeline shouldn't have ventured out without him. Someone was still trying to kill her.

At least she'd had enough sense to bring Kent along for protection.

To his mother's house.

Gabriel bounded up the stairs. There was no reason the thought of his mother and Madeline closeted away should fill him with such nervousness, but it did. What did they have to talk about? And why hadn't Madeline told him she was planning to visit during their drive in the park this morning? He'd been forced to discover her whereabouts from her butler.

He paused outside the door to the parlor.

His mother's voice was subdued, a far cry from her normal sunshine-laden tone. "They found her body laid out in a bed of a rented room."

The words hammered the air from Gabriel's lungs.

Susan.

Madeline had come to wheedle the truth about her from his mother. Damn it, he'd told her it was none of her concern.

Gabriel opened the door, startling both women. Anger heated his cheeks as he stared at Madeline, daring her to offer an explanation.

She had the grace to flush.

"Have you heard enough?" he asked. "Shall I tell you how she was laid neatly on the bed in a cheap rented room, her hands folded on her chest, her eyes closed? How her hair was plaited? How she was dressed in a new lawn night rail that wasn't even hers? How the bastard pinned this damned brooch under the purple bruises at her throat?" He drew the brooch out of his pocket. It fell from his fingers and clattered on the table

The newly blossomed color wilted on Madeline's cheeks, leaving them ashen. "Gabriel, stop."

"You came here to find out the tawdry details, did you not?"

"Gabriel!" This time the reproach in Madeline's voice punctured his tirade. He followed her agonized gaze to where his mother sat, her hand shaking so badly tea sloshed on her skirts.

His rage immediately extinguished, leaving only acute shame. "Mother." He took her cup from her fingers and gently placed it on the table. Then Gabriel knelt beside his mother, chafing her cold, trembling hand. "Forgive me. My behavior was inexcusable."

She patted him on the cheek. "Susan's story isn't yours alone. You may have lost your sister, but I lost my child. And neither did Madeline deserve to have her head bitten off for asking."

Gabriel exhaled slowly. Madeline knew he didn't want her interference. But he stood and bowed. He would do anything to soothe his mother's anguish.

Madeline's gaze didn't waver from the pin on the table, but she inclined her head in acknowledgment.

His mother rose. "You have to stop letting Susan's death rule you."

What was his other option? Let Susan's death go unsolved?

For the first time since her death, the burden of the case threatened to crush him. Her death had always weighed on him, but now it dragged him down like an anchor lashed to his leg. What would it feel like to not have it drowning him every moment?

Not every moment, he realized with a start. Several times in the past week, Madeline had banished all thoughts save those of her from his mind. She had the power to make him forget everything with the infinite pleasure of her touch, and more disturbingly, her company, but did he want to allow her that power over him?

No. How could he even consider such a thing? Another girl had been murdered. Both women deserved justice. The killer had to be stopped.

His mother shook her head in resignation. "It isn't wrong to let yourself have some peace. Contrary to what you think, I think your sister already has hers."

Gabriel could do nothing more than nod woodenly.

"I need to lie down." His mother paused by Madeline's chair and squeezed her shoulder. "I still stand by what I said, as much as he might try to prove me wrong. A week ago, he would have stormed out at my suggestion."

On that pointedly vague comment, his mother left, shutting the door silently behind her.

Madeline's hand shot out as soon as the door closed, grabbing the brooch. "Why was your sister in Paris?"

"Paris?" What the devil? "Susan was never in Paris."

"I saw this same brooch pinned to a dead girl in Paris two years ago." Twisting the brooch in her hands, Madeline held it up to the light. Her fingers traced the lock of his sister's hair sealed under glass in the center. "No, not quite the same. The brooch in Paris held blond hair." Madeline stared at him, her gaze intent.

"What did you see in Paris?" Every muscle in his body tensed as he awaited the answer.

Gabriel knew he must look like a madman but he could do nothing to temper his emotions.

"When the allied troops entered the city after Napoleon abdicated, I was assigned to whore myself—"

Distracted as he was, he refused to let her use that term. "Retrieve information."

Her lips quirked upward. "Call it what you will. I was assigned to retrieve information about a plot to free the emperor before he was sent to Elba. We were at a ball held in honor of the return of Louis the Unavoidable. I led my target to the room I'd prepared, but a man rushed past us as we entered. I assumed we'd surprised another amorous couple. But on the bed was a young woman." When Madeline placed the brooch back on the table, her eyes remained lowered. "She'd been strangled and positioned as you described."

The room dropped away and rushed back with blinding speed. The blues and greens adorning the walls roiled together and Gabriel sat heavily next to Madeline.

There was another victim.

Gabriel caught Madeline's hand. "Did you notice anything about the killer?"

She shook her head, the proud tilt of her chin ruined by two crimson blotches staining her cheeks. "No. I was . . . involved with my target."

Gabriel exhaled. To have come so damned close, only to be kicked back to the start, hurt a thousand times worse than not knowing at all.

"I'm sorry."

"It's not your fault." He rubbed the heels of his hands against his eyes.

When Madeline remained silent, he looked up. Her hands were clasped together so tightly her fingertips had darkened to purple.

"Isn't it? The man I was with was too drunk to realize what he'd seen so I just led him away. I didn't even tell anyone about the body."

"What would you have done? The killer undoubtedly left to avoid discovery."

"I could have followed him as soon as I saw the body."

Gabriel's regret disappeared under something very akin to panic. "So he could have killed you, too?"

"But that's not what stopped me."

Gabriel caught her hands, untangling her fingers. "I don't care what stopped you."

"You should."

"But I don't."

"Madeline—"

She jerked away from his hand. "Have there been any other murders in England similar to your sister's?"

Gabriel frowned. He could hardly return to sentimentality after the change in topic. "Two weeks ago, a schoolteacher, Molly Simm, was found strangled. Her body was arranged like Susan's."

"In London?"

Gabriel nodded.

"Do you have any suspects?"

"Yes."

"Then why are you protecting me and not investigating?"

"Her case was assigned to someone else. I was deemed too close."

"But you wouldn't be able to let that—" Her eyes suddenly widened and her lips parted. "You *are* investigating, aren't you? This and your sister's murder. That's why you wanted seven years of my bidders' financials."

"Madeline—"

"Some of my suitors are your suspects. You used my auction to cover your investigation."

Gabriel waited with his hands clenched at his sides. He deserved whatever recriminations she threw at him.

"Clever. Who are your suspects?" she asked.

Gabriel searched her face for some sign of her true reaction. "I shouldn't have kept the truth—"

She cut him off with an impatient wave. "It was a good plan. I would have done the same thing in your situation."

He couldn't believe his revelation didn't affect her at all. "I hid my intentions."

She raised her brow. "And I put you in danger by not telling you the truth about my past. Now, who are your suspects?" Her lips pursed slightly and her attention riveted on his face. "Judging by your actions, Lenton must be one."

"No longer, his whereabouts are accounted for the night of the Simm murder." Gabriel rubbed the back of his neck. "I believe it was Billingsgate. His family crest is the most similar to the sketch."

"Family crest?"

Even though he'd initially hidden his investigation from Madeline, he now found himself sharing every last detail. At first he spoke out of guilt for hiding the truth, but then he continued because he wanted to know Madeline's opinion and see if she could find anything he overlooked.

"The landlord couldn't tell you who rented the room the body was found in?"

"No, he said a street urchin had paid for it. These weren't places where the landlords bothered to ask questions."

"Yet obviously the killer wanted the bodies found or he would have disposed of them."

Despite the gravity of their discussion, Gabriel was entranced by Madeline's face as she examined the clues in her mind. The slight narrowing of her lips. The way she stared as if the answer was just beyond his shoulder. "I'll speak to Ian and Clayton and see if they remember him from Paris."

How could she not see how unique she was? How many women would sit and discuss the details of a murder when she had dozens of suitors waiting to fall at her feet?

"When exactly was Miss Simm killed?"

"Thursday the second. She left the school at four and her body was discovered at ten that night."

"I'll find out where Billingsgate was."

He didn't want her anywhere near him. He tensed as he realized there was one more layer to his deception. "Billingsgate is dangerous."

"In what way?"

"He is cruel and often violent to his bed partners."

Her reply took two seconds too long. "I suspected as much."

"I wouldn't have let him win the auction. I would have told you."

She shrugged. "Why? Catching a murderer is more important than my silly auction."

"I'd never have let it go that far."

She laughed, but the sound was hollow. "Why are you so worried about my feelings? I already told you I understand. I've done this most of my life, remember. I'm used to the mission, or in this case the investigation, taking precedence."

Gabriel wanted to shake her until her calm shattered and she railed at him as she must long to do. "I never did anything that I thought would endanger you."

"Enough. Do you want me to scream and fall apart?"

"Yes, if that is what you want to do."

She smoothed her skirt. "I don't. I never fall apart while there is a task to be accomplished."

Gabriel recognized this mask and knew he'd lost even more ground than he'd feared. "And after that?"

"That is my concern. Now as I said, I will get the information on Billingsgate."

Could he let her? It might be his best chance. She could get information he'd never be able to. But if Billingsgate *was* the murderer and he discovered what she was doing . . . A horrific possibility slammed through him. "Could the murderer have seen you in Paris?"

She tilted her head as she considered. "Perhaps."

"Could it have been Billingsgate?"

"I suppose. I don't remember him being there, but quite a few Englishmen were to celebrate the fall of Napoleon."

"The man who sent the threatening note said he knew you from Paris. What if he didn't know you from your past as a spy but from that night of the murder? When you came to London and hired me—"

"It would have appeared as if I had gone straight to the man who was hunting him."

"But then a week passed and nothing happened. He realized you didn't know his identity."

Her body went utterly motionless in the way that masked her agitation. "The man at the ball. He might have taken some of my hair. I thought my hair had snagged on one of his buttons. Or that he'd just been cruel." She tucked a strand of hair behind her ear. "But if he's the murderer, then everything would make sense. I would need a brooch, after all. But why didn't he leave after he recognized me the first time?"

"Perhaps he made plans but didn't see the need to follow through with them. Or perhaps he saw the chance to tie up loose ends like he did with Bourne."

A few heartbeats of silence passed before Madeline reached for her cup of tea and sipped it, a near feline smile curving her lips. "Your killer has left behind far more loose ends than he thinks." She held up her fingers as she ticked off her points. "Noblemen are never alone and if he's cruel, we will find someone who will talk. We can track when he was in London and Paris. He needs to have a brooch made. And I already know Billingsgate wants me. If he's threatened me twice, that means he thinks he's far smarter than us."

Gabriel stared at her a moment, realizing yet again that he'd underestimated her strength.

Yet he would still be mad to let her help. It would put her in danger, and he couldn't lose her. He was no longer able to delude himself that he'd be willing to give her up at the end of the auction.

"You cannot lose this chance to catch him. I've been in far more dangerous situations before," Madeline said.

"But not because I put you there."

"I'm putting myself there."

Gabriel recognized the gleam in her eyes, the same she'd had the night when they tracked Toole. She wasn't only willing to help. She wanted to. Needed to. Madeline would never be a woman content to sit idly by. And if he tried to force her away from the investigation, he'd be tearing away a vital part of who she was. He would have to trust her.

But that didn't mean he couldn't also protect her. "From now on we tell each other our plans."

"Regarding the murder investigation. I don't agree to more than that. My auction is my business alone." But then she leaned toward him, her cool façade vanished.

His acceptance of her help had earned her trust and forgiveness in a way his apologies never could have. But that concession wasn't enough. But from now on he'd be content with nothing less than all of her.

Including her heart.

Chapter Twenty-nine

Madeline paused at the edge of the trees. Women in modest gowns smiled demurely at the gentlemen around them. They sipped bland punch and flirted. It could have been any society event, save one distinction—at the end of the night, a gentleman could take his dance partner home or back to the brothel to finish the evening. All for an extremely hefty fee, of course.

Lady Aphrodite was the hostess of the scandalous late night fete at Covent Garden. She'd invited Madeline with a single condition—that Madeline not arrive and draw attention from her girls until halfway through the party, and then that she leave before it ended.

It had been much more difficult to persuade Lady Aphrodite to allow Madeline to send an invitation to Billingsgate yesterday. Now Madeline's assignment was twofold, to prove him a murderer and keep him as far away from their hostess as possible.

Since the party had been under way for over two hours, the brightly colored paper lanterns adorning the trees had begun to droop from the moisture in the air. The sparkling punch bowls made of ice sat in lopsided puddles. But the event was a success, and the weather had done little to dampen the enthusiasm of those gathered. The champagne flowed freely and the resulting high spirits suited Madeline's purposes perfectly.

Her gaze swept the crowd until she found Billingsgate. He was leaning over a diminutive brunette, who waved her fan in quick, agitated flicks. The color of her cheeks indicated anger. Or perhaps drink. No, definitely fury. Her movements were too controlled and the color hadn't spread down her chest. Every time the woman tried to back away, Billingsgate crowded closer, his jaw tightening. Madeline didn't doubt this man enjoyed violence.

"Let's bring him to his knees," she whispered.

Gabriel stood a respectful distance behind her. Even though the separation was by her order, it set her teeth on edge. She slipped back so she stood shoulder to shoulder with him.

"All we need tonight is to gain access to his financials. Don't allow Billingsgate to lure you away."

Perhaps she and Gabriel could disappear instead. They could— Before the thought could fully form, she dismissed it. She had a murderer to trap.

And an auction to finish.

Madeline frowned. It had taken far too long to remember the auction.

Gabriel's hand rested on her arm. "Madeline, I need your agreement. I refuse to put you at further risk."

She blinked at him, only vaguely recalling what he'd asked of her. "Of course. I'll stay within sight."

"Madeline! Huntford!" Danbury strolled to her side. "I'd begun to fear you'd chosen another event."

Gabriel released her arm, and she smiled at Danbury. "How could I do that when you chose this one?"

He raised her hand to his lips. "How, indeed." Tucking her hand through his arm, Danbury addressed Gabriel. "Excited to be done with this? Only one more day, then her virginity becomes the concern of another man."

Gabriel's face remained impassive. "Quite."

"Well, I'll deprive you of her a bit earlier, if she's amenable to the idea?"

"Of course." Madeline let habit save her before she humiliated both of them by refusing.

"So have you picked a beautiful lady to bring home?" Madeline asked as he led her away.

"Only if you're willing."

Madeline smiled despite Gabriel's gaze burrowing between her shoulder blades. "You can't purchase me at an event like this."

"I was under the impression that even you had a price."

"But also a timeline."

Danbury laughed. "Fine, I'll wait to prove my point. But I will win you to save my friends from heartache."

Madeline batted her lashes, and led him closer to Billingsgate. "I like your nobility. Speaking of aching hearts, did you witness the horrendous rendition of *Othello* this season?"

"I had the misfortune of seeing it just the other night."

"Please tell me you were there two weeks ago when Desdemona tripped and fell off the stage, landing in the pit with her skirts over her head."

"No, I didn't have the good fortune." Danbury chuckled, then turned to Billingsgate. "You were there, right? I can always count on you to be cultured."

He released the other woman's waist and she fled. "Indeed, I am. But I was at my club that night."

She knew she was only supposed to charm him to gain permission to see his financials, but the chance to find gaps in his alibi was impossible to pass up. "Really? I thought I saw your coach by the theater. It had to be you. It had your crest."

"I don't have a coach with my family's crest. Not since my father's day."

Curse it all. Madeline studied him. Why lie about something that would be so easy to corroborate? And why would there have been a sketch of the crest in the coachman's room?

Lord Boyle spoke. "I wish you *had* been at the theater. You took a damned fortune from me at the club that night." She didn't think Boyle was Billingsgate's friend so she doubted the corroboration had been planned.

"Surely you regained some of it after he left," Madeline said.

Boyle sighed. "Unfortunately, he never did. He just kept winning until dawn."

Gabriel's suspect had an alibi.

Her training kept her from wheeling about to see if he'd overheard. This would gut him. He'd be back to the beginning of his investigation with no clues. She wanted to go to him and pull him away from all this and never look back.

As if her paltry presence would do anything to shield him.

Madeline plucked a glass of wine from one of her suitors and sipped it. Murder investigation or not, she still had an auction to win.

Billingsgate pressed closer, his hand caressing up and down her spine. His possessive touch was as annoying as it was repulsive. But she still needed his financials. Gabriel would want to be positive.

Billingsgate's hand clamped around her waist.

Madeline laughed and batted it away. "No sampling the goods without an invitation."

His eyes glittered. "You did invite me. Specifically, I believe." His hand inched toward her breast.

"Back away, Billingsgate. She's not interested." Gabriel's voice was cold as he strode to her side.

Madeline drew in a silent breath. Gabriel was cutting off his path for further investigation.

For her.

Billingsgate stepped back. "Why? The woman wants me."

Madeline remained silent.

A mottled flush spread up his cheeks, but he seemed to recall himself at the last moment and shrugged. "I don't mind if you play coy. It will make our night all the more enjoyable."

Knowing his taste for violence in the bedroom, his words chilled her. But he strode away.

Gabriel looked pointedly at him, then back at her, silently asking if she wanted him to go after Billingsgate. She shook her head. There was no reason for Gabriel to risk the man's anger. Gabriel stared at her a moment, then faded back through the crowd.

She turned to her suitors and smiled, changing the shake of her head into something more dramatic. "A coy woman has no intention of following through." She cupped her breasts through her bodice, drawing ravenous eyes, Billingsgate forgotten in their lust. But although she'd needed to draw their attention, the action felt wrong. Cheap. Dirty. "I have every intention of seeing this all the way to its climax."

Quickly, she lavished attention back on Danbury. Despite her lack of enthusiasm, years of experience allowed her to know the precise moment to lay her hand on his arm or slide her tongue over her lower lip. Which was fortunate, for while she tried to charm Danbury—handsome, rich, and interested Danbury—her mind focused on Gabriel.

She'd been willing to leave the party.

Had been willing? If it was up to her, she'd walk over to Gabriel and leave all this.

But it *was* up to her, and that was the terrifying thing. She could throw herself into Gabriel's arms and announce that instead of selling her virginity, she was going to give it away on a foolish whim of her heart.

Her heart pounded wildly at the fantasy even as she rejected it. Nothing had changed. That option brought nothing but a brief moment of passion followed by a lifetime of regret.

Did it have to end with regret?

Almost certainly.

Perhaps if she were a different woman, more noble, more innocent, more pristine, they might have had a chance. She preferred to live with pleasant thoughts of what might have been rather than with the agony of failure.

When had she become such a coward?

Risk had been the one constant in her life for the past ten years. Each day brought the threat of capture, torture, and execution. What did she risk if she gave in to her feelings for Gabriel?

Only two tiny things—her heart and her soul.

Madeline gulped more of the wine and bantered with the men now swarming around her, careful to avoid Billingsgate. She twitched her toes. The dew had soaked through her slippers, chilling her feet. She surveyed the men around her again. Now she'd drive them into a frenzy of bidding.

Any moment she'd transform into the dazzling coquette.

She inhaled, pulled back her shoulders and . . . nothing.

She didn't want to do this.

When one of Lady Aphrodite's girls drew Danbury away, she did nothing to try to retain him.

Heavens, she was that far lost? Her breath came high and shallow. It couldn't be love, could it?

Surely not. Love wasn't supposed to fill you with fear.

A hand rested on her elbow. "Madeline, darling, are you ready to come with me now?"

"Billingsgate." All extraneous thoughts fled. Her entire being focused on the man crowding behind her. A shift of her elbow allowed her to calculate precisely how far his body was from hers. Then she shrugged, the subtle movement gauging his intent.

His hand clamped and wouldn't let go. He lowered his mouth next to her ear. "I'm tired of your games. There's a pistol aimed at your back." An unmistakable circular outline bit into her spine.

She laughed, pitching her voice to carry to Gabriel. "A pistol in your pocket? That's a bit generous, don't you think?"

The gentlemen around her chuckled and offered descriptions of what filled their trousers.

Billingsgate's fingers dug into her arm as he pulled her back a step. "Forgive me, gentlemen. A fellow cannot let a slur like that go unpunished. Come, shall we go for a stroll?" The pressure returned to her spine.

Her drunken admirers shouted lewd suggestions as he dragged her toward the dark paths. Not one of them offered to protect her, not even in jest.

Well, she knew where she stood with them.

Madeline cast a glance toward Gabriel, but Billingsgate blocked her view.

"Your faithful hound won't be able to save you. A few of my friends are detaining him."

Gabriel could handle himself. But a shiver ran through her. Anything could happen if guns were involved. She barricaded her fear in a corner of her mind. If she wanted to help Gabriel, she had to free herself first.

Madeline allowed Billingsgate to force her down one of the paths, his hot breath on her neck testifying to his intentions. If the information Lady Aphrodite provided was correct, he'd most likely want her tied. She had only a brief window to act.

First, she needed him to draw his gun so she could disarm him. "This is a foolish plan." A man who needed his victims tied and helpless was unconfident at the core. She'd emasculated him by rejecting him. Further ridicule should be intolerable.

He pushed her between the shoulder blades so she stumbled.

"Are you so desperate for a woman that you have to force her at gunpoint?" she asked.

His teeth ground together. "I don't plan to kill you, but if you make it necessary, no one will hear anything during the fireworks."

She had to give him credit. It was a decent plan. But she had one of her own, so she pushed further. "What makes you incapable of attracting women? Insufficient . . . equipment?"

"I can have any woman I want." Billingsgate shoved her into a small alcove. The tall shrubs entombed a white marble bench. On the bench rested a coiled rope. "Pick it up."

A tendril of fear escaped her control and quivered through her like a discordant note on a violin. He'd planned this more carefully than she'd anticipated.

Billingsgate pulled a stack of banknotes out of his pocket and tossed it next to the rope. "I'm not unreasonable. That's five times the amount I would have paid any of the whores here. If you submit without any fuss, the money is yours. If not, then you forfeit the money and a good deal more blood."

Madeline snorted. "Did you actually believe that offer would work?"

"There's a small fortune sitting on that bench. Do you know what most whores would let me do for that much money?"

"Why would I want your small fortune when I can have a large one?" And she wasn't a whore. Her spine stiffened, muting the terror. Despite the fact she'd given herself that title a thousand times before, she no longer believed it. The money on the bench didn't tempt her. All she could think about was getting free so she could help Gabriel.

"I hoped you'd say that. Now hand me the rope."

She knocked it to the ground.

A cold smile flashed in the dark. "Pick it up."

She laughed. "Why? Do you need it to hold certain parts up?"

There was the metallic click of a hammer being drawn, and the gun emerged from his pocket.

Victory.

She bent over, but rather than reaching for the rope, she drew her knife. As it arced out of her hand with practiced precision, Billingsgate flinched toward a sound on the pathway. The knife embedded in the soft muscle of his shoulder rather than severing tendons.

Madeline swore as she lunged at him. She grabbed the barrel of the gun, twisting it toward him.

Billingsgate roared in pain as she wrenched the pistol away and tossed it into the bushes. His hand tangled in her hair. With a violent tug, he sent her sprawling on the ground. Madeline tried to scramble out of reach, but he was on top of her before she could roll away.

She slammed her knee upward but he blocked her with practiced precision. Pinning both her hands over her head with one of his, he forced himself between her legs.

Panic became a living thing, clawing inside her, robbing her of her breath. Madeline opened her mouth to scream, but his hand ground into her mouth, blocking the sound.

His eyes gleamed. "Who do you think will come for you? Your Runner? He's not coming for you anytime soon."

The thought of Gabriel gave her mind something to latch on to. Something to keep her sane. It gave her power to bide her time as Billingsgate pulled down her bodice and groped her breasts, pinching and twisting until she whimpered. She swallowed the bile rising in her throat, playing the details of her escape over and over in her mind—a technique she'd perfected.

His fingers fumbled with the buttons on his breeches. Lulled by her complacency, he released her in order to use both hands to unfasten them.

Madeline seized the opening, slamming the heel of her hand upward into his nose. Grabbing his ears, she twisted his head, rolling him off. Despite the white stars of pain exploding from the stitches on her stomach, she sprang to her feet.

She had to get to Gabriel.

But after a single step, Billingsgate's hand latched around her ankle and sent her sprawling in the dirt.

The first of the evening fireworks exploded overhead with a deafening rumble.

"Ah, how timely. Go ahead and scream."

A second burst of light illuminated a dark shape in the entrance to the alcove.

Gabriel.

He dove past Madeline and slammed his boot down on her attacker's wrist, allowing her to pull free. A flash of green exploded overhead, lighting Billingsgate's contorted scream.

Madeline scrambled to her feet. She allowed herself only a single deep breath to regain the strength in her knees before she returned to Gabriel's side.

Gabriel grabbed the man by his cravat and hauled him to his feet. "The two men you sent to find me were at a disadvantage. They feared making a scene. I have no such compunction."

Billingsgate clawed ineffectually at Gabriel's hand. "Let me go, damn you! How dare you lay a hand on me? I'm a peer of the realm."

Gabriel punched him. "Peers' necks stretch the same as anyone else's."

Madeline grabbed his arm. "He isn't the one, Gabriel. He doesn't know about Susan."

But if she expected his ire to lessen, she'd underestimated him.

Gabriel hauled him back to his feet with a growl. "Then the bastard will hang for touching you. Assault is a capital offense."

Despite the gasping sounds coming from his throat, Billingsgate scoffed. "What do you plan to do? A dozen gentlemen will testify she came with me willingly."

"I've made sure those same gentlemen know you tried to cheat them at this auction." Gabriel's smile would have done a hangman proud. "I'll see you in front of the magistrate. And I should warn you, he is quite fond of Madeline."

A flash of red illuminated Billingsgate's horror. The gentlemen who'd ignored his treatment of women wouldn't dream of tolerating a man who cheated. Even if he wasn't convicted, as a man who supported himself at the gaming tables, Billingsgate had just doomed himself to a life of poverty. Gabriel thrust Billingsgate away.

Stumbling, Billingsgate collapsed to his knees, clutching his mangled hand to his chest.

Her revenge would be more subtle. Flicking at the dirt on her dress and straightening the bodice, she laid her hand on Gabriel's arm. She swept Billingsgate a final look of disdain. Then she walked away without glancing back.

Billingsgate had lost. He'd lost so badly she didn't even fear him.

For a man like Billingsgate, that would be more painful than the broken wrist.

"Care to wager if he's there for you to arrest later?" she asked.

"The constables I sent for will see to that." Gabriel drew her down a side path.

Madeline paused. "He isn't the killer. He doesn't have a coach with a crest on it. And someone vouched for him being at the club. Unless there's something I missed. Tomorrow we can start—"

He caressed her cheek with the back of his hand. "Are you all right?"

She nodded, her voice stuck under the lump in her throat. She wanted to tell him what it felt like when he'd appeared out of the darkness to save her, but couldn't think of the words. And what few words she could think of, she didn't think she could say without humiliating amounts of tears. Under the cover of the rumble from the latest cluster of fireworks, she drew in a shuddering breath.

Gabriel cupped her chin. She flinched away, the touch of his hand and his compassion too much after Billingsgate.

Everything was too raw, too uncertain.

Gabriel must have understood. He stepped away without offering his arm. "You should go home."

"I have to be seen so my suitors don't think I disappeared with Billingsgate." But she stared down at her filthy, torn dress.

"Come away, Madeline. They're not worth it."

"No, I need to go back."

"Madeline—"

But Madeline ignored Gabriel and walked back toward the party. After a few seconds, Gabriel escorted her back to the party, retreating to his customary place behind her.

From the edge of the shadows, Madeline stared at the gathered crowd. Whether they'd been momentarily distracted by her absence or not, her suitors had quickly found solace in the arms of the other women.

Tonight she lacked the strength to hide from the truth. She didn't care about this anymore. The men or the auction. Not even the deliciously large amount of money she was about to throw away. "I am finished with this. Take me home, Gabriel."

Chapter Thirty

In the coach, Madeline perched stiffly in her seat across from Gabriel. Her eyes didn't waver from the hands clenched in her lap. With each jolt, Gabriel feared she'd shatter.

He should care more that he'd just lost his last suspect. And he did care. The failure simmered, dark and molten inside him. Yet he found he didn't care about that nearly as much as he cared about Madeline.

A passing streetlamp washed light across her emotionless features.

But she wasn't emotionless. He could see it in the white, bloodless color of her fingers and the tension in the muscles of her neck. He could hear it in the slight rasp that accompanied each measured breath.

After she'd flinched away in the garden, he'd thought it best to give her space.

But she looked so damned alone.

Gabriel hated the uncertainty dogging his thoughts. What could he say? How could he help her without driving her away? He should have been thrilled at her claim to no longer care about the auction. Instead, it worried him.

His heart beat with aching thuds. It wasn't normal for anyone to be so composed after a trauma like that. Not even a spy. She needed to let her emotions out before they splintered her to pieces.

He moved next to her, careful to keep from touching her. "Are you all right?"

She smiled her courtesan smile. "I can't remember when I've had such an exciting evening."

No. He wasn't about to let her retreat. "Billingsgate is a monster."

She drew against the wall of the coach, farther away. "He's not worth remembering." She unclenched her fists to wave her hand in what was, no doubt, meant to be an offhanded manner, but the tension in her arms reduced it to a jerky flick. Her hands stapled back together.

"But you do, don't you? I doubt you can get him out of your head. You'll feel better if you don't bottle him up inside there. Talk to me, Madeline. Trust me that much. Let me help you carry this."

Her mildly amused expression held fast.

Slowly, the expectant breath that Gabriel held deflated.

Give her space. Give her time, he reminded himself. Just because he could no longer deny his feelings didn't mean she felt the same.

Yet.

He'd woo her until she no longer doubted she was worth more than any amount of money.

Suddenly, Madeline twitched. The spasm came again, this time along with a pained inhale. A single tear glistened on her lower lashes until a desperate blink chased it over the edge and down her cheek.

To hell with giving her space. Gabriel pulled her into his arms.

A sob wracked her slender frame. "Curse you.

Why do you have to be so understanding and nice and—" Whatever else she was going to say drowned in a gulping breath. "I hate crying. I don't want to cry. I don't—" Her sobs started in earnest.

At first, Gabriel tried to catch her tears with his thumb, but there were far too many. Her body shook as if her soul were being harrowed up. She doubled over in his arms, her forehead resting on his thigh. She had to fight for each breath as if she were drowning.

What the devil had he been thinking? He knew nothing of what she'd experienced. He'd wanted her to feel better, not collapse under the torture of what Billingsgate had done. Gabriel continued to hold her, murmuring soothing nonsense over and over, cursing his own stupidity.

Finally, her head rested in his lap and her weeping eased.

He stroked back the tendrils of hair that clung to her damp cheeks. Never did he want her to go through that again. Never.

"Enough, Madeline. You said not to speak of ending the auction until I was ready to follow through. I'm ready now. End it."

Madeline jerked upright.

Not now. He couldn't speak of this now. Not when her defenses had been ripped into tattered shreds.

Her fine resolution at the party to end the auction was one thing. But it had been private. No one knew. Now Gabriel was asking her to admit her desires aloud. Ending the auction would be tantamount to declaring her feelings. Admitting her love would be handing him the most powerful weapon he could have over her. Did she trust him with it?

She felt as if she teetered on the edge of a cliff, and while flying for a few moments might be exhilarating, there'd be that horrific impact at the bottom. There always was.

Were the few seconds of joy worth it?

"We don't know who Susan's killer is." She refused to leap unless he was certain. "Our best bet is still Billingsgate. If it's not, there's a good chance the killer is one of my suitors. He was at the masquerade, after all. If I continue with the auction, perhaps we could find something."

"And give the killer another opportunity to hurt you. I'm not totally at a loss. Some suspects have been eliminated, and I have more clues now than I have ever had before, thanks to you. I'll track him based on those."

Madeline pushed away from him, wanting to see his face. "How do you intend to stop the auction?"

Gabriel's brows drew together. "Since talking sense into you has failed thus far, I'll drag you in front of the nearest clergyman and marry you."

Madeline suspected she resembled an owl, wide-eyed and skittish, but unable to do more than blink. Her heart battered her rib cage with audible thuds. Or maybe they were only audible because blood pounded in her ears as well. And in her cheeks. And fingers. Her entire body pulsed with a terrifying mixture of hope, joy, and pleasure. But even the deluge couldn't completely overcome her hard-learned caution.

"Why would you want me for your wife?" She nearly choked. "For the mother of your children?"

"Then I'd know you're safe."

That was hardly the answer she'd hoped for.

But then Gabriel exhaled harshly and dragged his hand through his hair. "And because you crowd my thoughts until I can think of nothing else. Of your wit and kindness. The way this eyebrow quirks slightly when you're bemused." He traced her right brow with his fingertip. "Your insistence on opposing me at every turn. Your bravery serving your country."

"That was hardly noble or disinterested. I did it to save my own life," she felt obligated to point out. For his sake, she should argue his suggestion of marriage.

"You could have disappeared after your first mission and never come back. But you didn't."

"Instead, I seduced other men."

"You did what you had to do to survive. I won't regret that." Gabriel covered her mouth when she would have spoken. "I'm a selfish beast. Even though I'm not overly wealthy like you desired, I want you for myself. I cannot stand the thought of a man claiming you who doesn't see past your beautiful face. In fact, I can't stand the thought of another man claiming you at all."

His fiercely possessive speech calmed some of her fears. Gabriel wasn't her father. "You told me you didn't want to marry," she said.

"My sister can't live her dream because a murderer stole the possibility from her. I'm done letting him steal my happiness, too."

He wanted her. Even knowing the darkness inside her, he still wanted her.

"Why did you leave the party before anyone saw you?" he asked.

She sucked in two deep breaths. Her heart shouted her answer—what she feared, and yet desired the most.

She loved him.

The words flitted like newly emerged butterflies in her mind, too fragile to speak aloud.

But she also couldn't deny them.

"I wanted to be with you," she whispered. Then Madeline tilted her face toward Gabriel. "There's an easier way to end this. I can't auction my virginity if I'm no longer a virgin."

Chapter Thirty-one

With a growl, Gabriel pulled Madeline into his lap, her hip nestling against his groin. But despite the possessiveness of his arms, his lips barely bushed hers.

But she wasn't in the mood for hesitation. She needed to be claimed. She needed to be entangled in his arms before she could remind herself of the hundred reasons that she was being a fool.

She twisted her fingers in his hair, the short strands sliding through her fingers as she tried to pull him down.

But he wouldn't allow himself to be tugged closer. "Are you sure about the auction? You're no doubt emotionally drained by the evening."

She nipped at his lower lip, trying to delay her answer, but although the muscles knotted across his shoulders, he didn't respond.

He truly cared about her response.

She smiled at him, feeling at once timid and emboldened. "I'm sure."

His mouth brushed hers, only to lift a second later. "Then you'll marry me?"

Yes! she wanted to shout.

But once she did, she'd be stripped bare. A quip with its oh-so-tempting protection escaped. "I don't know. There are many reasons I might be giving up the auction."

Gabriel glowered at her. "Such as?"

"Would you want to go to bed with Himbalt even for a fortune?"

Gabriel's mouth claimed hers. Tasting. Possessing.

His tongue stroked the seam of her lips, seeking entrance. She complied with a moan, drinking in the rich male flavor so uniquely his. If anything, it was more intoxicating this time. She'd thought that with the novelty gone, she'd be better able to control her response. But as his lips trailed down her neck, each kiss increased the tension inside her. It was as if her body felt not only the pleasure of these caresses but also the ecstasy from each previous one.

There was also comfort there, a familiarity that was as erotic as the physical sensations. She stilled, fearing the loss of her newly discovered belonging more than anything. For a woman who'd spent her life in constant upheaval, the emotion seemed far too fragile.

Gabriel pulled back, his finger tucked under her chin. "I'm obviously not doing my job. What are you thinking about?"

She stared breathlessly at him.

"I know your beauty and charm will always draw the admiration of other men." He cupped her face. "But I need to know that when we make love, my name will be the only one on your lips."

She clenched her teeth together to forestall her initial defensive sally. Gabriel deserved better from her. She could do this. "I'm yours, Gabriel. I want no one but you." The words emerged desperate and jumbled. But they had emerged, and that was the important part.

"You'll marry me?" he asked.

Madeline took a deep breath and plunged head-first off the cliff. "Yes."

She had only a brief second to glimpse the grin lighting his face before his lips seized hers. His tongue explored her mouth, as if he wanted to savor the taste of her as she did him.

Gabriel's finger gently brushed her breast. She'd been touched before, and yet it felt like nothing she'd ever experienced. Not even with Gabriel by the fountain. The protective layer she'd always covered herself in had been stripped away.

His touch felt more intense. More right.

His lips rubbed over the lace at the edge of her bodice where the delicate red fabric met her skin. Madeline's head tipped back. If his fingers felt like lightning, his lips set her ablaze. The hot throb that had started low in her stomach spread, flooding each nerve with blistering pleasure.

As the coach slowed to a halt, Gabriel placed a lingering, almost regretful kiss on her lips. "We probably shouldn't scandalize your neighbors."

She couldn't let him go. What if he came to his senses and realized his mistake in asking for her? She couldn't bear it. She needed the happiness to last just a few more moments. "Why not? This might be my last chance to shock anyone before I become a Runner's boring wife. I—"

"You think being married to me is going to be boring?" Gabriel flung open the door of the coach. His gaze didn't leave hers as he carried her past the man he'd assigned to watch the house.

Only as they passed her butler did he lift his head. "The auction is over, Canterbury."

Canterbury's voice was amused. "It's about time, sir."

Gabriel placed Madeline on her feet next to the bed and stepped back, afraid if he held her a moment longer, he'd devour her.

Madeline stood there as poised and regal as a virgin sacrifice. But a sultry gleam shone in her eyes. If she was a virgin sacrifice, she was looking forward to the ceremony.

"Madeline?"

Half of her mouth tilted upward. "I'm working on being respectable."

Gabriel lifted an eyebrow. "And how precisely does a respectable woman behave in the bedroom?"

"I'm not precisely sure, but from the complaints I have heard, I think it involves suffering nobly while you slake your base lusts."

Gabriel grimaced at the image. He'd give thanks every day he'd been spared from that fate. "Don't you dare."

Her bravado faded and she bit her lip. "I don't know if I *can* react like a respectable woman."

His heart twisted at the uncertainty on her face. To hell with the distance between them. Why did he keep thinking that would do any good at all? Gabriel wrapped his arms around her, resolving to keep her there. "You're passionate and responsive. It's part of who you are. And I quite like it."

"Truly?"

"Yes. And if you ever threaten to be respectable

again, I might have to take you over my knee." His hand splayed across the firm curve of her backside.

The tension eased from her spine and she squirmed against him. "Thank heavens. Being respectable was starting to irk me because I've been longing to do this all evening." She reached behind her back. The bodice of the gown dipped as she unfastened the buttons. The satin slid from her upper body but snagged where their hips pressed together.

He loosened his grip long enough to allow the gown to pool at her feet in a rustling whisper. Gabriel tugged on the laces that tied her stays and tossed that to the floor as well. Her shoes, stockings, and knife followed.

She wriggled her shoulders until the sleeves of her shift lost their tenuous hold. "As long as I'm not being respectable . . ."

Gabriel exhaled at the bruises starting to form on her chest. He ran his finger lightly over one and then traced the edge of the bandage at her waist, his jaw tightening. "I should have protected you better. Perhaps we should wait until—"

Madeline caught his finger and brought it to her lips. "Don't you dare stop. It doesn't hurt any longer." She laved her tongue over the pad of his finger, then slowly drew it into her mouth.

He searched her eyes for the truthfulness of her words. "Are you sure?" He needed to know that she truly wanted this. But more than that, he needed to know that she wanted it for the same reasons as he did. Not just because of the passion, but because he adored her, cherished her. Loved her.

She unbuttoned his jacket and slipped it off his shoulders. "Does that answer your question?"

No. Not the most important one. "Madeline, I don't want you to regret this."

For an instant, her emotions were as bare as her body. "I will never regret you."

As much as he desired her, he could have stood there, simply keeping his gaze locked with hers for the rest of the night, and never regretted a moment of it.

But Madeline wasn't content to wait. She skillfully stripped him of clothing, then led him to bed, falling back on it and pulling him with her.

Gabriel slanted his lips along the neat edge of her collarbone, careful to keep his weight off the bandage at her waist.

"Actually, I do have a regret."

Gabriel lifted himself so he could see her face.

She nipped him on the shoulder. "I regret not doing this earlier."

With a growl, he flicked his tongue gently over her taut nipple. "I wouldn't taunt me in bed." He moved to the other breast, relishing the way her hips shifted with each slow circle of his mouth. "You might find it's the one place I have the advantage."

Starting at her knees, he worked his fingers up the silken skin of her thighs until he finally reached the moist heat at their apex. Calling on years of self-restraint, he held his own desire in check as he slid his finger back and forth across the opening to her core. She arched into his hand, but he held back until her breath became broken gasps. Only then did he slip a finger inside her.

His name became a curse on her lips as he continued the same leisurely pace. "I swear I shall kill you for this, Gabriel. And that is no idle threat. I know quite a few ways to—"

He added another finger and then caressed the nub above it with his thumb. "You were saying?"

She moaned. "Nothing. I take it all back."

Every base male instinct told him that she was

ready and willing for him. But willing wasn't enough.

He wanted her begging. He wanted her stripped of any doubt that they both wanted this. More than food. More than air.

He replaced his hand with his mouth and Madeline screamed in climax, her fingers digging into his hair as she thrust madly against his questing tongue.

Gabriel reveled in each cry, the sounds of her ecstasy dragging over him like a physical caress.

When her hips stilled, her hand moved immediately to his straining shaft. "I need you inside me now."

He paused at the urgency in her voice. "We don't need to rush this."

She gripped him in her hand, adding pleasure to pleasure as her fingers played over him. "Yes, now."

But there hadn't been time for the pleasure to build in her again. This wasn't passion driving her desperation.

"What's wrong?"

She guided him to her slick center. "Does it matter? We both want this."

So much that he was questioning his sanity. But if she had any hesitation at all, he needed to know. "It matters to me."

She writhed, the motion sliding him across her tight entrance, but he wouldn't yield to his need to thrust forward. Not yet.

"Madeline, tell me. You're to be my wife."

"Only until you change your mind!"

Her anguish echoed through him. He rolled to his side and cradled her against him, his fingers tracing the lines of worry on her face. "You don't need this to bind me. I choose you. Freely. Completely. You will be my wife if I make love to you now or if you make me wait until I'm eighty."

Her eyes closed, and a tear dripped down her temple

and into her hair. When she opened her eyes, the fear was gone. She smiled as she dragged her finger across his lips. "Even if I make you wait until you're eighty?"

"Yes."

She pressed him on his back and slid on top of him, straddling him, bringing him the barest fraction inside her. "Eighty?"

Gabriel groaned. "I sincerely hope it's sooner."

She shuddered as she rubbed against him. "It was an empty threat."

He slid his hand between her legs, stroking until the flush spread again over her face and neck and her eyes bored desperately into his.

"Please, Gabriel. Please."

She would never regret giving herself to him. He would make sure of it.

He gently lifted her back under him and thrust his hips forward.

Madeline blinked at the new sensation. The momentary flash of pain hadn't made her flinch. She was used to pain. However, this feeling of fullness was interesting. It burned slightly as if she were being stretched too far, but there was also a small frisson of pleasure. Curious, Madeline swiveled her hips, experimenting.

If this had been a man from the auction, she would have been tossing about, panting and pretending to find pleasure while the man grunted and hammered into her. Instead, Gabriel poised above her holding himself perfectly still, every tendon standing at attention, sweat shimmering on his brow, while she learned to find pleasure in their joining.

She loved him.

Her chest ached with the weight of the words, and she almost found the strength to speak them aloud. Almost.

Madeline dragged her finger down Gabriel's chest to where their bodies joined. He shuddered as if with fever, and that small reaction chased away any residual discomfort. She shifted again, pressing herself upward. This time the motion brought a blissful moan to her lips that she didn't bother hiding. She lifted her hips again, filling herself completely.

Gabriel spoke through clenched teeth. "I was trying to go slow."

Madeline dug her fingers into his buttocks when he started to pull away, drawing him even closer, desperate not to lose the sparking tension inside her. "I don't want to go slow."

He nipped her earlobe. "Then you'll have to let go. Trust me, Madeline."

As her fingers unclenched, he began to move. She couldn't breathe for a few heartbeats. Couldn't think. And the glorious thing was, she didn't have to.

She abandoned herself to being loved by Gabriel and to loving him in return. The first time in the garden had been about pleasure; this was about love. Being cherished. She raked her hands over his back as hot, shattering sensations consumed her.

Ecstasy slammed through her, each wave more powerful than the last. She cried out Gabriel's name until the deep, throbbing bliss robbed her of her voice.

Gabriel tensed above her, thrusting deep and hard as he found his own satisfaction with a cry. After a moment, he collapsed on the bed next to her, pulling her tight against his chest before planting a kiss on the nape of her neck.

In the safety of his arms, as her eyes drifted shut, she took the biggest risk of her life. "I love you, Gabriel."

Chapter Thirty-two

When the mattress shifted suddenly in the darkness, Madeline grabbed for her knife. Even before her hand found her bare ankle, she'd realized it was Gabriel, turning in his sleep.

Gabriel's hand stroked her back. "You're not asleep," he said, his own voice remarkably clear and alert.

"Neither are you."

His hand skimmed over her waist. "Regrets?"

Madeline enjoyed his touch. "No." And she didn't. At least not precisely. She didn't regret making love to Gabriel for an instant. She didn't doubt Gabriel would make some woman a fine husband. She didn't fear in the least that he'd be like her father.

What she feared was her ability to be his wife.

Her first instinct in the middle of the night was to reach for her knife. What did she know about planning menus or mending socks or whatever it was wives did all day?

Gabriel's arms encircled for her again, pulling her against him. Madeline sighed and settled against the hard muscles of his chest. As he lifted the rumpled linen sheet over them, warding off the chill, his hands skimmed light and nearly weightless over her. When she would have sought out his lips, he stopped her. "I haven't had the chance to hold you. And if you move, I won't be able to resist ravishing you."

Madeline smiled. She wasn't used to being coddled, but it turned out to be quite pleasant.

She could make this work, couldn't she? Of course she'd responded the way she had when startled. The need for survival had been ingrained in her. Last night had changed her status as a virgin, not her past as a spy.

Neither had it changed her overactive brain.

"What are your plans for the investigation?"

"I think we need to go back to the beginning."

The *we* in his statement was the most romantic thing he could have said. Then she frowned. Shouldn't she be worrying about him? Nagging him about being careful? But how in the blazes could she be expected to do that when she intended to be at his side? The doubts about her ability to be a good wife returned to the edges of her thoughts. "Perhaps your witness was wrong about seeing the man before. Perhaps he wasn't the father of one of the students," she said quickly.

Gabriel nodded against her hair. "Or perhaps he was drunk and drew the wrong thing on the paper. I know. I've been playing through every possible option. Your life is still in danger and I have no bloody idea who is threatening you." His voice was harsh, at odds with his gentle hands at her waist. "I cannot shake the fear that I won't know who the murderer is until he has his hands around your throat."

Madeline hoped the bastard tried. She knew a few tricks she'd like to show him.

"I was too damned sure of myself this time. Perhaps Potts was right after all."

"Potts is a dolt."

That elicited a short bark of laughter from Gabriel. "You don't even know what he said."

"If it wasn't praising your incredible skill, he is a dolt."

Gabriel's lips found the sensitive spot at the base of her neck.

"You said the drawing was only a rough outline," she said.

Gabriel shifted as if to rise, then stilled. "The drawing is in my study at home. Otherwise I'd show you." The arms around her were tense, the sated languor was gone.

There was as little chance of his going to sleep now as there had ever been for her. "Your house isn't far, is it?"

His breath hitched for a moment.

"It's only, what, ten minutes?"

Gabriel exhaled. "Don't you mind me dragging you from your bed before dawn?"

Madeline grinned, climbing from the bed. "Who is the first one up?"

Gabriel groaned, his eyes swept her naked body with renewed hunger. "Remind me very quickly why we're getting out of this bed."

"The sketch." Positioning herself in the lone beam of moonlight filtering through the curtains, she slowly bent to retrieve her shift from the floor. While she might doubt her suitability as a wife, she knew her power as a woman. With Gabriel watching, the slide of satin going onto her skin was as sensual as it was coming off.

Gabriel swore. "We'll go in the morning."

Madeline peered at him from under her lashes. "We still have the entire carriage ride over."

Gabriel's snort of laughter sounded remarkably

anguished. "How long until we can have the coach here?"

By the time they had dressed, Canterbury had roused her coachman and arranged for the vehicle to be brought around.

Once inside, Gabriel settled her on his lap. He traced the bridge of her nose with his finger. "You look beautiful in this." He grinned and fingered the lace barely covering her breasts. "But I like you even more without it."

A horseman cantered past the coach.

Madeline had already straightened and slid from Gabriel's lap before she remembered she no longer cared what other men thought.

Gabriel studied her, his face suddenly serious. "No regrets about last night?"

"I already said no." Madeline shifted and yanked her twisted skirts free. "My reaction to the horseman was habit, nothing more." Another remnant of her training she'd have to free herself from.

His gaze searched hers. "We'll work on that."

She was glad the darkness hid the embarrassment in her cheeks. How many more things about her would she need to change?

Madeline peered out of the window with curiosity as the coach slowed. She'd expected Gabriel to have a bachelor's flat somewhere. Instead, the coach stopped in front of a charming row house.

The inside was decorated in dark woods and muted tones; the darkness hid the exact color. But despite the obvious care that had been taken by a housekeeper, the room managed to look unused.

"You aren't here much, are you?"

"Not in the past."

Madeline trailed her hand up a carefully polished railing as she climbed the stairs. What would she do while Gabriel was out apprehending criminals? She would have been faced with excess time after finishing the auction as well, but this seemed much more real. More worrisome.

What if she grew restless? Missed her life as a spy and the freedom she'd grown accustomed to? She loved Gabriel, but what if that wasn't enough?

She followed Gabriel into his study. He lit several candles, the flickering yellow glow revealing a desk covered in stacks of folders three-deep. But despite the number of files, the piles were neat and Gabriel showed no hesitation in selecting the one he wanted.

Madeline stood at the window and checked the street while he opened the pasteboard folder. "This room has a nice view of the street."

"You should see the perspective from my bedroom."

"You could just ask me up there."

"It actually has a clear view of the entire block."

She eyed the massive amount of information. "Let's start at the beginning."

Systematically, she began to question everything they knew about the Simm murder, ensuring she wasn't lacking any important details. Every person he'd spoken to. Every room he'd searched. Soon, Gabriel had dragged two chairs over to the desk so they could delve into the documents more easily. Finally, with the first light of dawn seeping in the window, she paused, rubbing ink-smudged fingers over her bleary eyes. "I'm not driving you mad, am I?" she asked.

He surveyed her with bemused fascination. "No, you're keeping me sane."

Madeline looked down at her notes again to hide the warm pleasure from his words.

"You shouldn't have carried Susan's case on your own for so long."

"It is my responsibility."

Madeline traced her finger along the crease in his brow. "Now it is mine as well. Where is the drawing you found?"

Gabriel pulled out a half sheet of paper.

Something about it— "The coachman didn't draw this."

Gabriel jerked forward. "What?"

"The handwriting. This was written by the same man who left me the note."

"You are certain?" He swore. "The murderer intended for me to find it. And I was so damned desperate I didn't even question it. I am too close."

"You aren't desperate. You're determined. Passionate. Thorough."

"Not thorough enough."

"I never showed you my note. Besides, if you hadn't insisted on continuing to investigate this case, no one would have made the connection between this sketch and the note threatening me. It is only because you were so dedicated that we found the truth."

"But I wasted far too much time investigating the wrong man. While all that time one of your bidders might be— Bloody hell. Your bid book."

She stared at him.

"All your bidders signed the book. We can compare the writing on your note and the drawing to the signatures in the book."

Thirty minutes later, they were huddled in the coach over the ledger. The first three pages of names didn't look at all familiar.

"He might have disguised his writing," Gabriel said.

Madeline nodded. "But there are usually traits they don't think to hide, like how hard they press the quill. The spacing of their letters."

She turned the page. It had to be one of the men who had come to the auction late— She slammed her hand over the entry. Some wild impulse made her want to tear the page from the book so Gabriel would never see it.

"My father?'" Both words were hoarse.

"No!" She took a deep breath and moved her hand.

Madeline stared at the writing that perfectly matched the letters in the drawing beside her.

The Earl of Danbury.

Chapter Thirty-three

*Everything about Gabriel was wrong, from his posture to the cold stillness of his hand as he took the ledger from her.

"Danbury's the killer," she said. The odds someone had used his handwriting to forge the other notes was low. After all, the killer might have found out that Billingsgate was one of the suspects, but Danbury was never under the slightest suspicion. "His name wasn't on the list of men who had children at the school."

"A few of the children are paid for anonymously. Or perhaps he'd met Miss Simm somewhere else. Bourne must have recognized him when I came to question him at the tavern. That's why he fled. I led the killer right to my witness." Gabriel was silent for a few moments, but when he spoke, his voice was harsh. "Hell, and I'll bet he never saw Billingsgate near the school. That was just another misdirection."

"How will we prove it was Danbury?" Only belatedly did she·realize that her words should have been ones of comfort. Perhaps she should have offered a faint hope that they were mistaken. But the lie hadn't occurred to her. Both of them had seen too much of life to believe it.

Or should she have railed at Danbury, decrying his betrayal? Yet that wouldn't have served a purpose, either. Her words would only be a pale mockery of Gabriel's feelings.

Instead, she took a silent breath and gave him the only thing she could. "I'm finishing the auction."

Gabriel's gaze jerked to hers. "Like hell you are. I'm not letting you anywhere near him."

"The auction is the only reason he's in London. If I end it now, he might get suspicious and leave for the West Indies where you cannot touch him."

The deep lines bracketing his mouth barely moved as he spoke. "I don't have to arrest him to stop him."

She was too experienced to show her shock, but she couldn't keep it from chilling her veins. "Or you can let me go through with the auction and use the time to find the proof to force the magistrate to order his arrest." The thought of Danbury's hands on her made her stomach clench until she couldn't breathe, but she'd learned to tuck her preferences out of the way for the greater good.

Gabriel's hand cupped her cheek. "You may have been forced to use your body on behalf of your country, but I refuse to let you do the same for me. You're to be my wife. I won't share you with another. Not ever."

Madeline's throat burned. No one had ever hesitated to use her for his own ends. "I won't go through with it, only make him think I am going to."

"It's still too dangerous. We have to assume from his threats he plans to kill you after the auction."

"I'm used to risk."

"But I'm not used to risking you."

She blinked away the annoying tears in her eyes. "What will you do?"

"I'll shoot him."

"So you can hang for killing a peer?" Her voice rose more than she would have liked.

Gabriel cupped her face. "That scares you more than facing a murderer who wants you dead?"

Yes. She'd faced murderers before. She'd never faced losing the man she loved.

The rage in Gabriel's eyes dimmed as he stared into hers. "I'll try to have him arrested before I attempt anything else."

He wasn't promising not to kill Danbury. She couldn't ignore the omission. "But if you cannot?"

"I will do what needs to be done." He loosened the pins in her hair and sifted it through his fingers. "I tortured myself for years for not listening to Susan when she wanted to tell me about her suitor. Now I find I introduced her to the bastard." The muscles along his jaw bunched. "He's killed at least four people already. I know my duty."

The trouble was, she understood. Her mind recognized his determination even if her heart did not.

But Gabriel had spent most of his life seeking justice. To kill a man in cold blood—even if it was a man he hated, a man who deserved to die—wouldn't be something he could hide. He'd turn himself in and walk without protest to the gallows.

She'd kill Danbury herself before she'd let that happen.

But it wouldn't come to that. She wouldn't let it. "He won't have a chance to kill anyone else." She couldn't offer comfort, but she could give Gabriel something better. A plan to catch the monster. Slowly, her thoughts fell into place.

The thoughts coursed through her, stirring uncertainty in her chest. She'd been so sure she needed to give up the characteristics she'd developed as a spy. But what if they weren't the hindrance she thought?

What if her life as a spy wasn't something she had to reject but rather something she could build upon?

She stared at his resolute face and then placed a kiss on the hand that still pressed possessively on her cheek.

Gabriel would never approve of the plan.

She was tempted not to tell him. To let him discover her plan only after it was in motion. After all, a spy didn't reveal her intentions to anyone, let alone the person most likely to derail them.

She was no longer a spy.

But how brave was the woman without that façade?

The question resonated deep within her. Could she trust him to believe in her?

She was about to find out. "I have a plan."

Chapter Thirty-four

Madeline lounged on the polished oak counter at Naughton's, her crossed legs exposing a fair amount of silk-clad calf.

With slow deliberation, she inched up her skirts to her knees. "My hem rises with the bids."

The crowd howled encouragement to where Danbury, Lenton, and Wethersly hunched next to the betting book. The ledger rested untouched for several minutes until the cheers of the crowd got the better of Wethersly. He snatched the ledger and increased his bid. That set off a flurry of movement as the other two fought over the right to outdo him.

While everyone's attention focused on the bidders, she scanned the room again, using her carefully selected vantage point to see over everyone's heads to the entrance.

Gabriel still wasn't here.

Madeline turned her attention back to the men overflowing the gaming hell. Sensible black coats rubbed against puce and lemon as men shouldered their way forward for a better view. Only Naughton's burly footmen kept the crowd from sending her tumbling back over the edge of her wooden perch.

Madeline tugged on her skirts again, this time to keeping her fingers from tensing and betraying her nerves. She'd only ever run one mission with Gabriel, so why did she so keenly feel the lack of him now?

She glanced at the gold pocket watch that had been donated by one of the men standing near to her. Five minutes remained on the auction.

She could wait no longer to put her plan into action.

Madeline slid off the counter and glided toward Lenton. She rolled her shoulders, drawing his attention to her barely contained bosom, then dragged her finger down the valley between her breasts. Lenton's lips slackened and his eyes took on that slightly protruding look.

Yet rather than approaching him, she wandered toward Wethersly, letting her backside brush across his thigh. Breath wheezed out of the older gentleman, and if she hadn't known his reputation, she would have feared he was suffering an apoplexy.

"Sweet heavens, I cannot wait to get out of this dress." Tugging on the fabric of her bodice, she provided both gentlemen an unobstructed view down her dress.

Lenton nearly knocked the ink to the floor in his haste to grab the book. The crowd shouted encouragement. Wethersly puffed in outrage and reached for the book at the same time as Danbury.

Madeline flounced directly into Danbury's path, blocking him. "Do say you are about to bid again." She placed her hand on his cheek. Her first three fingers aligned with the scars on his cheek, the pale marks suddenly infinitely more ominous than they'd been the week before.

She trapped the fear lacing through her veins and twisted it into anger. Yet she kept both emotions from her face as Danbury's hands slid down her arms and lifted her from his path. "Of course I'll bid. I planned to win all along."

As Danbury moved past her, she felt the humming awareness of Gabriel's eyes on her. Silly, when a hundred men fixated on her like starving dogs, but the sensation tingled down her spine.

He was here.

In response to her beseeching smile, one of the footmen placed her back onto the counter. She searched the crowd until she found Gabriel. He stood by the main entrance, speaking with a dark-haired Runner.

After the other man hurried outside, Gabriel strode to her side and pulled the watch from her fingers. His hand slid over hers in a gentle contact that was far too brief.

"Where were you?" Madeline asked.

"There was something I had to take care of." He turned to the crowd. "Five seconds remain."

"There's—" Madeline stopped. It hardly mattered if he ended the auction ten seconds early.

She started the count. "Five . . . four . . ."

Lenton tried to wrest the book from Danbury, but Danbury blocked him with his forearm.

Danbury grinned. "Trust me. It's for your own good."

Wetherly stood back, the wrinkles on his face rearranged into angry slashes, but he didn't try to fight the book from the younger, larger man.

The crowd joined in on cue. "Three . . . two . . . one!" They surged forward, straining to see the unassuming black leather book.

Gabriel held out his hand and Danbury passed him the book. After a quick jotted note at the bottom, Gabriel tore the page free and held it high. "Earl of Danbury wins."

The gathered men erupted into cheers, pounding congratulatory fists on Danbury's back and onto the bar. The wooden planks under Madeline vibrated with the celebration. Wethersly stomped away, his lips clearly forming a few choice blasphemies. Lenton, on the other hand, blindly accepted a tankard of half-finished ale and gulped it without pause.

Danbury's arm snaked around Madeline's waist, the weight of his embrace tight and controlling. "Well, gentlemen, I'll take this creature off your hands."

The crowd shouted its approval, peppering it with ribald suggestions for deflowering her.

"You're free, too, Huntford," Danbury said.

Gabriel folded the page with crisp lines, then tucked it in his waistcoat. The muscle at his jaw twitched, but when he looked up, his gaze was empty. "Actually, I'm required to see to the matter of payment first."

Madeline had to raise her voice to be heard. "Shall we go somewhere a little more private?" She tipped her head toward the door leading outside.

Thirty minutes later, Gabriel and Danbury stood around a desk in her study.

Danbury wrote his bank draft with a flourish. Gabriel examined it, then nodded. "I will see this delivered to your bank, Madeline. Good day." With a bow, and without a glance back, he left. His step echoed through the front hall and down the front stair.

Danbury pulled aside the curtain and watched him leave, then with a slow smile he turned to her, his eyes gleaming with anticipation.

The lighter notes of Madeline's laugher floated over the deeper murmur of Danbury's voice.

Maddox's heavy hand on his shoulder was the only thing that kept Gabriel from charging back into the study.

"Fine, but let's share a drink before we depart," Madeline was saying.

The heavy wooden door muffled Danbury's reply.

This was insanity. Hadn't he learned his lesson with Billingsgate? He shouldn't have let her out of his sight.

"If you don't let her do this, she'll find some way to do it on her own," Maddox said.

That was the reason Gabriel had agreed. He knew what she was capable of. But he had insisted on some modification of her plan. Despite her protests, he'd be there to protect her the entire time.

As Madeline's voice whispered through to the adjoining parlor where Gabriel waited, his hand dropped to the doorknob.

"—in Paris?" Madeline was asking. Glass clinked as she poured drinks.

Gabriel's hand tightened on the smooth brass.

"I haven't been to Paris in a long time." Danbury's response was lazy and unconcerned.

"Really? I could have sworn I saw you there. At a ball."

"Well, I hate to contradict a lady, but you're mistaken." The first note of suspicion entered his tone.

Gabriel gave Maddox a curt nod, and with serpentine grace, Madeline's friend slipped from the room.

With a slow exhale, Gabriel forced the knots from his shoulders.

"I hear you saved young Evans from that fortune hunter that had latched her claws into him," Madeline said.

Danbury's voice regained its swagger. "We gentlemen need to look out for each other."

"Women apparently do, too. Did you hear they found a girl strangled two weeks ago? And she was a decent girl, a teacher. They think the murderer might have other victims."

"Not everyone is as decent as they appear," Danbury said.

Gabriel twisted the knob silently and pressed it forward the merest fraction. Danbury had begun to realize he was being purposefully interrogated.

As they'd planned.

"Surely you heard about it," Madeline said.

"No."

"But you've been to all the places where the murdered women were found."

"You *do* remember, you little liar."

Madeline gasped in pain.

Gabriel exploded through the door, his pistol already in his hand. Danbury held a fistful of Madeline's hair; her body was bent backward at a painful angle.

The gun was supposed to be used for effect, but it was loaded. Gabriel barely kept his finger from tightening on the trigger.

Danbury yanked Madeline against him and clamped his hand around her throat. "Ah, Huntford, I feared you'd be behind this."

"Let her go," Gabriel ordered.

"And allow you to blow out my brains? I don't think so. Drop it."

Gabriel hesitated. Madeline had told him he mustn't appear to give in easily. Danbury had to believe he'd won. She could handle whatever Danbury decided to do to her.

Madeline's face darkened under the constriction on her neck. Her chest convulsed as she tried to breathe, rapid spasms across her ribs and stomach.

Enough. Gabriel dropped the gun.

"Kick it under the desk."

Danbury released Madeline. As she sucked in a rasping breath, he drew his own gun from his jacket and pointed it at her. "Sit, Huntford."

When Gabriel hesitated, Danbury cocked the gun. Gabriel sat.

"Get your rope." Danbury thrust her forward. "Did you think I wouldn't notice that you had one hidden under the table?"

Madeline walked with small, halting steps to the rope.

"Let her go. Your quarrel is with me, Danbury."

Although Danbury's attention wavered from Madeline, his gun did not. "Quarrel? I have no quarrel with you."

"You killed my sister."

Danbury shook his head wearily. "All I've done is protect my friends from trollops."

"My sister was no trollop."

"I thought well of her, too, until I chanced upon her in the park. She flirted like a shameless hussy. On our second outing, she panted while I put my hand in her bodice."

Only the gun pointed at Madeline kept him in his chair. The perverted bastard. "You took advantage of her. Then you killed her for it?"

Danbury shifted slightly. "I never said I killed her. Only that she pretended to be a virgin when clearly she was not. It was a test and she failed."

"You had no right to judge."

"No right to judge a woman trying to dupe me?" Danbury sounded like a tutor who'd been given a particularly foolish student.

"You're the liar."

"No, Madeline and others like her are." His eyes were wide and earnest as he waved his gun at Madeline. "Can't you see that? She isn't a virgin. None of them are, yet they try to trick you into believing it. And she's worse than all the others. Flaunting it. She almost succeeded in bamming all of London. The brightest minds produced by Oxford and Cambridge, felled by a harlot."

But Gabriel didn't believe his noble claims for a moment. "If you were trying to protect your friends, you'd be killing women of your own rank. Loose women fill the ballrooms of London. Instead, you pick poor women on the fringes of society without powerful families to protect them."

Danbury's lips thinned. "I never said I killed anyone. But no man deserves to discover that his intended is a whore. That she gave herself to a bloody footman. That she thinks a tearful confession will spare her."

Gabriel stilled. The earl's fiancée. Hell, he'd helped Danbury drink himself into oblivion over her death.

Madeline spun to Danbury. "You know I'm not a virgin, so perhaps I can tempt you to let me go—"

Danbury's eyes filled with triumph and he met Gabriel's gaze over Madeline's head. "No, the only thing that tempts me is saving some poor soul from you in the future. Now tie him."

Angry red fingerprints encircled Madeline's throat as she walked toward Gabriel. Her hands shook as she secured his wrists behind the chair. That might have been an act, but when her hand clasped his for the briefest moment, her palms were damp. Even she couldn't have feigned that.

She was frightened.

Madeline's plan was a good one, but he was finished allowing her to risk herself.

No matter what Madeline thought, she was far more important than bringing Danbury to justice. Gabriel let the small knife slip from the sleeve of his jacket into his palm, and began to cut through the knot she'd just securely tied.

Chapter Thirty-five

"So what now?" Madeline lightened her breathing to frightened pants. The rapid tempo of her heart, however, didn't have to be exaggerated.

She could guess with great accuracy what Danbury would do, but there was always uncertainty.

Danbury's expression was a mixture of satisfaction and distrust. "Now I check the knots you tied."

Madeline slid an inch closer to the door.

"Don't move," Danbury ordered. "The gun is still trained on you."

She stopped with a jerk. She didn't think he'd use the gun. Given his record, she suspected he planned to mete out his more personal form of justice. But her goal was to maintain whatever illusion he chose to hold. The man had approached her twice to threaten her. He must be eager on some level for her to know the truth. She just needed to make him feel empowered enough to share. "Just let me go. Please."

Danbury smiled as he walked over to Gabriel, his gait measured. It wasn't the swagger of a man who knew he'd won, it was the careful approach of a man who'd spent years protecting himself. Yet he still thought he had them in his control, which placed him squarely in hers.

And he still had no idea what she had really been doing in Paris.

He was about to find out. She just needed to lull him a touch more.

"If you're trying to rid the world of liars and cheats, why do you only harm defenseless women?" Gabriel asked with a taunting smile.

Danbury stopped.

She frowned. What was Gabriel doing? Danbury wouldn't calm completely until he'd checked the knots. Besides, she was supposed to be the one facing the barrel of Danbury's pistol. -

"It bothers me that you misunderstand why your sister had to die. Just trust me when I say I am doing you a favor by freeing you from Madeline."

She tried to quell Gabriel with her gaze, but he continued to press. "You have no reason for this other than your sick enjoyment."

Danbury shook his head slowly. "You haven't seen what it does to a man to live with a whore. You never saw the mockery my father faced because of his slatternly wife. Did you know she had a daughter? She even had the audacity to give birth to the whelp. Flaunting the fact that she made him a cuckold. At least he had the sense to make her get rid of it. I visited the school a few times to make sure the girl was being raised with morals. But a few weeks ago, I found her teacher was eager to welcome any man with a cock into her bed. "

The last piece fell into place. Danbury's connection to the school. His name hadn't been on Gabriel's list because the girl had been placed in the school by her mother and probably anonymously at that. The

killer hadn't been a father of one of the students. He
was a half brother.

She moved toward the door again. Even if Gabriel
had decided on new tactics, she still needed to play
her role.

And draw that blasted gun away from him.

She took another step, and the gun swung back
toward her.

"Let Madeline go," Gabriel repeated.

"Let her go? She is the worst liar of them all. I
have a duty to remove her." His words were all the
more chilling for his calm.

"Stop with the delusions. You could have discred-
ited her if you wanted to. But you didn't. You want
this, you sick bastard. Who do you think they will
blame when they find her body?"

Danbury pointed his gun at Gabriel's head, his
finger notching back the trigger. "They won't find
where I leave her body. Not like the others. She
doesn't deserve to be remembered as a virgin."

That was close enough to the confession she
awaited. Madeline lunged for the door, her hand
grasping the handle, commanding the gun's attention again.

"You will be leaving with me soon enough."

"Like hell she will." Gabriel exploded from the
chair.

Danbury flailed the pistol in Gabriel's direction.

Not part of the plan! Madeline abandoned the
door as she leaped toward them, drawing her knife.
It flew from her fingers even as she knew it would
never reach them in time.

The deafening sound of the gunshot exploded in
the parlor.

But it was Danbury who stumbled backward, Gabriel at his throat. Her knife clattered harmlessly to the ground as Gabriel landed on top of Danbury and slammed his fist into his jaw.

Danbury swung his pistol, catching Gabriel in the side of the head and using the momentum to switch their positions.

A good Englishman would let Gabriel handle his own fight. A good Englishwoman would probably swoon.

Madeline kicked Danbury in the head.

His head snapped sharply to the side.

Gabriel didn't hesitate, using the advantage to flip him onto his stomach.

Danbury tried to buck Gabriel off, to no avail. "You have no proof. It will be the word of a bastard Runner and a whore against mine. No one will listen."

"Wrong," Gabriel said. Madeline retrieved the rope and tossed it to him. "I spoke to the captain of your ship. He verified that you were in Paris two years ago. And I imagine that after my inquiries, we will soon have reports of other dead women around your family's plantation."

"Women die all the time."

Gabriel's eyes narrowed to feral slits as he lashed the earl's arms together. "You left physical evidence as well. The night rails you used for my sister and Molly Simm are the same as the ones you gave to the lightskirts at Lady Aphrodite's."

Madeline blinked. She'd forgotten Lady Aphrodite had mentioned Danbury's habit of bringing new night rails for the women he slept with. Recreating his victories, no doubt.

Danbury paled. "There are thousands of plain garments like that all over London."

"No, there aren't. I've looked. You forget that

most women cannot afford even simple embroidery, let alone three pearl buttons."

"You planted the evidence. Everyone knows you've hated the aristocracy since your sister died."

Madeline returned to the door, half expecting to be struck down for the amount of unholy satisfaction that filled her. "I thought you might be fool enough to try something like that." She threw open the study door, revealing the appalled faces of Lenton, Wetherly, and also half a dozen men who hadn't participated in her auction. Ian and Clayton stood behind them, their faces carefully neutral.

Danbury kicked his legs in an attempt to stand. "It was a trap, surely you all can see—"

No sympathy entered the assembled faces.

As Gabriel hauled Danbury to his feet, a somber Canterbury escorted Jeremiah Potts and several burly constables into the room.

"Huntford! Stop mauling that gentleman."

"That gentleman just confessed to murder." A man stepped forward looking as though he'd been interrupted in the middle of dressing. His waistcoat was unbuttoned and his cravat missing. He stepped to the front of the men.

Madeline studied him. Something about him was familiar, but she couldn't recall seeing him in London.

Because she hadn't. She had seen a much grimier version of him training Greek rebels on the streets of Constantinople.

"And who are you?" demanded Potts.

"The Duke of Abington."

Potts sputtered and lumbered into an awkward bobbing bow. "I beg your pardon, Your Grace. What are you waiting for?" he asked the constables. "Seize the murderer and take him to prison."

"You might want to check his pockets before leaving," Madeline said.

One of the Runners reached in Danbury's pocket and pulled out a brooch containing her hair. No one listened to his sputtered protests as he was forced from the room.

Potts questioned the assembled men. Following the duke's example, the gentlemen were quick to condemn Danbury.

Madeline used the chaos to attach herself to Gabriel's side. She needed to throw herself into his arms. She needed to rub her cheek on his chest and hear his heart beat. Then she needed to hit him for not following her plan.

"We were supposed to lure him into confessing, not provoke it out of him."

"You were nearly strangled. It was my turn to bear the risk."

"You weren't supposed to fight him," she whispered. "I was just supposed to throw open the door."

"He made the mistake of pointing his gun at you again."

"That was my intention."

"*My* intention was to keep you alive. I didn't know what he'd do when you opened that door. There was no way in hell I was going to let him have a chance to shoot you."

"If you'd followed my plan, you wouldn't be bleeding," she reminded him.

"Or nearly as satisfied." Gabriel drew a handkerchief from his pocket and pressed it against his cut cheek. "At least for once, you aren't the one bleeding."

The inches that separated them were still too much. She tried to content herself with the heat of him warming the skin of her arm. The slightly quickened sound of his breath.

But she wasn't content.

She wouldn't be until she placed kisses on every inch of his uninjured body. But for now, a slight step brought her hand against his thigh. He shifted toward her, increasing the contact.

The dark-haired Runner from Naughton's entered the room and went directly to Gabriel. "The night rails from Lady Aphrodite are a match to the ones from the murder."

Madeline felt her eyes grow wide. "That was a bluff?"

Gabriel shrugged. "Not anymore." He nodded to the other man. "Thank you, Coulter. I believe Potts might appreciate your help taking statements."

As Coulter left, Ian sauntered over to join them. "Only you would be smiling during a murder investigation, Madeline."

As much as she loved Ian, she wanted to throw him and every other person that wasn't Gabriel from the room. Using great willpower, she said, "I expected you all to burst in at the gunshot."

"On the contrary I had to use all my talents of persuasion to keep them from fleeing. Well, except for Abington. But I told him to wait for your sign."

"Abington is a duke?"

"I know. Fortunate, was it not? I was shocked to see him strolling into White's."

"Strolling into White's?" Madeline glanced pointedly at his undressed state and rather bloodshot eyes. The man didn't look entirely well.

"Well, that's probably where he was going eventually. I owed him a favor."

"That you repaid by dragging him to witness a murder confession?" Gabriel asked.

Ian sighed dramatically. "If you put it like that, I suppose I owe him another one."

"Thank you for your help," Madeline said.

Ian looked away. "Anything for you, little one." But then he grinned. "Although now *you* owe me a favor, as long as we are mentioning such things."

"I'll owe you two if you can clear this room of everyone save Gabriel and myself in under ten minutes."

Ian bent as if picking up a gauntlet. Nine minutes later, he winked as he ushered the last of the men from the room.

Madeline didn't even wait for the door to shut before she twined her hands around Gabriel's neck and pulled him to her. Her words were muffled against his mouth. "I'm sorry. I'm so sorry. I won't ever risk you again like that."

Gabriel's lips stilled, then a breath of laughter escaped. Then another. He cupped her face in his hands. "I was about to apologize to you for the same thing."

"Oh." Madeline swallowed.

Gabriel cupped her face. "I love you, even if we'll be fighting over the chair with the clearest view of the street for the rest of our lives."

Madeline grinned. "Perhaps we can sit in the chair together. Although I don't suppose we'll be paying attention to the street."

With a growl, Gabriel scooped her up and sat her on the desk. She pulled him until he was between her knees. He slowly tugged the hem of her skirt up past her knees, then with feathering strokes, traced the line of her calf to the delicate skin on the inside of her leg.

She slipped her hands inside his jacket, smoothing them over the planes of his chest. As her hands swept downward, she brushed the corner of a paper sticking out of his waistcoat pocket, knocking it onto her lap.

The last page of the ledger from Naughton's.

Would it be more satisfying to tear it into small pieces or toss it into the fire? No, either of those would take too long. She picked it up to toss it aside, but stopped mid-throw.

At the bottom of the ledger, in distinctive, bold slant, was Gabriel's name.

She placed the paper back on her lap and smoothed the page open. Next to Gabriel's name was a bid nearly twice the size of Danbury's.

"You're worth far more to me than that," Gabriel said. "But it's all I could come up with in the time I had."

"This can't be a real bid." The words sounded distant.

"It is. Only about a third of that is mine, and the rest is from my—" He cleared his throat. "My father."

"You went to him?" Madeline tried to cover the fact that she was clutching the paper to her chest like a sappy imbecile.

"This afternoon, before I met you at Naughton's." A touch of color bled across Gabriel's cheekbones. "I couldn't let anyone else win you. Not even in pretense."

Madeline blinked against the salt stinging her eyes. "But the auction was over before you wrote anything."

"No, everyone thought the auction was over. I wrote my name at the bottom with three seconds to spare." Wiping away a tear that ignored her commands, Gabriel raised his brow. "Now I believe you owe me a night that exceeds my wildest fantasies, correct?"

Madeline braced her hands behind her on the desk, letting the heat she was feeling enter her eyes.

As Gabriel leaned in, she stopped him with a

finger on his chest. "I've arranged for you to spend the evening fighting a killer in the house of a former spy, who also happens to be your betrothed, while a duke listened outside the door. I think I've surpassed any fantasy you have ever had. I've fulfilled my obligation to the auction." She crumpled the paper and tossed it over her shoulder. But then she wrapped her legs around Gabriel's waist. "But my obligation to my heart—that's another matter entirely."

Gabriel's kiss left her breathless before he pulled back, his expression serious. "You're my wildest fantasy, Madeline. I love you."

His green eyes held hers, and in that moment, finally, she believed.

Epilogue

"The coach is ready, Mrs. Huntford."

Madeline glanced up at the butler's retreating back. It was still vaguely odd to see a butler without Canterbury's flourishes, but Canterbury had refused to displace Gabriel's old butler and instead accepted an offer of employment from Clayton. Not that she could blame him. Clayton's investments had paid off. He was well on his way to being wealthy enough to buy and sell the Bank of England. Yet he was still angry and bitter at the world. Especially at the woman who had sent him to the gallows. And Ian had disappeared, intent on tracking down the man who had betrayed her to Einhern.

Sighing, Madeline glanced at the clock, then started. "Heavens, it's late." She hurriedly tucked the case files she was reading back into the desk. "But I really think your best bet is to interrogate the maid again. I don't believe her when she says she doesn't remember a plate with a different china pattern coming through the kitchen that night. I was a scullery maid once in Seville. As intimate as I was with those dishes, there was no way I would have missed it."

"I'll follow up with her later this afternoon." Gabriel helped her to her feet, even though the small bump on her belly hardly showed yet.

"Tomorrow. Your mother will never forgive us if we miss any of her wedding festivities."

Gabriel placed his hands on Madeline's stomach in a gesture that was at once awestruck and fiercely protective. Her heart leaped as it did every time.

"I still say once she accepted Northgate, she should have obtained a special license and exchanged vows in front of the nearest vicar. It worked for us."

Madeline smiled. "That's because we couldn't manage to keep our clothing on long enough for anything more elaborate."

"Speaking of clothing—"

She gasped in pleasure as Gabriel's thumb brushed the underside of her breast, but she tried to focus on the conversation at hand. "She's had thirty years to imagine what her wedding might have been like. She has every right to make it as extravagant as she desires. Although I think the most elaborate plans came from your father."

Gabriel raised his brow. "I believe society realizes he's not ashamed of us. Hell, the entire world is probably well aware he's not ashamed of us."

His words were gruff but Madeline could hear the growing affection in them. Even if Gabriel wouldn't admit to caring for his father, the mutual respect between them definitely showed the promise of something deeper.

Gabriel's lips traced the edge of her bodice. "Now back to the topic of your clothing . . . How much time did you say we have?"

Madeline's knees trembled, but she forced them to steady. "Not enough time to get me out of this dress and back into it."

"Well then, what if it happened to become a bit creased in the carriage ride over?"

Madeline smiled, lifting her lips to his, her heart aching with happiness. "Some things just can't be avoided despite the best-laid plans."

K.I.S.S. and Teal: Avon Books and the Ovarian Cancer National Alliance Urge Women to Know the Important Signs and Symptoms

September is National Ovarian Cancer Awareness month, and Avon Books is joining forces with the Ovarian Cancer National Alliance to urge women to start talking, and help us spread the **K.I.S.S. and Teal** message: **K**now the **I**mportant **S**igns and **S**ymptoms.

Ovarian cancer was long thought to be a silent killer, but now we know it isn't silent at all. The Ovarian Cancer National Alliance works to spread a life-affirming message that this disease doesn't have to be fatal if we all take the time to learn the symptoms.

The **K.I.S.S. and Teal** program urges women to help promote awareness among friends and family members. Avon authors are actively taking part in this mission, creating public service announcements and speaking with readers and media across the country to break the silence. Please log on to ***www.kissandteal.com*** to hear what they have to share, and to learn how you can further help the cause and donate.

You can lend your support to the Ovarian Cancer National Alliance by making a donation at:
www.ovariancancer.org/donate.
Your donation benefits all the women in our lives.

KT1 0912

**Break the Silence:
The following authors are taking
part in the K.I.S.S. and Teal
campaign, in support of the**

Ovarian Cancer National Alliance:

THE UGLY DUCHESS
Eloisa James

NIGHTWATCHER
Wendy Corsi Staub

THE LOOK OF LOVE
Mary Jane Clark

A LADY BY MIDNIGHT
Tessa Dare

THE WAY TO A DUKE'S HEART
Caroline Linden

CHOSEN
Sable Grace

SINS OF A VIRGIN
Anna Randol

For more information, log on to: **www.kissandteal.com**

AVON

An imprint of HarperCollins*Publishers*

Ovarian Cancer
National Alliance
We work to save women's lives

www.ovariancancer.org
www.avonromance.com • *www.facebook.com/avonromance*

KT2 0912

3 1901 04105 2673